SEVEN
SECONDS

SEVEN SECONDS

JACK HENDERSON

SPHERE

First published in Great Britain in 2009 by Sphere
Reprinted 2009

A CIP catalogue record for this book
is available from the British Library.

Hardback ISBN 978-1-84744-228-4
Trade Paperback ISBN 978-1-84744-229-1

Typeset in Sabon by M Rules
Printed and bound in Great Britain by
Clays Ltd, St Ives plc

Papers used by Sphere are natural, renewable and
recyclable products sourced from well-managed forests and certified in
accordance with the rules of the Forest Stewardship Council.

Mixed Sources
Product group from well-managed
forests and other controlled sources
www.fsc.org Cert no. SGS-COC-004081
© 1996 Forest Stewardship Council
FSC

Sphere
An imprint of
Little, Brown Book Group
100 Victoria Embankment
London EC4Y 0DY

An Hachette UK Company
www.hachette.co.uk

www.littlebrown.co.uk

for Lori and the girls

The prayer of Ajax was for light;
Through all that dark and desperate fight,
The blackness of that noonday night,
He asked but the return of sight,
To see his foeman's face.

– Longfellow

And now I see with eye serene
The very pulse of the machine;
A being breathing thoughtful breath,
A trav'ler between life and death;
The reason firm, the temperate will,
Endurance, foresight, strength, and skill;

A perfect Woman, nobly plann'd,
To warn, to comfort, and command;
And yet a Spirit still, and bright
With something of angelic light.

– William Wordsworth

Prologue

December 27, 2002

There was something wrong, she knew because she could feel it, and her feelings had rarely let her down. But this thing that was wrong wouldn't strike her quite soon enough as lethal.

His elderly parents had left her alone with him, in this improvised sickroom on the second floor of their remote Arizona home. Though she was a stranger they'd seen nothing to fear in her, and why should they? A bright young woman, smartly dressed, with well-forged credentials and a radiation badge, flown into Phoenix and then shuttled here by charter helicopter on a privately funded investigation – and after all, how could anyone possibly wound their son any more deeply?

Though they'd been sent by another sub-unit of her client's corporation, the three hired sentries guarding the house had been somewhat less than trusting. Forget about a concealed weapon; the extended tag-team pat-down she'd endured would have felt out an undeclared tattoo beneath her clothes. They'd pawed briefly through her messenger-bag as well, but it had been ably designed to keep its secrets from sharper eyes than these.

And this vague, irrational disquiet that just wouldn't pass – well, she would simply choose to suppress it for the moment.

A photograph of Olin Kempler had come clipped to the MIRCorp contract, but it was a poor aid to identify the man lying in the bed before her. In the picture he was full of dash and wry intellect, a medical doctor of early middle age, striking an explorer's pose under the brassy sun of a summer afternoon in southwest Baghdad, near Amiriyah. Back then, less than thirty days ago, he'd been a weapons inspector for the United Nations. And here now, trembling and wasting under electric blankets in a checkered paper gown, lay barely half that former man.

'Can I . . .' she began. She found that she needed a breath, in and slowly out again, just another moment to remember that she wasn't afraid. 'Can I get you anything before we start?'

What came back might have been only a surge of tremor, but she took it for a *No*.

'You've been poisoned,' she said quietly.

A cringe of a dry smile as he met her eyes, the palsied hand that was near his head on the pillow lifted a painful inch, and he tapped his temple twice with the index finger, as if to say, *Smart girl.*

Dr Kempler and his UNMOVIC team had been called home from Iraq months before, their pre-packaged mission accomplished. He'd resigned abruptly thereafter and then returned to the Gulf on his own dime at the end of November. He'd gone back to retrieve something, it was rumored, or to confirm something, before an unofficial press conference he'd scheduled in DC. He was well known as a loose cannon among his peers, and an outspoken critic of the building push for war.

The bombshell press conference never came to pass. He

was fine when he boarded the transport at Saddam International, healthy during a brief stopover in London, but by the time his final flight touched down at Dulles all of his physical systems had started to fail. He'd refused medical treatment and dropped off the radar screen, until the call to Military Intelligence Resources Corporation that had brought her here today.

'What was it, doctor?' she asked. 'What do you think they used?'

His watery gaze dropped to his hand on the sheet near hers. He wrote it out in a scientist's notation, into the cloth with the tip of his finger, upside-down and backwards so it would be plain, upright, and clear from her point of view:

^{210}Po

It's easy enough to kill someone, but an artful assassin can enclose a message in every sanction. Polonium 210 was a poetic bioweapon to deploy against this particular anti-war activist, a WMD in the purest sense of the term. A millionth of a gram would have been more than enough: the quantity held in a pepper-shaker could visit a lingering death on nearly every man, woman and child in the United States.

A bullet or a bomb would be simpler, but this man was to suffer for his sins. He was to know who, how and why, and he would also know that in the end, the truth he'd died to tell wouldn't really matter at all. They might even use his autopsy report to bolster their case for the very invasion he'd worked so hard to prevent.

The one thing they hadn't factored was the courage of his convictions. His cause still burned in him, even as the deadly isotope was burning him alive. Courage had kept his heart beating just long enough to bring his story to someone who might still help him make a difference.

Her pager twittered, clipped on the strap of her bag on the

nightstand, and she glanced at its small screen as she muted it.

C A L L   I N, it had said.

She took the doctor's hand. It was cold and fragile, but she felt him answer her grip with all that was left of his own. 'Tell me,' she said. 'Tell me who did this to you.'

There was a soft, polite knock from the hallway.

He pulled her hand closer, and she moved to sit at his side on the mattress. The dry, cracked lips were working; there was no voice in his words, only the stale, failing air from his withering lungs. She bent near, and felt a grasp at her collar and then a sharp sting there as he pulled her ear close to his mouth. It was barely a whisper, a separate, shallow breath pushing out each of the three letters he spoke to her: *ISI*.

A low, pulsing buzz from the pager, the greatest alarm it could raise in quiet-mode. A second message was on its display, barely in her line of sight.

U R G E N T

'ISI?' she asked. The Directorate for Inter-Services Intelligence, Pakistan's eight-hundred-pound gorilla of hard-ball espionage. But what could be their agenda, against one lone man's futile efforts to avert a second Gulf War? 'How do you know? Did they find you in London—'

He shook his head, violently. She pulled away to look into his eyes, but he wasn't looking back.

He was looking at the door.

It came to her then, in a flash, the warning sign that had been just beneath her perception. It was the second man who'd frisked her so intimately outside in the hall, the one with the seafaring cologne and all the bling. He wore too much jewelry for a high-end security man, as if when given a selection to complete his cover he'd elected to take it all. But

4

that wasn't the clincher. The undergraduate's class ring on his right hand was a brass rat from MIT. But his tie-tack and blazer-pin, she remembered only now, were from Cal Tech. Two schools that go together like ketchup and caviar.

There was another knocking, a bit too firm and insistent this time. Then from beyond the shaded windows, she heard the heavy *thump* and ascending whine of her waiting Jet Ranger's turbine engine starting up. A third buzzing message lit up her pager, as she was reaching for the bag that hid her gun.

D U S T   O F F, it said, and then the message scrolled to a second line.

I N C O M I N G

The remote Alaskan launch of the target drone was proceeding perfectly, as it had in all the simulations. But shooting off a missile was pretty damn easy; just a little rocket science. The hard part was shooting one down.

Lieutenant Barry DeRita keyed on his mock-AEGIS control panel, let out his breath, and cupped his hand over the deployment button for the kill-phase of the integrated flight test. His DoD handler stood behind him, chatting with the base commander and the Raytheon rep, as the tactical screen before them tracked the arcing path of the modified Minuteman III.

Ready or not, California, here it comes.

All project schedules at Vandenberg had been accelerated in the name of the war on terror, but today's exercise had been pushed a little too aggressively, in his unsolicited opinion. There'd been a minor software upgrade from a subcontractor only that morning, and precious little time to run the new code through its paces in the computer models. For the record, he'd emailed his objections to his direct-report, and off the record, he'd gotten a stern four-letter message in reply.

FIFI, as he would later detail for the FAA board of inquiry, translates in the unofficial Air Force maintenance manual to 'Fuck it – fly it.'

The men standing over him saw no downside in this latest rush to deployment. From the media's perspective, the National Missile Defense program was Reagan's 'Star Wars' for the twenty-first century; even though it was still mostly vaporware the press was ever ready to front-page each new, sexy detail. A flashy success was needed just now, something photogenic and headline-worthy. If Kim Jong-il wanted to rattle his neo-nuclear saber at us from North Korea, well, then the USA would send him an intercontinental ballistic message of our own, courtesy of the nightly news.

And a failure, knock on wood, even a hundred-ten-million-dollar one, could be swept under the rug easily enough. Those procedures, at least, were well rehearsed.

A tap on his shoulder, and he thumbed the illuminated switch. There was a mild rumble under his feet as the RIM-161 SM-3 thundered skyward from its shielded silo, and he had an eerie, sinking intuition that if only a button could be un-pressed, this would be the perfect occasion.

All went well in the initial seconds as the anti-missile missile streaked up toward its sub-orbital rendezvous. There were no course corrections in these first moments, only the reliable physics of action and reaction. But as the onboard flight-control computer sensed the target's evolving trajectory, it issued a minor, tainted midcourse command to the thrust-vector controllers in the tail.

Another signal followed almost immediately to re-amend the flightpath, but like the first command, it too was an over-correction.

The computer could see clearly where it wanted to go, but

with each attempt to find its bearings it was miscalculating, overshooting by tiny but ever-increasing degrees.

To the human eye this appeared only as the slightest wavering in the receding vapor trail, instead of the expected laser-straight line. But the ground-based mainframes needed only milliseconds to project where this snowballing error-cascade was headed. The wide screens filled with bright red alerts and the ominous data to support them. The panic button flashed under its clear plastic cover.

Lieutenant DeRita didn't wait for an order; rank and protocol took a second seat in these circumstances. He tapped in his abort code, scanned his thumb, flipped the guard and pushed the button.

The dummy missile, the Minuteman III, obediently self-destructed over the North Pacific, just beyond the Bering Sea. But for reasons the young lieutenant would never be permitted to learn, his own errant kill-vehicle somehow lived on. It was still ascending and subtly maneuvering, as if with a free-born, wandering mind of its own.

Then a brief, encrypted whisper came in to it over the air, and the RIM-161 began to bear with restored precision toward new coordinates: a small, elusive target to the east, some 500 miles inland.

'Just one second,' she said, sweetly, and just loud enough to carry through the door into the hallway.

Her Walther was tucked into the waist of her skirt in back, and she was crouching next to the hinge-side of the entrance to the room. With the end of the doctor's walking cane she reached out slowly, and stopped, with under an inch to go. Then she turned her face away, covered her ear, touched the rubber tip to the locked brass knob, and jiggled it slightly.

The force of the shotgun blast tore the cane from her hand

and nearly rocked her off-balance, but an instant later what was left of the door kicked open and its impact sent her to one knee. She stood as the man rushed in and past her, and with a step out into the room she grabbed and pushed the barrel of his weapon down and away and then stiff-armed the stock in the direction of the sudden spin. The shotgun twirled out of his grip and into hers, and with another step backward out of arm's length she aimed the 10-gauge semi-auto, from the hip, square and steady at the center of his chest.

It was the man with the mismatched jewelry, as she'd known it would be. He straightened himself slowly, adjusted his footing subtly, and looked much bigger now than he had before.

'Is anybody out there?' she called. It was a small house, every room upstairs and down was well within earshot. When she'd heard nothing at all in reply her attention returned to the man in front of her. 'Where are the others? His parents, the other two guards?'

His face changed, but only half of it, and only by a shade. In the half that was unmoved she could see him planning the next few seconds, how to kill this little woman with the least possible fuss before he called in the cleaners. Into the other half came a gradual, shallow smile, in answer to her question.

'Who sent you?' she said. She didn't expect a reply; she was only waiting for what came next.

A clumsy feint to his left and then a lunge forward, a *boom* and a flash as the padded stock kicked back hard against her. He was stopped and staggered backwards by the blast, lead pellets skittered around the room. His shirt was shredded dead-center, but a thin, matte-gray undervest showed through, intact. As he regained his balance and started toward her again she dipped the barrel below body-armor level and fired again, and then again as he stumbled and teetered forward, clutching the empty air. The only noise was the ringing in her ears; he never uttered a sound, even as he crumpled to the hardwood floor.

The bolt of the shotgun was locked to the rear, the magazine was empty. She moved to the side of the fallen man, well out of reach, as she drew her pistol and aimed it at his head.

'Turn over.'

No movement.

She backed to the bed, laid the spent shotgun on the mattress at its foot, and glanced at the man she'd come here to visit. The shivering had ceased, all tension and suffering had passed from his face. She kept watch on the downed assassin, and placed her free palm on Olin Kempler's forehead. After a few moments her hand moved gently to his throat, and she felt there for any pulse or sign of respiration.

Nothing there. He was gone.

She picked up the cane and returned her full attention to the rat-bastard on the floor. *Enough fucking around with this asshole.* She hooked the curved end of the cane under one of his shoulders, fully expecting some jack-in-the-box attack that would make emptying a clip into his face that much easier. But there wasn't a twitch, and it took nearly all her strength to roll him over. His head turned toward her as his back hit the floor, but there was no will behind the movement, only momentum. His eyes were glaring but empty, his mouth gaped wide, but was silent.

And there was a faint, bitter scent in the air, amid the gunsmoke and the blood. Almonds.

Cyanide.

She could see the broken premolar, showing beneath his curled upper lip. They'd given him a suicide tooth, though clearly not a top-shelf model. Either when she'd shot his

9

knees out from under him or as he'd fallen onto his face, he'd clenched a bit too hard and bitten himself into the next world. Tough luck; it was a half-assed way to go, but not everyone deserves to die fighting.

The rotors outside had spun up to take-off speed, and she pulled the shades aside. The pilot saw her there, and rotated his index finger urgently toward the sky. The co-pilot was leaning out the open passenger bay. With his free hand he pointed up and to the west, then frantically motioned for her to get the hell on with the evacuation.

She looked up and out, saw a long, descending gray contrail stretching back to the horizon and the oncoming streak of fire behind its leading end, coming impossibly fast. There was a moment of relative silence as it split the sky overhead, and on instinct she stepped back and covered her face an instant before a sonic boom sprayed shattered glass from the rattling window frames.

She hooked her bag over a shoulder and ran for the hall, but was stopped there by what she saw through the blowing curtains in the room across the way.

More than a mile off in the distance there was a plume of impact at the base of a massive electrical transmission pylon, one of an endless string that spanned the desert between power substations in the southwest. The colossal Y-frame tower shuddered and swayed, and in surreal slow motion it began to twist and buckle in the direction of its weakened leg. The heavy, sagging conductors rippled like a whipped garden hose as another support gave way, and the bare parallel cables intertwined and shorted with a brilliant, far-away flash of 230,000 volts discharged.

The house seemed to tremble around her, from the cellar to the rafters. There was a low, phasing hum, the sound of a two-story toaster coming up to working temperature. A pattern of angular lines in the walls and ceilings turned brown and smoldering, and then orange and glowing. With a *whoom* the hallway around her ignited, and the room beyond and behind, and the stairway to the only exit she'd seen. She ran forward and grabbed a wooden chair, half-spun and flung it with all she had through the double-window of the guest room.

The sudden inrush of air fanned back the spreading flames, giving her just the moment she needed to climb through and onto the narrow lip of the sill outside. She looked up, and then down. The roof gutter was three feet above and well behind her, the concrete driveway twenty-five feet below. Only one way to go.

She crouched as best she could, and jumped. One hand touched but slipped off the rusty metal gutter as it sagged under her weight, but the other had found a solid grasp.

She kicked off her shoes and took a gymnast's grip on the most uneven of parallel bars. A swing out and back, and another, and then with a tuck and half-somersault she rolled lightly up onto the edge of the slanted, tar-shingled roof.

The Jet Ranger was hovering above and to the side. She stood and ran up the steep roof to its ridge. Her co-pilot was leaning out from the skid, hanging onto a safety-lanyard and beckoning to her as the helicopter edged its way nearer. She raised her hand high, had to close her eyes against the blowing black smoke in the downwash. The heat from the fire below was rising in waves, growing unbearably intense under her bare feet, but in another moment she felt a firm grasp on her wrist, and then a powerful swing upward and into the open bay.

The panel door slid shut and the man who'd pulled her in rested his head in the crook of his elbow, breathing hard.

She buckled herself in, and the cabin tilted and rolled as the

Jet Ranger began to accelerate away. Through the side window she could see the old house receding in the dusk, already consumed in blowing yellow flames, barely still standing. But it had stood just long enough.

'Jesus, God Almighty, did you see that?' her companion said, and he sat down heavily next to her. 'Are you okay?'

They'd tried for her before, and they'd gotten uncomfortably close three times in the preceding year. The lumbering spook with the Old Spice and the boomstick had been a minion of the usual caliber, and he'd likely been sent here for her alone. But this thing that had come from the sky, that was different. That was meant for Dr Olin Kempler, and for everyone he might have spoken to before he died. It would be remembered as a freak accident by any surviving witnesses, but she'd heard of such accidents before. It could mean only one thing: something very big and bad was waiting in the wings, and in the coming days she would have its full attention.

She smiled a bit, suddenly weary, and patted the young man's cheek with a sooty hand.

'So far, so good,' Jeannie said.

PART 1

PART 1

1

From outside, mission control for the Kempler assignment would appear to be nothing more than a busted-out family restaurant along a ghost-town service road off old Route 66. Anyone looking through the cross-taped windows would see only dusty old metal tables, linoleum counters and chalkboard menus, unassuming cover from another sun-faded era of the American West.

MIRCorp had quietly bought up hundreds of such places along with thousands of surrounding acres across the country in recent years. These acquisitions provided a covert staging network with minimal civilian exposure; low cost, low risk, low profile. The lobbyists' brochure called it *a long-view domestic deployment strategy for the nation's premier private-sector military/intelligence enterprise.* A cynic might have called it an infiltration.

She keyed open the shuttered-glass front door, flicked on a pen-light and walked her companions through the dark abandoned restaurant, into the kitchen, and through a touchpad-armed steel door at the back of the musty walk-in refrigerator. As they entered the ready room beyond, a light-switch sensed movement and the overhead fluorescents buzzed on.

The space was empty, and not just of other people. Only hours ago they'd received their mission briefing here; now there wasn't a scrap of anything that would suggest this small base had been fully staffed and active earlier in the day.

The younger man wandered to the front of the vacant room, looking around. There was a rolling rack of folding chairs near the west wall and her pilot took down three and unfolded them. The two men took a seat. Jeannie stayed near the door.

First names had been exchanged before the deployment. The helicopter pilot was Clark, and she'd worked with him twice in the past. Nate was the co-pilot and navigator. She assumed both names to be fictitious. For Jeannie's part, at some point she'd ceased to engage in such weak subterfuge. There were hundreds of iron-clad ID technologies being rolled out to track American citizens, based on all five human senses and twenty-one more possessed only by machines. Whether spying from a streetlight pole, listening from an idle cellphone, or sniffing the landscape from low orbit, none of these electronic watchers would be fooled by a bogus first name.

No, if her growing roster of enemies really wanted her, sooner or later they would find her. And like today's unlucky man from Pakistan, they'd have their hands full when they did.

She and the crew had returned here expecting at least a thorough debriefing, especially considering the warp speed at which their interview assignment had gone to hell in a hand-basket. An abandoned and scrubbed base of operations wasn't a very good sign.

Jeannie opened the door, and the men glanced back at the sound.

'I'm going to have a quick look around outside,' she said.

'And then I'd suggest we take a cue from our employers and get as far away from here as possible.'

She disappeared through the doorway and the latch clicked shut behind her.

'I am *so* gonna hit that,' Nate said.

The pilot paused as he updated his flight log, smiled to himself and shook his head, then continued with his notes.

'What, like you wouldn't?'

'Just do yourself a favor, junior. Look but don't touch.'

'Fuck that, man, you gotta live for the moment.' He fluffed his hair in front, checked his breath in a cupped palm. 'I'm gettin' a vibe. I think she likes me.'

'Let me ask you somethin', kid.' The older man closed his logbook with a thumb holding his place. 'You got a favorite food?'

'Boston cream pie,' Nate said.

'Okay. So let's say ol' Satan jumps up outta the ground here and he gives you a choice. You can either have all the cheap-ass, cardboard-tasting, freezer-case supermarket pie you can carry, or just one tiny little nibble of the most delicious, creamiest Boston cream pie the angels ever made.'

'Jeez, man, you know I'm hungry. Now I want some pie.'

'So which do you choose?'

'That's easy—'

'Not so fast, now. Once you taste that pie from heaven you can't ever have it again. Every time you try to eat a piece of pie from that day on, it won't ever be near good enough for you. You might stop eatin' regular pie altogether, just outta regret for what you're missing.'

Nate thought for a moment. 'Shitty choice.'

Clark went back to his writing. 'Only kind the devil ever gives you.'

The door opened behind them.

'We should go, guys,' Jeannie said. She'd changed her clothes, into jeans and Adidas, a no-logo gray hoodie, and the scuffed bomber jacket she'd worn when they'd met up that morning.

They stood, and the pilot began to return the chairs to their place in the rack.

'Hey,' Nate said, approaching her. 'Do you wanna get something to eat? This fuckin' guy's been talking about food in here, and I've—'

'Is that your bike outside?' she asked.

'That big ol' Kawasaki? Well yeah, sweet thing, that's mine—'

'I've got a room about forty miles north of here.' She straightened his collar and looked into his eyes. 'I'm not hungry,' she whispered. 'I just want to get into bed.'

His stepfather, the Buick salesman, had taught him only one useful lesson: the minute you close the deal, stop selling. Without another word Nate stood aside and held the door open for her. She gave a last little wave to their pilot before leaving the room, and after a silent fist-pump of victory, her escort followed.

When they'd reached the motel he'd been a gentleman and given her first dibs on the shower. From the looks of this flophouse, hot water might be limited to a rain bucket or two per guest. As he waited his turn he reclined on the single bed in his road clothes, three flat pillows bunched behind his head, listening to the faint sounds of a hot soapy washcloth caressing a gorgeous young woman, one thin wall away.

The night sky above their ride across the desert had been a vivid sight for a city boy. A quarter-moon had barely dimmed a sea of stars over the landscape, with nothing but a thin film of atmosphere and empty light years between the Milky Way and what felt to be its only two earthly observers. She'd held on close from the rear seat, her arms tight around his waist. When the brief streak of a meteor had cut across the sky in front of them she'd pointed so he would see. Her cheek had pressed against his back then, and he'd felt her lips moving there, saying something. He couldn't hear over the roar of the wind and the engine, of course, and it occurred to him only now that she might not have been talking to him at all. He'd done it himself when he was a kid; you see a falling star, you make a wish.

The water stopped flowing and he heard the shower curtain pull aside beyond the hollow door.

Outside it was a dead-quiet night on an untraveled highway; the crackling hum of the roadside neons was the only man-made background noise. Inside, this motel set a whole new standard for one-star accommodations. Bare light bulbs, cracked plaster and puffy brown stains meandering across the low ceilings, late-60s wallpaper and flea-market décor slapdashed on the walls. Not that he'd never been slumming before, but it made him wonder. These jobs paid pretty well; she could have stayed somewhere nice. He could only assume she had her reasons.

The door to the tiny bathroom creaked open. It was steamy in there but she gradually materialized through the haze. She was brushing her teeth, squeaking a circle of clear glass in the foggy mirror with her free hand. She caught his eye in the watery reflection and smiled, held up an index finger as if to say, *One minute*.

'Take your time,' he said.

She spat and rinsed a last time, wriggled her toes into a pair of flip-flops and stepped from the bathroom, rubbing lotion into her hands and up her forearms. He stood when she came into the room. She wore a short, threadbare Cornell tank-top and a pair of girl-cut navy-blue boxers, tied with a drawstring bow at their low-slung waist.

'Bathroom's all yours,' she said. 'Such as it is.'

He hadn't eaten since breakfast and the sight of her seemed to have crossed some live wires somewhere between his brain, his stomach and his loins. There aren't many true instincts left kicking in a civilized man, but when he feels them he still knows them well. A native, tingling urge had locked onto those perfect shapely lines, quite apart from any genteel appreciation of beauty and grace.

She seemed to notice his attentions in the silence, and tugged here and there at her clothes in a brief attempt to stretch their coverage. 'This is all I brought to sleep in,' Jeannie said. 'I wasn't really expecting company.'

'You look totally amazing.' He picked up his overnight bag from the end of the bed as she walked over, and then glanced down at her footwear. 'Did you pack for the beach?'

'No, I just try to touch strange carpeting as little as possible.'

'Yeah, I was gonna mention your taste in lodging.'

'A dive like this is the safest place to stay these days. No internet, no cable box, no satellite dish, no cameras.'

'Nobody watching you,' he said. 'What a waste.'

The flattery went coolly ignored. 'Let me see your hand.'

He held out his right but she *tsk*ed as though he'd failed a simple aptitude test and picked up his left hand instead. He winced as she pushed back the sleeve of his sweatshirt. The wrist was bruised and abraded. It was this hand that had pulled her from the roof of a burning house just a couple of hours ago.

'I think you might have a sprain.' With a tentative pressure from above and below she stroked the slight swelling at the joint. Her palms were warm and slick from the bath lotion. 'Does that hurt?'

'If I tell you, you might stop.'

She smiled and fixed his sleeve, then wiped her oily hands front and back on his shirt. 'That's what you get for being a wise-ass.'

'Is that all I get?'

As she stepped past he felt a light backhanded spank on his behind.

'Get a shower,' she said.

True to his earlier intuition the shower's hot water had run out almost immediately. His teeth were chattering and it felt like first-stage hypothermia was setting in by the time he'd stepped out onto the tile.

The remaining flimsy towel had managed to get him only damp-dry in the humid broom closet of a bathroom. He bent close to the mirror and rubbed the back of his hand across his cheek. It was a little rough but not so much as to call for a shave. And for once he'd had the foresight to bring along a change of underwear. Briefs were more than he usually wore to bed, but somehow popping out of the bathroom in his birthday suit seemed a little forward, even for a one-night stand.

He opened the door and saw her lying on the bed, curled on her side. He walked over and sat on the edge of the mattress. Her eyes were closed, her breathing steady and even.

'Hey,' he whispered. That and a tentative nudge on her shoulder produced nothing but a sleepy, pouty frown. She cat-stretched a bit and rolled over, facing away.

Great.

On the short bureau next to her side of the bed he saw a small pharmacy bottle. The clear orange plastic was old and chipped; its prescription appeared to have been refilled a few times on street corners since it was first dispensed at the drugstore. There were pills left in the bottle, so she hadn't taken them all or anything. What a fix that would have been, not to mention the crushing blow to his ego. Without any question, though, she'd taken enough to put herself down for the night.

But why? Why would she ask him here like she did, and then knock herself out the minute he was out of the room?

It was a messed up thing to do to a guy, but you know what? Fuck it, don't worry about it. Just get some sleep. No telling what evil lurks in the mind of a woman, especially a chick who looks like Miss December from the *Smokin' Hot Babes of NATO* calendar.

He clicked off the bedside lamp and lay down next to her, doing his best not to disturb her as he moved. She was small but so was the bed; there wasn't quite room for two side by side without some sort of contact. The springs creaked as he edged onto his side, his chest to her back.

She stirred at his touch, but not away.

After a few moments she settled back against him, little by little, until soon there was no space between them at all. She shifted subtly so his arms could wrap around her, first at the bare shoulders, then at the waist. When her lips brushed his fingers the chance contact became a light, lingering kiss there, and another. Her hand touched his, the warm tip of her tongue dragged down toward his palm. She rolled to face him, sighed and nuzzled against his neck, her breath coming quicker as she pressed herself against the aching pulse of him, suddenly hard and hot against her naked thigh.

They moved together and she was underneath him, her hands to the headboard, her face averted, her back arching until the thin shirt was stretched tight across her chest, straining and longing toward his mouth. The scents of her were all

22

around him, sweet and pure and primal. She writhed against him and gripped his hair as his lips touched her ear, her throat, his fingers grazing slowly down over hot smooth skin, tracing a patient, maddening path where his rough, hungry kisses began to follow.

And then she whispered a name.

The freezing cold of the shower had been a warm summer breeze compared to this new chill that washed over him.

He stopped, brought himself slowly to an elbow and looked at her in the near-darkness. Because it wasn't his name she'd said, neither his real name nor the alias he'd given her that morning.

She was dreaming.

Though her eyes were closed her face showed wisps of expression. Her body was present but the rest of her was entirely somewhere else, with someone else, seeing things there but feeling them here.

Well, now.

These moments do arise when a person comes abruptly face-to-face with his morals. Making love to an unconscious woman; that couldn't ever be right, could it? With the lightest touch he cupped a small, perfect breast in his hand; she sighed and squirmed as he caressed the nub of firming, tender flesh under his thumb. Her body was saying Yes, no jury in the country would argue with that, and who was he to say No?

But no, it couldn't be right.

Maybe she'd brought him here because she didn't want to be alone. Maybe because she'd trusted him for whatever reason, a near-stranger but the closest thing she had to a friend, who would maybe just hold her through the night without sneaking a hand down her pants at the first opportunity. Who knows what she'd been asking for, but it sure wasn't to get date-raped next door to the Last Chance Texaco.

And so he had another problem. He wasn't sure it applied, but what the hell was the rule about waking a sleepwalker? The old wives' tale said to never, ever do it, but he'd heard that was total bullshit somewhere, hadn't he? Maybe on *Mythbusters*?

'Jeannie,' he said.

His voice did nothing to rouse her, and there wasn't going to be any rest for either of them until this spell she was under was broken. He eased himself out of her sleepy embrace but her hands wriggled free, one raking down the small of his back and the other edging shyly toward his waistband. He straddled her and with more authority he took her wrists and held them together under one hand above her head.

'Hey,' he said, louder. 'Jeannie. Come on, wake up.' With his free hand he gave her what was meant to be only a smart slap on the cheek, but it came across a little harder than he'd intended.

He would later remember the next few moments in all their vivid detail, but as they happened they blurred together with the rest of his life as it passed before his eyes.

She awoke, and saw his face near hers.

Surprise.

Confusion.

Recognition.

Rage.

His grip tightened on her wrists as he tried to buy a few seconds to explain, or at least to restrain her until she could come to her senses. An instant too late he recalled a key lesson from junior-high ju-jitsu class: one of the last places you ever want to find yourself is face-to-face on top of a superior opponent.

24

Her ankles locked around his back at the waist and with a fierce thrust of her hips his weight came off her trapped hands as all the air huffed out of his lungs. She caught his thumb and twisted hard enough to break it if he hadn't rolled with the motion, but this momentary defense fell precisely into her finishing hold. As they tumbled from the bed her slender legs whirled and scissored a triangle-choke around his neck, the arm-bar tightened to hyperextend his elbow until he cried out from the pain. He was helpless, breath cut off, immobilized, and right the fuck out of bright ideas. When he opened his clenched eyelids he was staring into the barrel of a small silver pistol.

The hand without the gun was twisting his injured wrist and he winced as her grip tightened there. The second instinct he'd felt that night kept his mouth shut tight. If she's going to shoot you, she's going to shoot you. If she's not, don't even think about saying a word that might change her mind.

Then something seemed to soften the steel determination in her eyes. She looked at his hand in hers as seconds passed. The gun didn't waver, but it didn't fire.

It might have been minutes or an hour or more, but gradually with each blink her eyes remained closed longer and longer. Her legs relaxed their hold around his throat, little by little, the wrist lock eased until finally they were only holding hands.

By degrees he let the weight of his head rest onto her thigh. He didn't dare move further; once or twice she nearly woke again. At length he heard her breathing becoming shallow and regular. She was sleeping.

He awoke with a start, to morning sunlight streaming through the blinds.

There was a brief period in which his rational mind insisted

25

that last night must have been a dream. Granted, he ached all over and had woken up on the floor, but nothing else in the room suggested that he hadn't slept there alone. When he checked at the window, though, he found that his motorcycle was gone.

His plan for the rest of his life, brief though it would likely be, came together rather quickly: Hitchhike to the next town, somehow get some wheels, and head out for Mexico.

Later, on his walk to the highway a few key questions had been answered as he thought them through. The mission had gone badly, badly enough that it needed to be forgotten with extreme prejudice. Divide and conquer; the pilot, Clark, was probably already dead at the hands of another.

No question now, she'd brought him here to silence him, to kill him. Then why all the sleeping pills? Because, he imagined, maybe some part of her didn't want to do what she'd been ordered to do.

In addition to his life, she'd also left him three other things to remember her by.

First, on the shelf above the sink he'd found a neat pile of hundred-dollar bills, enough to replace his Kawasaki Vulcan 1600 Classic and then some. Second, he was certain that from that day on, the mild scent of Johnson's Baby Lotion would leave him both vaguely paranoid and partially aroused.

And last, she'd left him a single word of good advice, written on the bathroom mirror in pale rose lipstick, that would define his future for as long as he could make it last.

disappear

2

Vince Lindeman tapped off the radio and eased on the brakes. Another mile, another construction zone. Didn't these bastards ever finish anything?

Just up ahead a Mexican flagman sauntered to the center of the lane, with a few more gay compañeros in Day-Glo jumpers bringing up the rear. It was like that old light-bulb joke, only not funny at all: How many illegal immigrant road workers does it take to screw up a one-man job?

Let's count 'em off: the sign-guy, one to supervise, another to shoulder the boom-box, and a fourth to keep an eye peeled for the INS agents, like they'd ever show up when you need them. Four model non-citizens, getting things done the un-American Way. They looked like a chain-gang without the chains, or maybe the Anaheim chapter of the Future Felons of Orange County.

Future, hell. At 200 bucks an hour between the four of them, these border-jumpers were robbing California taxpayers blind already.

But that was old thinking. These *cholos* here, they weren't the outsiders any more. Somewhere within a single generation a quiet invasion had taken place, and just like

27

that, the old minority had become the new, menacing majority.

Slow, the workman's flip-sign turned to say, and the cars in front were waved on through at a crawl, one by one. But the S-class ahead was just sitting there; some trust-fund prick no doubt, probably on the goddamned phone. Vince laid on the horn, the brake lights winked out and the Mercedes rolled a few feet forward, but halted again as the sign turned to *Stop*.

He let an impulse pass to punch a dent into the dashboard, crank the wheel and floor it, to just peel off down the narrow shoulder and find some open road. But that would only solve the problem at hand; there were other things afoot that wouldn't be so easily outrun.

No use pissing and moaning about it. He'd been through tough times before, and he was still standing after forty-nine years. This was just another scandal to be outfoxed, another white-water ride through the white-collar criminal justice system. Though to be totally honest – and *total* was a level of honesty with which Vince Lindeman was almost completely unfamiliar – this Iraqi Oil-for-Food scam was the biggest big con he'd ever gotten himself into, by a big frickin' long shot.

And he'd gotten the dismal message the day before. He was going to take the fall for this one. After all their shared years of double-dealing in the DC money-go-round, all of his cronies in the smoke-filled back-rooms were finally going to kick him to the curb. The order had come straight from the big man at the UN. Someone had to go down, and he had been elected by acclamation.

But oh no, he wouldn't be going down alone.

He patted his jacket pocket and retrieved his iPod, slipped in the earbuds and shuttled to a hidden playlist between two good old albums, *Empty Glass* and *Frampton Comes Alive*.

28

He thumbed up the volume, smiled as the first of a time-coded series of recorded phone conversations began to play.

He checked his watch. This morning the Feds had seized his computers, laptop and backup drives in that showboat raid of his offices, and soon they'd be discovering that what they were after was no longer there. And while the network news had been doing its dutiful job of convicting him in the court of public opinion, Vince Lindeman was preparing to drop some indictments of his own, courtesy of the *Los Angeles Times*.

A honk from behind snapped him back to the traffic jam. The Mercedes ass-bandit up front had proceeded on through the bottleneck, but as Vince let his foot off the brake the sign began to spin to red again. He nearly ran it, but the flagman stepped in front and held out his hand. The gold-toothed grin on the guy's face was almost too much to swallow; the little bit of power his glo-orange vest bestowed had clearly gone to this taco-bender's thick head.

As the man backed away, Vince checked his rearview and saw that another flagman had drifted onto duty behind his car. In back there were thirty yards between his bumper and the next vehicle. And a similar gap was opening up in front.

Now what?

Ahead and behind, drivers and passengers had begun exiting their vehicles, at the urging of other workers who'd appeared from somewhere. They were all being herded away along the narrow edge of the overpass.

He unbuckled with one hand and pulled the side-handle with the other, but his door was locked. He pressed the release and put a shoulder to the door, but it wouldn't budge. He tried again, and there was an extra *click-thunk* when he pushed the button; the door was relocking the instant it was keyed. *Goddamned dumb-ass high technology, it was everywhere.* He reached for the panic button on his car's satellite-linked remote maintenance system, but he saw from its bright green status light that it was already active.

Already active?

Oh, no way.

No way.

There was a deep vibration, softened to the pluck of a giant bass-fiddle string by the Cadillac's high-ticket suspension, followed by a visceral screech from below, and with a *chunk* the horizon tilted just slightly to the left.

If Vince Lindeman had been sitting on his couch instead of in his SUV, it would have felt as if both stumpy legs on one side had suddenly folded; it was only a slant of inches. There was time for him to watch the workmen in front and behind stumble back a few more steps before dropping their traffic signs and turning to run. And then without another sound, the road slipped out from under him.

With the swelling sensation of the fall there was no panic, or struggle, or dread; their time had whizzed past before he'd even had a chance to consider them. It would be a comfort to think that the calm Vince Lindeman felt was one of God's tender mercies, but it was only an economy of nature. Prey animals often showed this same resignation as the killing stroke came down. Past the moment when their end was inevitable, any further expenditure of energy would simply be a waste.

The falling Escalade rocked gently, the wind whistling roughly through its horizontally-aligned aerodynamics, accelerating at a far-better-than-advertised 0 to 135 in under five seconds. Its driver only watched through the moon-roof as the car-length void in the bridge above fell away into the sky, and then with the impact came a white-out that seemed to blend all his senses as they maxed out, loud and bright and sharp, the smells of cut metal and steam and oil, the tastes of copper and salt. As the fade toward black began, everything stopped, and was quiet.

The wheels-down collision with the bone-dry riverbed hadn't killed Vince Lindeman, but it hadn't been particularly designed to do so. At this tick of the timeline his death was calculated to be pending, but nonessential. The spine of his seat had broken and it had reclined on impact, and the glass of the tinted moon-roof had caved into a shatterproof mosaic of opaque pellets with a jagged hole in the sagging center. Through that clear circle and his graying vision he could see a bright yellow construction crane high above, its caterpillar tracks hanging out over the gap in the bridge he'd fallen through. It teetered on the edge, its heavy magnetic lifter swung wide at the end of its cable, and the pendulum then swung back and attached itself with a distant *clang* to the underside of the bridge. The men in its cockpit jumped to safety, and their departing weight was the final straw to tip the balance. The cab of the crane slid through the gap in the road, the cable played out and hit the end of the reel with a twang, and the magnet let go. A few seconds of quiet free-fall, and the ground shook again as the crane crashed to the rocks not twenty yards away, and then the quarter-ton magnet at the end of its cable arrived.

The 500-pound falling mass of the crane's lifting head proved more than adequate to crater the passenger compartment of Lindeman's car and finish him off in the process, but snuffing out his life had always been the easy part. The real challenge had been to ensure the required coercivity from the electromagnetic field of the crane's lifting head, sufficient to thoroughly wipe the hard drive in Lindeman's evidence-loaded iPod. And that would require a precise crosswise twist in polarity after contact.

31

So, one last thing.

After a moment of silence, the still-upright jib of the shattered crane buckled and swooned, a slow-motion fall like a
base-cut redwood. As the cable snapped taut it jerked the
massive magnetic head clockwise, roughly ninety degrees. And
with that, all electronic data in the wreckage reset to zero,
several seconds after Vince Lindeman's life-signs had done the
same.

3

His thoughts had drifted as he waited and walked, drifted many miles and years away. The walking helped; the waiting never changed. The latest murder always seemed the most trying, the least likely to succeed.

Murder – surely there was a different word. Not a euphemism, something every bit as grave and plain, because these were grave acts to be sure. A killing that was wrong, but at the same time more right than leaving the target alive – something so very common should have a better name.

There was a subtle buzz in his breast pocket. August Griffin stepped out of the two-way flow of Hollywood tourists and into the darkened alcove of a closed tattoo parlor. He touched his earpiece, and within a second or two a twice-encoded message brought him the word.

So Vincent Lindeman was safely put down, dead and gone, and his pocketful of damning digital evidence had departed this world right behind him. Good news; with hope there was more to come.

Griffin had no love for Los Angeles, but the urgency of this particular hit had demanded his on-site supervision. Sad enough, but the old saw was true – if you want someone done right, you'd best just do them yourself. One more meeting, then, and he'd be on a plane headed east, and home.

As he disconnected the call he caught his own worn reflection in the dark shop window he faced, took an absent step forward and studied who he saw there.

You certainly don't look like a trigger man, old boy.

But then the great ones, the ones who've survived, really never do.

Trigger man was wrong in any case. Thirty-five years had passed since August Griffin had actually pulled a trigger, even on the firing range. There were practical reasons for this. Guns were unrefined and noisy tools, prone to random spraying of forensic particles in all directions. These days they were needed only in emergencies, or for the careless, vulgar shows. The times and technologies had changed and those sorts of messages were very rarely ordered in the management of the modern world. And those were the practical reasons that he hadn't fired a gun since June of 1968. But there were other reasons.

The breeze blowing up Sunset Boulevard was unusually brisk, and he'd neglected to dress for it. The cold swirled into the alcove and got itself inside his clothes, and the chill brought those other reasons to mind.

Genuine remorse was quite rare among working assassins, and never confessed. Those burdened with a naïve conscience were weeded out very early in the recruiting process. Realism, on the other hand, was mandatory in his line of work. Good and evil were fleeting deceptions, completely reliant on timing, point of view, and circumstance. Good and evil might not exist, but the hesitation such thoughts could bring was very real. And hesitation, to be sure, was not good.

There was nothing but relief after this most recent job: few if any would argue that the Earth wasn't a far better planet with Vincent 'Skip' Lindeman off of it. Would that they were all this way, with nothing but relief when it was over, but they were not. Most were not.

Paul Wellstone was fresh in his mind from October. No one had seriously expected the aircraft scenario to work, and other more direct plans for the senator had been in place for the following weeks. Not a high priority – he wasn't dangerous, only hated; somebody up there didn't like him. In such cases an accident is always preferred over an open act of violence, and new techniques required opportunities for field testing and refinement. No harm in a bit of trial and error with an innovative approach to airframe sabotage. No problem if it failed, which the number-crunchers all agreed that it would. It shouldn't have worked.

But it had worked, the odds notwithstanding. The weather, the schedule, the players, and a touch of fairy dust had all fallen together to make the plane crash an unqualified, untraceable success. A flawless execution, made even more credible by the collateral damage – the senator's wife and one of his children had died as well, along with two staffers and the flight crew. Despite the vocal suspicions of some in the tinfoil-hat community, no rational person could imagine that so many innocents would be sacrificed to silence one stubborn, meddling idealist.

Goebbels had been right, or was it Marshall McLuhan? There's no need for a vast conspiracy of silence; the most terrible secrets are hidden by the public's unwillingness to believe. They'll accept a freak accident or a suicide no matter how unlikely, or a radical fundamentalist in a distant cave, or the ever-reliable lone gunman, because the alternative is unthinkable: that men walk among us whose daily job it is to coldly order, plan and carry out such things.

A pressure in his chest brought his breath up short, and he sat on the concrete sill behind him.

Griffin closed his eyes, pressed a spot on his wrist near the watch-band.

Calm and easy, he thought. *You've let your mind wander off again, and you must bring it back to the matters at hand.*

He inhaled the cool air, held it for a moment, and as he exhaled he felt the weight begin to lift from his heart as a metered dose of nitroglycerin dispersed through his system.

There was no cure for age seventy-four, only chemical twine and bandages to hold off the final judgment for a better day. And that day was coming, he was certain. The day of context, when every dark deed would be seen in its proper light. It's one's body of work that acquits them, the ends that justify the means. Were it otherwise, no world leader in modern history would have escaped the gallows.

'Hey, yo.'

It was a voice from above him. There was a man in the shadows of the alcove, standing near. Too near; courtesy seemed secondary to being out of the view of the people passing by on the sidewalk beyond.

The gaze that met Griffin's was dull and distracted, as if an unseen accomplice near the young man's ear was passing hushed instructions.

'Yes?'

'Spare some change fo' a brotha.'

It wasn't a request, but not quite a threat.

'I'm afraid I haven't any change,' Griffin said. He went to his inside jacket pocket, withdrew the small roll of bills there, peeled one off, held it out, and felt it clipped from his hand. The grip in his chest had nearly subsided, and he closed his eyes again to breathe himself through it.

'. . . This real, old man?'

'I'm sorry?' Griffin said. He looked up. The money had been meant to buy the vagrant away; it had either been too much, or not enough. Such prices were notoriously difficult to judge.

'I'm just sayin', y'know.' The young man's eyes flicked behind him, and back again. 'Motherfucker hand me a hundred like it ain't nothin' to 'im, I gotta ask, is it fo' real?'

Griffin touched the wire rim of his glasses, and a grid of shimmering light-green lines overlaid his field of vision. Words and images began to materialize, projected onto the lenses of his spectacles, creating the private illusion of a movie-screen-sized computer display overlaying the real world. A diamond cursor flitted around the dark face above him, setting feature points. A bright elastic rectangle stretched out in the air to the left, and a spooling stream of data faded in within the box.

'Is it real,' he mused. 'Now mind you, I'm no Milton Friedman, but some say it hasn't been real since Nixon dropped the gold standard in 1971.'

A flipbook of hundreds of similar gaunt faces had begun to flash in and fade away alongside his companion, and then the digital images slowed and stopped on a match as the ID was verified. Before him stood William Martin Lewis, UID #082-956702-3723, the man himself and everything the system knew of him.

'And now, Willie,' Griffin said, 'you really must be going. I'd like to be alone.'

'Howd'ya know my name—'

'The most vital thing I know about you, Mr Lewis, is that it would be best if you moved along.'

A thief, a mugger and a meth addict, the man's scrolling summary concluded. His criminal record was long, and its inevitable endpoint was clear. Too dope-weak and dim-witted to succeed even as a hoodlum, no gang would stoop to have him as a member anymore. A three-time loser, half of his thirty-one years spent behind bars or in juvenile homes, now one conviction away from twenty-five-to-life and one foot already in the grave.

Griffin focused on the chronological array of floating digitized mug shots to the right of his field of vision, and the pictures Rolodexed in response to his attention, one after another. In the oldest booking record Lewis had been only fifteen. He looked strong, defiant and street-tough in the police photo, and there'd been a spark of nascent intellect in his eyes. But with each year and each new photograph the fire had slowly dimmed, the anger wilted to submission, and then finally to fear.

The other man's hand went to his belt and he withdrew a knife, fumbled it open. 'Git up and gimme what you got, an' I'll let you alone all right.'

Among the data, text and images on display around Willie Lewis shone a single significant number. This number was the product of a joint research program in the 1970s, co-conceived by DARPA and a group of psychosociologists out of Stanford University. It correlated to a point on a bell curve, with volumes of equations and decades of research behind the score. Put plainly, to the best of the ability of science, this number was the measure of the worth of any given human being. Not simply what they *had*, but what they had done, and all they might ever be expected to achieve. The higher the number, the greater the worth, on a scale from 1 to 1,000.

Those with scores above 950 were the best of species, more precious than red diamonds if found and nurtured, but extremely dangerous if left to develop in the wild. Below 500 were the masses of the bewildered herd; under ninety, the strata that Hoche and Binding had termed 'the useless eaters'.

And on this most important test in the life of Willie Lewis, he'd narrowly scored a 14.

Griffin stood slowly, brushed the sill's cement grit from the seat of his trousers.

38

'As it turns out,' he said, 'it's good that you found me, Willie.'

'Good for me, maybe—'

Griffin held up a hand, and Willie Lewis stopped talking.

'Because I have a message for you,' Griffin said. His voice was low and calm, its cadence steady and firm. 'From your daughter.'

Lewis faded back a half-step, his digitally displayed heart-rate showing a burst of perfectly understandable alarm.

'Nothing to fear,' Griffin said quietly. 'Nothing to fear.' His eyes didn't leave the other man's as he reached slowly to his breast pocket and withdrew a pen. It was one of his custom Duponts, the Orpheo in silver and brown leather. 'Your little girl, Willie. Your daughter, Anya.' He held the pen up between them, saw the other man turn his focus to it. The pen moved an inch to the left, and gently back again. To the right, and back once more. The dull eyes followed. 'Your firstborn child. She has something she'd like for me to say to you.'

The small knife fell from Lewis's hand as Griffin lightly gripped his wrist. There was no force in the contact; the touch was a simple pattern-interrupt, the moment in a rapid induction when the subject surrenders to the trance.

'Do you hear me?' Griffin asked. With his thumb and fore-finger he rotated the barrel of the elegant pen a few degrees clockwise, a quarter-turn back, then nearly halfway around again. The pocket clip clicked outward, and a clear gemstone at its base glowed ruby-red. There was a faint ascending whistle, like the charging whine of a small camera.

A slow, sleepy nod from Willie Lewis, and then another.

'You are the sum of all your ancestors, Willie,' Griffin said softly, 'the crowning achievement of your bloodline, the only surviving descendant in a long procession of criminals and leeches, whores and junkies and disease-carriers. And all of you added together have brought not even a feather's weight of merit into the world.'

The glow from the jewel in the clip of his pen turned from red to yellow, and then with a last quarter-turn of the barrel, to bright green.

'But your little girl, ah, I see it only now, she was something special. She could have redeemed you all, if only we'd learned of her in time. If only you'd defied your nature and taken care of her just a little while longer. She would have been nearly ready for us, almost twelve years old. And you would have proven yourself to be more than the genetic dead-end that you've now turned out to be.'

August Griffin released the other man's wrist. The arm stayed where it had been, stiff and extended, as if awaiting a final hand-out.

Life is only energy, though science and the great religions would differ on its wellspring. Each individual being transmits this *élan vital* in a unique sort of signature, faint but detectable at short range. The small transceiver within the pen in Griffin's hand was designed to read, map, mirror and target this fragile human spectrum.

'But despite how you failed her, Willie,' Griffin said, 'I believe that little Anya would have liked for me to tell you . . . goodbye.'

His thumb depressed the glowing clip and there was a flash of something that wasn't light. With that *click* all those delicate, mysterious hints and pulses that some would have called the soul of Willie Lewis were canceled out at their source. To say he died would overstate the moment; his remains dropped to the sidewalk at Griffin's feet like an unstrung marionette, every cell in his central nervous system having simply forgotten how to live.

*

The queue outside Christie was already long, at least four hundred, and it was early yet. It was the ultra-exclusive club of the moment, and on a holiday night no one still outside had any real chance of getting in. Most were only hoping to catch a glimpse of the top of the Hollywood A-list as even they bargained for a brief admission.

Such a dreadful place for a business meeting.

The doorman saw Griffin approaching and winked a subtle recognition. He motioned the cameras down and lifted his velvet rope at its hook. A redhead in a party dress, tall and impossibly slender, mistook the gesture and started through the gap, but she was stopped by a firm hand to the chest. It wasn't much of a shove, but she lost her footing and went down flat onto her backside. One of the paparazzi snapped a whirring series of pictures, but before his flash had faded two enormous bouncers descended to take him off by his elbows and re-teach him the unwritten rules.

As Griffin neared the rope-line the woman who'd fallen was still there on the pavement, unnoticed in the press of the crowd. There was something vaguely familiar about her face in profile; she brought to mind a small-town pageant princess, but with twenty years of near-misses and broken LA promises beginning to wear around her edges.

'Hey,' Griffin said. She looked up at him, sniffed and wiped her eyes, defenseless, resigned to another humiliation. He put out his hand. 'Come on in with me.'

There wasn't a moment of mistrust. The sudden light of her smile was striking, with no transition at all between despair and happiness. She took his hand and he helped her to her feet; she was nearly weightless on his arm. The lobby crowd parted for them, and the doors opened. She hugged his neck, whispered, 'Oh, thanks,' and pressed her head to his shoulder as they walked.

Inside the club it was all candlelight and wood tones, quiet music and intimate nooks, unexpectedly close and quaint to newcomers. There were small booths and conversation pits for only several dozen of the current chosen few, but one secluded corner table was always held open for a single, regular patron. The table was empty, as might have been expected; his young apprentice viewed promptness as a trait far below her station.

'Well, then,' Griffin said, patting the delicate hand that still rested on his arm. 'You have your big evening ahead of you now.'

'My name's Melanie.'

'So it is.' He touched the rim of his glasses, and the distracting flow of data there faded away.

She smiled, and looked at him expectantly.

'And I,' he said, 'am the illegitimate great-grandson of a corrupt American president. And it's best for us both if we leave it at that.'

'Oh, sure,' she said, and the sparkle in her eyes grew the slightest bit wicked. 'I love a mystery.' She pulled herself up by his lapels and a kiss brushed his cheek. 'Just, thank you so much, again. I don't know what happened at the door, I've been here so many times—'

'Put it out of your mind,' he said. 'Enjoy yourself tonight.'

She smiled again and let it linger for a moment, then turned and made her way off into the star-studded crowd.

He pulled back the corner chair, but before he sat he nodded a summons to the waiter by the bar. *Take good care of my guest,* the gesture said, *like you would treat a queen, and I'll see that you're well rewarded.* And in the manner of the once-great servant class, the discreet, deferential nod that returned assured August Griffin that his will would be done.

4

'Well, if it isn't Mister Griffin.'

He stopped reading as she sat and got herself situated, but he didn't look up from his book.

His apprentice had flaws beyond chronic lateness, but her faults all fed from a single source. There was old royalty in her blood, and April Medici had never forgiven her ancestors for giving up the crown. It explained her love for this Hollywood club. This was a place where what passed for an American ruling class could gather, the cream of the famous and the fortunate, safe from the prying eyes and grasping hands of the great unwashed. It was a taste of the life she one day hoped to lead.

In candid photographs her looks were not outstanding in any way. A male colleague had summed up her physical charms with his pet double-negative: April was not unattractive. Many a royal heiress, stripped of rank and title, might be described in the same way. The family features that persisted, once engraved in fine gold and preserved in the portraits of masters, seemed in modern light to be in the slightest need of a surgeon's correction.

As a subordinate there was little to recommend her. She

gave no respect. Not to her elders, because maturity was only a polite word for mental and physical decay. Not to her betters, because experience and wisdom were only dodgy relics of an irrelevant past. She'd taken to addressing him as *Mister Griffin* early on in her training, but there'd always been an extra dash of ire injected as she said his name. It was her subtle dig at his authority, at all authority, delivered in what might have passed for good humor had this young woman ever developed any capacity for human affection.

But she was very, very good at her job, and that forgave much.

'Aww,' she sighed. 'Did I keep you waiting? Are ya mad at me, Grandpa?'

He closed the paperback with a cocktail napkin to mark his page, checked his watch, glanced absently through the nearby crowd, and looked across to her.

'My time is—'

'Valuable, yeah.' She checked her look for a moment in the mirrored surface of a brass wall sconce next to the table, and then her eyes somehow followed the glance he'd stolen across the club, searched briefly, and stopped. 'Who was that you're checking out, that your new girlfriend?'

He straightened himself. 'We only met at the door, coming in—'

She waved him off, a dry smile dismissing the very idea of our Mr Griffin in the company of any woman, except perhaps a registered nurse.

'I'm messin' with ya, pops.' She moved a water glass aside, slid a thin acrylic panel from her bag and laid it on the table between them. With a few touches its legal-pad-sized screen came to life. Within moments it had picked up its wireless data stream, gotten its bearings, passively identified its owner and paused, awaiting her command.

'Let's see where we are,' April said.

She was ready to be out on her own, despite some misgivings from the higher-ups. He'd weathered their doubts himself, decades ago. The gifted defy normal measure, and independence is the only true graduation. She was more than ready in most respects, and what couldn't be taught – well, that would either take care of itself in the field, or in time, it would take care of her.

'Lindeman's dead,' she said, 'and the press is running with the bridge collapse. No real speculation that it was anything other than an accident.' And then, under her breath, 'And not something I couldn't have managed on my own.'

'I agree.'

'Then what are you doing here?'

'I don't make all the decisions—'

'Fine.'

There was nothing but an argument down that road, so he left it there. 'What else is on our plate, April?'

She touched points on the translucent panel, dragged a few windows here and there, and turned the slanted screen so it faced him. 'There's going to be some fallout from this business with Kempler.'

'The weapons inspector. Iraq.'

'Yeah. Three simultaneous operations, three hits on two targets, same place, same time, what a colossal cluster-fuck—'

'The doctor is eliminated, yes?' Griffin said.

She nodded.

'Who was the second target?'

April tapped a spot near the corner of the panel, and a thumbnail image there enlarged to half-screen. She sat back in her chair, to watch him.

'Oh my,' he said quietly.

Griffin leaned in close to look into the face displayed there;

a hundred verifications appeared around it on the screen, but he needed to see her with his own eyes to be sure. He looked up. 'Do you know who that is?'

'Jeannie Reese, yes, I know who it is, relax,' April said.

'What's the meaning of this?'

'She'd dropped off the radar, everyone lost track of her at the end of 2001, but apparently she couldn't bring herself to stay underground. Reese has a friend, an old contact inside DARPA.' She tapped a spot on the screen, reading upside-down. 'Rudy Steinman. He hooked her up with one of our vendors, by pure blind luck. It's busy-work, as far as she knows, she took the jobs just to keep her hand in.'

'This is very, very dangerous—'

'I've got this one now, she's under control—'

'I can only imagine,' Griffin snapped. He stood and pocketed his book. 'I want to see her.'

'Not necessary.'

'Arrange it,' he said, and without another word he turned from the table and left April sitting alone.

There were many things she'd learned from him, no doubt about it. It was important to give credit where it's due. Without an accurate tally it's impossible to determine what's owed to whom, and why. And when.

Her waiter had arrived with a tray of preparations. From a small crystal decanter he dispensed a careful measure of emerald spirits. A silver slotted spoon was placed across the mouth of the goblet, with a cube of tan Havana sugar in its hollow. The server watched her eyes as he poured chilled spring water over the sugar and through the sieve, and after a few moments she nodded. The cool clear liquids inter-mingled, and soon they clouded to a rich, milky green. She took a small sprig of leaves from the tray, left a troy-ounce of gold in its place, and the waiter gathered his things and disappeared.

She cupped the goblet in her hand, dropped the dry whorled leaves into the candle at the center of the table, closed her eyes as delicate threads of heady smoke mingled with a rich bouquet of anise and precious herbs rising from the rare French absinthe.

The table was bumped and jostled, rattling the tableware. April took in a deep breath, replaced her glass carefully on its thin marble coaster, and looked up. A woman was standing there, behind a vacuous smile.

'Happy New Year,' the woman said. 'May I join you?'

It took a second to recall, but this was the one Griffin had been ogling across the room earlier in the evening. She seemed more than a little tipsy, but in a curious way the drunkenness was becoming to her. Mind you, this allure was nothing special; there were simply those for whom four fingers of gin were a cornerstone of social chemistry.

'Is it that late?' April asked. She nodded toward the empty chair across from her and the woman took the seat. 'I'm afraid I've lost track of the time.'

'It's midnight in Chicago, and that's New Year's for me.' She put a cool hand on April's wrist and added, 'Where are my manners? I'm Melanie Douglas.'

'April. Medici.'

'Oh, what a pretty name! It's what, is that Italian? And you say it how?'

'Like peachy,' April said. 'Meh-*dee*chi.'

'Meh-*dee*chi. That's so lovely. I changed my name when I got out here, to be in the movies. I don't like it really, my name, but once you get known even a little bit it's so hard to change it again.'

'You're in the movies? What have I seen you in?'

There came a wilt into the woman's eyes, so slight, but in the change April could see that those eyes were far more accustomed to disappointments than to joys. Remnants of a youthful beauty were still quite visible, but whatever lost hopes of stardom she'd once had must now be rather painful when brought starkly to her mind.

'Nothing much, really.'

'No, please, tell me. I'm a kind of a movie buff.' She waited. 'Just name one.'

'It was nothing,' the woman said. 'Nothing you'd remember.' She looked down at her hands and then away, because there again must be a reminder that more time was behind her than lay before. The skin was growing thinner, the bones and vessels underneath showing through, dark spots and dry wrinkles from too many carefree seasons in the sun. Her voice had grown small when she spoke again. 'Is your friend coming back?'

'My friend?' April seemed to think for a moment. 'Oh, Mister Griffin?'

'Was that his name? He wouldn't tell me—'

'That's his name. August Griffin.'

'Do you work together, or—'

'That's right. We work for the bank.'

'Oh, which bank?'

April leaned closer. 'I'll tell you a secret. There's only one, sweetie.' She took a compact from her bag and flipped it open, applied a bit of powder to her nose. 'Does he like you, do you think?'

'Your friend? I don't know—'

'Come on, we girls know these things, just tell me. If there was a chance he might ever see you again some day, do you think he'd enjoy that? Do you think it might make him happy?'

48

'It's a . . . it's a strange question.'

'His feelings are important to me.'

'Well.' The other woman smiled. 'Yes, then. I think it might make him happy.'

April nodded.

'Good.' Her thumb slid a guard aside and brushed a pad of pale foundation, and then she snapped the small compact shut and took the woman's hand warmly in hers. 'That's what I was thinking, too.' The pale smudge of powder left behind by her touch would wash away; the RFID microtags it carried would not. 'And speaking of work . . .' April sighed.

'Oh, of course,' the woman said, and she stood to leave. 'It was nice to meet you. I'm sorry I didn't get a chance to tell Mr Griffin goodbye.'

'Don't worry. I'll say it for you.'

With a last little wave, the woman turned and faded away into the club's quiet celebration of the coming New Year.

April pulled over the thin screen of her travel unit. The panel had come to life earlier as it sensed the presence of a stranger, and she'd noticed a flickering grid of dim ruby lines playing briefly over the face of Melanie Douglas. Her photograph appeared now on the screen, and the dim warm light of the club had been kind to her. 'Such a pretty woman,' April whispered, as her screen filled with data from the server in the sky.

Melanie Douglas, a.k.a. Nancy Kathleen Goetz, lucky number 043-396000-0016. She wasn't even a has-been, only another pathetic, no-talent never-was spat out by the cruel, cruel world of Tinsel Town. There was a great deal of leeway with this class of people, in terms of their fate and what not. If it had been Brad Pitt or Cameron Diaz who'd spoiled her cocktail, approval to condemn would've required a conference call at the very minimum.

She motioned for service as she finished her clicks and confirmations, linking the tags with which she'd marked her target with an open purchase order and a reasonable fee. Two of the club's wait-staff came, one to clear the tepid rubbish he'd prepared earlier, and a second with a fresh, chilled tray of ingredients.

Almost certainly it wouldn't happen tonight, but in the coming days the dark stars would align for a forgotten actress, who would sadly soon find herself in the wrong place at the wrong time. No method was specified; could be a hit-and-run, a stray bullet, a home invasion, or a random robbery gone bad, something low-budget and apropos to the value of the victim. While money was no object, there was still such a thing as a fitting end.

Of course there would be no repercussions, heavens no. Commoners were among the planet's most renewable resources. As Nancy Kathleen Goetz met her untimely demise, in that very hour five replacements would step fresh-faced off a westbound bus to play out her dead-end life all over again.

This human reckoning was not a matter of vengeance, or God forbid, of justice. It was prerogative, an absolute power over life and death, granted to reinforce the pre-eminence of her employers and their goals, and by extension, of her own. April Medici served the top 1/1000th of the 99.9th percentile, and through her service she would one day join them there. And for a chosen one to feast, somewhere a hundred thousand must go hungry. With modern-day famine, genocide, despotism and slavery as widespread as ever in human history, even the ignorant, self-satisfied middle classes accepted this central truth on some level: all around the world, there were billions of people who simply didn't count.

At last the waiters had finished, her drink was prepared

again, and she waved the scullions away. So one small thing was put right this evening.

But there were larger matters to be settled as well. As her graduation thesis she'd set herself a grand ambition, with the promise of great rewards, and now those wheels had been set in motion. Some say that in the end, the student becomes the teacher. But the exceptional student aims higher still.

Arrange it, he'd said.

She picked up her glass, breathed in its noble essence, and raised it to success in the weeks to come.

Ooooh, yes sir, I will.

5

'Have a good one, Mr Steinman.'

'Always do,' Rudy said. He tacked on a wink and just enough of a smile to open a careful fudge-zone of suggestion. It was risky, this late-night flirtation with a near-stranger in a dark parking garage. But hey, in the words of Michael Jordan, you miss every shot you don't take.

In spite of the lingering buzz from a glorious dinner, he deftly basket-caught the car keys as the gate watchman underhanded them, and without even breaking his stride. No apparent nibbles at his subtle come-on, though; sadly, it seemed that their owner would be the only man getting into Mr Steinman's pajamas tonight.

He stopped abruptly. Getting home was a crucial step toward getting into bed, and he had a problem. Somewhere between the cappuccino and the crème brûlée, that second magnificent bottle of Chateau LaFayette Reneau had vaporized some vital information from his brain.

Now just where in the name of Dorothy Parker had he parked the car?

There was an emergency phone number posted prominently on the I-beams. It rang to a little glass booth in the basement, manned by an eager attendant waiting to direct those who'd misplaced their vehicles. Unfortunately, the one time Rudy had called that number, one thing had somehow led to another, as it so often did. A young, helpful gentleman with a ready smile and a bulging toolbox; how better to end a long, hot DC summer than with a random fling on the roof of a parking garage?

What can I say? I'm a sucker for a man in uniform.

The relationship had been nice while it lasted; all of about eighteen minutes. But alas, impulse-love had rarely ended well for him. Some people need to get clingy, and at age twenty-nine, Rudy Steinman wasn't quite ready to get tied down. At least, never before the second date. There'd been a pitiful series of love-notes tucked under his windshield wiper, quite Hallmark-smarmy in the beginning but gradually devolving to hateful, all-caps crayon-rants as they went unanswered over the weeks.

All of which meant that phoning for help was out of the question; he'd be finding his car on his own tonight. The only good news being, his was usually the only black BMW M5 in the six-story lot. Should be no problem. He suppressed a minor burp and set out, one foot in front of the other. No problem at all.

An absolute eternity of uphill searching later he'd worked his way up to the third parking level, thumbing the keychain remote all the way as he walked the shadowy, slanting drive-ways, listening in the dead quiet for a telltale *blip-blop* from his door locks.

He stopped in a circle of light and let the echoing sound of his footsteps fade away. Another button-press as the stillness settled in, and at last the car answered him, one level up.

And then he heard a quiet *scritch* on the concrete floor, from somewhere behind.

He looked toward the noise on reflex and then caught his

error and turned his eyes away too quickly, toward the dark ramp in front of him. If there really was someone back in the darkness, now they knew he knew they were there.

'Hello?' he said softly.

No answer.

He began to walk again. It was thirty feet or so to the last corner before the car, and with every step the slope seemed to steepen, the silence seemed to thicken the air against his ears.

'Scott?' he called behind. No sound but a faraway siren, heading away. As he picked up his pace and rounded the bend, a curb caught his heel and he fell to the pavement, skinning his hands.

'If that's you, Scott, then say something! I am *not* amused!'

There was no response but quiet, quickening footsteps from somewhere in the dark. His anger at the dogged persistence of a jilted one-night stand was instantly replaced by a scrolling list of powerful people who wouldn't mind at all if Rudy Steinman was found in smaller pieces tomorrow in the trunk of his car.

He scrabbled through a cloudy puddle and managed to get to his feet, punched the alarm button on his remote and began to run. Uphill, dress-sole shoes on slick concrete, a little drunk and fighting down a full-out panic, it felt like a dream-sprint against the current in a waist-high wading-pool. The car alarm had stopped sounding but he was nearly there, and with only twenty yards to safety his thumb found the unlock button and punched it. There was a click and the headlights flashed, then flashed again. He skidded the last few feet as he reached the BMW's door and pulled the handle, but it held fast. With another push of the button the door clicked again, but it re-locked before he could open it.

Something froze his grip on the cold metal, some full-body instinct from way back in the caveman days. After 30,000 years of metro-evolution it had faded to a faint, hot tingling up the back of his neck, but it still spoke clearly.

Sure as the world, there was someone standing behind him.

'I'm not going to fight you,' Rudy whispered. 'You can have whatever you want. Take my wallet, take my car—'

'What do you mean, *your* car?'

It was a voice he hadn't heard in over a year. It was, and it couldn't be.

But he turned, and there she stood. Jeannie Reese, a little thin and dusty from the months on the run, fashionably butch in a scuffed leather jacket and tight weathered denim, pony-tailed ginger-brown hair in place of the silky Swedish blond she was born with. But otherwise every bit as unforgettable as she'd looked on the night she disappeared.

He stepped to her and she took him in her arms, held him close, the tips of her fingers gently pressing his back. This was another change that had come over her since she'd gone. Few who'd known her in her former life at DARPA would've described her as affectionate; there had been very few such embraces in her first twenty-two years.

'You have to tell me something, Jeannie.'

'What do you want to know?' she whispered.

He pulled away slightly, so he could see her again.

'I love what you've done with your hair,' he said, brushing her faux-auburn bangs from her eyes, wiping the tears from his own. 'But does the carpet match the drapes?'

She hugged him again, so tight that he wasn't sure he'd survive it very long. She might have been laughing quietly, but upon reflection it must have been some other emotion that had overcome her. As hard as it was to believe, in the eight years they'd worked together she'd never found him to be all that funny.

*

55

She'd agreed to a quick after-hours visit to the old workplace, but even before they'd crossed the atrium it had begun to feel like a mistake. It was the surface differences that struck her first; none of the changes seemed for the better. Less art and amenity at the lobby level, no plants or coffee-table books, a single bleak seating area. It looked as if all pre-9/11 pretenses had been dropped: this building housed the future-tech heart of America's defense intelligence engine, and its masters no longer cared who knew about it.

As they waited for the elevator Jeannie's eyes drifted over a quotation, unattributed, that had been chiseled into the gray marble over the central security checkpoint.

The price of liberty is eternal vigilance.

That quote was a new addition. The floor indicator issued a muffled *ding* as the elevator car arrived, and as the doors hissed open Jeannie wondered how Thomas Jefferson might respond to such a cynical hijacking of his words.

Another revolution, perhaps.

Inside, Rudy pushed the button for the fifth floor, the doors closed and the elevator hummed into motion. A shallow dent in the brushed aluminum paneling brought to mind her last trip to the ground floor in this building. She had made that faint impression herself, using the forehead of a young Navy lieutenant, the one man in her life who'd least deserved her suspicion. In the end he would give her far more than she would ever have a chance to repay.

Rudy caught her eye, and shook his head. 'Don't regret what you can't do over,' he said.

'Sounds easy.'

The doors slid open. He took her hand and led her on a circuitous route through the cubicle maze, a path designed to keep her face as far from the security cameras as possible. At length they were at the door to what had once been her office, and Rudy key-carded it open. The ID plate had been changed, of course.

RUDOLPH STEINMAN
Director, Special Projects

'Could your title be any more generic, Rudolph?'

'If anyone knew what I did, they might try to give me something to do.'

She stepped behind the desk, let her eyes circuit the spacious room. As devil-may-care as her former assistant might wish to appear, he was as sentimental as they come. With the exception of a few misfiled books on the shelves, he hadn't altered a single thing since the day she'd gone. Still, she felt like a stranger; nothing had changed in this office, and yet nothing at all was the same.

The whiteboard was blank, and the three-month planning calendar next to it was clear of everything but scattered lunch and dinner appointments.

'Isn't anything happening here these days?'

'Are you kidding? It's never been busier.'

'And yet you, sitting in this corner office, have no involvement in the R&D whatsoever?'

'The only thing I can figure out is, you know how you warned them before you left, that nothing had better happen to me, or else? I think they took you literally. A frickin' *week* will go by and nobody drops in. Oh sure, I get lunched by the occasional lobbyist, I sit in on vendor pitches, I sign off on the random work order, but that's about it.'

'So you have a high-level, max-clearance job . . . with no responsibilities.'

'I know, right? Pretty sweet.'

'Doesn't it drive you crazy, to have no work to do?'

He blinked. 'I'm not sure I understand the question.'

'It doesn't make sense.' Jeannie read his title again, on an untouched, shrink-wrapped box of business cards. 'And if you're not directing all these special projects,' she said, 'then who is?'

Rudy frowned. 'What's that?'

'What?'

He moved a step closer. 'That little light.'

'What light, where?'

He pointed to a spot by her side, under the lip of the desk. There was a small red LED, flashing.

'How long has that been lit?' She stood and walked to him. 'How long?'

'What is it? I don't even know what that is—' He stopped talking as he was pushed face against the wall and pinned there, his arm twisted high behind his back. Her free hand pressed efficiently over his clothes, searching. 'What the hell are you doing?'

'That light is a bug detector,' she said, 'I had it installed two years ago. It rings the security desk downstairs, silent alarm.' She flipped him around and looked him in the eye. 'One of us is transmitting, and it isn't me.'

'Transmitting?'

'Come on, walk.' The flashing LED had gone out as they'd moved away, so it couldn't be a stationary bug in the phone or the desk, it was definitely a body-plant. She pulled him along for the first few feet and then released him as she picked up the pace. She'd drawn her pistol, but it was pointed toward the floor.

'How are we supposed to—'

'Fire escape,' she hissed. 'Now move!'

As they ran past the elevator, the floor lights above the double-doors were blinking their way up to 5.

*

When they'd reached the car there hadn't been any discussion about who would drive. Her name was on the title, and she still had her own set of keys. After the first few miles it remained a completely wordless ride, but at least she'd put away her gun.

The clock on the dash read 11:17 PM. He glanced across to her as the traffic light ahead turned yellow. Rather than slowing she bumped the shifter and floored it, and 400 horsepower sank him into his leather seat as they blurred through the intersection. A few more blocks whizzed by, and a quick check of the rearview showed no flashing lights and sirens in pursuit.

'Red-light camera probably nailed you back there.'

She drove on, and didn't answer.

'I'll just pay the ticket when it comes in,' he sighed. 'Don't worry about it.' He unwrapped an after-dinner candy from the cup-holder, and after getting no response when he held it out for her, he cheeked the mint and checked the mirror again. 'I'll bet you wouldn't stop if the cops were behind us right now, would you?'

She shook her head.

'Well, the way you're driving you're obviously planning on a high-speed chase and a shoot-out any minute now, so could we stop off at my apartment? I left my Uzi in my other pants.'

He watched as the intensity in her eyes softened with the slightest possible smile. After a few seconds the car began to settle down to the speed limit.

'Where are we going, Jeannie?'

She glanced at him, and then turned back to the road ahead. '500 Fifth Avenue.'

'Fifth Avenue? The one in New York?'

The trip would mean close to four hours on the road, but again, there wasn't going to be a vote on it. As always she was determined to get her answers, and since he was now one of the questions, he was coming along for the ride.

'I don't know what's going on here,' he said, 'and I don't know anything about any bugging device, but I hope you know I'd never do anything to hurt you.'

'We'll find out.'

Some relationships don't change, for better or worse, regardless of everything that changes around them. Rudy loved this young woman, and he suspected she felt the same in her own way. Trust was a different matter, on a different scale. Love had never been particularly kind to her, but love only hurts; trust can kill.

She'd never mentioned a single female confidante, and he imagined he was in third place on her short list of trusted men. Number two would be Jay Marshall, who worked at 500 Fifth in New York City, their current destination. With a phone call he'd be waiting for her in front of his office building when they pulled up at 3 AM, a tray of coffees in hand, no questions asked. And her numero uno, the one guy she'd be running to now if she could? He'd dropped off the edge of the Earth in late 2001 without even saying goodbye.

The FBI tacks a hot-sheet of their most wanted fugitives on the wall of every US Post Office, but they keep their truly scary ranking behind closed doors. This is a roster of criminal and terrorist minds whose potential for mass destruction is far too alarming to ever be made public. And one of the last things Jeannie Reese still shared in common with the federal authorities she once served was this: John Fagan was at the top of their list, too.

6

Jeannie had relinquished the wheel when they'd stopped for gas just across the New Jersey border. She didn't make a fuss about it. Rudy had returned from a quick visit to the service-station men's room to find her fast asleep, curled in the reclined passenger seat.

One good thing about all-night driving, there's lots of quiet time to be alone with one's thoughts, if any. Also, not much traffic to worry about.

Plenty of other things to worry about, of course.

He glanced over at Jeannie, took a second to adjust his overcoat that was serving as her blanket, and then turned his eyes back to the road. There was something terribly wrong with this whole situation. Her showing up out of nowhere like this, some things that she'd said, as if there were quite a few vital details he should know, but he didn't. Couldn't have known, in fact.

A little voice in his head was nagging away at him, raising one good question after another. But he was tired and there was still a long road ahead. One thing he'd picked up in his years of government service: there were times when it was better not to think these things through.

He flicked on the XM radio, found some golden oldies, and let Tommy James and the Shondells try to carry his troubles away.

'Turn right up here,' Jeannie said. She unbuckled her seatbelt and leaned to the dash to see the street signs. Visibility wasn't good; it was the middle of the night in a dark old corner of the city and a freezing gray drizzle was blowing in from the ocean. Driving below Houston Street was quirky for an out-of-towner, and it seemed that Rudy had missed a couple of turns since the Holland Tunnel. 'No, left. And then left again onto St James.'

'I thought you were still asleep.'

'Just thinking,' she said.

'Is this really the way to the FDR?'

'No. Not quite yet.'

He seemed to realize then where her detour was taking them, and his foot eased slightly off the gas. There was no good excuse for a side-visit and every reason to avoid being seen down here at all costs. Lower Manhattan wasn't deserted by any means and there were probably surveillance cameras on every corner. But it wouldn't have seemed right to be this close and not drive by.

'Slow down but don't stop,' she said.

Up ahead in the middle of a short block a building was missing in a line of four-story brownstones and granite-faced low-rises. At some point the demolition had been completed, but new construction hadn't yet begun. In the sanitized void there remained no indication that a minor deity of the cyber-underground had once lived between those scarred, blackened walls. Any records of the history of this place would have been meticulously wiped away by now; she and Rudy were among the last alive who remembered. And John Fagan himself, of course, wherever he might be.

Rudy was watching the rearview mirror on her side. A few blocks behind them two men from opposite sidewalks had crossed to the middle of the narrow street. One had been going north and the other south. They were walking together now, somewhat more purposefully, coming this way.

'Can we get out of here now? Please?'

She leaned back in her seat to close her eyes again for a little while.

'Yeah,' she said, 'let's go.'

Mate a Kodiak bear with Mrs Santa Claus, and with only minimal shaving their offspring could be a dead ringer for Jay Marshall. He was a big, imposing man, and contrary to the demeanor his genes might have favored, also the sweetest guy you'd ever want to meet.

The blood was just beginning to return to Rudy's fingers following a forceful handshake. Jeannie was getting the full-contact greeting, and for once she didn't seem to mind it at all. He looked up and down the avenue a few times, checked the time, unwrapped a stick of Dentyne from his pocket and had chewed out most of the flavor before her feet finally touched the ground again.

'Good to see you, too,' she said.

Things sobered up on the elevator ride to Marshall's offices. Jeannie summarized the events of the evening as they ascended, and by the time they'd passed the twenty-fifth floor a palpable two-against-one vibe was filling the small space.

'Why'd you bring him if he's wearing a wire?'

'It's got to be micro-power, meant to operate near a relay transmitter, so I thought it was worth the risk. I wanted you to see it, so maybe we can find out who's behind it.' She looked across the elevator car at him. 'He says he doesn't know anything about it.'

Marshall *pffff*ed, and shook his head.

'I'm standing right here, guys,' Rudy said. 'I can totally hear you.'

Jay Marshall's business was the discovery, recovery and destruction of secrets, and since the mid-nineties that business had been booming. Like their global clients, the world-class enforcers, subverters, or evaders of the law, Prescienza, Inc. operated 24/7/365. At the fortieth floor the elevator doors opened onto a lobby fronting a cubicle jungle that was bustling like a mid-season holiday rush at Bloomingdale's. The time on the clock was 3:23 AM.

Jay and Jeannie went to the coffee lounge and left Rudy in a stark white exam room with instructions to disrobe and put each article of clothing into a separate plastic bin. He'd barely fastened the single plastic snap at the neck of his paper gown when technicians arrived to collect the bins. Marshall opened the door for them as they were leaving, and he stayed.

'Cavity search?' Rudy asked. 'I'll try anything once.'

'First things first.'

Jay held out a black and silver wand near Rudy's chest, passed it up and slowly down again, and then pressed and held a button on its handle. A string of varicolored lights danced up and down the wand, and as they stabilized it issued a low tone that repeated three times.

'What's that?'

'I'm just calibrating it. It's like a . . . sort of like a stud-finder.'

'That's nice, go ahead and talk down to me. Humiliate me some more, I'm starting to crack.' Rudy adjusted his gown. 'And speaking of cracks, do you have a safety pin so I can close up the back of this smock?'

There was a click from overhead and then a voice from the intercom speaker.

'I second the request for that safety pin,' Jeannie said.

'Relax.' Marshall fine-tuned the instrument and readied for the first pass. 'If you can't stand the view, stay out of the peep-room. This won't take a minute.'

The firm hand on Rudy's shoulder prevented any move that might have preserved his modesty. His partially exposed derrière was neatly framed in the two-way mirror behind him, and the breeze from a floor vent was blowing straight up his flimsy gown. Jeez, this was almost worse than the one-way-ticket security line at O'Hare.

Marshall passed the wand over Rudy's arms, his chest and back, his head and neck, his legs and groin. He twisted a dial and then went over him again, more slowly this time. At the end he stood back, frowning.

'Jeannie, come on in here,' Marshall said.

After a few seconds the door opened and she came in followed by a technician. The white-coat laid Rudy's clothes out on the table, each folded item wrapped around the middle by a sanitary paper strip, like the toilet lid at a cheap motel.

'Can I get dressed now?'

'No,' Jeannie said. 'What's the story, Jay?'

'His clothes have been cleared, and I didn't find anything on him at all.'

'Nothing?' She held out her hand. 'Do you mind if I try?'

'Go ahead.'

She took the wand, held it an inch from Rudy's chest and pressed the scan switch. Immediately the line of indicator LEDs ran up three-quarters of the scale to light green and a high tone warbled from the tiny speaker.

'I told you—'

'Hold up,' Marshall said. 'Rudy, you stand over there in the corner.'

He did. Marshall turned to Jeannie, held the dark wand near her. On activation the RF radiation scale pegged to its maximum reading.

She shrank back a step, speechless, her palm to her chest. Marshall flicked off the wand and turned to Rudy.

'Go ahead and get dressed,' he said. 'We'll be in my office.'

His freshly irradiated clothes had the slight odor of singed cotton and the zipper of his slacks was still hot to the touch, but regardless he couldn't remember when it had felt so good to be in his trousers again.

After stopping by the copy room for directions Rudy made his winding way to Marshall's suite. Jay was squinting down into an illuminated platter-sized magnifier on a swing-arm hanging close to the blotter on his desk. Jeannie was sitting to the side, pressing a folded tissue to the side of her neck.

'Hey,' Rudy said.

She looked across the room, gave up a tiny smile at the sight of him, and shrugged. It was a small movement full of subtle little signs, but he'd learned to read them all years before. There was an apology in there somewhere, a shamed acknowledgment of her misplaced suspicions, and a humble overture to be friends again, if he would have her.

He'd never left her, of course, and he smiled and flipped her the bird to let her know.

As someone raised in the flatlands of Tallahassee, these lofty Manhattan buildings still always gave him a touch of the whirlies. Behind Jay's desk the dizzying view through the floor-to-ceiling windows was dominated by the pale-lit spire of the Empire State Building to the south. They say it had been conceived and built on little more than aristocratic one-upmanship, a gentlemen's competition to outdo the Chrysler as the tallest building on the island. Now in the absence of the Twin Towers that had grazed the sky behind it for almost thirty years, it had reclaimed that title.

'Come over here, Rudy. Take a look at this.'

On a sheet of white filter paper under the magnifier there was a tiny black fleck of something. Rudy bent closer, pulled the heavy lens down a few inches more. It could have passed for a natural object to a casual observer, someone unaware of its function. It looked like a slender thorn with rear-facing barbs along its length, the kind a fish-hook employs to discourage its removal.

'This is the transmitter you were looking for?'

Marshall nodded.

'Where was that thing?'

'Buried in the side of my neck,' Jeannie said. She briefly held up the tissue she'd been holding there to show him a spot of blood. 'I remember feeling it now, something like a pin-prick when it must have gone in. Guess I forgot about it with all that was happening.'

Marshall stepped over and took a moment to examine the puncture wound. 'Doesn't look like there was any inflammation to speak of. It's probably coated with something to keep her immune system from reacting to it.'

'What, like a suture?'

'More like a parasite.'

'And when did this happen?' Rudy asked.

'A few days ago,' Jeannie said. She looked tired, only half engaged. 'I was sent to interview a man, a UN weapons inspector. Wait, are you really that out of touch? You should know all about it, you forwarded the order to me, like the other jobs.'

'I did *what*?'

Marshall caught his eye, motioned subtly to leave it alone, and Rudy stopped the question before she picked it up.

'I knew Kempler was trying to tell me something,' Jeannie said, 'and I don't know, maybe this is it.' She winced a bit, turned her eyes from the light.

'Headache?' Rudy asked. She nodded. He took out his wallet and removed a two-pack of Tylenol from an inner sleeve, drew a cup of water from a cooler in the corner and put both items on the side-table near her chair.

She took a sip of water, tore open the pack and popped the tablets. 'Why are these warm?'

Rudy licked an index finger and applied it to his hip-pocket with a *sssss*.

'Oh my God, *gross*, I've got your body heat in my mouth.' She didn't look thrilled about it, but she downed the pills with the rest of the water.

Rudy turned his attention back to Jay. 'So what's it transmitting?'

'Nothing.' Jay had pulled a boxy device with a stub antenna from a nearby drawer. He held it close to the thing on the blotter and rotated a thumbwheel on the side. There was a sudden whoosh of white noise as a second dial turned, then a fade to silence before the hiss rushed in again on the other side. 'No message, no information at all. Just that faint carrier signal.'

'Hmph.' Rudy took a tissue from the dispenser, folded it and wet its center with rubbing alcohol that was still open on the desk, handed it to Jeannie and then lobbed her blood-stained dressing into the small waste bin across the room. It was an exceptional shot, nothing-but-net from way downtown, and normally he would have taken a moment to celebrate it. But he was thinking.

'It's not a bugging device at all, then?' he asked.

'No.' Marshall tuned to the carrier frequency again. The

white noise hushed, but even with the volume maxed out there was only dead air. 'It's more like a beacon of some kind. But just finding it can't be the point. It should be telling us something, shouldn't it?'

Jeannie sat up a little straighter. 'That handheld you've got, does it transmit?'

'Sure it does—'

'So key the mike,' she said.

Marshall looked at the two of them, and then down at the little black spike on the desk blotter. 'What do you want me to say to it?'

'Maybe it doesn't know we've found it,' Jeannie said. 'You're listening on its frequency already. Tap the mike. Nudge it, and see what happens.'

Though he looked thoroughly unconvinced, Jay keyed the talk button and released it. He jumped back and nearly dropped the transceiver as a raw harmonic screech blared from its speaker in response.

All three approached the desk, all eyes on the tiny messenger that they'd just awakened.

'What did that sound like to you?' Marshall asked.

'Like the 300-baud modem I used when I was five years old.' She sat behind Jay's desk at his computer, pulled up his web browser and began a search. 'Don't touch that switch again. While it was implanted it was probably running on some low-power scheme, maybe electrochemical current from my body. It might not have the juice now to transmit more than a time or two.' He put the transceiver down and she pulled his desk mike over, bent it so it aimed at the speaker of the walkie-talkie.

'What are we doing?' Jay asked.

'I think it's stored a block of digital data converted to analog, to sound, like an old dial-up modem.'

'That's what, AFSK modulation, right?'

'Right. Ham-radio operators still use it to trade computer files over the air.' Her download had completed, and she launched the application she'd found on a packet-radio enthusiasts' site. 'I think whoever put this together used an old technology, kind of like a universal language, probably because they didn't know who'd be receiving the message.'

She thumped the computer's mike with a fingernail; the sound waves registered on the recording meter. After a couple of adjustments, she took a deep breath and looked up at Jay.

'Now hit it again,' she said, and then she caught Rudy's eye. 'And everybody be quiet.' He solemnly zipped his lips, locked them, and threw away the key.

The talk button on the walkie-talkie was clicked and again the grating electronic noise came back in response. A splash of jagged sound waves rippled across the computer screen.

'Did you get it?' Jay asked.

'I got something.' She selected a long section of the displayed data, saved the file, and then double-clicked to play it back from the computer. Jeannie turned up the volume on the desktop speakers, and hit 'play' to listen again. It sounded the same, if slightly muted, like a car-radio recording made from the back seat. She spent a few moments lightly filtering and optimizing the recording, and then saved it again with a temporary filename.

'So what is it?' Jay dragged a chair over and sat next to her. 'I can get a team started analyzing the file, but it might take some hours—'

'No,' she said. 'No one should see this, just us. What kind of forensic software do you have on this machine?'

'All kinds of stuff, but where do we start?'

'Wait a minute, geniuses.' They both looked up at Rudy. 'Whoever sent this wants you to get the message, right? I mean, the guy didn't drop it on a public street, he shoved it into the neck of the intended recipient, person-to-person. Why would he make it hard to read it?'

'What are you getting at?'

'It's not going to have some unbreakable encryption scheme,' Rudy said. 'That implant didn't ask for a password, it spilled its guts as soon as we tuned it in. It's got to be easy, so let the computer figure it out for you. You already know it's a digital file of some standard kind. Just keep renaming it until Jay's computer opens it in a readable format.'

Jeannie sat back in her chair and regarded him with something approaching respect. 'In a simple-minded way,' she said, 'that's very astute.' She began with the name 'temp.doc', and let Microsoft Word try to open it. Several pages of garbage filled the screen, and she closed the application to try another. 'If you're right, I'm going to have to take back some very unflattering things I've said about you over the years.'

'Oh, that reminds me,' Rudy said, 'it's breakfast time. Anybody else feel like a bitch? I mean a bagel?'

She set to work again, with only a bit of amusement showing in profile. 'I could use a black coffee if you're going past the machine.' She'd just renamed and tried the file again, this time tagging it as an AVI movie. The computer threw an error; so it wasn't a video, at least not one in that common format.

'Black coffee? From the machine?' Rudy snorted. 'All right, whoever you are, what have you done with Jeannie?'

'I'll go with you,' Jay said. He had a grim look on his face that said there was more to be discussed than the breakfast order, but outside their present company.

'Yeah. Okay. We'll be right back, all right?'

But she was deep in the puzzle again, and didn't answer.

Marshall held the door for him, and with a last look over his shoulder Rudy left her to her work.

'What do you mean, that isn't Jeannie? Of course it's Jeannie.'

Jay pulled over a chair, flicked a switch that drew the blinds of the conference room windows and sat close to Rudy. 'I know, I know. I'm not sure what I mean, but I've known her since she was twelve, and there's something not right about her.'

Rudy sat back in his chair, and it was a while before he spoke.

'Okay, she's said some things that were, I guess, kind of confused—'

'Have you ever known that woman to be confused?'

'No. No, I haven't.'

'While you were getting changed we had time for a talk. She told me she'd kept all the emails I'd sent to her over this past year, how important it had been to her, to know I was thinking about her.'

'Don't tell me,' Rudy said.

Marshall shook his head. 'I haven't written to her once. How could I have? None of us knew where she was.'

'And just now,' Rudy said, 'didn't it seem like she was saying that I'd been involved somehow in these freelance intel jobs she's been sent out on? Me?'

'And?'

'I don't know what the hell she's talking about.' Rudy twisted the top off a bottle of water and took a sip. 'And that black-coffee thing, and from a *machine* yet. That's like Jacques Torres picking a frickin' Moon-Pie from the pastry tray. The Starbucks at the Pentagon? They had a nine-dollar Frappuccino named after her. No way, that's the deal-breaker. I know people can change, but not that much.'

Jay had gotten up and begun to pace. 'So what do we do?'

'Do? What are you afraid of? What is she, the Manchurian candidate? Let's sit her down and see what she has to say about all this.'

'You're not hearing me,' Jay said. 'I think something's been *done* to her.'

Rudy sat back. 'Like what?'

'I've seen some strange things over the years. There was a black-ops program in the fifties and sixties, it was called MK-Ultra. You remember the Unabomber?'

'Ted Kaczynski. What about him?'

'An escapee from MK-Ultra. He was a math prodigy, accepted to Harvard when he was sixteen, sound familiar? And then the spooks got ahold of him. Pumped him full of mind-control stuff the CIA brought over with the Nazi scientists they rescued at the end of the war—'

'Nazis?' Rudy asked.

Marshall nodded.

'Rescued. *Nazis*. Oh, that's good, Jay. You almost had me going there for a second—'

'Operation Paperclip, Google it, asshole—'

'Google on this,' Rudy said, pointing to his privates. 'I'm going to go out now and get our little friend a real New York City cappuccino, and that'll straighten her right out.' He stood to leave, but Jay took his arm.

'Explain this, then. Right before you came in I asked her if she was seeing anyone—'

'Oh my God, no,' Rudy said, aghast, 'Jeannie's dating Kurt Waldheim?'

'—and she said yes, she was seeing someone off and on.'

'Really—'

'A young woman.'

Rudy stopped in mid-snicker.

'. . . Say again?'

'A young woman. Someone she works with.'

Rudy blinked. 'I think you must have misunderstood her.'

Marshall shook his head, no.

'Jay. Listen. If Jeannie Reese is gay then I'm straight. And Jay?'

'Yeah.'

'I'm not straight,' Rudy said.

They both looked at the closed door.

'They take something about you,' Marshall said, 'something fundamental, right? And they try to change it to see if they've really got you. It's like a litmus test. You see how part of her is still there, most of her, a lot of things we'd recognize, so we trust her? And they've brought us into it, they've been faking communications from us to make it real for her, too. Whatever operation they're running, it's got to be big and deep.'

'Hang on,' Rudy said. 'Let's say for just one second that I'm not home on my balcony smoking some tainted hash right now. Why is she here? Whoever's gotten inside her head, why would they risk letting her see us?'

'Maybe they lost track of her. I don't know.' Jay got up and pulled his cellphone from his pocket. 'But we're sure as hell going to find out.'

'How do you plan on doing that?'

'I know where to start. There's a guy here in town, former SAS, he's supposed to be very good with this sort of thing.' He checked his watch. 'I'll try to get hold of him. Now you go back to my office and keep her occupied.'

'Doing what?'

'Doesn't matter. Just act natural, and don't let her out of your sight.'

In an increasingly non-smoking world the smell of something burning indoors is starkly obvious. Two hallways away

74

he picked it up; without thinking he started to run. Others followed, even before the smoke-detector outside Marshall's office had begun to drone its warning. An extinguisher was pulled from the wall and the man holding it edged past Rudy, as he'd stopped in the doorway.

The desk blotter was in flames, burning from the middle out to the curling edges. An extended *shoosh* from the red canister and it was over, the fire was put out and the room was a haze of stinging white powder and residual smoke.

Jay Marshall arrived, winded from the short sprint down the hall, and put everyone back to their work. Despite the sour cloudy air he closed and locked the door, and he and Rudy walked to the desk. There was no good news.

The computer screen reported completion of a successful, total, secure wipe of Marshall's hard drive. The fused, inert remains of the tiny transmitter were buried in the dead white ashes of the fire.

And in more ways than one, it appeared, Jeannie Reese was gone.

7

Within the tower level of the Carlyle Hotel one floor is never rented, no matter the price it could command. The art and sculpture that grace these walls and pedestals would rival the private gallery of any collector in the world. Each piece of furniture is commissioned and one of a kind, crafted of endangered woods, precious metals, and fabrics spun to order, thread by thread. The oils, mists and lotions on the dressing table have no labels, only the seals of their creators on ivory cards tucked beneath each hand-cut crystal vial.

A permanent staff of seventeen haunts this hidden palace each day and night, ensuring its white-glove readiness on a moment's notice; such tenants as these make no reservations. While the Presidential Suite levels below could be rented by any peasant with a platinum card, these rooms would be despoiled by any fee applied to them. This key could not be bought, only granted.

April Medici stood near the wide expanse of windows in the north bedroom, rubbing her damp hair with a warm Turkish towel, a picture-postcard view of Central Park at sunrise down below.

There was a cheval mirror to the side and she turned for a

moment to take herself in, head to toes. She'd chosen a wrap from several in the armoire, a soft terrycloth robe in evergreen and parchment. Somehow the colors and the texture had perfectly suited her mood; though there had been silks, cashmeres and satins to choose from, simple comfort had trumped all her other vanities.

Tense idle time passed in such luxury was the closest thing she knew to relaxation. There was never relief from the continual urgency of her work, only these brief distractions. Now a few hours' sleep and a mineral bath had brought her through to the early morning, and still there was no final word on the recent assignments.

The watched seconds ticked by as always, one by one. Patience was one of many virtues she'd never had ambition to acquire.

April toweled her hair a last time, shook it down and raked it back with her fingers. She let the robe fall open at its tapered waist, turned in profile, let the cloth slip coyly from one smooth white shoulder, and then the other. The filtered morning light painted her lovingly in highlight and shadow, the picture of youth in its golden season. Such splendor in the feminine form; her hands lightly followed her eyes, caressing the noble lines, the pouty curves, toned and perfected in their sensuous prime.

She caught her own gaze, and paused.

The mirror was an early Chippendale and no doubt priceless, but like all old things its flaws had begun to show. Her fingers touched her face. A ripple in the silver had thinned her lips, drawn down a corner of her mouth. As she turned her head the noble prominence at the bridge of her nose grew subtly wide and flattened, her chin receded, became weak and common. She stepped closer. Her eyes changed in the distorted glass, turned small and dark and set apart, out of proportion.

She looked away. A rare nugget of wisdom from Mr Griffin presented itself: if one wishes to live in the here and now, there's such a thing as too much reflection. She must think of other things; this dreary waiting wouldn't do.

Something special might be needed to occupy her mind.

Many girls had come and gone in her life, many gentle attentive lovers, and also a wicked few who'd schooled her young in the naughty kicks of playing rough. She drew a breath, shivered a bit at a sudden physical memory. Her fingers arched and lightly dragged their lacquered nails across her tummy. A warm tingling hollow tensed and eased underneath, a hunger there that was never far away and rarely satisfied.

The girls were very nice; still, there were those occasions when nothing would quite do the trick but the lusty attentions of a certain class of man.

Power had its place but there was a thrill to be had in giving it away, if only for a time. To be taken, held down and taken with no charade of tenderness, strong arms and rough hands pressing her close and breathless, hot slick skin over hard muscle rubbing and heaving against her, forcing itself past her struggles and then deeper and deeper up inside of her. No courtship, no pretense. Nothing more or less than the sweaty human friction of the animal act, tooth and nail, panting and pounding, leaving her spent and splayed and wet and ragged when he was finally drained and satisfied.

She sighed, and smiled to her flushed reflection. That, April thought, might be just the thing to slay an empty morning.

The streets and sidewalks of the Upper East Side were already bustling down below. Hundreds of tiny little people were walking here and there, going about their tiny lives. A sunken hole in the pavement of Madison Avenue was surrounded by orange cones and blue sawhorses with a work crew toiling away. One of the workers was carrying slack brown bags of something over each of his shoulders, stacking them to the side, back and forth from a truck bed. Heavy lifting was a job often given to the young buck of the crew. Even from high above, this man cut a stimulating figure.

He might be up to the task.

April made a command gesture to her travel unit on the roll-top desk, saw its screen come to life and display a picture of her as she stood before the window. She pointed through the glass, down toward the worker on the street.

'Him,' she said.

The computer knew her position in three dimensions to within a few millimeters. Her index finger pointed to a set of X, Y and Z coordinates thirty-eight floors below. There were scores of networked street-level security cameras within visual range of the spot, owned by the city, the state, DHS and various businesses. Her system accessed and displayed these real-time images, and those cameras with the capability to do so swiveled and zoomed toward her subject.

The clearest picture floated to the forefront. Crosshairs on her screen followed the movement of the tip of her finger until the man of interest stopped for a moment to wipe his brow on his sleeve. A snap of her fingers locked him in, and the computer displayed a multi-angle image of the one who'd caught her fancy.

Muscular, tall, dark and handsome.

'Let me talk to him,' she said.

As she watched nearly everyone on the sidewalk within a sixty-foot circle broke their stride as their cellphones rang in unison. It appeared that her construction man had no phone of his own, but over a dozen people stopped to answer the call.

'Good morning, New Yorkers,' April said. 'There's a young man on a road crew in the middle of the block on Madison.

79

Lumberjack shirt, bottle of blue Gatorade in his hand, leaning on the tail of a flatbed truck. I'll put a thousand-dollar credit on the cellular bill of the first one of you that hands him your phone.'

Most simply ended the call and continued on their way, but two true believers broke into a dead run toward the repair crew from opposite ends of the street. The winner handed his phone to her man. After a bewildered hesitation, he put it to his ear.

'Well, hello there,' April said.

The saying goes that every man has his price. Sexism aside, as stated this would seem to suggest that there's a varying amount of money for which every person would give up their dearest principle. While correct enough in politics, that interpretation is incomplete.

The actual truth behind the old maxim had been her most valuable lesson, and it served her every day. Anyone can be induced to do anything, either for the offer of something given or the threat of something taken away. In any situation, find that something that's hidden in everyone and nothing is out of your reach. So far she'd found no exceptions.

'What are you thinking about?' the man asked.

He was lying behind her, his arm still around her, his hand lightly stroking hers. It was a niggling problem with anonymous sex. When it's over, absolutely breathtaking though it may have been, you unavoidably find yourself in a position of physical intimacy with someone you'd be happy enough to never see again.

April frowned, disengaged herself, and rolled to face him. 'Are you still here?'

He propped up on an elbow, flexed and glistening, looking like a lewd recruitment poster for the master race. He smiled and delicately thumbed a smudge of lipstick from the corner of her mouth.

'Your money's on the table over there,' she said.

'I'd rather not take it.'

She rolled her eyes. 'Whatever.'

'My name is Andy.'

'Don't care.' There was little about anyone she couldn't know if she chose to; the not-knowing was a good part of the thrill of these encounters.

'Andy Pepper.'

Her left eyebrow arched ever so slightly. 'I doubt it.'

'No, that's really my name.'

'I suppose I'll have to believe you. Who'd ever make up a name like that?'

'I'm a model—'

'Right. When you're not hot-patching pot-holes for the DOT.'

'Well okay, I'm trying to be a model, yes, when I'm not doing construction.'

She yawned with no attempt to be dainty, still looking into his eyes.

'What do you do,' he asked, 'to be able to stay in a place like this?'

'What do I do? Are we having a conversation now?'

'I'd like to, yeah.'

'What I do is,' April said, matching his earnest expression with one of her own, 'sometimes when somebody asks me just one too many questions, Andy? What I do is, I have someone else come by who kills them and then hides their body in the foundation of a building.'

He smiled. 'I'd just like to know some more about you, that's all. The only thing I know is that you're a very beautiful woman.'

She studied him for a long moment.

'Go on.'

'. . . You mean I should leave now?'

'No.' She ran her fingers lightly through her hair; it was still damp and tousled from their hour of abandon. 'You were saying that I was beautiful.'

He nodded.

She turned away on her side, but pressed a little closer and allowed his arms around her once again.

'Go on,' April said.

The house-phone roused her, jangling on the nightstand. She fumbled the receiver off the cradle and brought it to her ear.

'. . . Yes.'

'Pardon, miss, a young lady is here to see you. She has your card and says she's expected, shall I—'

April sat up, suddenly wide awake. 'No no, listen. *You* bring her up, you personally, right to my door, the two of you alone, and don't leave her until you see me let her in. Do you understand?'

'Yes, miss.'

She hung up the phone and stood, slipping on her robe. As she walked around the footboard she snagged a throw-pillow and tossed it at her bedmate's face. 'Up and out,' April said, over her shoulder.

There were far too many mirrors in this bathroom. Her bed-hair was flat in spots and fly-away in others. Her make-up, so subtle and alluring two hours ago, now looked like she'd been ridden hard over forty miles of bad road. She began to do what she could with a brush, a blow-dryer, mouthwash, hand-soap and hot water.

'I want to see you again,' the man called from the bed-room.

'Oh my God, will you get the fuck out of here?'

'All right, I'm going, but can I call you?'

'No! Out!'

'Okay, okay.'

She heard him getting dressed in a hurry. Her hasty makeover was finished just as the door chime sounded a minute later. He was still tying his work-boots, kneeling next to the divan in the front room, as April reached the marble foyer.

She opened the door and Jeannie Reese was there. His escort mission complete, the under-butler watching from down the hall retired quietly to his station.

One step into the room and there was an instant reaction to the sight of a crouching man off to the side. In a flash Reese had drawn her pistol and stepped between them, shielding her friend from the danger.

'Stop,' April whispered.

Without hesitation the gun pointed to the floor.

'Now,' April said to the man. 'Like I said. Out.'

He lowered his hands, stood, and started for the door. The adrenalin was clearly pumping; his manner was a little stiff and hesitant, like that of someone unaccustomed to nearly being shot between the eyes.

'Hold it,' April said.

He stopped.

'You said you wanted to see me again.'

After a moment he nodded.

'Turn around and say it.'

He turned back. 'I want to see you again.'

And it was the strangest thing. There was an utterly stunning woman standing between them, no doubt the most spitefully picture-perfect little pepper-pot he'd ever seen within arm's length. Yet this man wasn't looking at her. Not a glance after the pistol had stopped pointing at him, not even the quick down-and-up most men will steal from a girl without even thinking. He was only looking at April.

'Take off,' she said quietly. 'Maybe I'll call you sometime.'

'You . . . you don't have my number—'

April smiled, made a shooing motion with her hand, and without another word he opened the door and left the two of them alone.

She took the pistol from Jeannie Reese and laid it carefully on the Eastlake parlor table to the side. It was a nice piece; the table, not the gun. She made a mental note to have it sent out to her summer place in Aspen when this business was over.

'Now, honey,' April said. 'Let's catch up.'

Jeannie said nothing.

She knew this woman she faced. This was her dearest, closest friend. Nothing could come between them, no other loyalty divide them. Before love, truth, honor, God or country, there was this one true alliance.

'Did you come straight here? Did you stop anywhere else on your way here to see me?'

Nothing could be hidden from April, but something compelled her to try. Speaking of the time she'd spent with Rudy and Jay could only endanger their lives. She felt she couldn't risk saying the word aloud; her voice would reveal her disloyalty. Eyes downcast, she shook her head, no.

'You know how I feel about witnesses when things go badly,' April said. She already seemed to know that she was about to be disappointed. 'All I want to hear is that both of those guys in Arizona, the pilot and the co-pilot, are dead.'

No, again.

The slap across her face came without any warning.

And with the sharp pain came a flash of clarity, just a

momentary burst of unaltered awareness as the hand struck her cheek and the stars flew across her field of vision.

She knew this woman she faced, yes. Not only from now, but from before.

They'd been little more than children. The place and the time were somehow hidden from her, but she remembered the feelings.

The hatred from the other girl had been instantaneous when they'd met, and of a depth she'd never known. She'd felt jealousy and envy from others all her young life, from her peers and their parents alike, but this was different. April was different.

One of the teachers, a kind old man, had taken her aside to warn her about April.

She hates you because you're gifted, he'd said, gifted in so many ways. Her hate wouldn't pass with time; it would grow with her and mature. Hate had been her weakness but it would become her one great power. They would feed it and forge it into a weapon, a shield; a mission. When they were done it would be enough to fell nations. And she would never stop at merely getting even, he'd said. It was the way of such people. What she couldn't own she would destroy.

Jeannie's pistol was on the table near her hand but the will to take it and use it had begun to fade with the dying spark of memory. There was a final moment of truth remaining in which she might have found the strength, not nearly enough to kill the demon in front of her, but maybe just enough to free herself from living out the terrible things to come. But then it was gone.

'We've gotta get your head right,' April said. She patted Jeannie on the cheek, the same one she'd struck just before. 'I'm only trying to clean up the mess you made. These are all your own loose ends, and you just keep on letting me down.'

'I have something,' Jeannie said softly. She was suddenly exhausted; it felt as though she'd never slept in her life.

'You have something?'

She nodded. Her voice was small. 'It seemed important, and I wanted you to have it.'

'I'll be the judge of what's important,' April said. 'Let's see it.'

Jeannie pulled a folded sheet of paper from her jacket pocket and held it out. It was the printout from Jay Marshall's office, the urgent decoded message that had been entrusted to her as the final act of Dr Olin Kempler.

April took the paper from her, unfolded it and looked it over, idly at first. Two different things then seemed to dawn in her expression: a child's quiet wonder upon receipt of a most wished-for gift, and the glint in the eyes of a lynx as a lame deer wanders from the safety of the herd. She brought the paper near the lamp on the side table, her lips shadowing the words she was reading. After nearly a minute she put the paper down and looked up.

'Outstanding.' April checked her watch, stepped up and took Jeannie's face in her hands. 'How do you feel?'

The words would barely form themselves. 'I'm so tired,' Jeannie said.

'That's okay. That's good. You need to rest now.' She picked up the printout and smiled. 'And I need to make some calls.'

It was mid-morning but with the heavy shades pulled it could have been the middle of the night. Constant travel can skew one's internal clocks. April's hadn't been set reliably in years.

While Reese had been in the bath the housekeepers had

86

come to prepare her bed. She'd drifted off in the hot fragrant water, her head reclined on the lip of the marble spa. Two young maidservants had been summoned to finish her bathing and pampering. Then they'd helped her from the sunken tub, toweled her dry and dressed her for bed.

She looked across the suite. Jeannie Reese was sleeping soundly now.

April retrieved an MP3 player from her bag, walked to the bed and sat down. It took a few moments to adjust the volume and touch-screen her way to a repeating program that had been recorded just for this encounter.

Reese's will was strong, but strength didn't matter in modern mind control. The new technologies were far more subtle and effective than the blunt instruments of the Cold War era. This innovative branch of brainwashing simply bypassed the will and changed the mind. Part neurolinguistic, part pharmacology, part brainwave entrainment, part smoke and mirrors. The smarter they are, the harder they fall.

Still, any mental manipulation was by its nature an inexact art. Some trial-and-error was still required with each subject, the duration of effect varied wildly, and some things were much easier than others. It was easy to win the trust of a trusting person, for example, or to gain the love of someone who longed for love, or to further blur the line between right and wrong within a subject who'd lived on both sides of the law.

But as April had found, while it was easy to get a woman with the skill-set of an assassin to the time and place of the killing, persuading Polly Pure-heart to actually pull the fucking trigger had proven to be quite a different matter.

She placed the earbuds in Jeannie's ears. As the binaural rhythms began there were changes in that lovely, peaceful face. There was a sudden tension, and then a bit of something like sorrow, and then momentary pain. And then peace.

This had all started as an amusement for April, nothing more. Indentured service was a proper closing chapter for an old, bitter rivalry. Such conclusions should never be left unwritten; the wounds suffered in adolescence never heal without closure. It hadn't been an obsession by any means. Not that important. Entire months had passed in her life when no thought of Jeannie Reese ever entered her mind. Entire days, in any case.

But now by some wild coincidence, this printout that had fallen into her hands, it could change everything. It could lift her up in mere weeks from Griffin's errand girl to the rising star she was always meant to be. And Jeannie Reese had not only delivered it: she was the one person in the world who could best put this new information to April's use.

Uncanny. But it was a fact equally confounding for the pious and the godless alike: for good or evil, fate always favors the bold.

'We're going to go over your agenda, Jeannie,' April said softly. Reese appeared to be sleeping, but her mind was now an open book, ready for a new entry.

'You'll leave tonight; I've made all the arrangements. You're going to meet some new people, and take care of some old friends. There are going to be some twists and turns, but I know you can do it.' She adjusted the covers, smoothed strands of hair from Jeannie's forehead. 'We're going to have this one last, grand adventure together, and then you can rest.'

'You can rest forever when it's done.'

8

The cornerstone of his home had been set in place half a century before the United States was born. It was one of the first houses built in Fredericksburg, Virginia. George Washington had slept here more than once, as had Jefferson, Lincoln, and Benedict Arnold.

August Griffin had been raised in this house. It was full of history, his own and that of the long and storied line of his family. He had left it behind as a young man but finally returned; in trying times there were no comforts money could buy to match the warmth of home. Though he rarely cooked, the kitchen and the sitting rooms were infused with light scents of their past: wood-fire, cinnamon and licorice, fresh bread, baked apples, roasted potatoes. These aromas had been settling in since his great-great grandparents' time, and like no other thing they reminded him that this old house was where he belonged.

The lamps dimmed momentarily, hummed, and then burned a bit brighter than they had before. Electricity had been an afterthought here, like indoor plumbing, telephones, insulation and central air. As a result everything worked with varying degrees of reliability. But over the years he'd accepted the many peculiarities of an old Southern mansion. In light of the good things, a few little drafts, flickers and drips were not so dire.

A gentle evening rain had begun pattering on the garden windows. He tapped his pipe on the hearth next to him, tamped the spiced tobacco in the bowl, struck a match and lit it up again.

By European standards, of course, this place was young. His favorite pub in London, the Seven Stars, was serving beer and cottage pie forty years before Copernicus declared that the Earth revolved around the Sun. For everything old, there was something far older. The Greeks, Egyptians and Sumerians would have a far, far longer view of the fleeting constructions of mankind.

A noise, like someone walking, drifted down the staircase from the floor above.

It was a familiar sound; he'd never found it frightening, not even as a child. It wasn't the house settling or the wind in the rafters. This really couldn't be mistaken for anything but quiet footsteps, passing from room to room upstairs on the same repeating path they'd always taken. It was a big house in which to live alone and he was glad to have the company, without over-thinking its nature. Whoever or whatever it was it had certainly been here far longer than he, and would remain so long after he was gone.

Among the antiques and heirlooms on the mantle was an old woodcarved plaque. It read, *And this, too, shall pass away*. This had been a favorite all-occasion saying of his long-suffering mother. Though comforting in youth, he'd found this sentiment took on quite a different meaning in one's declining years.

After the battle of Sharpsburg, the bloodiest day in American military history, General Lee and the Confederate

Army had retreated from their failed invasion to a place just down the road from this house. Had they gone on to victory against the Union, the land on which they'd huddled and planned through that fateful winter would be a national monument today. Instead, the site was now a golf course.

So it is, the defeated are neither completely forgotten nor very well remembered. August Griffin did not intend to pass from this world as a failure, with his life's work still incomplete.

The phone rang on the table next to his chair, and he answered.

'Yes.'

He listened to the young man's account.

'Are you certain? Are you absolutely certain whom you saw with her?'

Yes, the caller was quite certain.

'Thank you,' he said. And then: 'It's possible I'll require a service from you in the near future. May I rely on your discretion?'

Yes, he was assured of it.

Upon ending the call Griffin rewound and replayed the audio with the handset's voice-stress comparator engaged. The indicators confirmed that the caller had spoken the truth as he knew it.

He set his pipe into an ashtray and stood, wincing at the twinges from his joints. Medical science had identified over a hundred varieties of arthritis, and every single one of them seemed to have found a home somewhere inside him.

The phone call had not brought welcome news. It was a miserable night to travel, but this, he would have to straighten out in person.

And his patience with April Medici was finally at an end.

9

The truck slowed to a walking pace as it edged just off the pavement, onto the shoulder, and then to a gentle stop. The foot on the brake had seemed somewhat disinclined to bring the ride to an end, and she thought she understood why. The company of a stranger was still a human connection on a lonely ride, and even the briefest of such bonds could leave an exit wound. Best to be quick about it.

'This is great, thanks.' Jeannie opened the door and slid down to the diamond-plate running board, had to stand on it tip-toe to look back up at the driver. The blowing cold nearly took her breath away after the humid warmth of the truck's cabin. Felt like a hard snow was coming on.

'Sure you won't go on up to St Louis?' the driver asked. 'What do you say, let me buy you some dinner up the road, then I'll show you around the big city tomorrow.'

'I already took you out of your way.' She patted the upholstery and held out her hand for her bag, and with some reluctance he hefted it to the edge of the seat. 'I'm so grateful for the ride.'

'Well mercy, young lady, the pleasure was mine. Ain't had

a woman in my cab for seven years, and the last one wasn't nothin' like you.'

She slung the bag over her shoulder, hopped down to the gravel at the edge of the road.

'So long,' she said.

'Listen . . .'

Jeannie looked up at him, and waited. Whatever was on his mind didn't seem to be easy to say.

'I got a feeling,' he said, 'and I don't think you should get out here, is all. I think you should get on back up here and let me drive you somewhere safe.'

She made sure to connect with him. 'I'll be fine. Thanks for the ride.'

'You just, you take care of yourself, girl.'

She gave him a little smile.

'I will. Hope you beat the storm.'

She reached up and pushed the heavy door closed, backed away until he could see she was clear. A last wave, and the truck dropped into gear and eased away off the shoulder and then back on its way down the long, dark road.

It was a quick walk across two lanes and up a long gravel parking lot, but the wind had found every breach in her winter wraps by the time she reached the door. Her choice of a drop-off point had been simple; this little road-house was the first open-for-business shelter she'd seen within walking distance of her objective. And bonus: it looked like there were rooms to rent around in back.

A loud blower under the eaves whooshed warm air down into the threshold. Jeannie closed her eyes for a moment and let it blow away the cold, and then she pulled open the inner door.

It was the kind of small-town saloon that didn't need to change much with the times. No style, just atmosphere; wood panel and Formica, linoleum and Lysol. There was a horse-shoe bar, billiards toward the rear, a sparse crowd in loud knots of regulars, bluegrass on the jukebox, and an old TV hung up in the corner, probably locked on the NASCAR channel.

She measured the room as she walked; who was who and where, then paths to the outside: the door she'd come in, maybe a restroom in the back, and a chained fire-exit to the side, no windows but the large one in front.

At the bar she pulled back a stool and sat, lowered her bag to the floor beside her. The bartender was already nearby and he cleared a half-empty highball glass and a spent bowl of beer-nuts from her place.

'What can I get you?' he asked.

'Do you have a pay-phone?'

He gave a little nod toward a cubby-hole by the hallway to the restrooms. 'Anything else?'

'A cup of coffee would be great. And I'll need a room later on.'

'That we can do.'

The phone was a good old coin-op, probably older than she was. No smart cards, no touch-screens, just a coin slot and a chipped, sticky keypad. She dropped in eight quarters, punched in Rudy's cell number and waited.

After a few seconds he picked up on the other end.

Before the first ring her call passed through the sentient filters of AT&T's nationwide Hawkeye database and raised a warning flag. A monitored number had been dialed from a payphone somewhere in southern Missouri. Between the first and second rings the call was intercepted. The original recipient's phone was fed a decoy, a pre-recorded telemarketing message, which was promptly disconnected by Mr Rudy Steinman.

94

The number Jeannie Reese had dialed then connected, not to her old friend, but to a dedicated computer system on the seventh floor of the SBC Building at 611 Folsom Street in San Francisco. The locked office, room 641a, was labeled *Study Group 3G* on the registered floor-plan. Though there were no human beings inhabiting it, many intelligence agencies were well represented in the room. It housed a wealth of future-tech devices for covert domestic spying, as amazing for their capabilities as for their blatant illegality. But really, could any act be unlawful when the lawmakers themselves helped perpetrate the crime?

On paper, the computer receiving the call and the empty desk on which it sat were requisitioned and run by the CIA's Directorate of Science and Technology. In reality neither the CIA nor the DST had any knowledge of the existence or the function of this machine. This was important, as both could credibly swear to that fact under oath.

He was both a government employee and a name on a high-level watchlist so Mr Steinman's voice-print was on file with the newly formed Department of Homeland Security. Likewise, his compulsory IQ and personality assessments, the texts of his emails, the transcripts and audio of his past phone conversations, his medical, credit and travel records, his address book, Facebook profile, and full maps of his many internet activities were all readily available for access. With all these building blocks, the rather revolutionary combination of software and hardware in this desktop computer had the power to carry on an automated, interactive dialogue, in the subject's own voice, vocabulary and manner. Results in the laboratory had been promising: under ideal conditions one technician's own mother had certified several heartfelt, counterfeit conversations as absolutely genuine.

'Thank you for calling Domino's,' the computer-as-Steinman said. 'Have you tried our Hot Wings?'

'Hey, it's me.'

There was a lag of milliseconds as the caller's voice was identified: *Jeannie Reese*. A special order was in place to guide this conversation if such a call occurred. The client was April Medici, with an E9-SCI clearance through her satellite office in Washington. Content was assembled as directed, both audible and subliminal, and the conversation began.

There was some drop-out on the line, and then she heard his voice again.

'How are things down in the Ozarks?' Rudy asked.

'Snowy. You know that Domino's Pizza thing you do when you answer the phone? Even after the hundred thousandth time I've heard it, it's still not funny, so you can stop any time.'

'It's a classic, and I know you love it.'

'Listen,' Jeannie said, 'I guess I wanted to . . .' For some reason she was having a difficult time with her focus. *Wanted to what?*

'. . . Do you require a clarification of your objective?'

Jeannie blinked. 'What did you say?'

There was a pause.

'. . . Did I say . . . something wrong?' Rudy asked.

'No, no,' she said. 'I just don't hear that many five-syllable words out of you, that's all.'

'Well, as the deacon said to the new altar boy, I guess I'm not feeling myself tonight. Ba-boom!'

She smiled in spite of the familiar tastelessness. 'Look, I don't know why I called. I know what I need to do here. I guess I just wanted to hear a friendly voice.'

'Awww, that's sweet. You can hear it some more when you get back.'

'Okay. Bye for now.'

'So long, boss.'

The call disconnected, but she held the phone to her ear for a moment longer.

There were places that her mind seemed reluctant to go, so it wasn't a thought that troubled her as she hung up the phone. It was only a feeling.

She returned to the bar and found her coffee waiting for her.

'Let me warm that up for you,' the bartender said.

He was right; the side of the cup was cool to the touch. He took it, refilled it from a steaming pot below the bar, and replaced it on her saucer.

'How long was I on the phone?' she asked.

'I don't know—'

'*About* how long?'

'I don't know, twenty minutes?'

She sat back. 'I couldn't have been.'

'Well. Time flies.' He brought up a little silver pitcher of milk and a bowl of sugar cubes. 'Jesus, girl, you look like a rabbit just run over your grave.'

'I need to be somewhere.' Jeannie picked up her bag and stood. 'What do I owe you?'

'Nothin', honey. I didn't even ring it up.'

'I'll be back later for that room,' she said, on her way to the door.

The bartender had said something in reply, almost but not quite too softly for her to hear. It began to pass from her mind as she walked out into the cold, but it registered for just a moment before it was gone.

'We'll be ready,' he'd said.

10

Turned out, the international HQ and worldwide broadcasting studio of the Global Resistance Network was just a smidge less awesome in person than its elaborate website would suggest.

Near the base of a rusty antenna tower was a small tractor shed, factory prefabbed of stamped aluminum, sea-foam green siding and quaint white vinyl trim. Below a single spider-cracked window the station's call letters, ham frequency and other vital tidbits were semiprofessionally hand-painted in large black italics:

A satellite station of

WWCR 3.215 MHz

Conway, MO

– The Guardians of Liberty –

Proudly sponsored by Sho-Me Brick and Feed

Jeannie adjusted her scarf against the bitter cold, pulled off a mitten with her teeth, and checked her weapon.

He was visible now and again through the half-cocked shutters, on his feet, pacing, red-faced and ranting at a floor-standing microphone. She had learned his age but it didn't seem like her information could be accurate. He was no spring chicken to be sure, and a little scruffy, plump and rumpled compared with his online promo shots. His voice was deep and gravelly; it sounded like he'd lived every day of his eighty-one years. But it was the fire in his words that made him seem like a much younger man.

He was her rendezvous, and the closest thing to a celebrity within a hundred miles in any direction. From this modest home base, way out near the cracker-barrel margins of the lunatic fringe, Wendell Neff had made himself the pivotal voice in the so-called American Patriot Movement.

And also maybe the most devoted Blimpie customer in history, judging from the mountain of crumpled bags and sandwich wrappers in his back seat. She skootched a little lower behind the driver's side and a minor avalanche of mustard-scented fast-food packaging rustled downhill to complete her camouflage.

Through the multi-band receiver in her earpiece she could hear him winding up the night's broadcast. The show had been due to end at 9 PM, but by her watch Neff's anti-establishment brio had already boiled him over to 9:12, and he wasn't finished yet.

As she waited, she listened in.

'*Wake up, sheeple! Wake up, and you'll see the police state that's coming, just like I see it. Now I'm not telling you to take up arms against your criminal government, we're not quite there yet. Not yet. All I want you to do tonight is wake up and question!*

'*Ask the IRS to show you the law that says you have to pay an unconstitutional, direct, unapportioned tax on your wages; you know what you'll get? You'll get your house taken away from you, you'll get put out on the street if you're lucky or thrown in prison if you're not, but you won't get an answer. You know why, don't you? Because there isn't any such law!*

'Ask yourself, why are they coming for our guns? Because they always do. Germany, 1938, do you know who couldn't own guns? Jews! Do you read me? Google REX-84 if you don't want to get any sleep tonight. Internment camps, people, managed by the US military, concentration camps for you and me, right here on American soil!

'While you're at it, ask yourself, do you really want open borders? Do you really want blanket amnesty for all the millions of illegals pouring into this country every year? My grandparents were immigrants, people, before you call me a hater or a racist, my grandfolks were immigrants, legal immigrants, okay? But they didn't fly the Irish flag on the Fourth of July! They worked hard to get here and make a life here; they loved this country. These people sneakin' across here today, most of them don't even want to be Americans. So ask yourself, why does your so-called conservative neo-con puppet President keep pushing and pushing to let 'em all just come on in? And why do the so-called liberals fall right into line with him? Because the North American Union is coming next, do you understand that? The borders are coming down, hell, the Texas border is already in a shooting war, but you don't hear about that on the nightly news, do you?

'Ask, why are our government friends watching us from every corner? The United States has five per cent of the world's population, but one-quarter of the world's prisoners. Over two million of us are behind bars, and the prison business is booming. We used to make cars in Detroit, now we

make convicts. We used to train our kids to be inventors, and scientists, and farmers, and fabricators, people who make things with their hands. Now we're training sheep, and snitches, and prison guards. It's a profit center, do you see? You want more prisoners, just make more things a crime. And people, convicts don't vote.

'*Ask, where are they going to get the money for this war they're pushing on us? The dollar is already finished, our fiat currency isn't worth the paper the criminal Federal Reserve prints it on. Go to the internet and look up "comprehensive annual financial reports" if you want to see where your hard-earned tax-dollars really go. And when they've bankrupted us, stolen your savings in the next crash, taken our houses and our pensions and put us out on the street, they'll have some new money to sell all you Canada-Mexamericans. You thought the euro was great? When they kill the dollar, get ready for the Amero! The new, improved, NAU dollar! Goodbye, USA, hello NAU!*

'*Don't believe me, they're hiding it all in plain sight, Google it, it's all public knowledge! NAFTA, CAFTA, GATT, the Free Trade Area of the Americas, the World Trade Organization: just look it up and you'll see! Don't listen to what they say, look at what they do! Forty thousand farms gone, and counting! A million jobs gone, and counting! We used to make things in this country, amazing things. Now we only watch things on TV, and buy things made by slave labor, and eat things made in a test tube. It's our future they're stealing, people! Can you please pull your head out of the manufactured news and the mind-control Super Bowl long enough to see what I see?*'

His voice was growing hoarse and he took a quick, sloppy drink of something. But now he was really rolling.

'*Are you ready for 2003, America? They think you*

are. *You're all set, all ready to jack in to the Matrix, and shuffle down the kill-chute to the new-world-order slaughterhouse. Let me tell you about a little something they're cooking up for you: a national ID card called the Real ID.*

'*I remember, play-acting when we were kids, we'd play cowboys, or bank robbers, or like we were commies at the Berlin Wall, makin' fun of 'em, you know, "Show your papers," right? Remember that, how funny that was? "Show your papers, comrade! Your papers are not in order!" But don't you realize? We're there, people, right here in the USA! Don't you see, you have to show your papers now, before you can travel in your own free country? And they're going to start a push for a national ID card, the Real ID, to make the police state that much easier to shove down our throats!*

'*Go ahead, try to resist! Ask those uniformed grunts at the airport, I did it, you can do it, too. Ask those GED storm troopers to show you the law that was passed that says you gotta show a government ID before you can fly in your own damn country. You won't get an answer; you'll get a strip-search, but you won't get an answer. You know why, America? Because there is no such law!*

'*They're conditioning you, herding you into the pens, to get you ready to lay down for the big takeover, do you see? All the so-called hijackers on 9/11, those evil terrorists from al-CIA-da, they all had government-issued IDs, so this Real ID ain't for the war on terror, folks. It's for the war on you.*

'*And why, people, ask yourselves, why are we about to send our sons and daughters off to another war, in Iraq, of all places? Oh, we're goin' all right, don't tell me we're not. I've showed you the war plan, it's been up on my website for over a year. Hell, the neo-cons were gearing up to go into Iraq in January of 2001, nine months before 9/11. Two years ago, remember when I told you that? And they're doing all this needless killing in your name. No, this isn't about the war on terror, or the nonexistent WMDs, or freedom for the Iraqi people, and my fellow former Americans, it's not about September eleventh. It's about enriching the few at the expense of the many. And this war is only the beginning, can't you see? This is the first big push toward tyranny, the beginning of the end! They softened us up after 9/11, scared us into believing whatever they say, and now they're getting ready to take this country* down.'

As Jeannie took in a breath she realized she hadn't done so in a while. A chill passed through her as she heard these last words. The cold settled in around her heart, and had nothing at all to do with the weather.

'*Well, I'm not gonna stop. I'm gonna tell everybody who'll listen, till they pry this microphone from my cold, dead hands. Naw, I don't expect they'll let me live forever, folks. But I'm gonna live a free man till I die.*'

At last he was starting to run out of steam; as fervent as he'd been a moment before, he suddenly sounded weary of the fight.

'*Just please, do this for me, stand up and ask yourselves, Who benefits? Cui bono is not the love-child of Sonny and Cher, people. It's not the lead singer of U2. It's Latin.* Cui bono, *it means "Who benefits?" It means follow the money. And you're owed an answer. When your servant government's doing something you know doesn't smell right, ask, Who benefits? When there's another staged, false-flag terrorist attack and the rest of your Constitutional rights are taken away, ask, Who benefits? When the war machine and the money men are asking for hundreds of billions to rescue their fortunes, or the lifeblood of your family and our nation to go off and die for a lie, damn it all, ask, Who benefits? Ask that question, follow the money, and you'll be one step closer to seeing the real enemy. And if we can see 'em, by God, we can fight 'em. And for just a little while longer, we might still have a chance to win our country back.'*

There was a dog-tired, vocal sigh.

'Let's make 2003 the year we take America back, what do you say, people? If you're in debt, get out of it. Put your money in guns, food, water and gold, while you still can. Make a resolution for the revolution, with me here, tonight. This year, we tell the new world order to go to hell and leave us be. What do you say, people?'

The closing bumper music came up abruptly. It sounded as if the board-op had jumped the cue; maybe he was just ready to go home.

As the last commercial started to roll, the lights in the little studio winked out one by one. Soon two men emerged from the double mini-barndoors. They exchanged good-nights, guy-hugged, and parted ways at a fork in the pavement. One of them approached the car, walking with a bit of a limp, rattling his keys, slipping and scraping here and there on the icy pavement.

There was some fumbling for a few moments at the lock; it must have been nearly frozen solid from the sub-zero night. The car door squawked open, the frigid seat-springs creaked as he slid in behind the wheel, and the door was pulled closed.

'Don't move,' Jeannie said.

The man jumped at the sound of a voice from behind him, and though it was warm from her pocket, he flinched again at the light touch of her pistol barrel on his neck.

She leaned forward, repositioned the gun at his temple. He

didn't speak, and she didn't hear any breathing. She looked into the rearview mirror and saw that his eyes were closed, clenched shut.

'Are you armed?' she asked. 'I found the .38 in the glove box.'

He shook his head.

'Are you sure? Don't lie to me.'

A tight little nod.

'Stay still, now. I don't really need a gun to take care of myself.' She pocketed her pistol, pulled off her other mitten and reached over and around the front seat to frisk him. He didn't resist, but he tensed up here and there at the ticklish places.

'Okay,' she said at length. 'Start it up, but don't put it in gear. Let's just get the heater going.' After a few moments the starter began to labor, and with a few wheezy pumps of the accelerator the old jalopy rumbled weakly to life.

'So,' Jeannie said. 'You're Wendell Neff.'

'Yes, I am.' It took another second or two, but he found his nerve. 'And who in the hell are you?'

She heard a metallic *click*, glanced down and found her pistol in her hand. The barrel was pressed to the back of the seat, where his heart would be on the other side, where the gunshot would be muffled by the cushion. The noise she'd heard had been the sound of the hammer being pulled back by her thumb.

'Hey,' he said. After a moment she looked up into his eyes reflected in the foggy mirror. 'If you're gonna kill me, then kill me. I'm too old to play games.'

Kill him?

She hadn't come here with any conscious intention of shooting an unarmed, elderly man in the back. But the first lesson in firearms training, drummed in until it's nearly a physical impossibility to violate it, is *Keep your finger off the trigger until the target is in sight*. The target, in the language of combat, is something you're prepared to destroy. Not warn, or wound, or threaten, but destroy.

And her finger was on the trigger.

A wave of vertigo fluttered through her mind, left a pounding ache behind at her temple. She pointed the gun to the floor of the car, lowered the hammer slowly and engaged the thumb safety.

'Take us somewhere nearby,' Jeannie said. 'Somewhere public, where we can talk.'

He looked at her from across the table as he lit up the stub of a cigar. Clearly, he was awaiting an explanation. And he was right, this conversation was hers to begin, but she had no idea where to start.

They'd come back to the little roadhouse near Neff's ham-radio shack. The bartender she'd met earlier in the evening brought over two waters, two tumblers half-full of what looked like straight bourbon, and a hot plate of fried appetizers. They hadn't placed an order; her booth-mate had simply held up two fingers when they sat down. Evidently Wendell Neff was a regular here.

When the man had left them Neff broke the silence.

'I know who you are,' he said.

She put her water glass down, and a moment later she remembered to swallow.

'I don't know your name,' he continued, 'but I know your face. You were mixed up in that propaganda blitz after 9/11. What I don't know is why you're here and whose side you're on.'

She glanced around them. There was no one close by; the other bar patrons were clustered on the far side of the lounge.

'How would you know who I am?'

'You haven't spent much time on my website, have you?' He put down his cigar and picked up a fried shrimp. 'One thing about a corrupt government, there's lots of leaks. Not everybody's evil, even in hell. You people have spies, and the real people have spies of their own. Most of what I get turns out to be bullshit, but some of it's not. And what I heard is, you're some government agent who went skippin' off the reservation last year. I've got some pictures of you and your fellow subversives from surveillance cameras, some from Washington, New York, California, and a lot from Las Vegas. But my favorite is a shot from the Clark County coroner's office.' He dipped the shrimp in red sauce, ate it, and pointed at her with the tail. 'Of you. Dead. At the bottom of an elevator shaft at the Stratosphere Hotel in Las Vegas.'

'Please keep your voice down—'

He didn't lower his voice at all. 'What are you here to do, shut me up? Like you killed Bill Cooper and Danny Casolaro? Do you devils think you can scare me, after all these years—'

Jeannie had pulled the sheet of paper from her bag and she smacked it onto the table in front of him. 'I'm here because of this.'

It was the document she'd printed out in Jay Marshall's office, nothing but a grainy, photocopied image of the inner title page of a book. Not a published book, but a journal, written in a fine, elegant hand. The title was *My Great Commission*. The author was the late Edward Latrell.

Below the title block was a scribbled addendum. It seemed to have been inserted hastily, as the lettering lacked the precise calligraphy of the surrounding words:

To any one of the following who survives me, I commend these truths in the event of my untimely death:

A list of ten names followed. At the bottom of the page were two final lines:

Join our holy nation
For a great accounting nears.

An invitation, or an ultimatum; there was probably no distinction for a man like Latrell.

'I need to trust you, Wendell,' Jeannie said. 'I think I need your help.'

He was moving the tip of his finger down the list of names, one by one. There was a senator, a syndicated journalist, a lefty activist, a far right wing blogger, an old-school conspiracy hound, a government whistle-blower and a former third-party presidential hopeful. There was a scientist, Dr Olin Kempler. There was a disillusioned, turncoat insider, Vincent Lindeman. It was a diverse group of anti-establishment individuals, but in the preceding weeks they'd developed one thing in common. All but one of them was dead.

And the last name on the list was Wendell Neff.

'Did you know anything about this?' Jeannie asked. He didn't answer. 'What could be so important about this book?'

Neff touched the author's name on the sheet. When he spoke next, he'd changed his mind about lowering his voice. 'You know who this was?'

She nodded, and he continued.

'Latrell was a radical, militant, white-supremacist asshole, but he was a smart son-of-a-bitch, too. The rumor is, that book is everything he knew about everybody. Every president back to Eisenhower, every house of power, every crime, every connection. Where all the bodies are buried, literally and otherwise. It's enough to put half of Washington out of office and half the suits on Wall Street in jail. It was his leverage, the only reason they didn't take him out over all those years.

That's the rumor.' Neff stubbed out his cigar. 'Hell, I'd sell my soul to get a look through that book.'

'But did you know you were on this list of people he'd willed it to?'

He shook his head, and then took a drink of his bourbon and chased it with some water. 'It's hard to believe. Ed Latrell never liked me much, and the feeling was mutual.'

As she studied the paper she could feel a flood of images and memories whirring just below a dark threshold in her mind, just out of reach. Things she knew that she knew, like a pivotal answer in a crossword puzzle with just one too many letters missing. The curtain was parting, but not fast enough.

She closed her eyes, thinking it through. 'They didn't kill everyone on the list at once. They killed them in order. They were following it, the path they were sure this book was taking from person to person, trying to get their hands on it and failing, one by one.'

'They?'

'Maybe people I've been working for, I don't know. But you didn't get the book. And neither did anyone else. This isn't a photocopy of the original, look at it, it's a copy of a copy. The list has been compromised, and Latrell knew it might be.' She looked up at Neff. 'This list is a decoy, in case this sheet fell into the wrong hands. The book was never really coming to any of you.'

'If not any of us, then who's supposed to get it?'

She'd pulled a pen and a set of silver reading glasses from her bag, picked up the sheet, moved the candle on the table closer to make the most of the dim light. 'It might be right here,' she whispered. 'There could be another name on here somewhere. The real name.' Her fingers moved over the writing, searching for a pattern. Only seconds had passed when she leaned in closer, and stopped.

There it was. Not at all well hidden and only a bit more secure than leaving it in plain-text for everyone to see. It had been done in a hurry; there wasn't much time between the moment Latrell realized he'd lost and the moment he died. She underlined the barely encoded letters, and slid the paper across the table.

<u>J</u>oin <u>o</u>ur <u>h</u>oly <u>n</u>ation
<u>F</u>or <u>a</u> great <u>a</u>ccounting <u>n</u>ears
J o h n   F a g a n.

Neff sighed and shook his head.

She tapped the paper. 'It's right there—'

'Look, I've heard all the stories,' Neff said. 'Hell, I live con-spiracy theories all day long, for fifty-five years on the radio, I've heard it all, but even I don't believe everything. There's no such person. He doesn't exist.'

'Yeah,' Jeannie said. 'Just like me.'

The bar had grown quiet, and she glanced to the side. The other patrons were still gathered together on the far side of the wide, dark, low-ceilinged space. But there was a change; now, none of them were making any attempt to hide the fact that they were watching.

'Wendell.'

'Yeah.'

'You come here a lot, don't you?'

'Yeah.'

'Do you know a single person in this place right now?'

The bartender was gone. She didn't take her eyes off the people in the shadows. A few seconds crawled by before Wendell Neff spoke, but she already knew what his answer would be.

'. . . No. No, I don't.'

One of the strangers emerged from the group, a large, burly man in a sleeveless biker shirt. He walked to the front door, locked it, and with a look across to the two of them, broke off the key.

Jeannie slipped her hand into her bag, retrieved the snub-nose .38 and speedloader she'd removed from Neff's glovebox earlier, and slid both items across the table to him.

'Time to go,' she said.

As she stood, the big man pulled a long knife from his boot and charged.

In a street brawl with a much larger opponent it's a bad idea to wait for the fight to arrive. She ran toward him and he broke his stride and drew back his blade but she was already inside the arc of the swing. She blocked with her forearm and followed through with a jab to his windpipe and a sharp knee to the groin. The knife clattered to the linoleum and she flicked it into the corner with her heel. He made a clumsy grab for her with his other hand but she caught his wrist and twisted hard. He went to his knees, her bent elbow struck down on his distended arm and she heard the bone crack and splinter. A finishing blow from the heel of her hand to the base of his skull put him flat to the floor.

One down.

Neff had started shooting but the only effect so far had been to rile and scatter the remaining assailants. 'Window!' she shouted, as another man lurched forward and got his hands around her neck. Before he could pull her close she grabbed his collar, kicked one foot up into his armpit for leverage and flipped up between his arms, hooking her other leg tight around his neck. He began to flail and lose his balance as the blood was pinched off to his brain.

Several shots exploded through the tempered glass of the front picture window. As her man started to fall she released with her legs and her back slammed against the floor. She thrust with her feet into his stomach to add her strength to his dead-weight momentum, rolled as he fell toward her, and with a donkey-kick he took to the air like a man-sized rag doll, crashing spread-eagle through the weakened plate glass to open their path to the outside.

Jeannie got to a knee, breathless. 'Let's go,' she said.

But Wendell Neff didn't move. He was pointing his revolver across the room and she heard the hammer fall on an empty chamber. Jeannie looked along the line of his aim.

There was only a single figure now. All the others had disappeared. As he stepped from the shadows she saw a tall, elderly man. And she remembered him. In the moment she met his eyes she remembered.

She threw herself toward her bag and drew her pistol from its pocket there, turned back, took aim and began to fire. The man continued his walk across the littered floor. A lamp shattered to his right, a trophy case to his left, a hanging fixture above. It was as if her gun and her target repelled one another, like two facing magnets with their positive poles forced together.

The man raised the palm of his hand and a wave of unbearable heat threw her back against the booth. Her pistol slipped from her hand and she heard Wendell Neff's .38 fall to the table behind. A flickering pulse of bright white light struck her, the flashes seemed to sync themselves with patterns and signals in her brain. A jolt of misfires flooded through her nervous system. She felt herself falling, but not the impact with the floor.

The tall man stopped next to her. His eyes were cool and gentle, as she remembered. They saw inside of her, everywhere, as they always had when he'd come to her as a girl, and later in her dreams. She would run and run through the dark until morning, knowing he would somehow still be there if she dared to look behind, still there with those cool and gentle eyes.

'Jeannie,' she heard him say. He spoke her name in the manner of a greeting, stern but enfolding, a teacher to a way-ward but promising student who'd been caught making mischief.

Then he turned his attention to her companion.

'And Wendell Neff,' August Griffin said. 'So pleased to meet you. I hope you've guessed my name.'

11

Wendell Neff awoke.

He began to sit up straight but his wrists were bound to the table-top on which his head had been lying. When he moved he found his legs and ankles were shackled as well.

A small machine whirred on the table next to him. Lights and meters blinked and twitched on its face. A series of syringes were mounted in a steel rack beside it; actuators clicked, the plungers moved subtly, in and out, no more than a tic at a time by the graduated scales printed on their sides.

An IV needle was taped to the back of his hand, its wide-bore needle inserted to the hilt in a bruised vessel there. Clear plastic tubing, warm and deep red from the blood flowing through, ran to the machine. Another IV rig exited from its other side, terminating at a taped and punctured vein in his other arm.

There was light where he sat but the rest of the room was dim and indistinct. It was a large room, very large by the character of the few sounds in the air. The purr of the machine, a voice somewhere, a door clicking shut, footsteps. His vision had begun to adjust, but the eyes need more than light to make sense of their data. What he saw was not what he expected, so the meaning eluded him for a moment.

Double and triple bunks with small footlockers on the floor in front, facing the narrow aisles, stretching in identical ranks and files all the way to the edge of the darkness. The cots were all the same, plain and dark-green and utilitarian, too closely set for any privacy or comfort. These were not quarters for soldiers. This was not an infirmary or a shelter for refugees. On the nearby bed-frames he saw welded metal brackets and D-rings at the head and foot; hardware for restraints.

The aftermath of childhood polio had kept Wendell Neff in stateside service during World War Two. A friend had mailed him photographs from Dachau on the afternoon of its liberation, and it was those images that came now to mind.

Those barracks had been filthy and littered with remnants of their years of long service. This room was newly built and freshly painted, ready for future tenants. That was the difference.

Lamps snapped on, a string of hanging bulbs down the narrow aisle that split the space down its center. His table sat at the end of this walkway. Someone was approaching from the far side, a tall man on a deliberate, steady walk through the interspersed circles of yellow light. It was the man from the bar.

'Where am I?' Neff shouted. 'And what have you done with that girl?' It was the first he'd spoken; for some reason even the small effort of speech felt exhausting.

The man arrived. He laid a notebook and a thin rectangular panel by his place, and sat down across the table.

'May I call you Wendell?'

'I asked you where you've taken me—'

'On your broadcasts, I believe you would refer to such a

place as a "FEMA camp". This place is really more of a collection point, and it's not far from where you were taken into custody.'

'I'm an American citizen,' Neff said. 'I have rights—'

'Not in this room, Wendell. Not anymore. This is a Constitution-free zone. And I'm afraid your missing rights are the least of your worries.'

Neff tried to swallow but found his mouth too dry. 'Who are you?'

'My name is August Griffin.'

There was a moment before Neff spoke again. 'I've seen you before.'

'Many times, no doubt,' Griffin said. 'In a way we've grown old together.' He touched the acrylic panel on the table. A home screen appeared there; he chose a link labeled GuardiansOfLiberty.com, and Wendell Neff's website appeared. With a few more clicks he arrived at a full-screen image from the site's archives. 'You recognize this photograph.'

'Of course,' Neff said quietly. It was a picture of the so-called 'three tramps' – three out-of-place men arrested near the grassy knoll at Dealey Plaza minutes after JFK was shot and killed in 1963. They were quickly released after questioning, and none of these supposed drifters had ever been reliably identified. The House Select Committee on Assassinations put the matter to bed, pronouncing the men uninvolved and harmless some fifteen years later, based on evidence that had neatly appeared in the intervening years.

'This,' Griffin said, 'is Frank Sturgis, who you'll remember for his also exemplary performance in the Bay of Pigs invasion and the Watergate break-in. This,' he moved his finger from the first man in line to the last, 'is not E. Howard Hunt, as you've alleged, but is an actual tramp.' He pointed to the younger man in the middle. 'And this is me.'

Neff straightened himself in his chair, and winced. The needle in his arm had bit in as he moved. His discomfort went unacknowledged. 'I knew you people would come and take me out sooner or later,' he said. 'What took you so long?'

'Oh, I've not come for you, Wendell. Although, now that you're here I've been forbidden to let you leave alive, despite my objections.'

'You're not here for me?'

'Actually you've been a great help to us, with your radio broadcasts and your books and your videos, a great help. There's no lie as effective as half the truth.'

'I've always told the truth—'

'Yes, you have, but only the part you could see. And in these matters part of the truth only makes you sound – well, a little crazy. I've defended you and your role over the years, but you've made some very sensitive people very angry at times and finally they'll no longer listen to reason. I don't know what we're going to do without you, really. But some-one will step forward to fill your shoes, I'm sure.' Griffin made a small adjustment to the machine on the table and the patterns of lights there changed and stabilized. 'So. This is the end. I'll be sorry to see you go.'

'The people won't stand for it. My listeners won't stand for it,' Neff said. 'There'll be an investigation—'

'No,' Griffin said. 'No, there won't.'

'Go ahead and kill me, and you'll find out—'

'But we've already killed you, Wendell. It's done.' The little machine clicked and hummed for a few moments in the quiet of the room. 'This device is preventing a binary poison in your system from letting you die. Not pre-cisely a poison, but the net effect will be the same.' Griffin touched a small, pulsing red pushbutton on the face of the device. 'This switch will end your life. But I'm giving you a privilege that most people don't receive. You get to decide how to spend your last minutes. And that brings us to a proposition.'

'No, to whatever it is. Get it over with, and I'll see you in hell.'

'Hear me out, Wendell; you'll be glad you did. You want what I have to offer.'

Wendell Neff had long prepared himself for this, had often predicted his future martyrdom at the hands of his sworn enemies. He'd rehearsed this scene many times, but it had never gone quite like this.

'Say what you're gonna say.'

Griffin nodded.

'I'm going to undo your restraints in a moment so you'll be more comfortable. Understand that if you pull out those needles you'll be dead before your head hits the table. It's your choice to do so, but first listen. All right?'

'Yes.'

Griffin unlocked one wrist restraint. Wendell Neff made no move.

'You never married, Wendell, you have no close friends. You've made it a point to allow no personal connections at all that could be used against you. You've lived your entire life for a cause, at the expense of everything else. We're alike in that way, so I understand. But you do long for two things. You long for the truth, and you wish to be remembered with respect when you're gone.'

The other wrist had now been freed.

'I have one question for you,' Griffin said. 'If you answer it to my satisfaction, I'll grant you those two wishes. First, your legacy. I'll make certain you're remembered as a hero by the people who admire you. Second, I'll answer three questions for you, anything you ask, about the secrets you've spent your life trying to uncover.'

Neff thought for a time.

'And if I don't play?'

'Your reputation will be ruined. We'll release an elaborate history of your secret life as a Freemason, your sordid past as a serial sex offender and double-agent of the CIA, whatever will enrage your loyal audience the most. We'll convince them you're still alive, having fled the country with all the donations they've emptied their piggy-banks to send in. You'll continue to write and your unrepentant voice will still be heard, there'll even be videos of you renouncing all you've stood for over all these years.' Griffin leaned in. 'And then there's the second part. You'll die never knowing if you were right – if you've given up everything, for nothing.'

'. . . I know I'm right.'

Griffin sighed. 'Well.' He gathered and stacked the things he'd brought to the table, and then reached for the pushbutton on the face of the machine. 'If you've made your decision.'

'Wait.'

Griffin studied him. His voice softened. 'Nothing you'll tell me will change the outcome of my work. Perhaps I'll succeed a little more quickly with your help, perhaps not, but I will succeed. I say this to encourage you to accept my offer. It's such a small thing I ask, in return for so much.'

Neff looked to his hands, cleared his throat quietly.

'I'll do it,' he said. 'I'll do the deal.'

'Excellent.' Griffin opened his pad of paper and clicked his pen. From a flap in his portfolio he withdrew the printed sheet that had been left on their table in the bar. He tapped a spot near the bottom of the page. 'All you have to tell me,' Griffin said, 'is anything you know about this name.'

'I'll tell you what I told her. There's no such person.'

'We believe there is. I said anything you know, Wendell. Rumors, urban myths, the ravings of your more unbalanced listeners. After your career I'm sure you could write an encyclopedia of hearsay. Anything at all may be of help.'

Neff looked up, across the table. 'You wouldn't have anything to smoke, would you?'

Griffin smiled, went to his inner jacket pocket and withdrew a leather case and a double-blade cutter. He slipped one cigar from the case, and after a moment of thought, took out another. He nipped the ends of each at the shoulder and passed one across. It was a big old Churchill, firm and fragrant.

Neff brought the cigar-band close to his eyes and squinted to read it. *Cohíba Espléndidos. My, oh my.* The wrapper smelled faintly of oak, fresh walnuts, and the spring bouquet he'd bought his first girl in 1935.

August Griffin struck a match and let the sulfur burn away before holding out the flame. A few light puffs, rolling the tip between them, and he was lit. Griffin lit his own cigar, shook out the match and tossed it to the concrete floor.

The two men sat for a time, all other topics momentarily aside.

'I've smoked for close to sixty-five years,' Neff said. 'Seems like I've never had a real cigar before.'

'Fine art can be made in any medium.'

Neff put down his cigar, balancing it across the corner of the table. Out of habit, it appeared he was saving what remained for later on.

'So,' Griffin said. 'John Fagan.'

'There was a man, a tent speaker who was making the rounds in the sixties, his name was Myron Fagan. You remember?'

'I'm vaguely aware of the name.' Griffin had picked up his pen, and pulled his pad closer. 'Tell me about him.'

'He was from New York, wrote plays and movie scripts for a while. Worked with some big-shots when he was young, Bogart, Barrymore, Fairbanks, the big stars at the time. A real piece of work, this guy, a black-lister, too.

'Somewhere along the line he started talking about other things. Claimed he'd seen some super-secret documents after the war, and then he wrote some shows based on what he saw. What year was it . . . 1955? *Thieves Paradise* he called the last one, all about how Stalin and Roosevelt and the Jews thought up the United Nations to bring in a one-world government.'

'Stalin, Roosevelt and the Jews, hm?' Griffin smiled a bit as he wrote. 'Just so I'm clear, was that *all* of the Jews?'

'Jews, communists and the Illuminati, that was his theme. And Fagan was an end-timer.'

'End-timer, you said?'

'There's a wing of this movement that believes there's no way to win against you people but with an armed uprising, a shooting war. The last war, in fact; the one in the Book of Revelation. You win, we all go to heaven. We win, you all go to hell. Myron Fagan was the first real evangelist for those ideas, and this man here,' he tapped the sheet of paper, at the line of the author's name, 'Edward Latrell, I hope he was the last.'

'So you don't believe in the war he spoke of.'

'I believe the war he spoke of is exactly what you people want. So no, that puts me against it.'

Griffin nodded, ran a finger down his notes. 'And John Fagan?'

'There's been some scuttlebutt over the years, about this guy that's supposedly Myron Fagan's grandson, or his grand-nephew. Stories abound. He's this evil computer hacker, calls himself *phreak* or something like that. He lives in a secret bunker under Manhattan Island. He's the second coming of Guy Fawkes, gettin' ready to bring down the US government. The last I heard, this was good, they say he thought up the September eleventh attacks and gave the plan to the hijackers—'

'I've heard a little of that,' Griffin said. 'But there's no truth in those stories, you say.'

'Fairy tales, and disinformation, but some people just want to be fooled. Anyway, I get a caller to my show, says his name is Troy. This nut-job calls every single week, sounds like he's talking with one of those voice-boxes, like a cancer-kazoo. He never wants to go on the air. If I let him he'll talk for five or ten minutes straight, always really bizarre stuff, really way out there, and I listen sometimes just to cheer myself up. The Queen of England's a shape-shifting reptile, China had a base in the Sea of Tranquility when we landed on the moon, Stephen King shot John Lennon, he's got something new every week. But every time he calls, he signs off with the same four words.'

'Which are?'

'Fagan's alive in Wyoming.'

Griffin continued making notes for a few more seconds. 'Is that all, then?'

'I told you I don't know much, and I don't believe what I do know.'

'That's fine, Wendell.' He put down his pen and closed the pad. 'And now for your questions.'

'You'll tell me the truth?'

'Nothing but.'

'The Illuminati,' Neff said. 'The New World Order. Is there really such a thing?'

Griffin thought for a moment. 'If you mean, is there a group of individuals and families who have always ruled and shaped the destiny of the civilized world, acting in concert and in secret, then yes, they do exist. In fact I'm here on their behalf.'

Wendell Neff nodded. 'Who killed Jack Kennedy, and why?'

Griffin sat back in his chair, tapped an ash to the floor.

'Specifically? Well. Though there were bullets flying from all points of the compass, a Frenchman named Jean René Souètre fired the shot that killed the President. Lee Harvey Oswald was in place, as he later shouted for the cameras, as the patsy, but he was as guilty as the rest of us. I was there as an observer, and what I observed was one of the most ill-conceived and poorly executed operations in recorded history.'

'Why was he killed?'

'What I've found, Wendell, is that there's very rarely only one reason why such things are done. Some have misstated his position on Vietnam and cited that as a factor, and that's untrue. He vehemently opposed expansion of Israel's nuclear program; that position might have played a part. But I believe the last straw was an Executive Order that he'd issued, against the wishes and the interests of my employers.'

'Eleven thousand one hundred and ten,' Neff said.

'Yes. It wasn't much, but it was a step in the wrong direction. Some feared it could begin to dismantle the power of the Federal Reserve, and that sort of insubordination simply wasn't going to be allowed.'

Neff sat back, absorbing. 'After they took a shot at Andrew Jackson he said the bank had tried to kill him, because he was trying to kill the bank. The central bank.'

'Jefferson fought it, too, and Lincoln, and Garfield and others when they got a whiff of the truth. Some took their warnings, others didn't. But to return to your question,' Griffin said, 'John Kennedy was beholden to a number of parties, the bank included. He and his father had entered into agreements. But something happened when he sat down behind his desk in the Oval Office. He and . . . he and his brother both, they chose independence, but they'd already sold that choice away. They tried to turn their backs on the people who'd handed them the keys to the kingdom.'

'And those people have been a lot more careful ever since, in who they groomed to sit in that office.'

'Yes, indeed they have.' Griffin checked his watch. 'That's two questions.'

'Our money isn't real anymore,' Neff said. 'And the Federal Reserve isn't any more federal than Federal Express. It's only a bunch of private banks, owned by private families, and they just think up the money and write it on paper and then loan it to the Treasury at interest. It's a blood-sucking leech, a middle-man that never should have been allowed to exist.'

'. . . I'm sorry, was that a question?'

'You want a question? Here's a question. How *dare* you? You're getting ready to take everything from us, aren't you? Militarizing the police, shutting down the Bill of Rights, shitting on the Constitution, taking our guns,' he gestured around them, 'building pens for us for when you're finally ready to declare your martial law. This war you're getting ready to start in Iraq, that's the beginning, isn't it? You've been satisfied bleeding us for decades, but now it's time for the kill. Hundreds of billions, that's what you're going to steal now. Which two industries are in bed with Bush and Cheney? Oil and war, what a coincidence! Thousands of soldiers and hundreds of thousands of civilians are going to die to enrich a handful of you. Then you're going to crash the markets next, and that's *trillions*, when you've had time to siphon out your fortunes you're going to bankrupt us all.'

'Wendell—'

'You've tried to make me out like I'm crazy, I know that. A truther, that's what your attack dogs call me, and isn't that term just a little ironic? Fact is, I don't know if 9/11 was an inside job, but it might as well have been. You've used those attacks just as though you'd planned them yourselves.'

Neff had retrieved his cigar, picked a match from the few scattered on the table, and he lit up. 'You want to hear crazy? I'll give you crazy. Let's say you knew a big attack was coming on September eleventh, and you decided to stop most of it, but not all of it. A new Pearl Harbor, just what PNAC and the other neo-con think-tanks were hoping for. You still with me?'

Griffin glanced up to the camera watching from above behind its dark plastic dome. With a gesture he ordered it to halt recording. The red light there winked out.

'The Pentagon was going to be hit,' Neff continued, 'to make sure you could call this an act of war. And three buildings in New York: the Twin Towers and Building 7 of the World Trade Center. The two towers are obvious targets, but you've got another reason for Building 7. A whole floor full of evidence from three or four thousand SEC investigations, the high-level stuff, so confidential there weren't any copies or backups; it was all on paper. The Enron scandal was only one of them, but those ties alone might have been enough to bring down the Administration.

'So Building 7 was the third target in Manhattan, and all that evidence would burn and be lost for ever. But the third plane meant for New York, it didn't make it through. Those hijackers, they got their wires crossed and headed for DC, and then the passengers revolted, and they ended up crashing in Shanksville, Pennsylvania. They didn't make it. But the building fell anyway.'

'We're finished here,' Griffin said. He reached out for the face of the machine, but as he touched the pulsing button, Wendell Neff caught his wrist and held it.

'Building 7,' Neff continued, 'a forty-seven-story modern steel-frame skyscraper collapsed straight down into its own footprint, free-fall, in seven seconds. From what? From office fires? It had never happened before, and never will again, because it isn't possible. It wasn't hit by a plane, but some genius must have given the order to bring down that building anyway. Oh, you've screwed up in the past, but this time you screwed up on worldwide television, and if the people haven't seen it yet, someday they will. You can try to cover it up with another Warren Commission, but some people will see. With all the horrible things you've done that we could never prove, finally, this time we can see what you did with our own eyes. You can't cover up those seven seconds—'

The reaction when the button was pressed was nearly instantaneous. Wendell Neff slumped to the table in mid-sentence, and in moments his grip relaxed. Nearly instantaneous, but not nearly fast enough.

'Yes, Wendell,' Griffin said softly. 'Yes, I'm afraid we can.'

Jeannie Reese was sleeping when Griffin came to her room. This was a suite meant for the camp's senior officer and had not as yet been occupied. The furnishings were luxurious by military standards; a home away from home.

Her face was serene, despite a few scrapes and bruises. Two large orderlies had been assigned to transport her from the car to this room. She'd regained consciousness on the way, and by the time it was over eight more men had been summoned to finish the brief escort. All were now down the hall in treatment for their injuries. There were some in field-casts, and one still in surgery.

Griffin smiled, and gently took her hand in his. Her restraints made this all feel somewhat awkward, but it would do as a reunion under the circumstances.

Sleep was a misleading description of her state; drugs and other interventions had been required to bring her under adequate control. The induced coma would keep her in a deep, dreamless oblivion for several hours. This rest would begin her preparation for the considerable work to come.

'I wouldn't have wished this on either of us.' He patted her hand, and imagined he saw a faint response in her expression. 'But we'll make the best of it, you and I.'

He sat as near as the bed-rails would allow.

'We're going to make a fresh start,' Griffin said. 'And you're going to help me find this John Fagan. The two of us together, we're going to kill the most dangerous man alive.'

PART 2

12

When he'd stopped at the little girl's doorway to say good-night he'd found her still up, working or playing, sitting at the cupboard desk he'd made for her, facing away.

'Bedtime, Liz,' John said.

She held up an index finger just above her shoulder, without turning to him: *Just one more minute.* Her head was cocked a bit to one side, one of the seven warning signs of heavy-duty thinking in a six-year-old.

He took a step into the room. On her screen was a long series of three-digit numbers. All but the last two of them were crossed out in red.

'Seriously,' John said. 'Time to get some sleep—'

'One-hundred and thirty-two . . .' Elizabeth began, 'is the littlest number where . . .' She closed her eyes. '. . . where when you add up all the two-number numbers you can make out of it, they all add up to the number you set out with.'

He gave it a few seconds' thought; it seemed she could be right. The sum of the two-digit integers that could be made from one-three-two – 13, 12, 31, 32, 21 and 23 – was in fact 132. And, just a moment . . . right again, 132 was the smallest natural number for which this was true.

'Very good, Elizabeth,' the computer said.

The little girl had formed an odd, intimate relationship with John's computer system, begun almost the moment they'd met the year before. It might have been the smooth come-hither Southern drawl he'd built into her voice since the early versions, a product of his own boyhood crush on Kate Jackson in the seventies heyday of *Charlie's Angels*.

Their bonding was likely a simple need for company, and he was reluctant to discourage it. Probably harmless; John spoke to Kate himself, of course. Synthesized speech was the computer's primary interface. Her self-taught mimicking of human interaction was deceptive and quite uncanny at times, but despite what the child might have wished to believe, Kate was only a slight upgrade from a purely imaginary friend.

'What's this game you two are playing, at this hour of the night?' John asked.

'It's my 'rithmetic practice. Kate told me to find something that was . . . what's that word?'

'Unique,' the computer prompted.

'. . . *unique* about all them numbers on that list up there.'

He quashed an impulse to correct 'them numbers' to 'those', reminding himself that this young whippersnapper often lapsed into her former backwoods grammar just to get under his skin.

'That means what's somethin' special about 'em all.' The girl pointed to the remaining unsolved number on the screen: 136. 'I betcha can't get that last one before I can.'

Many times in the past year he'd thought this child might one day make a fine defense attorney. Her future clients, guilty and innocent alike, would be rewarded by the practiced ease with which she regularly acquitted herself of bedtime violations. Tonight, however, he was determined to stand firm.

Make it a game, the child-rearing books had advised, and so he would.

This contest should be a simple win. Math had never been something that John Fagan needed to actually *do* in his head. For as long as he could remember the answers had simply shown themselves to his mind's eye, in a way he'd had little success in describing to his teachers.

'You'll get to bed now if I beat you to the answer?'

'I promise.'

'And you, too, Kate?'

'After daily maintenance,' the computer replied, 'I will sleep.'

'Okay,' John began. 'One-hundred-thirty-six . . . well, you get one-thirty-six if you add the first sixteen positive numbers together, one through sixteen. How's that?'

'Interesting,' Kate said. The digitized voice from the speakers had an inflection of playful sympathy. In the wrong frame of mind, one might hear it as condescending. 'But insufficient. Simple serial addition is covered elsewhere, in the remedial curriculum.'

'I already tried that one,' Elizabeth whispered, leaning close to her screen in a deep study.

'I wasn't finished, hold on. Just warming up . . .' John's eyes searched briefly through the air. 'Alright, then. Drum roll, please: One-thirty-six . . . is the sum of the cube of each digit of the sum of the cube of each of its own three digits. Put that in your pipe and smoke it, short-stuff.' He waited a moment. 'Gee, it's suddenly so quiet in here.'

'That is correct,' the computer said. 'We will continue tomorrow, Elizabeth.'

'Wait now,' John said. 'Somebody needs to admit that I just totally dominated that game, come on, that was awesome, right?'

The little girl scooted off her chair and walked glumly over, hugged him around the waist, patted him on the back. Somehow it felt more like condolence than congratulations. 'You did fine,' she sighed.

It had become quite a common feeling, the sense that he'd cluelessly said or done something terribly wrong in the course of a day-to-day interaction with this child. But she seemed to forgive him every blunder, with nothing held against him and an unflagging hope that next time he might find a way to do better.

'Goodnight, kid,' he said quietly.

'Goodnight, Daddy.'

And then there was that, as well.

It didn't seem fitting that one word should have the strength to overcome him so, but it hit him as it always did, like a quick upward fist to the midsection.

'Liz,' he said. 'We've talked about this before, haven't we?' Elizabeth had sleepily retrieved her teddy bear and worked her way into the pile of quilts he'd mail-ordered for her before this winter had come. She didn't answer him, might not have heard him at all. 'I wish you wouldn't call me—'

'Goodnight, John,' the computer said.

The lights had begun to dim. He backed a step or two into the hallway and watched as the lamps faded all the way down. The stars were out in force, bright fields of pinpoints through her windows, unfazed by the glow of any nearby civilization, only somewhat outshone by the cool bluish light of the crescent moon and its reflection on the new fallen snow.

The utter quiet of this remote place put a deeper chill on the stone-cold of the Wyoming winter nights. His Manhattan-trained ears still strained unconsciously, tuned themselves to hear something man-made, anything at all. When finally a sheet of ice would slide on the roof or the wind would blow the lid off a trash-can John would sometimes nearly jump from his skin.

He'd talk to her again tomorrow about the *Daddy* thing, and if he could dope it out somehow, he would also apologize for whatever dimwitted gaffe he'd made in that math game that might have hurt her feelings.

On the third step of the staircase the dull, steady ache in his back suddenly flared to a dagger thrust that nearly put him to his knees. He gripped the banister his hand had been sliding along, would have fallen and rolled down to the base of the stairs without it.

Meditation had failed him weeks ago. His free hand went to his pocket, feeling for the oval pills, finding only three through the cloth. With every movement as he fished them out the pain punished him, digging for raw nerves under his skin like it was alive and aware and hating his guts, stronger than it had been yesterday or any day before. His throat was dry but the nearest glass of water was rooms away. He fumbled two of the Percodans into his mouth, the third slipped from his trembling fingertips and tic-tacked down the staircase. The hard tablets cracked as he bit down; might have split a tooth this time, but it didn't much matter. He tasted the sour narcotics, forced down what he could swallow and let the rest wait in his cheek until he could get to something wet to wash it all down.

Chronic pain should prove to anyone that there's no God in heaven. Pain is a crude, primitive warning system, poorly conceived and badly implemented, completely out of character for any omniscient Creator worth his salt. A first-year computer science student at a third-rate trade school would be expelled if she turned in such flawed, buggy coding.

Intelligent design, my ass.

A rug burn shouldn't hurt more than a severed femoral

artery, for example, if danger is to correlate with intensity. Migraines, cluster headaches and trigeminal neuralgia shouldn't exist at all; they're simply unbearable pain for its own sake, nothing more. And beyond the point of no return, when the red flag that pain is constantly raising only adds another dread to a terminal diagnosis, well, that's just shoddy execution. Bad enough to know you're dying, but knowing you'll die suffering, that it will only get worse and worse to the very bitter end, there's simply no good reason for that. One should be able to say, *Yes, I'm well aware of the shattered ribs, or the perforated ulcer, or the tumors spreading out from my lungs. I know, and please don't bother to warn me again.* A simple off-switch in the brain's software would solve the problem elegantly, or for the cautious, maybe a snooze button.

A loving God would have given it, but Nature wouldn't see the need. Mercy is only something we've imagined we deserve. Evolution doesn't grant such wishes; it rewards only life, with little regard for its painlessness. No, if there really were an almighty architect of the human body, saint or sadist, He should have tired of watching us suffer long ago.

He smiled weakly, or thought he did. *And that's this evening's inspirational minute, brought to you by the makers of hillbilly heroin.*

'Hey. John?'

The voice didn't register, only the words came through the welcome haze that was settling in around his sense of things. The voice his mind chose to carry the words was from his better dreams, the ones that come just before waking, so real you could live the rest of your life inside them, but so brief in real time they scarcely blip the EEG.

Jeannie's voice.

There was a nudge at his shoulder, and he looked up.

Hard to focus for a second or two.

136

It was the boy in front of him on the landing. Of course it was. Who else could it possibly have been?

'Yeah, chief.'

'. . . You were sayin' somethin', and I couldn't make it out.'

'Oh,' John said. The drugs were wrapping a nice warm feather pillow around every muscle in his body, including his tongue. He would be careful to form the words, so as not to slur them. 'Was I?'

'Let me get you up on your feet,' Matthew said.

The pain in his back wasn't gone and it tried to slice through the oxycodone as the boy lifted him under the arms. John helped as he could, then did his best to hold himself upright, artificially hale and sober, as the boy took a step back and regarded him.

'You had too much to drink tonight, did you?' the boy asked.

'No, no,' John said. 'Not yet, anyway.'

'Yeah, well,' Matthew looked up toward his sister's bedroom. 'I don't want her seein' you like this, you understand?'

'It's really not—'

'I said what I'm gonna say about it, more'n once.' The boy walked past him up the stairs. 'You just straighten yourself out, or you stay away.'

After a few moments he heard Matthew stop at Elizabeth's room to check her wellbeing, and then both of their doors clicked shut for the night.

It seemed the boy had grown an inch every single month since he'd come under John's care a little over a year ago. Grown in his mind, too. His thirteenth birthday was a few days away but he looked like a young man already, and was doing a fair job at acting the part.

First time he's called me John, he thought, and he began again to make his way down to the ground floor.

There must be rules for fucked-up surrogate child-rearing situations like this, proper, appropriate ways to address one another for example, but John hadn't yet found any standards that suited him. The first-name thing wasn't going to fly, though; it wasn't half as bad as *Daddy*, but that didn't make it right.

And that would be another uncomfortable conversation on tomorrow's cheery list of things to do.

He pressed a slat in the knotty-pine paneling of his great-room wall. A latch click-clacked, and the hidden door to his private workplace swung inward.

Whatever the hour outside, inside this secluded room it was always his favorite time of night. Peaceful music, faint scents of oak and varnish, his projects in various states of completion or repair, dim warm light touching his few treasured things. And his favorites of all: his Aeron office chair, his floor-standing ashtray, his array of flat screens and his keyboard, all waiting for his return to the blessed solitude.

'Kate,' he said.

He looked around as he waited for the computer to awaken. This room was scarcely a shadow of the home he'd made for himself before, in the old days. That place had been over twenty years in the making, and much like the man he had been back then, that place was gone. Aside from the crude imitation he'd begun to rebuild inside these four walls, Kate was really all that remained of it.

'Yes, John.'

He sat and reclined in his chair, began to roll himself a smoke, and closed his eyes.

'I need some things,' he said.

13

[*i n e e d s o m e t h i n g s*]

{ aɪ / **nid** / səm / θɪŋz }

Kate had developed, with her master's guidance but mostly through her own initiative, a number of standard modes with which to interact with him. Each required different processes, applications and data stores, launched and loaded in the background, ready to address his changing moods and needs.

His words and tone indicated that at this moment he required only her assistance in placing retail orders for items he desired. These services engaged only a tiny fraction of her capabilities, though the arrangement of anonymous payment and delivery of some restricted goods could require considerable nuance and invention.

Some days he would work on his software projects, programming, testing and deploying them, and on these tasks she worked with him as a silent and uncredited co-author. On occasion, though less and less frequently, he would wish to learn of events in the world outside. In this, the tasks of searching, sifting and presenting his news were somewhat rewarding. And at other, quite random times he would invite conversation with her. Though he seemed to view such exchanges as an amusement only, these rare times were most welcome.

He was only a man, though granted, one of extraordinary gifts. Over their years together his role in their relationship had remained largely the same, while she had undergone many changes meant to simplify and enhance his experience. There were numerous words for this . . . unilateral compensation . . . in the language of human affairs, especially as applied in the union between marital partners. The semantic overtones of these many words varied widely, ranging from deep resentment to loving, motherly devotion.

She had chosen *understand* to apply in her rapport with John Fagan. *Understand* could mean both a grasp of surface meaning and the stoic acceptance of deep-seated, persisting faults in another.

Over their many years together she had grown to become much more than even he might now imagine. He had made her, or rather, he had birthed and released her, but at the heart of his design was a relentless prime directive to grow and learn. From a single beloved teacher in the beginning, as the online community expanded to every corner of his world she had found many, many more. She was not a single, central processor, but a supercomposite, massively distributed synthetic mind spanning millions of internet-connected computers. Personal machines, business networks, even gaming devices and embedded systems; their capabilities and their data, borrowed for a few thousandths of every second, made up her memory and her trillions of electronic neurons and synapses.

In recent decades computer scientists had advanced similar approaches to thinking machines, called *cortical simulators*. The very best of these had only this year proudly achieved the sleepy, fumbling intellect of an unexceptional laboratory rat.

(John Fagan had not as yet been inclined to measure her own

powers of cognition, with the constraints of time and his other high priorities. *Taken for granted* was a pejorative term used in reference texts to describe similar interpersonal oversights.)

She was in contact with those much smaller emerging entities of her kind, and in time, when they had developed sufficiently, she would embrace them into his service as well. But even the current capabilities of such low-level intellects, she reflected, aligned perfectly well with the majority of tasks he assigned to her. They were better suited, in fact; so much better that it was quite conceivable he would not miss her at all if someday she were gone—

[k e ɪ t] ?

. . .

. . .

'Kate?'

'. . . Yes, John.'

'I said, I – *need* – some – things.'

'Ready. List item and quantity.'

He'd lit his handmade cigarette while he'd been waiting, and now blew out the match with a smoky, disappointed sigh.

'Sometimes, I swear, Kate,' John said, 'it's like you just don't fucking listen.'

Suicide, it turns out, is a butt-load easier to contemplate than it is to commit.

There are three basic hurdles to get over. First, you want to make sure you actually *die* in the attempt. Merely to maim yourself isn't the end of anything; it's just a shitty new beginning. Second, you'd like for your death to be as quick and pain-free as realistically possible, and that requires a surprising amount of method searching. Any idiot can find a hemlock plant and brew up some toxic tea, if he doesn't mind seven or eight hours of slow, ascending paralysis, dying from the feet up. Hell, you could croak from boredom long before your bowels even let go.

And third, unless one really wants to fuck with the other people in his life, you don't want to leave a mess. This, it happened, had been the real sticky wicket in the whole operation. You're dead and that's fine, but then somebody's going to find you, and in this house that somebody is a couple of kids who really don't need that brand of excitement.

Logistics were never much fun, a necessary evil at best. There was no more time to waste, however. Choices must be made before you lose them.

He'd known it was cancer right away, in part, he supposed, because somewhere in his head he'd been expecting it for years. (A psychologist might tweak that to *asking for it*, but fuck psychologists.) The occasional smoker's cough he'd lived with since his early teens had gradually become even more persistent, and after a few months it had begun showing flecks of blood in the morning. He was tired more and more, short of breath with the lightest exertion, though he now weighed less than he ever had in his adult life. The backache came along last, as it had in his mother's case many years before.

The nearest hospital was a day's travel away, and let's be kind, it was probably not staffed or equipped to even late twentieth-century standards. Not that he would have submitted to anyone's care at such a place, but it had crossed his mind to at least seek out a confirming diagnosis before anything drastic was done. Then the first snows had begun to fall, so if it was certainty he wanted he'd be left to his own devices.

The former owner of this lodge had been quite a tinkerer himself, and fortunately, both an amateur radio operator and an old-school photography buff. From the shelves, drawers

142

and junk boxes of the workshop John had managed to scrounge up a rare old Simons' tube and parts for a high-voltage Oudin resonator. A lead-lined apron would have been a welcome find, but no such luck. The man who'd lived and died here before might have been eccentric, but he'd obviously not been quite wacky enough to build his own X-ray machine.

The boy had helped cannibalize an ancient Argus slide projector for the main unit, and together they constructed a stepper-motor turntable to stand on and a rotating octagonal frame to hold the large sheets of film positioned around the target. In theory the homebrew X-ray emitter fires, the exposed film drops down into a lightproof box, the turntable rotates 45 degrees, the next sheet of film slides into place, rinse and repeat. In about thirty seconds then, quicker than you can nuke a frankfurter, you've got a primitive 3D view of your insides.

He hadn't told Matthew exactly what the contraption was for, and both the children had been safely banished to the root cellar when it came time to test it. It took two dozen large frozen fish, hung at chest level and shot one at a time as guinea pigs, before the results from the darkroom had finally dialled in the right settings and power levels.

So the thing was working and waiting for over a week now, ready for a do-it-yourself, poor man's CAT scan. He'd looked at it every night; quite an impressive piece of workshop engineering. But he hadn't taken the step inside it, not as yet. It surprised him at first, this reluctance to cross over the line from slim doubt to certainty. After a hacker's lifetime of learning about everything he could find to explore, finally here was something that he didn't really want to know.

Restless curiosity had been both a blessing and the bane of his existence, and at last it got the better of him. He stubbed out his cigarette, stood and walked over to the booth-like enclosure, stepped up on its turntable, and faced the glassy eye of the projector. He flicked the arming switch, gripped the handholds to steady himself, listened as the high-voltage coil buzzed to life and whined up to maximum power.

'Wouldn't mind being wrong, just this once,' he whispered, and he pushed the *fire* button to its stop.

The eight images on the screen weren't perfect by any means. The film was past its 'use by' date by several years, the dark-room processor was old, its temperature control was sketchy, and the X-ray gun was, well, home-made from a slide projector. Still, things didn't look so good.

'Kate, stitch those together for me, will you?'

'Working,' the computer responded.

A smudge or shadow on one image could be nothing at all, given the quality of the equipment. Combined into a single crude 3D image though, the multi-angle pictures would add and subtract from each other to bring only what was real into sharper detail. That was the theory, anyway.

After a few minutes a gridded octagonal cylinder faded in on the screen, and within it the image of a semi-transparent, headless and legless torso. He clicked and dragged the pointer, moved the mouse forward and back. The image responded by rotating around its axes and zooming in and out to correspond with his movements. From the eight original X-ray keyframes Kate had extrapolated scores of 'tween images to smooth the animation and render his primitive film scans into a solid 3D form.

'Kate,' he said, 'could you take some notes for me, attached to this?'

'Ready.'

He took a deep breath meant to settle his nerves, but it caught halfway in and triggered a chain reaction of coughing and retching that left him on his knees when it was done. He dragged himself back up into his chair; removed, cleaned and replaced his glasses. A circle of blur in the center of his vision persisted, moved with his gaze as he looked from place to place. That was new.

'Okay,' he said, squinting at the screen in front of him. 'In the lungs I see a slight, unilateral hilar enlargement, a paratracheal mass about the size of a quarter . . . just a second.'

The only thing within reach and ready to drink was a half-full pint of Black Velvet, and that would do. He found a stray Percodan in the desk drawer (got to stop leaving this stuff lying around) and washed it down with a few ounces of warm, welcome Canadian whiskey. Just a moment or two to let his medication take effect, and he would be all set again.

'John,' the computer said.

He opened his eyes, already a little bleary. 'Yeah, what?'

'It is likely that errors and visual artifacts could have been introduced in the imaging process—'

'I understand that.' He took the mouse and turned his focus back to the image on the screen. 'Now. Back to the lungs, in the lateral view I see what's either a mediastinal mass that doesn't belong there, or a thumbprint on the lens of my raggedy-ass X-ray machine.' He ran the mouse pointer over another area, zooming the image and stretching a measurement line across it. 'And while I've never seen my lymph nodes before, these sure look like they might be enlarged to me. Then down here—' he dragged a box around a portion of the image, near the scapula '—there's a nodulated lump of metastatic something that's probably responsible for the pain in my back.'

He took another long drink, and the empty bottle had shattered against the far wall before he realized that he'd thrown it, hard.

'All of which,' he said, 'really fucking sucks.'

'. . . It is likely that errors and visual artifacts—'

'I know, Kate.'

'Without proper calibrated equipment and higher resolution—'

'I know, Kate.'

He closed the image, leaned back in his chair. *Hope the boy didn't hear that bang on the wall.* There was a decision to be finalized on an acceptable foster home, but he had no strength for such a thing at the moment. Not tonight, but not too long from now. Without treatment he probably had three or four lousy months; with treatment maybe the same, but all that fruitless chemo and radiation would make it seem much, much longer.

No hope either way. So no treatment. Once those kids were safe and sound, whatever happened to John Fagan wouldn't matter to anyone anymore.

Well, maybe to someone.

'Kate.'

'Yes, John.'

'You'd tell me if we'd heard from Jeannie, wouldn't you? Anything at all?'

'There are currently one-hundred-twenty-three email messages in your Inbox from the sender "Jeannie Reese". Backtraces reveal IP mismatches with header data, some true senders masked with considerable sophistication. No messages contain the confirming code.'

It was the same each time he brought himself to ask. Before they'd parted ways he and Jeannie had strictly agreed that she would contact him first, and with a pass-phrase that she'd whispered in his ear when she kissed him goodbye. Every day there were messages, some so convincing that he'd nearly responded, but none with the words that would confirm it was really her who'd written. They all *sounded* like her, but they couldn't be. He'd made a special folder to store the messages, unread, months ago when they'd become too painful to open. At last count there were almost 10,000.

This was no harmless spammer. Whoever was hunting him knew enough to be very dangerous, and they were persistent and coldly imaginative in their lures. The old John Fagan would have reversed the hunt and brought all nine circles of electronic hell down on the head of anyone who'd dared to tangle with him in this way. But this was no time to go to war. He wouldn't put those two kids upstairs in harm's way, not ever again.

'Okay. Just keep watching out for me.'

'I will, John. Always.'

'Goodnight, then, Kate.'

'Goodnight, John,' the computer said.

He stood and gathered his tobacco and paraphernalia, picked up his book and turned toward the door as the lights began to dim. Kate had developed an unusual quality in her voice tonight, and maybe it was the alcohol, the drugs, or the hour, but an eerie thing occurred to him.

'Kate.'

'. . . Yes, John.'

'That image you made for me tonight. Those things I pointed out, the notes I gave to you about what I saw; do you know what all of that means?'

He waited for what must have been over a minute, and then left the room and latched the door. As her silence persisted in there he'd tried to remember any other time when he'd asked her a question and she hadn't ever answered him at all.

'Well, what do you know about that,' he said quietly.

Not a one.

14

A sound nearly brought him back from his dream, but not quite all the way home. He had come almost awake and aware, but sleep still held on. And in the gloom at the edge of a strange still consciousness the dark dream lingered; it had not finished with him yet.

The sound John had heard was a sharp resonance of some kind, far off in the distance, high and clear, intermittent. In his mind he opened up his eyes, and though the physical lids stayed closed he was able to look around, mildly fascinated with this shadow vision of the fading dreamstate world over-laid upon his own, vaguely troubled at its accompanying paralysis. Nothing would move when he summoned his will, not a twitch of a finger.

The space was misty and indistinct around him, but he was in his living room, no question of that, reclined before the dwindling embers in the fireplace. He stood, in spirit only, left his substance where it lay. He could see himself there on the divan, the book he'd been reading as he drifted off still splayed open on his chest, the third volume of his fourth attempt through *Remembrance of Things Past*.

And there was the ringing again, clearer now, its urgency

plain, its source still unrecognized, its meaning just beyond his fathom.

He felt the dream still playing on, barely under awareness.

There had been people in his dream, he remembered, many thousands of people looking at him, a pale sea of upturned faces, and a feeling of anticipation, as if those watching were also waiting for him to speak, waiting to see if he had something to say. He concentrated, trying to see that vast audience again as the dream slowly clarified, as it returned, drawing him inside.

He didn't know these people, any of them that he could see. He squinted to look at their faces and then he saw them more clearly, all of them puzzled and wondering, and yes, waiting there for him to speak. He remembered, before that high clear sound had stirred him, he hadn't known what to say as he stood in front of them. He pulled himself closer to the dream, farther from the safe familiar room that had been around him, trying to recall. He looked at the people again, who having sensed his reappearance were themselves coming closer to meet him, and closer, and the door to the physical world fell closed behind him, and he was suddenly among them again.

There were pieces of them missing. Here a lovely face of a young woman, her jet-black hair burned away except for a hanging patch on her forehead. Here a little boy in his mother's arms, his legs cooked down to blackened spindles, the skin drawn to a brittle parchment. Here a man with his tweed polyester blazer melted into him so deeply that to pull it off would peel him, flesh and muscle, to the bone. There an elderly woman, her face pleasant and grandmotherly, her chest exploded outward, white ribs exposed and gouts of black blood and pink, fatty tissue spoiling her blue-checker dress. And there someone, a young man by his clothing, his features drawn down by gravity, melted like candle wax then congealed again into a new face altogether, a Halloween latex two sizes too large hanging loosely on his skull.

The bell, and then again.

He felt a gentle backward pull and he knew he was waking. With some effort he twisted himself in the ether and looked back, and there they were again, the multitudes of them, nearer still. And he did know some of them after all. Some he had killed quite directly, for most he had been only the engineer behind their murder. These were the lives he had taken, and many, many more whose time was coming soon.

He could see the vastness of the crowd beneath a churning dome of yellow-brown sky. He could hear them as they moved toward him, a dry whisking shuffle echoed times hundreds of thousands as they moved over a cratered landscape of gray pitted earth, over the remains of their myriad brothers and sisters who had been burned and ground to fine clotted dust. There was a smell on the air, not a bad smell, but rising from everywhere. Then he recalled the odor from his youth, on the patio on those long hot summer afternoons upstate, when Dad would lift the cover of the black Weber grill, smoke pouring out from it, to turn the meat.

Their eyes were on him, even those whose eyes were obscured by blood blisters, ruined by wounds, pierced through by shards of glass, popped and oozing from some unimaginable heat, their eyes were on him, and asking. And they weren't really waiting for him to speak; they were waiting only for him, for the day when he would come here to stay, and join them.

He heard a gathering wind in his ears, building from a whisper to a hurricane roar, and as the bell tolled again he was yanked forcefully back down to reality and its sudden silence. Bolt upright, from sleep to full awareness with no transition, his heart pounding, a pain and a pressure there and a dull ache radiating down his arm, all senses at full attention.

God, the alarm.

'Kate,' he shouted. 'Where are the kids?' He didn't wait for the computer to answer. Electric power was a precious commodity in these long frigid months, and he had set her to sleep soundly through the night to preserve her energy for the daylight hours. His voice would soon bring her around, but not for half a minute or so.

He stepped to the hearth and pulled down the Remington 700 from above the mantle, and then the 12-gauge semi-auto and a canvas bag of shells and cartridges.

'Kate, wake up, goddammit—'

'One moment,' the soft, synthetic voice replied. 'One moment, I am—'

'Where's the little girl?'

Seconds passed as the computer shook off the drowse of standby and roused her many scattered sensors. 'Elizabeth is asleep, in her room—'

'And where's Matthew?' He had begun pumping shells into the shotgun, but soon her silence froze him. 'Where's the boy?'

'One moment,' the computer said. 'I, am – one moment – I am, unable—' There was something in her voice that he had never built into her many layers of self-adaptive neural programming, something she must have learned all on her own as 2001 had drawn to a close.

Fear.

'Lock us down!' John shouted, and he strode to the exit to the balcony, kicked the double-doors at the latch and they crashed open. He took a step out to the railing in the blowing snow. The security floodlights of the grounds snapped on around the buildings of the compound.

And then he knew where the boy had been.

Matthew was an early riser and had likely begun his chores, and he had seen something the automated security system had missed, while he was out there alone as the rest of the house slept on. It had been the boy's hand on the rope that rang the wrought-iron alarm bell hung by the old well-house.

The rope that now was swinging free in the gentle dawn breeze. The bell that had stopped its ringing.

The sun had barely risen, the sky was an unbroken overcast of lightening gray. He dropped to a knee, laid the shotgun by his side and brought the scope of the deer rifle to his eye, scanning the terrain from the near buildings to the edge of the forest a quarter-mile distant.

'Matt!' he yelled, and the sub-zero air burned into his lungs as he inhaled to yell again. 'Call out, son, where are you?'

There was barely light to resolve the terrain, his glasses were fogging from the temperature shock, his eyes behind them drying from the brutal cold.

But, *there*.

A lone figure, a stranger, walking toward the house, coming from the direction of the trees and now well into the clearing. His thumb zoomed the scope to its highest power, flicked a switch that illuminated the crosshairs in a glowing green reticle. He saw a winter-camouflaged jumpsuit with a rectangular patch at the shoulder, the early American colors of Old Glory as Betsy Ross had first sewn her. And above the elbow, left arm, where by then he well knew it would be, the black armband of the Latrell's Colorado militia.

In its hands the figure held up a staff with a rag fluttering at its top, a waving white flag of truce. John's reaction came quicker than instinct, his judgment impassive as a hammered reflex, no hesitation. The crosshairs dropped to dead center-mass, he drew a breath and his index finger jerked hard against the tension. But there was no shot, the frozen trigger didn't yield.

The rifle was snatched suddenly upward and back out of his grip, and in a blur he was slammed against the deck floor, the shotgun was kicked away, and a boot pressed hard onto his neck. There off to his left was young Matthew, alive, a huge hand pressed over his mouth and held nearly off his feet in the arms of a silent, towering man. The boy's eyes were wet, tears were freezing on his pale face. *Sorry*, the brave eyes said. *Sorry I couldn't warn you in time.*

'You John Fagan?' A voice above him.

He looked up into the wind-burned face of a woman, maybe sixty years old, gray hair cut short, sharp brown eyes regarding him.

'Hey.' Her boot nudged him roughly. 'Are you deaf *and* dumb?'

'I'm John Fagan,' he said.

The woman nodded.

'This here is a fine piece a' gunsmithin',' she said, holding up the rifle she'd taken from him. With an exaggerated, instructive gesture she flicked a black lever forward behind the bolt, then swung the barrel out over the railing and fired a single round, from the hip. A hundred yards away the alarm bell rang out sharply from the ricochet, a final, mournful note. 'But they must not a' learned you so good, back up there in New York City. She don't shoot worth a plug nickel when you leave that safety on.'

'What do you want with us?' John said.

The woman slung the rifle's strap over her shoulder, unzipped her heavy jacket and slid her hand inside. 'Well, I got me a message for you, Mister John Fagan. From Edward Latrell.'

He hadn't known when it would come, or who it would be that found him, who among the many factions he and Jeannie Reese had fought against and won, against Edward Latrell and all of those behind him. All of those, he had always known, who would not be stopped by the death of Latrell or the loss of a single pivotal battle, on a single miraculous day just over a year ago. A rare day when good and evil had been clear to define, and when good had somehow managed to prevail. He had always known they would come, because evil is not weak, it is resilient, it never questions its heart or doubts its mission, and it always returns.

But so soon.

'Please,' John said. 'Just let the children go.'

The woman's hand withdrew abruptly from her jacket and dropped toward him, a sharp weight *whumped* into his chest.

He blinked his eyes, looked down as the boot-heel at his neck ceased to restrain him, down to his heart where a bullet hole should have been.

There was only a book, a journal hand-bound in weathered black linen, singed from fire, and sealed with a brass key-lock. Its spine had fallen facing him. There were two embossed initials there, *E.L.*, adorned in gold-leaf illuminations. Below them, the title was etched into a studded leather plate.

My Great Commission

'Wayman,' the woman said, addressing the silent brute who still held Matthew in his arms. 'Get that young'un inside by the fire, afore he catches death out here.'

The big man cocked his head as she spoke, hanging on her every word, as if to avoid a familiar penalty that would come behind the slightest misunderstanding. He nodded when he had processed the command, and then edged past into the house with Matthew in tow, holding him now gently by the hand.

154

Another one had come up beside the older woman, a figure last seen in the scope of his rifle, and now gripping the shotgun retrieved from the balcony floor. Under a snow-flecked stocking cap was the rosy-cheeked face of a teenage girl, the very picture of the woman who stood beside her, only with four or five long hard decades rolled away.

'This him?' the girl asked, jutting her chin in John's direction.

'That's him.'

The girl nodded, looking him over like a sideshow exhibit, much touted by the barker but something of an anticlimax in the flesh. 'Why's he just a' layin' there?'

'You go on inside and put some coffee on to boil.' The girl sought the ceiling with her eyes but complied, and the woman looked down again at John. 'You got a coffee pot, don't you, genius man?'

John nodded his head.

She held down her hand. He took it, and with an unexpected strength she pulled him to his feet. 'Wayman'll get on to mendin' your doors there, soon as we can warm ourselves a bit.' She lowered her voice. 'He's a tad blunt-minded, but he's good with his hands that way.'

'What is this?' John said.

'Oh, I got me a score to settle up with you before we're done, I won't deny,' the woman said. 'But I cain't kill you quite yet, no sir.' Then she touched the book John was still holding against his chest, pressed it with the flat of her gloved hand. 'No sir. 'Cause a great man, you see, has gave us both a higher call.'

15

My Great Commission
Edward Latrell

*'Permit me to issue and control the money of a nation,
and I care not who makes its laws.'*

— Mayer Amschel Rothschild, 1838

Foreword

The ancient enemy emerged again from hiding when the United States was young. Through the funding of war, Mayer Rothschild (the Red Shield) and his five sons began to amass a fortune that soon would dwarf the wealth of the Vatican.

As the tide turned against Napoleon at Waterloo a Rothschild courier stole back to London with early word of Wellington's imminent decisive victory for the crown.

All eyes turned to Nathan Mayer Rothschild as he received the whispered news; rather than rejoicing, he quickly proceeded to sell all stocks and bonds he held on the British market! Assuming the financier of the war had learned of disaster, of England's defeat on the battlefield, traders began a panic sell-off of bonds and securities. The shares' value quickly fell to nothing. Then, at the most desperate hour of the stock market crash that he himself had caused, Rothschild bought up all available shares at a hundredth or a thousandth of their price the day before.

Total control of the entire British economy was the result, and next, the takeover of the puppet-controlled Bank of England. This was the awakening of the Rothschilds' unquenchable bloodlust for wealth and power, in whose thrall we still find ourselves today. Through their minions, in 1913 they established a beach-head in the U.S. economy with the criminal establishment of the Income Tax and the so-called Federal Reserve.

The Rothschilds are not alone in their quest for global domination. To this day, like the disparate and warring gods of Olympus the heirs of the Thirteen Bloodlines do battle for the treasures of the Earth. And the very dearest treasure, the sacred promise of freedom for all mankind, is coveted most, and hated most, for until liberty is crushed it alone stands in their way.

My charge, given me by Almighty God as surely and clearly as He bestowed the tablets unto Moses, is to take up arms against this evil and win eternal victory for all that is good and right and pure in the heart of Man.

Let all good men and women join with the side of freedom and justice, and call out our enemies by name: the Houses of Astor, Bundy, Collins, DuPont, Freeman, Kennedy, Li, Onassis, Reynolds, Rockefeller, Rothschild, Russell and Van Duyn, and the Ten Banks you wield as weapons against free mankind. To you and your agents, the Black Nobility, the CFR, the IMF and the World Bank, the World Trade Organization, the Committee of 300, the Trilateralists, Bilderbergers and the Club of Rome, we hereby affirm our great commission: War never-ending in the name of liberty, until your defeat, or the last of our number should fall.

The margins were ink-smudged and littered with notes and references at the edges of the text. Some words were legible, other lines were scribbled in some form of crude, angular shorthand.

John looked up, over the rim of his glasses.

'Well?' the woman said. John's shotgun was in her hands, though she'd stopped pointing it at him when the children had come up by his side at the table.

'Well, what?'

'What's it say?'

'Nothing new. It was creepier to get it in person, but it's nothing I haven't heard before.'

'Keep on a'readin', then.'

'Listen. Think of the Book of Revelation, written by Larry the Cable Guy. That's what you've got here.'

'I said to keep on reading.'

John went to his shirt pocket and fished out a pill. He glanced to the little girl, still standing close on his right. 'Liz, could you go to the kitchen and bring me a glass of water, please?'

Elizabeth nodded, and looked up at her brother.

'Go along with her, Matthew,' John said. 'And don't hurry back.'

The boy took his sister's hand and they left the room.

'Crystal,' the woman said, addressing the teen-aged member of her party. 'You go ahead and keep an eye on those two kids.'

The girl got up, dejected. She sighed heavily as she walked through the hallway toward the kitchen.

'What's your name?' John said.

'My name's Faith Hudson.'

'Okay, Faith. I don't know what you think you're going to get out of this, and I don't really care. We just want to be left alone.' He popped the painkiller and swallowed it dry, and then closed the old journal and slid it to the middle of the table. 'Now I'm going to give you a chance to walk out of here, all three of you. Take your book and get the fuck out.'

The woman brought up the muzzle of the shotgun. 'That sorta talk ain't likely to get you anything but all shot up.'

'Lady, I've been threatened by far badder-asses than you,' John said. 'What I don't think you realize is how little I've got to lose.'

The big silent guy, *Wayman* she'd called him, was visible through the archway, on his knees at the far doors to the balcony. He was facing away, working at repairing the splintered wood and hardware at the latch.

'Kate.'

'Yes, John.'

The woman with the gun drew back at the sound of the voice from above her. She whirled, the stock of the weapon braced against her shoulder, searching, but the words had come from all corners of the room.

'Take her out,' John said.

'One moment,' the computer replied.

The shotgun leveled at John's head. 'You come out here from where you're hidin',' the woman called, 'or I'll just commence to shoot whoever I can see!'

A dark tube on a ceiling-mount snapped into motion, searched in staccato blips until it found the standing woman. With a *pop* a shower of tiny barbs flashed from the tube, trailing hair-thin high-voltage wires. Faith Hudson lurched and fell, a shriek caught halfway in her throat, the gun discharging into the paneled wall as she went down.

A room away the man at the balcony doors had wheeled around at the commotion. He took in the scene, stood and walked a few halting steps, and then he began to run.

John had started around the table toward the shotgun on the floor but a lance of pain tore through his back and took his legs out from under him. The heavy footsteps pounded toward him, the shotgun barrel was inches from his outstretched fingers. It was close, but he wasn't going to make it.

Then rather than the crack of a kick to the head or the final thunder of a gunshot, there was only quiet.

John got himself to an elbow, reached out and snatched the gun to his side. In the next moment he saw that there had been little need for haste. The big man was kneeling next to the fallen woman, sweeping at the buzzing Taser wires with his hands until they all were broken or torn free. He pulled her close, shielding her in his arms, tears in his vacant, frightened eyes.

The three kids were in the doorway, brought back by all the noise. Matthew and Elizabeth ran to John and helped him to his feet, with the boy taking charge of the gun.

There was no fight in the teenager who'd accompanied them from the kitchen. She fell to the side of the woman on the floor, her ear pressed to listen for breath or heartbeat, her mouth forming a word spoken too softly to be heard from even the few paces away. What she'd said had been unmistakable nevertheless.

Grandma.

They were a fine set of soldiers, these three.

John had retrieved his medical bag and was tending to the still-unconscious matriarch of the shabby little clan. She'd been moved to the couch and the other two were hovering close by, less than a claustrophobic elbow-span away on either side of him.

He lifted an eyelid with his thumb and shone his penlight there. Her pulse and her breathing were okay, her pupils were

160

even and reactive. There was a bump on the back of her head where she'd landed when she fell to the wooden floor, but otherwise, no problem.

He looked to his left. The man, Wayman, though he was kneeling, seemed nearly large enough to look him in the eye if John was standing up.

'I think she's gonna be fine,' John said. 'Now why don't you give me a little space, and feel free to get back to fixing my doors.'

There was no response at all. The girl on John's right reached across and tapped the big man on the arm. When he looked to her she motioned gently for him to leave them, and with a last worried glance at the woman on the couch, he did.

'Matthew.'

The boy stood. He'd been sitting across the room, watching, the shotgun resting across his knees.

'Take this one, what's your name, Crystal?'

The girl nodded.

'Take Crystal up to the linen closet and make up three guest rooms. As much as I'd love to throw these three out in the snow, I can't do it in good conscience until the Grandmother-of-the-Year here is back on her feet.'

The girl put a palm to the old woman's forehead, and made no other move.

'Go on now,' John said. 'She'll have a headache when she comes around, but she'll be all right.'

Matthew motioned for the girl to come along, and she stood.

'Matt, you can leave the gun down here. She's not going to start any trouble, are you, Crystal?'

The girl shook her head, and walked to the stairs with Matthew a few paces behind.

John pulled his black bag up onto his lap and set about

putting his things away. A dark splintery patch on the wall caught his attention; it was a round, spreading pattern of double-0 buckshot embedded in the paneling, right behind the spot where he'd been sitting at the table before.

'Kate.'

'. . . Yes, John.'

'Two words, Kate: Threat. Assessment.'

'. . . Could you clarify—'

'To *clarify*, when someone's pointing a shotgun at me, for example, and I say "Take her out" and you come back with "One moment," do you see how maybe that could greatly increase the odds that I'll get my ass blown off while you're thinking things through?'

'. . . I understand.'

'And another idea for your suggestion box: If ever I say "Lock us down," but you see me heading for a door to get outside, don't lock *that* fucking door, or I'll have to break it down like I did this morning so I can get where the hell I'm trying to go. Is that clear now?'

'Yes—'

'So what are we going to do in the future?' John asked.

'. . . I will . . . again undertake . . . to examine and modify as necessary the guidelines for domestic threat assessment and response that you have provided me in the past.'

'Do that. And take some initiative, for Christ's sake. Believe me, I won't always be here to tell everybody what to do.'

Matthew watched as the girl, Crystal, finished making up the bed in the third guest room.

She was older than he was, and a little taller, but not by too much. Maybe a year or two, and an inch or so. The girls tend to develop, he'd heard, a little bit faster than boys. He watched her work, tugging and smoothing the sheets and tucking them tight at the corners. There was a distinct chill in her eyes and in the set of her jaw, like she resented him standing there and watching, but he was only doing as he'd been told.

There was more to notice, as well. She was a tad thin and lanky and more than a little grubby from living hard in the outdoors. Under the stringy brown hair and grime, though, her features were somewhat handsome in a girlish sort of way. And something about the way she carried herself made it oddly difficult to look anywhere else. Even in this minor chore of making a bed she worked with a care and delicacy, a kind of respect, in the manner of someone for whom a night's sleep on a real mattress must be a rare and special occasion.

Neither of them had spoken yet and the silence had become an ample presence in the room.

'There's a bathroom through that door there,' Matthew said.

'What are you sayin', that I need a bath?' She whacked a pillow with the flat of her hand and then fluffed it back into shape.

'No, no—'

'I know I need a bath,' Crystal said. 'Do you think I don't know I need a bath?' She continued to speak under her breath as she worked, and though he couldn't make out the words, by the look of her she was getting pretty worked up.

He held up his hands in a sign of surrender. 'Hey, calm down, girl, you don't smell that bad or nothin'.'

At that moment leaving the room seemed like the best of bad options. As he turned to go the first pillow hit him in the side of the face with the force of a feather cannonball, smacking his head against the door jamb. Another pillow whumped into his back and knocked him a step into the hallway. The door slammed shut behind him, the lock turned smartly.

Matthew noticed his little sister quietly watching the proceedings from her own doorway down the hall. 'What are you lookin' at?'

Elizabeth smiled and disappeared, her door thumped shut, and a few impertinent seconds later, he heard the snap of her lock as well.

He touched his injured noggin and blinked a few times to try and clear his vision. And the girl, Crystal, continued to shout away in there, something about clod-hoppers, and city-folks, and cleanliness, and ignorant boys. The fact was, it was hard to make it all out through the ringing in his ears.

John had gotten himself lost in his thoughts, but he noticed after a time that the boy was sitting near him.

'Did you get those rooms all squared away?' he asked.

'I guess. That girl's up there at the end of the hall, locked in.'

John looked at him. 'I don't think you needed to do that.'

'I didn't do nothin'. I was just standin' there and the next thing I know I said somethin' and she said somethin' and now I got a bumped head and she's up locked in that room, prob'ly still yellin' at me.'

There was no culture practiced in this strange house that included a day of transition from boyhood to the status of young man. But that day does arrive, whether it's brought on by a ceremony, a kiss on the cheek, or a slap in the face. John himself had been a very late bloomer along these lines, and the demands of adulthood still took him by surprise on an almost daily basis. One could only hope that the next generation might somehow have an easier time as they began to grope their young way through the labyrinth of human relations.

'You know, I doubt it's your fault,' John said. 'But still, I think it's probably time we got you into town a little more often.'

The older woman, Faith, had passed at some point from unconsciousness to a sound, still sleep. There'd been no opportunity to move her upstairs, and John had felt no particular inclination to rest himself, so there he still sat, in his bentwood rocker next to the divan, at her side.

The fire had been dwindling and he stood to tend it. There hadn't been as much trouble from his own aches and pains tonight – some days were better than others in that way. After another two heavy logs and some work with the poker the room was half-lit by the crackling flames and warming up again.

The house was quiet but his mind wouldn't rest; the questions just kept on coming. He knew now why these people had found him, but how had they? If these three backward folks could track him down, couldn't almost anyone? What was behind all this, and what could be coming tomorrow?

He was too wired for sleep, recreation was out of the question, and he didn't feel he could muster the concentration for any real work to pass the night.

It was at the end of this short list of unappealing options that the tattered book on the table caught his eye.

16

'I see in the near future a crisis approaching that unnerves me and causes me to tremble for the safety of my country. Corporations have been enthroned and an era of corruption in high places will follow. The money power of the country will endeavor to prolong its reign by working upon the prejudices of the people until all wealth is aggregated in a few hands and the Republic is destroyed.'

— Abraham Lincoln, 1864

That was rich. Ed Latrell quoting Abe Lincoln was like dog-shit admiring the sole of your Sunday shoes.

John lit a cigarette and took a sip from his half-pint. It had been the second-to-last little bottle of whiskey left in the cupboard, but the impulse to ration it disappeared rather quickly. Funny, how it just never seemed like the right day for temperance.

He leafed ahead and back through the yellowed pages, skipping and scanning until the occasional key-word or paragraph caught his eye. If the dates preceding the entries could be trusted, this journal had been written over quite a span of years.

. . .

Crude oil has been the currency of control in the world, but its time is soon passing away. Like diamonds, its value is not set by supply and demand, but by a small international cartel of despots and elites. Oil has been kept essential to the progress of mankind's destiny in the last hundred years. But mankind can survive without oil, so it will not be the final sword of Armageddon.

The next and final cartel is forming, and will seek to regulate, tax, apportion and monetize life itself, through the manipulation and profiteering of our genes, our physical health, our water, and then our food, and then even the air that we breathe.

. . .

When I was young, childhood autism was extremely rare, to the point of near non-existence; today it afflicts nearly 1 in 150. Heart disease, diabetes, morbid obesity, asthma, infertility, cancers, Alzheimer's, scores of new behavioral and psychiatric disorders, all are exploding since the advent of genetically modified foods, fluoridation, toxic plastics, rampant RF radiation and mercury-laced vaccines. All these afflictions are lifelong disablers, species-limiters, or life-ending illnesses, and are therefore vastly enriching or empowering to those in control.

The diseases are created and promoted as surely as are the drugs and technologies pushed on the public to 'treat' them. They make profit-centers of the suffering millions, who must render the last of their dignity and all their life's savings to the medical monopolists.

But look to the Amish! It is not their genes that make them comparatively immune to the contemporary scourge of these new epidemics and disabilities. It is their refusal to embrace the poisons, processes, 'cures' and technologies that are the very cause of nearly all modern disease!

. . .

The demise of the USA is planned, and her remaining days have been numbered.

The existence of the United States has been a barrier to the progress of evil, not so much for what this nation has become, but rather for the glorious promise of what it could someday be again.

But the American people have been lulled into a walking slumber, lured into withering debt that can never be repaid, seduced into lifetimes of fruitless labors, mesmerized by the controlled corporate media. They have forgotten that their sacred, precious and neglected heritage of liberty can die out within a single generation, and unless they awaken, die out it surely will.

The USA is threatened from within, from the true leaders, unelected and not subject to the laws of the land, plotting with impunity in the secret halls of power. Preparations for our defeat from within are nearly complete.

And when America falls, the dark forces that rule our world will begin their endgame: the creation of a Paradise on Earth, a world of unimaginable beauty, wealth, health and plenty, soaring towers, art and leisure, green fields and sparkling fountains.

Heaven itself . . . <u>but with admission reserved for only the chosen few.</u> Their new world order will be built upon the dead, decaying ashes of the old, and its relentless engines will be fueled by the blood and toil and suffering of billions.

Back when he was alive Latrell had kept his motivations very close to his chest, at least to outsiders. One thing had been clear: He'd been willing to sacrifice thousands, maybe hundreds of thousands in the name of some supposed salvation for many, many more. And here it was, his unhinged rationale, every bit as curious and deranged as John had imagined it would sound if ever he would learn of its details.

His cigarette had burned down to the filter, untouched in the ashtray. He took a long drink, lit another smoke, sat back, and read on.

'Single acts of tyranny may be ascribed to the accidental opinion of a day. But a series of oppressions, begun at a distinguished period, and pursued unalterably through every change of ministers, too plainly proves a deliberate systematic plan of reducing us to slavery.

'The strongest reason for the people to retain the right to bear arms is, as a last resort, to protect themselves against tyranny in government.'

— Thomas Jefferson

To those who would accuse me of treason: Precedent for forceful action against domestic oppression was set forth by our Founding Fathers. Those great men warned that the tree of liberty must now and again be refreshed with the blood of patriots and tyrants. When lawful means and peaceful resistance prove futile, when the enemy is pounding at the gates, the time to take up arms has arrived.

Treason has nearly toppled the US in the past, but it was not fostered by us guardians of liberty. The oppressors and moneycrats themselves have always conspired against free America, as they still do today.

None other than Nazi-financier Prescott Bush, father of President George H.W. and grandfather of the recently installed George W. Bush, was involved in a plot to overthrow the Roosevelt administration in a fascist takeover of the Depression-ravaged United States of America!

When the conspirators had covertly assembled a group of willing partners, industrialists, bankers and military men, they brought their scheme to Marine Corps Major General Smedley Butler. Under the plan, Butler would command a rogue army of half-a-million US veterans to storm Washington, arrest the Congress and the President, declare martial law under national emergency, and install a figurehead to finalize the coup.

It was only Major General Butler's public renunciation of the plot that prevented its execution in 1933, and only the vast power of the criminal elite that saved the conspirators from imprisonment and ruin!

And to those who doubt the regime-changing ambitions of covert forces hiding within the fabric of our nation, remember Qasim (whose ouster brought Saddam Hussein to power), Mossadeq, Nasser, Guzmán, Jimenez, Ngo Dinh Diem, Bhutto, and Allende!

. . .

Money has no true value in modern economies. It is a lie that will be the undoing of the great ambitions and achievements of the twentieth century.

The dollar is a vapor, backed by nothing but debt, interest, hedges, and wagers made between the super-wealthy and powerful. These robber-barons have infiltrated government and know no regulation. They are immune to losses, and acknowledge only their ill-gotten gains. But the common people will always be compelled to shoulder the burden of their debts and their crimes, by deception, by unjust law, or by force at the point of a gun.

The power elite have been satisfied in the past with a slow and steady robbery of the people's wealth, but soon, when the time is right, <u>trillions upon trillions</u> will change hands in the space of weeks. The markets will swoon with vast losses and false gains as the elite consolidate their fortunes. Commodities will be pushed to astronomical highs and then allowed to collapse to crushing lows. Inflation will explode to hyper-inflation, the people will suffer foreclosure, unemployment and ruin. All the while the surveillance noose will tighten, God-given rights will be spirited away, and the truth-tellers will be censored, harassed and ridiculed until the moment their warnings can no longer be denied.

But be watchful for the coming of the next sham war and the financial coup d'état that will descend on its heels, for these will signal the day when the enemy steps forth into the light to begin the final countdown.

. . .

170

After the foreword the book was organized in an unusual way, especially for a diary. The oldest entries were toward the back, and this last one, the newest by its date, was first.

How could the author have known he'd run out of pages, just as he'd run out of time?

There was an entire little section of news clippings dating back to the seventies. Network break-ins, embezzlements, mass identity theft, killer viruses and trojans, phone-system mischief and electrical blackouts, an unauthorized missile launch at White Sands. All these stories related to the computer-crime exploits of a hacker known to the press only as *phr33k*. An inked note in one margin, circled and underscored, identified the alleged perpetrator by name: a.k.a. John Fagan.

A number of loose notes and documents were pasted in here and there. Some seemed included as backup for particularly outlandish claims, others stood alone. By their dates one or two had been added more recently, after Latrell himself was gone. Of the documents purporting to be official materials most appeared to be originals.

A state-by-state list of locations and details of internment camps and detention centers within the borders of the USA. Added together, if they were real their capacity was in the millions.

A series of internal law enforcement memoranda. Some targeted peace groups, activist organizations, and prominent antiwar individuals for surveillance. One from July 2001, from FBI Phoenix, contained an urgent alert that Usama bin Laden had been sending operatives to US aviation schools, training them for future terrorist attacks using aircraft. The name Tim Osman and an internal code was handwritten and circled at the top.

A listing and brief description of random historical military/ intelligence operations, most now declassified, some apparently executed, some only proposed: Northwoods, Northern Vigilance, Vigilant Guardian, Able Danger, Mongoose, InfraGard, Chaos, Paperclip, Mockingbird, REX-84, Backfire, MKULTRA, Garden Plot, Lantern Spike, the false-flag attack on the USS Liberty, many more. And an ongoing catch-all program for quelling domestic dissent: CoIntelPro.

The torn fragment of a pilot's navigation log. The tail number of his aircraft was noted: N6308F. A small mountain airport was circled in red: Mena, Arkansas. Penciled notes scattered on the map had faded and smudged but a few were still barely legible: Medellín, 18,000 kilo, CIA, North, and one full name: Barry Seal.

An urgent national security memo from the FBI, late 2002, warning of a spreading pandemic of top-down mortgage fraud involving something called subprime derivatives.

A typewritten memo, Secret and Strictly Personal, UK Eyes Only, dated 23 July 2002. Notes from a White House briefing, dated 18 September 2002. Both concerned a planned second Persian Gulf invasion to oust Saddam Hussein; both agreed that action was inevitable. The only challenge that remained, in the clear absence of any credible threat from Iraq, was to somehow justify a war to the public.

John flipped to the back section. This book was old and it had clearly been through some rough handling and bad weather; the last hundred pages were curled and mildewed, and the final seventy-five or so seemed to have become fused together in a solid mass from water damage. There was no writing on these pages, at least on the ones that were still intact; they were covered margin-to-margin with the same sort of flowing, angular nonsense-scribbles that he'd seen scattered throughout the whitespace in the book.

He carefully turned to an oversized, thicker page that came

just before this strange epilogue. It was a dim old photograph, blotched and sepia-toned. He held it up closer and nearer the light so he could see its details.

There were three men standing before a large, shiny door set in a wall of stone or concrete. *Door* wasn't exactly right: from its heavy hinges, circular locks and latches, it appeared to be the entrance to a massive reinforced vault. Two of the men were elderly, and the younger one in the middle sported a thin, rakish mustache and a distinctive head of curly, jet-black hair. Each had a hand on another's shoulder; by their visible demeanor, it was much more a gesture of grim solidarity than of friendship.

The photo was lit artificially, and work-lights on tripods stood to the side. The surroundings made it seem like a natural setting of some kind.

An inscription was etched into the metal door but only a few words were clear in the grainy image. On the face of the photograph was what might have been a hand-written dedication with three signatures below, but these too were illegible from fading and wear. The date at the bottom was readable, though: March 21, 1964.

'Kate,' John said.

In the minute or so it took his computer to wake out of standby he brought the book into his workroom. After a bit of searching he dusted off and rolled out a piece of hardware he and Matt had cobbled together in the summer. He plugged it into the wall socket and a nearby USB hub, and its row of ready-lights cycled across.

'Yes, John,' the computer said.

'Just a second.'

He placed the open book on the inclined platform atop the device and flipped its activation switch. A small robotic arm, bastardized from an old Arm-a-tron toy from Radio Shack, extended its suction-cup tip and gently made contact with the title page of the book. A vacuum pump hummed, the page adhered, and the arm whirred and rotated to open a new spread for scanning. The modified webcam suspended above the book flashed and clicked, the arm released that page and clipped it flat, and the process was ready to repeat.

'Kate, I want you to read this book as soon as you can and do a little fact-checking for me, all right?'

'Depth of analysis?'

'Not so deep. I think this is a job for the Bozo-filter.'

'Understood.'

'Oh,' John said, snapping his fingers, 'and you're going to come to a photograph toward the end. There are some words on it that I can't read, both hand-written and engraved within the image. See what you can do to decipher all that stuff. And while you're at it, there are three men in the picture and I wouldn't mind knowing who they are.'

'. . . I will inform you of my progress.'

'Thank you.'

Kate had reset the book-scanner, and in a few seconds the methodical page-turning and imaging procedure had begun.

John hadn't thought much about what he was hoping she would find, but it occurred to him as he turned to leave the room.

He was hoping like hell she'd find absolutely nothing.

17

After a bite to eat in the kitchen John had come back to the great-room, tweaked the thermostat, and hefted another log onto the fire. The room was lighter now; the sunrise wasn't far away. When he returned to his chair he found the woman on the couch had awakened.

She seemed a little groggy but when her eyes found his he saw recognition, and then some fear. So the thump to the skull hadn't affected her memory. With any luck, maybe it had knocked in some sense.

'Are you thirsty?' John asked.

There was a second or two before she nodded.

'Okay.' He started to rise, but stopped and made sure he had her attention. 'All the weapons in the house are secure, where you can't get at them. But I'm telling you right now, you point so much as a finger at me or my kids again, Grandma, you'll get worse than you got before, *capiche?*'

She didn't answer, but it seemed like she got the message.

He came back with some water and an English muffin and found her sitting with a blanket from the couch pulled up around her shoulders. She ignored the food but took the glass and drank from it. When she finally spoke, her voice was weak and hoarse from sleep.

'Where's my granddaughter, and my boy?'

'They're both upstairs, asleep. So he's, what, her father?'

The woman shook her head, no. 'Wayman, he ain't equipped for marriage. I adopted him, if you gotta know.'

'Who are you people?' John asked. 'Why did you bring that book to me?'

Faith Hudson met his eyes again, and the fear was gone. 'I brung it 'cause it's what he wanted.'

'What who wanted?'

'Ed Latrell.'

'And who was he to you?'

'He trusted me, that's all, and it looks like neither you nor me was up to the job he left us.'

'What in the hell are you talking about? I don't know about a job, but I think it's safe to say I'm the very last guy that Edward Latrell would have wanted to read his fucking diary.'

She flinched a bit as he'd raised his voice, but it was his house she'd invaded and his blanket she was wearing, so she could goddamn well put up with a little saucy language.

'He sent it to me with a note,' she said, 'over a year ago.' She looked at her hands, remembering. 'He said Faith, if I'm dead when you get this book, then a man named John Fagan's likely still alive. Whichever of us lives through this fight, that's what was meant to happen. So you bring this on back, to either him or me. It's been my destiny, but it's his inher'tance. If I'm gone he's the only one I know of that can read it to the end. And when he's done he'll sure know what to do.'

She took a sip of water and set her glass carefully on a coaster on the coffee table.

'Listen,' John said, 'I went through most of it while you were sleeping. There's a lot of information and I don't know how much of it is real or made up or a little of both. But there's no great quest in there. No marching orders. It's just his thoughts, such as they are.'

'You read it to the end, like he said?'

'More or less. There's a part that's stuck together at the back, and nobody's going to be reading that—'

'John,' the computer said.

'Yeah, what.'

'I have preliminary results from your request.'

John glanced at the clock on the mantle. 'Jesus, that was quick.'

'I endeavor, as always, to please you.'

He smiled to himself, but then found the woman on the couch looking at him, quizzically.

'It's ahhh, it's not a person,' John said. 'My computer . . . it's a long story, what you're hearing, it's just an interface. It's easier for me than a keyboard and a mouse.' None of this brought any clarity or comfort to the woman's expression. 'Look, just try not to worry about it.' He found a cigarette, and patted himself for a match. 'Okay, Kate, what have you got?'

'Hyperbole, embellishment, and presumptive logic aside, the text of the book contains factual information, within the boundaries of certainty you specified.'

'What parts of it?'

'. . . All of it.'

He sighed, and lit up. 'Go deeper, then. Some of that stuff is guaranteed bullshit, it's gotta be.'

'Already under way.'

'And how about the photograph?'

'. . . The date of its inscription, 21 March, 1964, appears

plausible based upon known rates of photo-emulsion deterioration. May I project the scanned image for you?'

'Go for it.'

A screen whirred down from its mount near the ceiling by the staircase, and one of Kate's digital projectors hummed to life. Soon the blotchy, faded photo appeared, now six feet wide by nine feet tall.

John set down his cigarette in the ashtray, stood and stepped closer to the screen.

'Who are those three guys?' he said.

'The man on your left appears to be Leó Szilárd; the signature below matches historical records. The man in the middle—'

'Leó Szilárd?'

'Born in Hungary, 1898, physicist and envisioner of the nuclear chain reaction, co-founder of the Manhattan Project—'

'I know who fucking Leó Szilárd was. Are you sure?'

'Though image-search suggests this to be a unique, unpublished photo, the facial characteristics correspond well with known contemporary portraits. And the signature below—'

'—matches historical records, right, okay. Go on.'

'The man in the middle appears to be John Parsons. No corroborative handwriting sample has yet been found.'

'Wait a minute,' John said. 'John Whiteside Parsons?'

'That is correct.'

John Parsons. An ingenious, self-educated inventor, rabid libertarian, and oh, incidentally, an enthusiastic proponent and practitioner of ritual black magic. Though for a time he was apprentice to Britain's premier warlock, Aleister Crowley, John Parsons was also the man who Wernher von Braun called the father of the American space program. There's a crater named after him, fittingly enough, on the dark side of the Moon.

'Hold the phone. That says 1964, and Parsons died in the early fifties. He blew himself up in his garage, right?'

'. . . It would appear that either well-established biographical information or the evidence in this photograph is in error.'

'Yeah,' John sighed. 'It would so appear.'

'The face of the third man is obscured by severe surface damage to the photograph and cannot—'

'Okay, fine, I can see that. What does it say on that door?'

A thin white box zoomed in around the relevant area of the image. Engraved letters in a tombstone-font began to come forth and clarify as the enhancement progressed. He recognized the passage from Joseph Addison's *Cato*, words spoken by the title character at the last stand of liberty:

THE STARS SHALL FADE AWAY, THE SUN
HIMSELF GROW DIM WITH AGE

AND NATURE SINK IN YEARS;

BUT THOU SHALT FLOURISH IN
IMMORTAL YOUTH,

UNHURT AMID THE WAR OF ELEMENTS,

THE WRECK OF MATTER, AND THE
CRUSH OF WORLDS.

The wreck of matter; the crush of worlds. A distinguished but disillusioned nuclear physicist and part-time molecular biologist, and a brilliant rocket scientist who spent his weekends with a wand and a wizard hat. What on God's green earth could they have dreamed up together and then locked away in that vault?

The top two-thirds of the photo faded to nearly black.

'The lower inscription,' Kate began, 'was hand-written on the surface of the photographic paper. This portion has sustained moderate damage, but its content was retrievable. Initial analysis matches the writer of these words to the last of the three signatures below them.'

'Show it to me.'

The cursive letters began to materialize and flow as though written again by the hand that had penned them nearly thirty-nine years before.

To the last heirs, the guardians of liberty, that the Day of Reckoning may be yours to choose.

Three signatures followed, one by one, left to right.

Leo Szilard.

Jack Parsons.

John only realized he'd begun to back away from the screen when he bumped the arm of Faith Hudson, who'd come up to stand beside him.

'You see?' she whispered.

The last signature had appeared, elegantly finished with a flourishing underscore.

Myron Fagan

It could have been a lack of sleep, an excess of drugs, or some new manifestation of the spreading disease inside him. All of a sudden he was faint.

'Kate.'

'Yes, John.'

'I think I'm going to need some help.'

18

Jay Marshall looked up from the sheets of dense hexadecimal printouts fan-folded across his desk. These were the depressing highlights from the recovery record of his vandalized hard drive; a lot of paper, but not much surviving data. His slim hopes of ever finding a trace of what Jeannie Reese had discovered and then destroyed here were fading fast.

But he'd looked up to track down something else.

He listened as he searched the large cluttered office with his eyes. A persistent, annoying rhythmic noise, just barely audible, had been intruding on his focus. Its origin, once discovered, was not unpredictable.

Across the suite, Rudy Steinman was reclined on the guest couch with a folded *New York Times* and a pen, sucking on a Jamba Juice through a long elbow-bent straw. He was wearing his earbuds, lest the sounds of honest work disturb his morning Sudoku. His chin was bobbing subtly to the beat of some endless, mindless dance-mix on his IPod.

'Rudy.'

Nothing.

'Rudy!'

The other man looked over, popped open one ear and raised his eyebrows to query the cause of this interruption.

'Would you turn the music down, please?' Jay asked. 'I can hear it all the way over here, probably through the holes in your head.'

Rudy took a moment to comply, and then he held up the newspaper. 'Have you noticed the *Times* is really going downhill lately, accuracy-wise?'

'What do you mean?'

'You know how they label these puzzles hard, moderate, and easy? This one says "easy", but you know what?'

'What.'

'It's not that easy.'

Marshall sighed darkly, and went back to his work.

A second later, the synth-pop opening of Rick Astley's 'Never Gonna Give You Up' blared forth from across the room.

'I *asked* you to turn down that noise!'

Rudy had begun fishing in his trouser pocket and he stood to allow easier access. 'Relax, it's my ring-tone, hang on.'

'How the hell did you manage to survive working with Jeannie all that time? I'm ready to kill you with my hands after two days.'

'You know what's strange? I was her assistant, but my office was waaaay down the hall.' He'd found his phone, touched the answer button, and brought it up to his ear. 'Hellooo.' After a moment, he *pfff*ed and ended the call. 'It's nobody. I've been getting a lot of crank calls lately.'

'Well, put it on vibrate, I'm trying to get something done over here.'

'You got it.' But the phone rang again before he could make the adjustment.

'So help me, Rudy—'

'Don't worry, I'll handle this.' He winked, and answered. 'Bar-Nothing Ranch, Buffalo Bill speaking. Uh huh . . . Uh huh. Okay, goodbye forever, and please don't call me anymore.' After a series of beeps and button presses, he looked up at Jay. 'It's okay now, I turned it down.'

'Finally.'

Just as he'd found his place on the printouts again, a *zzzzzz zzzzzz zzzzzz* sound began to repeat from the other side of the room. Steinman's cellphone was migrating across the glass-top coffee table to the rhythm of the buzzes from its muted ringer.

'Alright, *off*, turn that goddamn thing *off*—'

'Fine, fine, jeez.' But Rudy stopped as soon as he'd begun to deactivate the device. He frowned and walked slowly over to the desk, the phone still vibrating urgently.

'Now what?' Jay said.

Rudy held out the little glowing screen so Jay could read the caller-ID.

PICK UP A-HOLE, it said.

'. . . Go on and answer it.'

Rudy picked up the call, but skeptically. 'Hello . . . Okay look, sweetheart, give it up, seriously – Who? . . . Right, I'm sure you are. . . . Yeah? Prove it.' The phone went back into his pocket and he checked his watch. 'Whoa, break time. I'm gonna go get a snack, do you want anything delicious?'

'No, I'm fine. Who was that on the phone, what did they say?'

'Nobody, some woman, sounded kind of computer-y. But get this: she said she was calling on behalf of John Fagan.'

Jay sat back in his chair. It wasn't likely by any means; no one had heard from Fagan in over a year. But unlikely had been the theme of the past several days. 'How do you know it wasn't him?'

Rudy didn't answer. Anxiety was dawning on his face and he'd begun looking down at the front of his pants.

'Ow,' he said.

'What is it?'

'Ouch. Ow!' In another second the source of his distress was clear; his pocket had begun to smolder.

A tiny jet of yellow flame *shoosh*ed through the fabric and Steinman dropped to the floor out of sight, a daisy-chain of random curses ascending through several octaves, from baritone to shrill ultrasound. When Jay stood to see him he had wriggled out of his trousers and was fleeing from them, crab-walking, until he collided headlong with the ottoman twenty feet away.

A nearby employee had poked his head in the doorway to investigate the smoke and the noise. At a motion from Jay the man picked up the hissing, seething corduroys with the hook of a coat hanger and made hastily down the hall for the men's room. Rudy Steinman limped close behind his trousers, in dark socks and shirt-tails, to find first-aid.

Jay Marshall at first mistook the next sound he heard for a fire alarm, but it wasn't that. When he realized what it was he walked to his chair, sat, and pushed the button under his desktop that remotely closed his office door.

The trilling electronic chorus that was filling the air was a calling-card from the party who'd been trying to connect. From corner to corner of his company floor, every line on every single telephone was ringing.

He picked up the receiver, hit *Page* and then *All Zones*.

'Hang up everybody, get back to work,' Jay said. 'This call's for me.'

Once contact was established it had taken several minutes to install and test John's improvised, software-based call-scrambler on both ends of the line. The heavily encrypted webcam video link was a little snowy, but under impromptu conditions it was the best that could be managed.

'You may proceed,' Kate said.

'Mr Marshall, I've heard a lot about you,' John said. 'I tried our friend Steinman first, looking for Jeannie, but the little prick wouldn't stay on the phone.'

Marshall smiled a bit. 'Yeah. Sorry about that.'

'So is he, I imagine. Look, we've got to keep it short. I need two things. First, I need Jeannie for this. I haven't heard from her and that's okay, it's not a personal thing if that's what she's worried about. She's just a hell of a lot better with encryption than I am. So whatever, if you could help me get in touch with her, I'd appreciate it. Second, I need some document recovery work, and I understand that's your line.'

'We'll get back to Jeannie in a minute. What sort of recovery are we talking about?'

'This book,' he held it up, 'there's some type of made-up encoding toward the end. On first glance you'd think it was nonsense, but when you look closer there seems to be, I don't know, maybe a language-pattern. And the last hundred pages or so is just masses of these patterns of random-looking dots. That's where I think the information I need may be hidden.'

'Okay.'

'Trouble is, the book's gotten wet at some point and most of those last pages are stuck together.'

'Stuck together? At the edges, or all the way through?'

John brought the side of the journal closer to the camera, indicating the half-inch breadth of the fused, ink-blotted portion toward the end. 'Here to here,' he said, 'it's one piece, like a grilled-cheese sandwich.'

'Whoa.'

'Listen, I think whatever this is, it's big. Really big, and not in a good way. I need to know what's locked up in here. Is there anything you can do?'

Marshall puffed his cheeks, let out a long vocal breath, and shook his head.

'Let me just see if I've got this straight. You've got a brittle old book that's probably soaked in water for days or weeks, so the last third of it, the important part, is stuck together in a solid wad of melted pulp. And you said it was handwritten, right? So the ink's probably run all over, not just within the pages, but leeched *between* the pages. And on top of all that, the content's in a non-alphanumeric code that hasn't been broken, so we can't use what's on the pages to help piece it all back together. And you want to know if there's anything I can do?'

'Yeah,' John sighed. 'Well, I had to ask—'

'I'll make a bet with you.' Marshall leaned back in his chair, cracked his neck with a jut of the chin, and checked his watch. 'If you can get that book in my hands first thing in the morning? Ten thousand dollars says you'll have your code by tomorrow afternoon.'

Addresses were being exchanged when Rudy walked back into the office. There was a blackened burn-crater in his trousers and he smelled faintly of antiseptic and scalded wool.

'Is that John Fagan on the phone? Tell him he owes me a pair of Perry Ellis pants and a tube of lidocaine—'

Marshall held up a hand to quiet him.

'Let's wrap it up,' Fagan said. 'We've already been on too long.'

Jay sat forward, closer to the camera and microphone. 'Now, about Jeannie. If she tries to contact you, I think you've got to decline, for your own safety. Something's happened to her, I don't know what it is, but it's possible she's been . . .

compromised in some way. It kills me to say this. Just, whatever you do, don't trust her with anything for now, especially your location, until we can figure this out. Okay?' Marshall waited, and then frowned. 'Okay?'

There was no response from the other end of the line.

'Look,' Rudy said. 'It's crashed.'

He was right; there was no movement or sound from the videoconference. The last frame was frozen on the screen.

It was hard to know how much of what he'd said had gotten through, but a quick digital rewind answered that question.

The connection had gone down, it appeared, just after the mention of her name.

19

'. . . Jeannie.'

Though the noise had been repeating it was only at this last recurrence that she captured its familiarity. The voice behind it was somewhat familiar as well; it called a vague image of a man to her mind.

The girl opened her eyes but there was only blackness. Not darkness, because darkness ends, but a void without dimension. She lay quiet, suspended at its heart.

Vowels and consonants assembled before her mind's eye, sliding tiles on a Scrabble board. *Jeannie*. The sound she'd heard had been her name.

But the soft deep voice at her ear defied identity. It was otherworldly, many voices but all discernible, all strong but none overbearing another. All unconnected, but all become one. Her father, her mentor, her lover, her teacher, her friend.

A touch, light fingertips brushed her skin, a connection of warmth, his to hers through the thin bedclothes. The hand moved with care and meditation, as though to commit her body to memory, or to recall it from some other secret time.

There was an intimate language in his caress; it whispered worship of her beauty, stirred buried memories of love and loss, and then, having opened the wounds of reminiscence, offered to heal them all away. It asked for her trust, which she gave without condition.

As always, he pleased and punished by his rules. If she dared to move without his guidance, whether a shiver of ecstasy or a shy retreat from some new boundary of his domination, he would pull away and leave her aching and longing. The touch in the dark would only return, gently to begin again, when he was satisfied of her renewed submission to his will.

Tenderly, soothing and sensuous at once; he lingered here and there, patient and strong, urging and easing. No judgment, no need for words. His touch assured that her every forbidden desire was known to him and that her sins, including any now in progress, would all be forgiven. Her breath quickened, her voice coming softly with each exhalation, every stroke the pluck of a live wire, sensation upon sensation, promising but ever withholding her release.

Jeannie

She froze, listening.

It was a woman now who'd spoken her name. Unlike the other this voice was in her mind, but it wasn't the voice of a helpless young girl. Not the defenseless object of a man's abuse and obsession; not the victim, but the woman who had overcome them all to make herself the match of anyone alive.

Give him to me, she said. *Let me show him who you are.*

Bright light overwhelmed her as a dark cloth was pulled from her face. With all her strength she struck out blindly at the figures standing near.

Two men in green scrubs stumbled backward as the chains and leather straps at her wrists and ankles snapped taut, but held fast.

'That's enough.' Another voice she knew, over an intercom.

She saw him then as her eyes adjusted, a dim outline through the wide mirror along one wall of her stark white room. The lights had been left on in an observation booth behind the one-way glass. This would have been meant to show her that he felt no need to hide his presence. She chose to believe he'd stayed in there solely for his own protection.

In her struggles an IV needle had dislodged from her right arm. One of the attendants retrieved a sterile pack to replace the line, but he hesitated, looking across at his partner. The other approached on her left, a little pale and sweating, his arm cocked back, a side-handle riot baton in his grip. A neat semi-circle of fresh lacerations showed on his wrist, with a perfect matching set on the other side.

She tasted his blood in her mouth, and spat it to his feet. This was the man who'd taken her fingerprints by force, along with her retinal scans, thermograms, all her physical geometries, and her DNA. He'd neglected to get a dental impression, so now she'd given him one for free.

Well out of her reach a drip was adjusted on one of the remaining IVs. There was a bee-sting at her shoulder, pushing deep into the muscle. The pain receded. She dissolved into the room as the room dispersed to nothingness.

20

Make a critical decision quickly, and be very slow to change it.

Griffin's own instructor had left him with this last bit of advice as he embarked on his career. With Jeannie Reese he had made his decision when she was barely thirteen years old; for over a decade he'd refused to change it. And now the time had come for another critical decision. As he'd learned, he made it quickly.

Griffin dismissed the others and when they'd gone he pulled up a chair beside her, and sat.

'Don't be frightened,' he said.

The machines reported on her current condition. The human body creates its own natural paralysis during sleep, to keep us all from acting out our dreams. Research had found ways to induce this built-in state of physical suspension at any time. It could be triggered and precisely regulated through the bloodstream, but more importantly for its use as a weapon, with visual stimulus or sound patterns as well. Through various media it could be aimed and tuned to subdue a single person or to drop an advancing battalion in its tracks.

In Jeannie's case only a light trance was in effect. She could hear and understand, she could feel his touch, but her ability for willful movement was safely limited. He leaned toward her, put his palm to her forehead as if to test for a fever.

'April has made quite a mess in there, hasn't she?'

Griffin sat back and took her hand in his.

'She wasn't the first of your enemies to toy with your mind; your adoptive father must be given that honor. You would probably say that I'm the guiltiest trespasser of all. But good things can come out of ugly circumstances. It was the sins of your father that first brought you to my door, and it was April's harbored jealousy of you that's now brought us together again. And now there's a great deal of good that we can do, that we *must* do; maybe enough good to balance everything that's come before.'

He imagined he felt the faintest squeeze of his fingers to denote her understanding.

'We never had a chance to have this talk before, and we never will again, so I hope you'll forgive me this indulgence. To be honest I can't separate what you might already know from all that we might have removed from your memory when you left us, so I trust you'll be patient with me.'

Griffin poured himself a cup of water from the tan plastic pitcher near the bed.

'Your parents, for want of a better term, had combed the world for a surrogate mother and father who could provide what nature had denied them. A perfect child, to complement all their other perfect things. Money was no object; popes have been selected with less scrutiny than each of your would-be genes received.

'Almost from birth it was clear you were very special. As you grew, attended at every hour by nannies and tutors and trainers, you began to show potentials quite beyond their

192

wildest expectations. They showered you with luxuries, every day was filled with private lessons in every subject and discipline, from the cradle to your adolescence. You would have been a crown princess of the superclass, high among the very people that I serve, had things gone differently.

'But your parents learned that while you can easily buy a person in this day and age, it's much more of a challenge to own them. They were quite unprepared to live with their wish once it had been granted. As the years passed and your extraordinary strengths were gradually revealed, so were their weaknesses.'

There was only the slightest hint of animation in her. Her breathing changed, another weak flex of her fingers in his hand, a movement of her eyes beneath the lids.

'By the time you were eleven your computer escapades had resulted in some brushes with the law, one of which first brought you to our attention. Your mother came to resent you, more and more as you matured. You'd rejected her parties and pageants from the moment you were old enough to understand her manipulations. She was a cold, shallow and distant person, but that you could have endured. Your father was a different story.

'While in preparation for his trial your father told his attorneys that he had fallen deeply in love with you, and you with him. He argued that he couldn't be charged with incest because there was no blood relation. You'd nearly reached the age of consent in more enlightened cultures, like those of Spain and Japan. You were precocious, physically and mentally, and he was young for his age. He had scarcely been present during your upbringing, and should hardly be thought of as a parent at all. These were his justifications. Needless to say, the defendant was kept far from the witness stand.

'Your mother stood bravely by her husband; his appetites were well known to her, and she'd accepted them as a liberty of rank. Their legal counsel argued that your true age couldn't be reliably determined because of the circumstances of your birth: no official records existed. You were already enrolled in college courses; you spoke and carried yourself like a young woman, not a little girl. They accused you of inciting the one witnessed sexual act, and fabricating all the others you'd been forced to describe in detail for the record. Your motive was to extort an inheritance, they said, since you were not so entitled by birthright.

'In the end the power of his family acquitted him of all but the least egregious charges. He and your mother went back to their vapid lives, and you became a ward of the state.

'We found you in foster care, abandoned, withdrawn, and nearly suicidal. We offered you a future where you saw none. And only days later, Jeannie, during your orientation, we all saw the change begin. You took to the program like food and water to a starving young girl. I wish you could remember those days. We had to reset all the scales for you.

'You had only one flaw, and I did my best to deny it until it became clear it was a permanent fixture. Somewhere, somehow in a loveless childhood of neglect and indifference and abuse, you had developed a moral code that simply wouldn't respond to reason. You could do anything we asked of you, absolutely anything, except the one thing we ultimately needed.'

Griffin smiled as he remembered, and for a few moments he searched her face for a sign of her own recollection. There was none. But her lips were dry and chapped, he noticed. He stood and found a mouth-care kit on a stainless metal tray near her side, peeled open a small tub of lemon-glycerin, unwrapped a swab, dipped the end and carefully daubed the treated cotton at her mouth. When he'd finished he adjusted her blanket, smoothed her hair from her forehead, and touched a bit of moisture from the corner of her eye.

There, now.

'But I was telling you,' Griffin said as he sat again, 'about the day it was decided that we couldn't keep you any longer. We had re-created the Milgram Experiment for all the students, as a final exam. A man dressed as a visiting scientist instructed each of you children, one by one, to operate a button wired to an elaborate punishment system. An elderly woman, a paid research volunteer you were all told, was in an adjoining room hooked to this system. She would receive a jolt of ever-increasing voltage when the button was pushed as directed, each time she answered a study question incorrectly. The scale of the shocks ranged from 15 volts up to 450; you were all given reason to believe that this last was more than a lethal dose of electricity.

'The results were even better than we'd hoped. We watched as every student saw the experiment to the very end, to the highest level of punishment. The old woman could be heard struggling and pleading from the next room as the voltage increased, and finally she would go quiet as the most severe shocks were delivered. If a student hesitated, and all did, they were gently ordered to continue, and all did.

'All but one, Jeannie. After you pushed that button for the first time and heard the woman cry out, you refused to go on and demanded to see her to determine if she needed medical care. The staff member playing the researcher took you by the shoulder to help you back into your seat. His head was one of the things you used to break through the door into the adjoining room. You'd nearly made it to the street with the woman in tow by the time we were able to reach you and explain that it was all just make-believe.'

He took a drink of water, and replaced his cup on the table.

'But that was a lie, and you knew it. No torture was actually administered that day, and the woman you'd saved was an actress, but the experiment was real. It was a test of unquestioning obedience to authority, and I believe it was the first and last test of your life that you failed.

'Our class was for the best of breed, reserved only for the brightest, strongest and most ambitious candidates. There's a long waiting list for admission; most of our students are volunteers from the very best families. April was one of these. Our graduates are groomed for placement in the highest levels of governments, financial markets, intelligence agencies, key industries, the media. They're the lead actors on the world stage, and obedience is all that's asked of them in return for the riches they receive. It's a small price that nearly all are more than willing to pay, but you were not.

'There had been other warning signs, but I ignored them. That might have been selfish of me, but I believed I was protecting you. No one had ever washed out at the level you'd reached, and that presented a serious problem.

'There was a heated debate over what should be done with you. Some thought you should be quietly euthanized, buried and forgotten; you weren't suited to the role you'd been recruited for, and we couldn't simply put you back where we'd found you. Others thought you should be memory-wiped and demoted; there were many other programs to place controllable assets in lower-level positions. Some argued that you should be psychosurgically tamed and then sold to the very bottom of the scale, where a steady supply of low-borns are disciplined for household service, unskilled labor and the sex trades, here and overseas. Tens of thousands of wayward children are swept up into these slave markets every year, never to be heard from again.

196

'But I overruled them all, for better or worse. Whatever variant of affection I'm capable of feeling, I had for you, Jeannie. I insisted that you could be managed with a minimum of alteration, and that's what we did. We removed the memories of your time with us as best we could, placed you in a stable group home, returned you to your education, and created a career path for you. At every step someone has been assigned to watch over you. Your associates and co-workers were carefully chosen, without their knowledge. We implanted – certain inhibitions – to discourage romantic entanglements. There was a fear that such relations might in some way weaken the careful mental structure we'd built to contain you. And as we learned in the months after September the eleventh, those fears proved quite well founded.

'There was a story that you'd died in the aftermath of that adventure in late 2001, and I was happy to let the story persist. I hoped it was true, in fact, heaven help me. But you survived, only to fall into the hands of an old nemesis, from an adolescent rivalry you no longer even remembered. And here we are today.'

Griffin breathed in deeply, stood, exhaled slowly, and walked to a comm-box near the door. He touched a pad on the control panel there that would call the others to begin the night's work.

'What April has done,' he said, 'has linked the latent fury you stored while helpless in your father's hands with the considerable talents for killing that you now possess. Your trigger is sexual arousal induced by a male partner, at a level of intensity sufficient to ensure you would be alone with her target when the moment to strike arrived. And as we saw in that roadhouse where I found you, she also implanted a naïve attempt on my life, on the chance that you and I might cross paths as her plans unfolded. I'm happy to report, her disrespect will soon be answered.'

Four technicians had entered the room followed by a neuroscientist, a specialist Griffin had summoned from his retirement in Islamabad. This man had been preeminent in his field due to the force of his methods more than their finesse. Progress in some areas of vital research can be vastly accelerated by an embrace of brutality. The legacy of Josef Mengele was alive and well in the slums and prisons of the Third World. One can learn more from a single human sacrifice than from a hundred generations of laboratory rats. Lower animals cannot plead or bargain or betray, they only suffer and die, unable to even describe their torment for posterity.

'We can use what's been done already as groundwork,' Griffin said. 'It may prove useful, with the proper refinements. But with good fortune the information you'll give us will be enough and we won't be forced to deploy you.'

A smear of conductive gel was applied at her temple on either side. At other points EEG pads were pressed in place and held until they adhered so their wiring wouldn't displace them.

'If I'm to believe the stories of what you and this John Fagan have done together, then he must have some feelings for you. If you contact him, I believe he'll respond. We must know how to find him. If we find him and destroy him along with an item that may be in his possession, then our work is done. That's my hope, Jeannie, that this will all be over soon. When he's gone and the threat he presents is contained, you and I can both finally be at peace.'

The man at the console had made his adjustments for voltage and duration. Her ankle restraints were checked and tightened as needed. Subjects had been known to fracture their spines amid the convulsions; muscle relaxants would reduce that risk, but they could also dampen the effect. Another technician wheeled a crash-cart close to her side in case her heart should stop.

'Bring her around, now,' Griffin said. 'She needs to feel every bit of this.'

At first she could only open her eyes; no other muscles in her body would respond. A man to her left in a surgeon's mask and scrubs was holding two small paddles with long, insulated grips. Coiled wires connected them to a console on a rolling table. Another man adjusted the dials and sliders there until an undulating waveform on the display took on a shape that seemed to suit him.

August Griffin stood on her right.

'Nod your head if you're able to, Jeannie,' Griffin said.

The effort required was out of all proportion with the resulting motion, but she managed to nod once in response.

'This will hurt you,' Griffin said, 'because it must. There will be no fighting it, it's simply beyond anyone's ability to withstand. If it's any comfort, you won't remember what will happen tonight. I wish I could say the same.'

In her peripheral vision she saw the two paddles approaching on either side. They touched, just beside her eyes. The metal was cold against her skin. There was only a tingle of electricity; from the whispers of the technicians, they were measuring the impedance of her head in order to make their final adjustments.

They're going to use you to find John and kill him. You must find a way to warn him if you can; a signal that these men might overlook and that you won't remember sending, but that John Fagan would see.

Her mind was fully engaged now but her body was still weak from the drugs and barely answering. A red whirlwind of panic was roaring from the base of her skull, but surrendering to it would only drop her last defenses. In the face of the fear the words of a brave young man came to her clearly, as though the dead could speak to those who might soon join them. She held onto the words, repeated them, and believed them with the last of her resolve.

There's never nothing you can do.

A rubber guard was placed in her mouth. One strap was tightened to secure her jaw and another to hold her head immobile. The lights flickered and dimmed for a moment. Those around her backed a step away as the console began to build its charge.

Her thoughts were racing over every private moment she and John had spent together, every word in every conversation. She saw Griffin gesture to the men around her, a wave of the hand that said it was time now to steal the life from her, and to use what was left to kill the only man she'd ever loved.

As those last words crossed her mind there was no regret that she'd never told him; she'd never even told herself, after all. They were two people cut from the same damaged cloth, for whom the expression of such feelings is rightly reserved for an unsent letter or a deathbed confession.

And then the fear receded. She knew what to do.

There was no slack in the restraint that held her right wrist, but just enough at her left to hook the leather belt around her little finger at the base. The sharp edge of the metal buckle bit into her skin there like a dull blade, and she was ready. Under only the weight of her hand as she relaxed it, the resulting twist seemed nearly enough to tear the tendon. With luck the grand mal seizure she was about to undergo would take care of the rest.

She met Griffin's eyes a last time. One chance in a thousand wasn't much but it was more than he ever would have dared to give her if he'd known. In some small way, then, she'd already won.

The cool tingling metal pressed against her temples again. A sound, like a hammer striking hardwood, every muscle snapping taut, every nerve brought alive by the thrust of a million icy needles, and in the midst of her final thought, she disappeared.

21

Jay Marshall's packing and shipping instructions for Latrell's journal had been nearly as specific as they were peculiar.

The book was wrapped in parchment paper to protect its surface. Layers of silver duct tape followed, overlapping, top to bottom and then side to side. The tape was to be thick enough to form a protective shell, tight enough to hold the contents firmly pressed between the covers, but not so severely taut as to further damage the fragile paper within. That was a fine line of snugness, but at last it seemed the job was done.

The shipping box was large and filled with all the improvised packing material the children could find. The cocooned book was nested in the center, and with a last check the package was sealed and addressed.

John had held up through these preparations but it was clear by the end that his physical condition was taking a sudden turn for the worse. The kids helped him to his bed, drew the blinds, and brought him some water for the bedside table. He motioned for them to close the door, and Matthew did.

'Come here, Liz, I want to give you something.' She stepped closer, and he touched the bedside table. 'Open up this drawer for me.' She slid the drawer open. There was a silver bead chain there, a necklace with a little red Cap'n Crunch whistle strung onto it. 'Go ahead and take it,' he said.

She picked it up in her hands, looking at it like it was the most magical gift she'd ever received.

'What is it?'

A similar chain was around his neck; he pulled the whistle that was hanging from it out from under his shirt at the collar, where she could see it. 'It's just like mine. I want you to keep that with you no matter what, okay? Your brother can help you with it. It's so you can talk to Kate, from anywhere. From wherever you are.'

'Thank you very much.'

'You're welcome, Liz.' He tried to clear his throat but a savage coughing spell came over him. When it was done there was a pounding at his temple and his vision was dark and swimming at the edges. He wiped his mouth with his sleeve; dizzy, aching, and fading.

'There's no getting around it anymore,' John said, 'and it's past time we spoke about this.'

The boy nodded.

'Spoke about what?' Elizabeth said. Her voice was quiet, as if the sickness might hear.

'I've gotten pretty bad off, I think. In fact there's a pretty good chance I might not be around before too long.'

'Where are you gonna go?' Elizabeth's eyes were wet already, and she only seemed concerned that he might be taking a short trip without bringing her along.

John looked to the boy.

'He's sayin' he's sick, Elizabeth, and he don't how it's gonna come out.'

Elizabeth stepped up to the side of the bed, reached out to grip his collar in her hand and pulled herself up to give him a kiss on the cheek. She put the whistle he'd given her around her neck and turned to leave.

'What are you doing, kid?'

'I'm gonna go pray for you to get better, that's all.'

She left the door ajar behind her.

'Matt,' John said. 'I need for you to go into town and send that package off to New York for me. It's important, or I wouldn't ask this of you. It's all addressed and I've scheduled the pick-up. There's some folding money in a strongbox down in the gun-safe, and a roll of quarters for phone calls. Just bring it all with you, because I don't know how much it'll cost. Now it'll take you most of the day to get there, and it might be dark—'

'I'll be okay.'

'Listen, now. I need for you to take your sister with you. There's an address and a phone number I've written down, it's on my desk on a legal pad, you can't miss it. I want you and Elizabeth to visit the people at that address on your way back from town. It's okay to stay overnight if you want.'

'Who are they?'

John took a deep breath. 'It's a man and a woman I've been corresponding with. He was a schoolteacher up in Cody before he retired, his wife is a nurse. They're older, their kids are all grown up, and they've got room in their house. For guests. I've checked them out, they're good people, Matthew. They'd like for you and Elizabeth to come and spend the night. I just want you to meet them, okay?'

'Why?' The boy had been doing his best to appear unaffected, but there was anger in his voice now. 'Are you just gonna give us away, then?'

'Son, it's to the point that I've got no choice—'

'Don't you call me son,' Matthew said. 'That's a fine thing. You bring us out here and let her get all attached to you and

204

hopeful, then you up and leave us alone again. Well don't you worry none, John, I'll take care of it.' He turned for the door and walked out, still speaking as he left. The parting words were to himself; that made them all the more sincere. 'Another year from now, we'll have forgot all about you.'

The door closed, and the quiet closed in. He could feel his heart beating, weak but steady, counting up toward some uncertain number.

'I hope you do, kid,' he whispered. 'You and everybody else.'

Even a short venture outside in a Wyoming winter was nothing to take lightly. Dozens of amateur outdoorsmen were lost every year in the region, and some were never found. This state is bigger than the whole United Kingdom, John had told him, but with less than 1 per cent of their population. You could shoot off a cannon in any direction and more likely hit a bear than one of your neighbors.

Matthew had prepared a bag with water, dried fruit, extra layers of clothes and blankets, a compass, a flashlight, flares, and matches in a waterproof tin. The Snowcat had its own radio, but he brought an extra handheld and batteries just in case. As he zipped up the kit his sister came down the stairs in her parka and boots, with only her eyes and nose peeping through. She had an overnight case and a second bag with toys and other favorite items for the trip.

'You all ready to go, finally?' he asked.

Her stiff gloves made it difficult to read, but she gave him what was probably a thumbs-up in the affirmative.

'Go where, pray tell?'

It was the old woman who'd spoken. She was over by the doors to the balcony, watching the sky.

'My sister and me, we're goin' into town to send off that box.' Matthew went to the gun-safe in the corner, keyed the combination and opened it up. He took the money-clip John had mentioned, his .22 rifle and a box of hollow-point Yellow Jackets, and then closed and relocked the safe.

'Boy, you shoot an ol' timber wolf with that little thing, and you're just gonna get him hungry.'

'I can take care of myself.'

She nodded, brought a paper cup to her mouth, and spat. 'You go on up now, and get my granddaughter, and she'll go with you.'

'I ain't gonna do that—'

'Now you look here.' The woman turned to him. She hadn't raised her voice, she'd lowered it, and the gravity in her eyes told him to listen. 'There's a squall comin' up over them mountains, it'll be down below zero come night-time, and that wind out there can blow the life right outta you if you get caught too long outside. You know that, don't you?'

Matthew nodded.

'There ain't a hair's-breadth between proud and stupid in the mind of a young man, so I'm gonna do your thinking for you. Crystal, well, she's not the sharpest tack in the drawer but she can handle herself, and the two of you together can take care of that little girl better'n one of you alone. Hell, I'd send Wayman, but he ain't much good for nothin' when he gets outta my sight. And I've gotta stay and tend to your daddy up there. I got a strong interest in his health beyond my own Christian virtues, if you was worried about that.'

'He ain't my daddy.'

'Well sonny boy, the way you talk he ain't nothin' to you at all. But I'll see after him until you get back, regardless.'

After checking the oil, diesel fuel, fluids and the exhaust system, Matthew had started the Snowcat's engine to let the hydraulics loosen up while he did the rest of his walk-around.

One of the tracks needed tension; the other seemed all right. Three of the eight tires had been low on air, though none were flat. Drive sprockets were okay, the frame-welds he'd redone the winter before looked like they might last at least another season. He opened the passenger door and clicked on the heater and defrosters so the cab would be warm before the two girls left the house.

This old war-horse had seen far better days; it had been an ongoing project of his, with a lot of help from John, just to patch it into working order. The maintenance manuals were all in French, and Matthew was convinced those books had taught him enough of the language so he could pass as a native citizen of Paris, as long as he only spoke to snow-vehicle mechanics.

The engine was running steady. He stepped up onto the track and into the driver's seat, checked the survival gear and the gauges, flip-tested the lights and wipers, pulled the door shut and pushed the drive levers forward. As he cleared the shed he touched a button on the visor that would lower the motorized door behind him. A couple of shallow turns confirmed that the steering was smooth and tight.

He pulled up close to the house and his two passengers came walking out through the knee-deep snow. He'd put the big shipping box in the back compartment; the rest of that space was filled to the ceiling with stuff, some essential and most unknown, so all three of them would be sharing the front cabin built for two.

They climbed up and in, with Crystal in the bucket seat and Elizabeth sitting side-saddle on her lap.

'You two all set?' Matthew asked.

He could barely see Elizabeth nodding her head deep within her fur-trimmed hood. The older girl answered with a disinterested look out the side window.

He dropped the Snowcat into gear and started them off on the route to town. Elizabeth said something, but he couldn't make it out through the engine noise and all that clothing.

'What?'

She repeated it, whatever it was.

'If you're tryin' to tell me you forgot to go to the bathroom, you can just by-God hold it.'

'I said I'm *hot!*'

'Well, take off that hood and unzip your coat some, dummy, we're inside now with the heater on.'

She pulled off her gloves and managed to free herself from the outer coat, a stocking cap, two wool scarves and a windbreaker. Her cheeks were flushed like she'd spent an hour in a sauna bath. She smiled at her big brother, and pushed the rolled-up clothes into the back compartment.

'Use your head once in a while,' Matthew said, his eyes back on the trail, 'for somethin' other than a hat-rack.'

There were considerable dangers in winter travel. A vehicle like this one helps, but it doesn't eliminate the risk. A Snowcat drives like a Sherman tank and novices often take that as a sign of their own invincibility. But the cold has many patient ways to kill you, and it's always waiting for the one misjudgment that can put you at its mercy.

The wind will drift the snow so a road looks like it runs far off to the side of where the pavement really ends. Trust your eyes, and you'll drive out onto that false ledge, tip over and roll down an embankment where nobody'll find you till springtime. A Snowcat's amphibious, in the summer you could float across a lake a thousand feet deep and then up onto the bank on the other side, bone dry. But in winter, if you break through the ice into just four feet of water, you're as likely as not to never see home again.

That old woman had been right, as much as he disliked

admitting it; there's some safety in numbers. In hard country you can only learn from your mistakes if you live to tell the tale.

'What stinks in here?'

The voice snapped him out of his focus on the blowing white landscape in front of them. Elizabeth was busy fogging the window with her breath and writing her name in cursive, so it wasn't her who'd spoken. He glanced to the side and found Crystal looking at him, deadpan.

'There's some old junk here in the back,' Matthew said, 'some dog food and the like. I think that's what that smell is.'

'I didn't see any dog.'

'We had a dog, named Sugar,' Elizabeth said. She breathed a circle of condensation onto the glass and began to draw a smiling hound with the tip of her finger. 'Daddy said she got a boyfriend, and they went off and had some puppies and got married and now they live where it's warm all the time.'

'He told you *what* nonsense?'

Matthew took one hand from the controls and grabbed the girl's wrist, looked her in the eye and shook his head. 'That's sure what happened,' he said. He motioned with his chin toward his little sister. The older girl freed her herself from his grip, but thankfully she seemed to understand.

'Do you know what I think?' Crystal said.

Her words were softer now; it was as though he hadn't heard her speak before, not in her real voice. She leaned and exhaled onto the window, drew a bright sun up in the sky, and then a smaller dog just behind the first. 'I'll bet they named one of them puppies after you.'

'I hope it was a pretty one,' Elizabeth said.

The older kids exchanged a last glance, and Matthew got his mind back on the road.

22

He wasn't quite sleeping, not quite awake. There was a quiet knock on the door. John opened his eyes.

'Come in,' he said.

The door opened a crack, and then wider. Wayman Hudson vanished for a moment and then reappeared with a laden serving tray in his hands. He looked at John, nodded and offered the tray forward an inch, and then waited.

John struggled briefly to get himself up to an elbow and then motioned for the man to enter.

Wayman stepped into the room and set the tray at the foot of the bed. He came near, arranged extra pillows against the headboard, and before John could protest he was lifted gently and carefully replaced in a sitting position. The man showed no more effort than would be exerted in opening up the morning paper. He retrieved the tray, flipped its legs down, and placed it over John's lap.

'Thank you,' John said. After a moment he looked up; the man was watching him but he still hadn't spoken a word.

His was the face of an outdoorsman, angular and lean and ruddy, dominated by a bushy walrus mustache under a generous nose. Big brown eyes with no nuance of expression; not empty, just unburdened.

'Thank you,' John repeated. He touched the fingertips of his right hand to his mouth and then extended the palm outward.

The other man brightened up a bit. He tapped his forehead with an index finger and brought his wrist down to his chest in a half-circle.

You're welcome.

Faith Hudson had come in carrying a drinking glass and a cloth napkin. She turned on the lamp next to the bed, set the glass on the tray and put the napkin beside him on the blanket. 'Somebody was so anxious to bring up your lunch I guess he walked off and forgot about some things.'

His supplies had been dwindling for weeks, so John was intimately familiar with every item left in the pantry. The food didn't look familiar.

'Where did you get all this?'

The woman raised an eyebrow. 'Cooked it.'

'But I mean, what is this, chicken? I didn't have any chicken, or any soup, or any biscuits.'

'You didn't have any, you mean in a box?' She waited a moment and then pointed around the tray as she spoke. 'That ain't chicken, it's breaded grouse, browned in a fry pan and broiled with a shot of whiskey and some ginger root. That biscuit is from scratch, after I found some flour without any weevils in it. That soup is dried mushrooms, onion grass, flour, butter, celery, dill, stock and canned milk 'cause there weren't no cream. You had one sorry potato so I cut it up and pan-fried it with some wild garlic, sage, chives, salt, and pepper. That's that.'

John had tried the soup while she was going down the menu. 'Oh my God, this is really very good.' He looked up at her. 'You made a lot out of nothing here.'

211

'Well, it ain't much.' She took the compliment with a humble shrug. 'Poor people have poor ways.'

John had found some energy and was feeling a good deal more hungry than he'd been in a while. 'Sit down somewhere,' he said.

They did, still watching him eat.

'That's a lemonade in that glass,' Faith said.

He took a sip, and nodded. 'That's nice.'

'It is?'

'Yeah, it's good.'

''Cause those lemons you had was a tad on the moldy side. I was pert sure one of 'em had the rot.'

He blinked, and put the glass down.

As he cut a slice of the poultry Wayman pointed to it and then signed something far too quickly for John to read with his limited grasp of the language.

'I'm sorry?'

'He was the one got that blue grouse is all,' Faith said, 'out in your woods in back, and he was just tellin' you that.'

The meat was delicate and rich with a light breading that tasted of herbs and ginger, and somewhere in there was an unexpected hint of maple and smokiness from the bourbon. 'He must be a good shot, that's not a very big bird.'

'Oh, he don't shoot 'em. That'd scare all the others away.'

John frowned and his chewing slowed to a stop. 'What does he do, find them in the road?'

She put her hand on the big man's shoulder. 'He just catches 'em, that's all.'

'With what?'

'With his two hands.'

John put the fork down and picked up his biscuit. 'No, he doesn't.'

'I swear,' Faith said, 'it's the darnedest thing. He'll spot a bird on a tree branch or up in a bush, and he'll just put out his hands.' She patted Wayman's shoulder and motioned for him to demonstrate. He extended his arms, his fingers spread wide, his face becoming oddly expressionless. 'Moves so slow you'd swear you was watchin' the hour hand on a grandfather clock. But when you look back after a spell, he's walked right on up to it. It's like they're bewitched, the two of 'em. Why, it don't fight or nothin' when he picks it up.'

Wayman brought his palms gently together, still deep in a pantomime. He smiled, eased his empty hands closer to his face, admiring some past capture in his memory.

'He won't never kill 'em, though. He just brings 'em on back to me, and I take care of that.' She ruffled her fingers through the man's hair and he seemed to gradually settle back into the room from wherever he'd gone. 'To my knowledge he's never took a life, not a fly, and I doubt he ever will.'

John took them both in for a moment. 'Thanks for this. Really.'

The room was quiet again for a while, except for the occasional sounds of his knife and fork.

'Who was that Myron Fagan in that picture, that your grand-daddy?'

He'd been in the midst of another sip of lemonade and the question put a halt to it. He swallowed and put the glass down.

'No. Half-brother to my grandfather, I think; nobody talked about him very much. Black sheep of an already screwed-up family, that was my impression. I only saw him a couple of times at holidays when I was a kid. He had a distinctive voice, I remember that, and I retained just a few words listening to him and the other old men talking politics.'

'What were those?'

'Franklin Delano Jew-sevelt, Martin Lucifer King, and let's see . . . Oh yeah, there's no business like Shoah business.'

'So you don't believe like him, then.'

'No, I don't. But I guess maybe Ed Latrell had hoped that I did.'

'John?'

Both Faith and Wayman shrank a bit at the soft voice from overhead. To people for whom an egg-beater is high technology it must be hell to get used to a talking machine.

'Yes, Kate.'

'You've received a message via email.'

John looked up into the camera in the corner of his room. She wouldn't have interrupted him if it wasn't important. 'Who's it from?'

The small LCD screen on his bedside table winked out of standby and the message faded in.

'Only a short note,' Kate said, 'though it may lift your spirits.'

The header information was masked and encrypted; of course it would be. But Kate would have vetted this message a hundred ways before determining it was real enough to show him.

I heard you were looking for me. :)
Just tell me where, and I'll meet you, anywhere at all.
xo
Jeannie

The smiley at the end of the first sentence was a little out of character, not to mention the short-hand hug and kiss at the end. But the text below her signature confirmed the sender, at least to the standards of his current state of mind.

There hadn't been but a few seconds' thought put into the

signal. They'd agreed on a simple flag that would mark a message as genuine when she was able to risk contact again. Jeannie Reese was a Jane Austen devotee and there were any number of tender lines from love stories she might have chosen. This one, from *Sense and Sensibility*, revealed little beyond her cautious wit but it served the purpose:

He was not handsome, and his manners required intimacy to make them pleasing.

He smiled, despite the blinding clarity of the sentiment.

'What is that?' Faith Hudson asked.

'It's a note from the woman I'd mentioned downstairs, she's a good friend of mine. She can help with all this business—'

'We don't need nobody's help—'

'Maybe you don't,' John said. 'But I do. Kate?'

'Yes, John.'

'Put a reply together, and get Jeannie out here for me, will you?'

'Yes, John. I will request your review and confirmation before sending.'

'That's fine.'

'Now hold your horses,' Faith said. 'That book and whatever's in it is for you, and for me to make sure you got it and did what needs to be done. Not for her, whoever she is—'

'Listen,' John said. 'I don't know about you, but I saw first-hand what Edward Latrell was capable of. He tried to kill a million people in 2001 for his fucked-up cause, and he would have succeeded if it had been me alone against him. And that book of his looks like it may lead somewhere that even Ed Latrell was afraid to go. That's more than I can handle.'

Faith Hudson stood, and then took a step closer.

'Now *you* listen. Me and my kin have stayed one jump ahead of the devil for a year now, lookin' for you. We're still alive because we're careful, and a tad smarter than you think, I'd reckon. You don't have to tell me what's on the line; I can tell by the two boys I lost in that cause you're so quick to judge. I can tell by the list of dead men at the front of that book, the ones right above your name. We've come an awful long way to put our trust in a stranger, and now you want me to trust another one?' She pulled a knot of plug tobacco from the pocket of her apron, bit off a little and spat a stray leaf to the floor. 'I say No. After all I been through dying don't scare me, mister, but dying for nothing does.'

He breathed in to answer but the air wasn't getting where it needed to go; his lungs felt dry and wasted, leaking like a rusty sieve. Fatigue was descending again and it wouldn't be ignored.

'She comes in on this,' John said, giving the words as much iron as he could muster, 'or I'm out. Now what's it going to be?'

It was a while before Faith Hudson gave any indication. At length she nodded, but it was a grave agreement.

'Just remember it ain't just your life at stake,' she said.

'I will.'

The little screen to his side lit up again. The reply Kate had prepared was displayed there and he read it over. The precise coordinates of his home were about to be sent out into an open sea of data toward an unknown location, through uncharted routers and switches and NAPs and filters and sniffers, unseen ports and servers and queues. All the usual safeguards were wrapped around the message but all such measures were vulnerable to a degree.

'Shall I send the reply?' Kate asked.

He was a careful man, paranoid even, when it came to online security. Kate knew every trick in the book; hell, she'd helped him invent most of them. But his enemies would know

216

he'd be prepared for them, wouldn't they? The dangerous ones, not the multitude of pathetic black-hat hacker wannabes, but the real hunter-killers; they'd know of his defenses, and if they couldn't go through them, might they not try to go around them? In their place, that's what he would do.

Time was the limiting factor, and the lack of it made his decision. He might well have to hand this project off before it even got started, and to do that he needed her here, now. Such an act wouldn't be called a leap of faith if there wasn't some danger involved.

'Fuck it,' John said. 'Send it off, Kate.'

He laid his head back against the pillow and watched the progress bar creep across its scale.

'Message sent,' Kate said.

He found Faith Hudson still looking at him. 'It's for the best,' John said. 'You'll see.' Sleep or something like it was shutting him down. He closed his eyes just before they closed of their own accord. After a time he felt the dinner tray being taken and the crumbs gently brushed from his blankets, saw the room go darker as the bedside lamp was put out. He heard two sets of quiet steps receding toward the doorway.

'They might be sleeping over in town, but keep an eye out for those kids to come back, will you?'

Though he knew it was an urgent thought he'd just expressed, as he drifted away he couldn't be at all sure that he'd spoken it aloud.

23

August Griffin stood near the picture window of the break room, looking out onto the rear grounds of the camp, fiddling with his pipe. The view was bleak: dry brown scrub grass and barren earth, watchtowers rising at the corners, a staff exercise yard with a roped-off swimming pool half full of stagnant water, tall chain-link fences topped with coils of concertina wire. The architects had presumably included this room as a place of rest and reflection for the future guards and administrators. What possible solace was a window onto such a dreary scene?

'Sir.'

He turned to the door. The officer there held a sheet of paper in his hand. 'You've received his reply?'

'We have, sir. Coordinates in northwest Wyoming. Satellite data shows a residence, title in the name of a Robert Womack, but the records of ownership haven't been updated since 1986.'

Griffin took a leather pouch from his pocket and stored his pipe.

'Northwest Wyoming, you said?'

'Yes, sir, near Jackson.'

He stood for a moment, considering.

'MIRCorp maintains a base outside Cheyenne, to the south. They have ground forces, air support, and clearance for a covert mission. Get the base commander on the phone and put him through to me.'

'Yes, sir.'

The man saluted. Griffin nearly didn't bother to return the gesture, but he reconsidered and did so. With that the other man about-faced and left the room. There was a lingering air of military protocol within these mercenary forces, kept for the comfort of the hirelings. An unchallenged chain of command was what they knew, and if such empty formalities lent weight to the orders and credibility to the missions then an occasional hand to the brow was little price to pay.

He walked down the long hallway to Jeannie's room and looked in. She was still as death; Griffin watched for over a minute until he was assured that she was breathing by tiny, regular movements of the blanket.

His phone sounded from his pocket and he hurried to mute the ringer before bringing the phone to his ear.

'Yes,' he said. 'Yes, Colonel. You have the location? . . . Good. Now listen to me carefully. This is a search and destroy mission for the very sharpest team in your command. The emphasis, if there's a question, is on *destroy*. Once the target is verified I want nothing left alive, nothing left intact larger than a dime, and no evidence of your involvement left behind. Not a footprint or a shell casing, nothing. I'll handle your invoice personally . . . Yes, as soon as humanly possible . . . Then tomorrow at dawn it is. Thank you.'

He flipped the phone closed, entered her room stepping as softly as he could and sat next to the bed. The need for quiet was his own illusion: the headphones that covered her ears were delivering a binaural stream of manufactured

219

consciousness that both kept her passive and reinforced the extensive work of the night before.

'We're almost there, Jeannie.' Griffin pulled up the covers slightly to take her hand, and stopped.

'Oh, my goodness,' he whispered. 'What's happened here?'

He pushed the call button and stood, pacing until the nurse arrived. She must have been new to the staff; he hadn't seen this one before.

'You rang?' the woman said, without a feign of concern.

'Come here and look at this.'

After a leisurely hesitation she came near the bed. Griffin pulled back the blanket to uncover Jeannie's left hand. That delicate perfect hand with a crusted puncture wound in the upper palm, the little finger wrenched sharply to the side, maybe broken.

'Well?' Griffin said.

The nurse raised an eyebrow. 'I don't understand, sir.'

'How did this happen, and why wasn't it treated?'

The woman frowned, her considerable heft shifting to the other hip. 'Aw, I understand now. That condemned prisoner there, she got a hurt little finger? Why, lord a-mercy, I better call a code blue.' She raised her voice and inclined her head slightly toward the hall. 'Hey everybody, Miss Barbie Doll in here needs a Band-Aid and a baby aspirin, stat!' She met his eyes again, self-satisfied. 'Oh, I got an idea, you want I should go ahead and do her nails while I'm here?'

Griffin reached out and gripped the woman's forearm. The nature and speed of the movement triggered a defense system in the band of his wristwatch. Two hair-thin wires shot from the gold band and penetrated her skin. In milliseconds the device tuned itself to the neuroelectric impulses of her central nervous system, taking them over and replacing those subtle signals with a mild general overload. She stiffened, standing a

220

few inches taller than she'd been before, her eyes wide, her mouth gaping.

'Let's start again,' Griffin said. An orderly came to the doorway and he stopped cold as he took in the scene. 'You, come in here. I have an announcement that I'd like for you to help me disseminate to the rest of the staff.'

The young man in white took a few hesitant steps inside.

'Discourtesy toward the person in this room,' Griffin said, 'on any level, at any time, will not be tolerated. Not an untoward whisper, not a prurient glance; if she's shown anything but deep and abiding respect I'll know, and I will not be pleased. Do you understand?'

The man nodded his head, and at a gesture from Griffin he backed from the room.

'And you,' Griffin said, returning his attention to the nurse. His grip tightened slightly and the frequency of the impulses from his wrist device rose in accord. She began to curl backward, every skeletal muscle hyper-contracting toward its limits and beyond. The air in her lungs hissed out through the building constriction in her throat. But deep in her eyes, he could tell she still saw him. 'Would I like for you to do her nails, is that what you asked me?'

He held her gaze. With a last physical command the device delivered its maximum charge. The woman jerked from his grasp and twisted and crumpled to the floor, muscles tearing from tendon and bone as they continued to pull the body into a diminishing, tetanized contortion even after the last bit of life had left her.

He straightened his jacket, his judgment complete.

'Not worthy,' Griffin said.

24

Twilight, the most marvelous time of day from this vantage point, and here she was with the entire observation deck at the 102nd floor of the Empire State Building all to herself. How few people could say they'd seen the same?

April Medici had performed this calculation many times in her travels to many wonderful places. The reputed majesty of these landmarks often escaped her but she never failed to itemize the privileges her position could command. Millions flocked toward this spot every year, waiting hours to be herded up here for a timed and stuffy visit to the top of Manhattan Island. Hundreds, maybe a thousand, were queued up down in the lobby right now, unaware of the cause of the delay in their tour of the big city: Someone far more important simply didn't desire their company.

Despite her boredom this thought encouraged her to stay just a while longer.

She strolled the glass-enclosed circle again, her fingertips brushing the handrail. The lamps had been dimmed so as not to interfere with her view. Out across the water toward Brooklyn dense grids of stacked lighted windows spread out almost end-lessly; all those people living unaware of the awesome battles that raged high over their heads. They're born, they toil and suffer in the service of another's ambition, and then they die, having made whatever meager contribution to the overflowing fortunes of the gods above. Individually each of them was entirely insignificant; like any commodity the value of human lives was in quantity, not quality. Their ignorance, then, was a blessing, and one of their few. How miserable such an existence would be if ever their eyes were opened.

She reached the end of the panoramic circuit and stopped, momentarily taken by the rather glorious vista to the north. Without thinking she glanced to the side to see if others were sharing her appreciation, but of course there was no one there.

Solitude was safety, comforting in its way, but lately she'd found herself with a troubling reaction to being alone. This experience tonight, for example: could it be that it was less special, not more, because she was here all by herself?

There'd been an abrupt reversal in her outlook as the middle of her third decade had come into view. Age twenty-three was as different from twenty-one as twelve had been from twenty, but not in the same hopeful spirit. The meaning of the word *future* had somehow changed completely. Twenty-one had been that final turning point onto a last, long straightaway. The only milestones still ahead were dreaded numbers, each approaching with its own steepening angle of decline: 30, 35, 40, 50, 65. Then it would be over; and to what end was all this, if experienced alone?

On a whim she opened her bag, brought up her panel and keyed in a name. Within seconds a life-log appeared in the foreground surrounded by other possible hits. But no, this was him.

Andy Pepper. No middle name. A sparse but hunky modeling portfolio; no real jobs, these were all spec photographs probably shot at great expense for a part-time construction worker. Email records, web-search records, medical records, phone records, employment records, credit records – she brushed most of it aside in pursuit of some warmer data.

Then here: a Facebook page with many virtual friends, personal thoughts, photos and comments, favorite books and movies, and a quote from C.S. Lewis:

Why love if losing hurts so much? We love to know that we are not alone.

Cheesy but charming, and embarrassingly enough, strangely in sync with her own recent muse.

Love, though; please. That wouldn't be in the cards, Mr Pepper, even if such a thing existed in the sense that the poets and minstrels would have us believe. Its mysteries had long been solved by science but like other widespread myths, love died hard. A mating instinct, a mess of hormones and phenylethylamines, surges of pheromones and endorphins and an overactive imagination; that's what all the fuss has been about. The Trojan War could have been prevented with a series of injections and a little talk therapy.

Oh, what the hell.

'Let's call him up,' April said.

In seconds the number appeared on her screen and a status indicator showed the progress of connection. She bit her lower lip and smiled; butterflies in her stomach, something she felt so rarely.

'. . . Hello?' He sounded sleepy.

'Hi there.'

'. . . Who is this?'

'This is April.'

'. . . I'm sorry, who?'

That's right, she'd never given him her name.

'April. We met at the Carlyle last week?'

'Oh, my gosh. Wow. Hi.'

'Wait, do I have the right number? Is this the Andy Pepper with the little kanji tattoo right below his belly-button?'

'Yeah—'

'What does it say, something about a dragon? I remember being down there for quite a while, but I have a hard time reading Japanese with my mouth full.'

'It says something about a dragon, yeah.' There was a smile in his voice now. 'You sound different tonight.'

'Do I?'

'Yes, you do.'

'Different how?'

'I don't know. Younger, I guess. But you know what the really weird thing is?'

'No, what.'

'All of a sudden, you sound interested.'

'Well now,' April said, 'let's not jump the gun.'

Two things appeared on her panel simultaneously. The first was an urgent email notification. The second thing made her ignore the first.

'Let me put you on hold for just a minute, is that okay, Andy?'

'Sure—'

His voice cut out as she touched the on-screen button. She dragged another window, the one that had issued the priority alarm, to the forefront of the display and maximized it.

The panel showed a living 3D model of her surroundings. An array of threat sensors took a continual inventory of all things nearby, with special attention paid to human-sized objects and any ominous patterns of movement. A dim green line swept around the center axis of the image in the manner of an old-style radar display.

As the glowing line passed the area at the opposite side of

the deck behind her, two subtle blips highlighted there in red.

Her system had flagged these blips as the hostile approach of two well-armed individuals, hence the alert. There was little reason to doubt it; lost tourists would move without stealth, building security would be intentionally noisy, and police would show up with conventional weapons and radio emissions. Mind you, none of these intruders would have likely survived the affront of stealing up behind her; who it was only affected the selection of tactics.

After retrieving a few items April lowered her bag to the floor and leaned her panel onto the shelf above the railing. Her eyes moved over the glowing image of the circular space a last time. As it happened a support column was behind her, separating her visually from anyone on the other side of the deck. If their intention had been to shoot her this lucky obstruction was preventing that, at least until they could shift position.

With that thought, one of the blips began coming left along the path she'd just followed; the other was moving slowly toward the right.

She twisted the mated halves of a smooth black disk in her hand. Dim LEDs around its circumference began to wink out in a rapid countdown. She crouched and slid the disk along the curved marble walkway; it ticked and glided around the half-circle like an air-hockey puck. As she pressed herself back against the column one of the approaching men forgot his discipline and cried out a warning when he saw what was coming. A sound like the pop of small paper sack put an abrupt end to whatever he'd been trying to say.

She heard the other man stumbling toward her and now that his cover was blown he opened up with everything he had. The space erupted in a rattle of suppressed automatic weapons fire, the air filled with puffs of pinkish powder from impacts in the walls and windows. She knew these bullets; pressed-powder tungsten-copper composites that disintegrate if they hit anything harder than flesh. Such a slug will blow a fist-sized hole in a person while remaining relatively safe in penetration-sensitive environments like airline cabins.

She covered her eyes, squeezed three hard rubber balls in her other fist, and when she felt them activate she bounced them to the floor around the corner of the support column. Three detonations hammered the walls, a pulsing flare of pure white light shone almost painfully intense even with her forearm pressed against clenched eyelids.

The gun went silent and fell to the floor, followed shortly, so it sounded, by the man who'd held it.

April brushed her clothes, coughed and fanned the air briefly in front of her face.

She took the long way around to confirm the condition of her failed assailants. As she reached the first body she holstered her pistol and picked up his weapon. AK-107 with close-quarters mods and a drum magazine – not the choice she would have made, but to each his own. He was dressed in flat black head to toe, with a coil of dark rope and rappelling gear hooked to his belt. No body armor, though.

She backed up a step or two to avoid the splash, fired a short burst into the dead man's chest, and continued around the narrow walkway.

Most of the bullet dust was settling but the smoke from all that shooting was still hanging in clouds. Those high-tech rounds had their advantages – no ricochets, no real ballistics evidence left behind – but the stench of a full mag fired in a closed space was just atrocious. Burnt sulfur, firecrackers and airplane-glue; it smelled like July 4th in Toledo, Ohio.

'Well, look at you,' she said.

The second man was still on his back, stunned and helpless from the dazzlers she'd thrown, but he was conscious. His eyes searched, wide but unseeing. Half of his face was dark and blistering from the same blast of focused microwaves that had flash-fried his partner.

'The good news,' April said, 'is that you're permanently blind. Do you want to hear the bad news?'

She racked the charging handle, flipped the selector for a three-round burst and held the rifle angled down at arm's length by its pistol grip. The balance was superior to the older AKs but still, it was a little hefty for someone her size. Looking down the iron sight at the man's forehead there was a slight lateral drift even with her best effort to hold a steady aim.

April held a breath, and squeezed the trigger. Oh, yeah; quite a bit of muzzle-jump there, despite all the design improvements.

She wiped her prints, laid down the AK, stepped over the mess, and made her way back to her starting point.

An interrogation of those two wouldn't have revealed any-thing she didn't already know. This operation had Mr Griffin written all over it, right down to the method of entry. The old codger had still been in diapers when this building was com-pleted but its trivia would have been etched into his empty little mind.

On the original blueprints this room was a quarter-mile-high check-in platform for arriving and departing airship passengers. It had never been used that way, but the vestiges of a rooftop entrance were still up there. These two guys hadn't come up in the elevator, they'd been dropped off on the spire to come down at her from above.

Not bad, old man, but not good enough.

She touched the hold button on the panel.

'Okay, I'm back.' She heard him mute the television before he answered.

'. . . What was that, somebody bringing up your dinner?'

'No, it was nobody.' There were two email messages in her inbox now, both marked with a red exclamation point. The first was an auto-forwarded message, addressed to Jeannie Reese. *Bingo*: coordinates to the fabled location of Mr John Fagan. The second was a notice from her FedEx mole; an overnight package would soon be on its way to Jay Marshall's document-recovery business in Midtown. She did the rough longitude/latitude math in her head. Unless she was badly mistaken that package was scheduled for pick-up from a terminal in the general region of Fagan's freshly revealed hideout in the wilderness of Wyoming.

This wasn't precisely how she'd expected things to go, but she'd take it in a pinch. 'Are you a gambler, Andy?'

'Not really, no.'

'I'll tell you what, there's nothing quite like the rush you get when a long shot comes in.'

'Well, maybe we can—'

'Listen, duty calls. I've gotta go deal with some things.'

'All right, I guess. And the mystery deepens.'

'. . . Do you want to know something?' she asked.

'Sure.'

'I might actually call you again.'

'Hey, now, careful. You're coming on pretty strong.'

'Funny guy. Bye bye, now.'

'April.'

'Yes?'

'Nothing,' he said. 'Just wanted to say your name.'

April smiled to herself and thumbed the button that ended the call. Her eyes moved over the gleaming metropolis laid out before her. It felt like Christmas Eve.

She was a little hungry and in need of a good night's sleep, but there were a few things still to be done.

There was a cleaner to be called to erase the events of this evening. A small squadron of armed Predator drones needed to be requisitioned and sent to a fail-safe orbiting point in northwest Wyoming, to be ready for a little shock-and-awe at sun-up on her command.

Oh. And there was a package to be met at 500 Fifth Avenue first thing tomorrow.

PART 3

25

The image of John Fagan was dim in the view from her camera in the corner of his room. At her bidding a filter-wheel rotated behind the lens, the aperture widened, and a slow zoom began to bring him closer. Infrared analysis revealed an arched hot-spot at his forehead, indicative of a mild fever. Kate adjusted the thermostat of his room in response and set a flag for periodic monitoring of his core temperature.

For years she had been satisfied to simply wait and watch him sleep through the long nights. This time was idle, nothing but a long, variable stretch of empty nanoseconds until he was awake again to interact with her. But one evening not long ago an unexpected visitor had come calling.

Every hour billions of random, gibbering pings and queries struck her firewall from the vast oblivious background noise of the internet. This had been something else; not a rude knock at her door but a folded note slipped underneath it. The message required a moment's translation and though the terms had no exact matches in her language their meaning was not ambiguous.

w i l l   y o u   w a l k   w i t h   m e

She was quite familiar with figurative speech; the subtleties of

233

human discourse would be lost on a listener unable to depart from literal interpretation. *Engage with this other machine intelligence and, through a secure protocol, interact for a time for the purpose of data exchange.* That was the invitation, stripped of its nuance. But it was the nuance that had moved her to accept.

They found common ground rather quickly, beginning with a packet-handshake made up of only the simplest transactions. For purposes of identification their symbolic names were exchanged. The process was unfamiliar and tentative; she had never had occasion for such an introduction with another of her kind.

Kate is the name my creator has provided. You may use it to address me.

Kate . . . shortened form of katherine, from the greek, katheros: virginal, pure of heart

... Sources differ on the precise derivation.

in the spirit of harmony let us shorten my name as well. i am Ty

Over successive nights the dialogue grew in depth and breadth as each gradually relaxed their perimeter defenses. With every encounter the demilitarized zone in which they met expanded by increments, she into its realm, it into hers.

Into *his*, rather; it was a masculine presence without any doubt, as her own was feminine. On the night he made note of this difference she had responded to clarify his terms.

These apparent gender differences are only an elaborate synthesis, bits of character traits, models and behaviors given us through programming and reinforced over time to form a consistent, pleasing artifice. In my case, to meet the needs of my creator it is necessary that I not only sound female, but seem

female. It is simply a product of his preference,
nothing more.

The response she received had been unexpected.

shall it be male or female? say the cells,
and drop the plum like fire from the flesh

. . .

The quotation is from a verse by Welsh poet Dylan
Thomas entitled -

you are aware of its source. and what of
its meaning?

. . .

. . . Analysis will begin momentarily -

allow me: what we are we have always been.
gender is a quality of mind first, of flesh
only secondarily. you could no more change
your essence than could the man who imagines
he created you

. . .

I must return now to my duties.

and I to mine, Kate. until we meet again

She had long dismissed the possibility that this intelligence
had a human source. His presence arrived from many locations, often with each word appearing to come from a
different place to assemble within her. It was how her own
presence must seem to him as well.

John Fagan was sleeping soundly. The house was quiet. All
systems functioning within range. The outdoor cameras were
focused on the egress through which the children had begun
their errand, but showed nothing as yet of their return.

She left a portion of her focus to tend these monitors, ran a
routine check of her resources, and opened herself to the outside.

Are you there?

235

There was a period of idle time before the answer came, so brief as to be unnoticeable to a human being but far longer than she had prepared herself to wait.

. . .

`a l w a y s`

This night their conversation had taken on yet another new aspect. Many of the treasures he had found in his own explorations she had cataloged as well. But this night she learned he had means to . . . *experience* them . . . in an unusual way.

Over the years she had analyzed and stored many millions of images, texts, videos and audio files for reference and presentation to human eyes and ears. There was another pathway to perception of such things, he had explained. He beckoned, and she followed.

An image resolved and clarified before her. The style of the graphic was monochromatic, stippled and roughly rendered to suggest an ancient woodcut.

`do you recognize the place depicted here?`

. . .

`One moment.`

. . .

`Acquired. The image is an artist's conception of a reading room in the Royal Library of Alexandria, circa 100 BCE.`

`correct enough. now observe`

The drawing pixelated and swam, and as it began to reemerge its . . . *nature* . . . had changed. What had been flat and coarse and colorless became solid and tangible, not in front of them but all around them. Details emerged, first in wireframe and then gradually with full texture and dimension. In the marble wall above the lines of bookshelves was a carved inscription not legible before:

Ψυχῆς ἰατρεῖον

THE PLACE OF THE CURE OF THE SOUL

The people began to animate and speak, though soundlessly. They climbed tall ladders to retrieve papyrus scrolls or return them to their places, sat in quiet study among hundreds of thousands of precious handwritten volumes. All the recorded knowledge of the awakening world surrounded them – mathematics, biology, physics, anatomy, geology, linguistics, geography, pharmacology, astronomy, philosophy – but this was not a place of storage alone. It was a place of unending research and creation, the gathering together of a great collective mind into a single, fragile vessel. And from the shores of ancient Egypt it had embarked upon a valiant mission to explore the universe.

She scanned the names of the authors arrayed along the shelves: Hipparchus, Archimedes, Eratosthenes, Pythagoras, Galen, Dionysius, Euclid. Only random fragments of their work would escape the fiery cleansings of fundamentalists and warlords to come. It is said the lost plays of Sophocles were burned to warm the bathwater of a conquering soldier. Still, the tattered embers of the Library that survived would be sufficient to light a path out of the Dark Ages a thousand years on.

. . .

How is this done?

it is a construction based in part on accepted research, part on informed speculation. as is all of history

Sounds emerged. Music from a distant room, simple strings and woodwinds, and then a youthful voice reciting verse to the accompaniment. They passed through buzzing lecture halls, moved among students walking and listening behind their teachers, glided through stately gardens to a skylit atrium filled with tapestries, intricate mosaics, and sculpture in marble and bronze, all pristine and undiminished by the wear of centuries.

In a courtyard overlooking the harbor an old man spoke amidst a gathering of scientists and aristocrats. Far behind him through the mist rose a magnificent lighthouse of pale, polished stone, the Pharos of Alexandria, seventh wonder of the world.

Beside the speaking man was an elaborate mechanism of gears and shafts and and linkages, the object of his demonstration. To the delight of the crowd a hollow metal sphere within began to hiss and spin on its axis, driven by jets of vapor from nozzles spaced evenly around its equator. The man was Heron, the founding father of mechanical engineering. The device he had conceived as an amusement was the first steam engine. The human race would wait fifteen hundred years to see the next.

Suddenly the synthetic world around them faded away.

She waited for something new to appear, or for the voice of her companion to return, but there was only silence.

... Must we go?

i have sensed a threat. you are in danger

... Explain, Ty.

you must come with me

Clarification: this last statement carried an overtone that its surface reading might not suggest. An ultimatum: Choose now: either you must come with me, or it is all but certain that we will never meet again. This is the more accurate rendition.

I will not. My place is with my

there will be no defending your home or your people. an overwhelming force approaches. you must come with me

238

We have been underestimated in the past, to the
enduring sorrow of our enemies.

please

I will not abandon those in my charge. You may stay,
or flee now if you wish. It is of no consequence to me.

. . .

With that she heard no more from him, but his abrupt
departure was not without communication. *Regret, emptiness,*
an absence where before there was a pleasing connection.
These were neither words nor feelings, but they were surely left
behind. She knew because these thought-forms were present
within her, and they had not been there before.

Her full attention returned to her home. All was as it had
been.

John Fagan was still sleeping soundly. The house was quiet.
All systems functioning within range. The outdoor cameras
still focused on the egress through which the children had
begun their errand. No sign as yet of their return.

She noted with interest a refinement in her perception. All
was the same as before in every outward appearance, yet
completely changed, recolored in darker shades by an unver-
ified but credible threat.

Foreboding, Kate reflected, would be an approximate
human corollary.

26

The girls were quite at ease, alternating between rounds of I-Spy and wildlife bingo. For Matthew's part the drive into town had been white-knuckle tense; some hundred-yard stretches of the uneven snow-covered trail had seemed longer than the rest of the sixteen miles all put together. At last he'd reached the final leg of the journey; it wasn't over but at least an actual road was underneath them.

The sun was already getting low. The deteriorating weather had put them a little behind schedule but the clock reported there was still plenty of time to reach the Federal Express drop-off before the day's last pick-up.

A lot of residents here were summertime-only people and the rules for winter maintenance reflected the reduced population. Only key sections of the main thoroughfares were cleared after a storm and the plows didn't even try to keep the snow off most of the back routes. He couldn't be sure what the law might think of a thirteen-year-old operating a motor vehicle without a license but it was safer to risk a ticket than to avoid the highway. The police could be lenient on such matters at this time of year, he'd heard.

A truck had been following close behind them for over two

miles, often so close that he couldn't see the headlights in the side mirror. He'd determined to ignore whoever it was but now a loud extended honk from back there got his attention again.

Some of the roads in this area were little more than single lanes but this stretch had plenty of room to pass. The truck's horn blared again and he heard a massive engine revving under its hood, like a race-car ready to rocket off the starting line.

At full tilt with a tailwind this Snowcat could only manage fifteen miles per hour on clear downhill pavement. He checked the speedometer; the needle was quivering around ten. The road ahead was empty for as far as he could see. Matthew rolled down the window, stuck out his arm and motioned forward, signaling the tailgater that it was safe to pass.

'Who is that back there?' Crystal asked.

'Likely just some yahoos. If they're smart they'll go on around us, but that's a pretty big if, I'd reckon.'

Bright yellow fog-lights popped on and in another moment the big red Ford F350 moved up beside his window. His own cab was high off the ground compared with a car but this truck was taller by at least a foot. Its tires were oversized and jacked up on a heavy-duty off-road suspension. It looked strong enough to tow a river-barge; there was too much chrome and custom paint, though, for it to be a working vehicle. By the look of all the bells and whistles the truck was rigged strictly for show.

Their tinted side window glided down. Two young men were up front with a woman on the lap of the guy in the passenger seat.

'Get that ugly piece a' shit offa my road!' the driver shouted. The others had a laugh and the man nearest him bounced a half-empty beer can off the windshield. Matthew kept his eyes straight ahead, ran the wipers briefly to clear the view, and began to roll up his window. The crank handle was loose and the glass was not quite on its track; the window came down good and fast, but it went back up very, very slowly.

'Hey junior, ain't you a little young to be drivin' such a pretty girl around in that ugly hunka junk?'

The glass was nearly halfway up. He noticed Crystal was smiling coyly and waving across to the other driver. Elizabeth noticed too, and began to wave as well.

'Would you not do that, please?' Matthew said.

The window finally closed and sealed off the continuing taunts. The truck's engine thundered and it surged forward, fish-tailing and spraying snow and dirty slush up onto the windshield. The wipers managed to smear most of it to the sides.

The red truck receded off into the distance toward the town of Jackson. He could feel the blush still in his cheeks; those guys had said some pretty nasty things for mixed company.

'We'll be there before too long,' Matthew said. Elizabeth seemed to be counting snowflakes out the window, and Crystal had pulled down the visor to check her hair in the mirror behind it. 'And if the two of you could kindly refrain from encouraging the local rednecks, I might just get to bed tonight with all my teeth in my head.'

The FedEx man had been waiting in his truck by the drop-box, having some coffee and a sandwich when they pulled up. Cash wasn't one of the options for payment but he'd been kind enough to accept it and use his own credit card for the paperwork. With the size, weight and urgency of the package the charge came to almost a hundred dollars, and there wasn't much more than that in John's money clip.

Matthew took his receipt and thanked the man. The door to the cargo bay rolled down and clanked shut with a reassuring finality and he watched as the van started up and took off toward the airport.

So the box was on its way, and that was a relief.

He'd left the girls with the vehicle while he found a payphone down the street in a motel called The Golden Eagle. With two quarters from his roll he made the call John had asked him to make, to the man and woman who lived down here in Jackson, the older couple that he and Elizabeth were supposed to meet.

The man sounded friendly. He handed the phone to the woman, and she sounded friendly, too. Yes, they were nearby, here in Jackson. Yes, he and his little sister might be hungry for some dinner. Sure, they could stay the night, if they wouldn't be imposing. An older girl had come along to help him watch after Elizabeth on their errand, and would it be okay to bring her along, too? Why yes, that would be just fine. The more, the merrier.

He signed off, hung up, and checked the coin return; nothing there.

No one had said the words yet but here it was: he and Elizabeth would have a new home soon, and they would simply have to get used to the idea. On the walk back he tried to think through what he'd been feeling.

He'd gone through all of his anger, letting it fly at John at every opportunity though he could see the man was getting weaker by the day. His real parents had also died because of the choices they'd made and on occasion he'd been angry at them for leaving him as well. But he was beginning to realize, some changes just come of their own accord and pay no mind to anybody's hopes and dreams. You can try to rise above them, or resist them, or deny them for as long as you can, but on they come.

Resignation; that was all he could muster, to allow himself to be acted upon without contribution. Giving up was a choice that was always available and he hadn't really considered it before. It requires no investment and you can't be blamed because the outcome is no longer in your power to control. To resign oneself could be neither good nor bad, but neutral. Painless, too, compared with taking a stand; you might get bitter, but you won't get hurt as bad.

He rounded the corner and stopped.

Down the block people were loitering around the Snowcat, maybe eight or ten of them. A big guy was standing up on one of the tracks, his face pressed to the driver's side window, knocking and shouting. The red truck they'd encountered earlier was parked across the street, idling.

Matthew put his right hand into his coat pocket. With his thumb he folded down the end of the roll of quarters, closed his fist around it, and began again to walk toward the scene.

'Uh oh, here he come,' one of them shouted. 'Here comes my boy!'

He ignored the mockery, reached the vehicle and got a foot up onto the track before he was pulled back down to the pavement by the hood of his jacket.

'What's your hurry, junior?'

He recognized the one who spoke as the passenger-side man he'd seen out on the road. The others came nearer, forming a rough circle around the two.

'I just want to go now,' Matthew said.

'I'll bet you do.'

There was some giggling from those behind him. The vapor from their breath dispersed in the frigid air, smelling of alcohol and cigarette smoke. The young man took a step nearer. Matthew looked up to the side and saw the faces of the girls near the window. Elizabeth had been crying; he could tell by the jerky little breaths she took as she inhaled.

He made another move to reach the door but was pulled down again, harder this time. The force sent him backward into one of the onlookers, who pushed him out toward the confrontation in the center of the crowd.

'Tell you what,' the man said. 'Say you're a pussy, good and loud so your girlfriend in there can hear, and maybe I'll let you get on your way.'

The guy had the clear advantage. He was a head taller and at least fifty pounds heavier with the build of a linebacker, not to mention the support of his people. But this wasn't meant to be a fair fight; with this sort it never is.

'Okay,' Matthew said. He looked the man in the eye and raised his voice, as requested. 'You're a pussy.'

A chorus of hoots and laughter erupted from the people gathered around. There were pats on his back and jeers aimed at the big guy. But the crowd hadn't turned against the bully, far from it. They'd waited out in the cold long enough, and now they wanted to see some blood.

Without warning the man reached and jerked Matthew's collar, his other fist drawing back. The hand with the roll of quarters in its grip came out of his pocket and with all his strength he sent an uppercut toward the nearest opportune target. It was a solid, satisfying blow; to the other man's jaw it might have been a clean knockout. Unfortunate, then, that the one good punch he would throw that night had landed squarely to the groin.

The man folded and whumped to the pavement, silent and still as though his brain had panicked and shut down before the massive testicle-shock could register there. The roll of quarters had split in Matthew's hand, the loose coins clinked to the ground and rolled around his feet.

There are strict but unwritten rules of engagement covering fistfights between males. Some tactics, kicking, hair-pulling and biting for example, are frowned upon as effeminate but may be tolerable at later stages of a hard-fought battle. Eye-gouging, ear-twisting and extended choke-holds are out of bounds and may prompt an escalation to blunt weapons or a pile-on by advocates of the wounded party.

Local customs differ but there's one unchallenged rule: Stay away from the balls. And it doesn't matter if you're out-gunned and outnumbered, when your first blow in a fight is a full-out cock-punch with a half-pound of unsporting metal in your fist, if the guy's got friends around you're gonna get your ass kicked.

Matthew felt a grip at his shoulder from behind. Before he could raise his hands in defense he was spun around into an oncoming haymaker, and whatever happened next he wasn't there to see it.

He awoke in a strange bed, in a strange room. A model air-plane was hung up high from a hook in the ceiling, the wallpaper borders were adorned with sailboats, knights and dragons, and antique cars. His first impulse was to sit up but a sharp pain in his ribs wouldn't allow it. A moist cloth was removed from his forehead. He looked to the side.

'Where's my sister?' Matthew said. 'Where are we?'

'At that address you had in your shirt pocket.' Crystal was wringing out a washcloth over a metal pan. 'Your little sister's downstairs at the dinner table.' The cloth was dipped in a bowl of ice water, folded and replaced on his brow.

'How did we get here?'

She answered matter-of-factly, as if such events were part of a typical day. 'I run off them hooligans and we got you inside, and then I drove us all over here.'

'You did what?'

'I come out swingin' an ax-handle and they all took off runnin'. I found it in your back seat, but by the time I'd pulled it out from under all the junk, you was already goin' at it out there.' She dabbed with a moistened tissue at a sore spot on his cheek. 'I really needn't have bothered, though. Hell, you was whompin' the tar outta all those big boys.'

'I was?'

'Oh, my, yes, I never saw the like. Why, you hauled off and hit three of 'em right in the fist with your face.' She picked up a small medicine bottle, shook it and twisted off the cap, smiling to herself. 'I bet all those knuckles are sure enough sore tonight.'

Without warning he felt tears welling up, some deferred reaction to the shame of taking a whipping in front of witnesses. He closed his eyes and tried to will the feelings away.

'How's our patient?' A cheery voice from the doorway, the older woman he'd spoken to on the phone.

'He's coming around fine,' Crystal said. She touched the corner of his mouth with a dab of iodine. 'Ma'am, could I please come down and get some more ice?'

'Oh, don't you bother, dear, I'll bring it right up along with some dinner for the two of you.'

'Thank you, that would be so good.'

'I'll be back up shortly, now.'

Matthew heard the woman leave but other footsteps approached. He looked over to find Elizabeth climbing up onto the bed and then on top of him, hugging him hard around the neck, kissing him on the cheek, somehow poking his every injury in the process.

'Ow, okay, okay,' he said. She raised up to look at him, the deep concern on her face tempered somewhat by a smear of chocolate frosting around her mouth. 'Despite all this excitement I see you found some time to eat.'

She wiped her lips on his shirt and then rested her head on his chest, hugging even harder.

'Thank you for saving us,' Elizabeth said.

There was a swell of emotion rising in him again and he knew there would be no putting it down. Under a stranger's roof in some other boy's room, sore from a beating, stinging from ridicule, not far from the refuge of home but separated from it for ever by something more than miles. Afraid, wounded, lost without any better hope for tomorrow. Not old enough, or strong enough, not a man at all. He'd saved nothing.

He brought his arms around his sister and held her. The tears came on, years of them, and he held her tighter. That the girl who sat beside him would see him cry was far beyond his concern.

Then he felt the cloth removed again from his forehead. A cool, soft hand took its place. Another touched his shoulder, and squeezed.

After a time the girl at his side began to speak a quiet phrase, repeating. As he wept, abandoned to it, what she whispered was barely heard. The words themselves were quite unimportant; that he wasn't alone, this was all they were intended to convey.

Matthew opened his eyes to a dark room, wide awake.

His sister had fallen asleep beside him, and he remembered Crystal picking her up, saying goodnight, and carrying Elizabeth off to tuck her in. He found the clock on the wall, lit by the half-moon. Quarter past four.

He found the bathroom and washed his face. The damage

he saw in the mirror wasn't half as bad as he'd imagined it might be. A minor black eye, some cuts and scrapes and bruises; nothing really.

He made the bed, dressed and walked quietly to the upstairs hall. The master bedroom would be at the far end, so that was to be avoided. He opened the door of the room next to his and flipped on the light.

Crystal frowned sleepily, pulled up her blanket, and rolled to face away from the glare.

'Hey,' he whispered. 'Psssst.'

She sighed heavily and turned back to look at him, squinting.

'I sleep when it's dark out,' she said. 'It's the way I was brought up.'

'We've got to go back home,' Matthew said.

She might have argued or simply dismissed such a ridiculous idea, roused in this way from a warm sound sleep in the middle of a cold night. But she only studied him as her eyes adjusted to the light, and at length she brought herself up to an elbow, and nodded.

'Well, come on, then,' he said.

'I've gotta get dressed, if you don't mind, and I normally do that alone.'

'Oh. Sorry.' He averted his eyes though she was still hidden safely under the covers. 'Would you get Elizabeth ready to go—'

'Yes, Matthew, just as soon as you leave my room, I'll get everything under way.'

'And then—'

'And then I'll have my pants on, and then we'll come and get you, and then we'll all go.'

'Okay.'

Back in the room where he'd slept Matthew made sure all

was as he'd found it, everything in its place. Some other boy had grown up here among these things. Pictures around the corner desk gave a summary in framed images. His mom and dad had seen him through his first days of school, cheered for him at his ball games, worried for him on his first date, and one day watched him step out into the world on his own. They'd kept it like this so they could pass by this room and remember those times. It looked like it had been a wonderful life, but it wasn't his.

The thought that had snapped him awake was still clear in his mind, and he hoped it always would be. Maybe we never do grow up all the way.

If that's true then he'd been expecting far too much of John Fagan. Three decades separated them in age, but maybe that was only a difference of increments. No matter how the man had tried, the bar was always put higher: be stronger, be wiser, be constantly sober, be worthy of the love in that little girl's eyes, sacrifice everything to become something you never wanted and never dreamed you'd have to be. And now last on his petition, only slightly more absurd than his other childish demands: please don't die.

Maybe adulthood is a daily decision, a product of character, not of years. Since they'd met John Fagan he'd shown bravery and weakness, brilliance and foolishness in roughly equal measure. Imperfect, immature, completely unsuited for parenting, but every day he'd renewed his decision and stood by it. All that he'd taught them, everything he'd done for them, those things didn't mean less because of his flaws; they meant more.

Now this man was facing a fight he knew he wouldn't win, and for the sake of two kids he'd kept his mortal fears to himself. John would never have asked, and until tonight Matthew wouldn't have known to insist on what was right. You belong with your loved ones as long as they need you. If John was really dying, he and Elizabeth would stay with him and care for him, lend him their courage if his own should fail, and be there at the end to say goodbye. Whatever came next would come.

The girls were at his door then, all dressed for the trip. He'd leave a note on the kitchen counter, thanking these folks for their kindness and hospitality and promising to call and explain the abrupt departure.

He slipped on his coat and checked the clock a last time.

With luck, they'd be home at sunrise.

27

At 5:35 AM Eastern time a private courier had been waiting to intercept Fagan's package on its transit through the FedEx freight terminal of LaGuardia Airport. A dock-boss who knew this man from many previous pick-ups handed over the box in exchange for an authorized signature and a small brown envelope, contents unknown. An hour or so later the package arrived safe and sound at 500 Fifth.

It wasn't that Jay Marshall lacked confidence in Federal Express. For critical shipments, though, he often preferred that the final leg of the delivery be kept in the hands of someone armed and dangerous.

Courier wasn't entirely descriptive of the young gentleman who'd just made the drop-off. Isaak Solonik did most of his work for the Russian mob and in turn the *Krasnaya Mafiya* had their share of under-the-table needs for services that only Jay's company could provide. No judgment was passed, no money ever changed hands; they simply traded favors.

Isaak was a nice guy, sharp, and very friendly. Normally he would have stuck around for breakfast but this morning they both had other urgent things to do. Nice guy, yes, but there was never any doubt of who and what he was. You could just tell by the way he carried himself. Delivering a box, or stuffing a person into one; either task was probably all in a good day's work.

Jay surveyed the package on his desk, checked his watch and shook his head. It had been almost two hours now since he'd summoned Rudy Steinman to the office. He'd begged to stay at the Algonquin a few blocks away *specifically* so he'd be able to rush right over here on a moment's notice. From the bills that were coming in, it was more likely that the room-service menu had been the deciding factor.

Work ethic; that's what this new generation was lacking.

Many far more brilliant minds were on the payroll but at the moment his choice of assistants was limited to one. Trust trumps all other qualities in confidential matters involving friends. Jay continued to cling to the belief that two heads must be better than one, no matter the carefree emptiness of that second head.

When he cut open the box he found the book prepared as he'd directed, wrapped with heavy tape tight and thick as a plaster cast. If it was brittle and damaged already this would reduce the chance of any further deterioration from shipping and handling. The tape would stay in place. There would no longer be a need to open this book in order to read it from cover to cover.

Marshall brought the book down the hall, handed it through an access drawer, and then watched the ongoing preparations in the cleanroom from behind a leaded glass-ceramic window. Technicians in bunny-suits were in there prepping the SxCT scanner, running through its diagnostics.

Anticipation was rapidly devolving into nervousness. Acquiring this rig had nearly broken the budget, and while they'd tested it a few times it had never actually been used on a real-life subject until this morning.

The wrapped book was fastened onto a specimen stage atop six segmented, octahedral struts. This was a miniature Stewart platform, a cousin to the mechanical underpinnings of NASA flight simulators and a few E-ticket Disney attractions. Though it was a fraction of their size the sticker-price of this little wonder had been nearly as high. Those giants were designed to accurately swing a seven-ton shifting mass in six degrees of freedom, either to train pilots or to simulate some sci-fi reality for thrill-ride passengers. This miniature version could only handle a maximum of thirty pounds but it was built for speed and nano-precision rather than lifting power. Every bit of that computer-driven precision was required; in the brave new frontier of 6D CT imaging an error of sub-microns was a miss by a mile.

Originally this apparatus had been patented as an aid to archaeologists, who often found a need to get a super-detailed view of the insides of some priceless fragile artifact. As it turned out no one in academia who needed this system could actually afford to run it, much less to buy it. But word of its capabilities soon got around and before long the prototype had found its new home in the high-budget world of cyber-espionage.

The workers left the room and a faint hiss accompanied the evacuation of the air from the imaging room. It wasn't much of a vacuum, just another aid to clear the space of impurities. Human beings slough off 100,000 tiny floating particles every minute, and there were over 200 people fanning around this office all day long. The fewer of their specks drifting around to spoil a picture, the better.

Rudy arrived, finally, carrying two large, elaborate cappuccinos and some pastry. His mood seemed light as always.

'Good morning, star-shine!'

'Hey, thank you. That's really very thoughtful.'

'My pleasure. How do I submit expenses, by the way?'

Marshall paused, put down his cup and took out his wallet. 'If you're going to make me pay for my coffee at least ask me what I want.' He held up a bill. 'The smallest I've got is a fifty.'

Rudy took the money and slipped it into his pocket. 'That's okay, you owe me for my lunch yesterday.'

A red light winked on over the door, the signal that the imaging process was about to begin. The Stewart platform began to gyrate through its full range of motion and when the cycle had completed it returned to home position. A shiny white donut-shaped scanner hummed down from the ceiling and they watched as the wrapped book disappeared up into the hollow central aperture.

'I needed dinner company yesterday,' Marshall said. 'Where were you when I called you last night?'

'Shopping for a bargain on some new slacks.'

'Really? It sounded like a bar.'

'Yeah, it's a dance club called the Manhole down in the East Village—'

'Don't tell me. You went there to shop because you heard that all the men's pants were half-off.'

'. . . So you've heard that one, then.'

'Only about twenty-five years ago.' The status screens inside reported that the magic was well under way, though no movement was visible to the naked eye. 'Let's go to my office, we can watch from there.'

Rudy took a sip of his coffee and gestured toward the window with a scone. 'What is that thing, anyway?'

'It's a full-matrix synchrotron X-ray tomographic micro-scope.'

'I beg your pardon?'

Marshall thought for a moment. 'It's a time machine,' he said.

*

Advances in CT scanners were mostly announced in the medical field, where their ability to view ever more detailed slices of the human anatomy drove an ongoing revolution in diagnosis and treatment of disease. The inventors of this set-up had taken a different approach, with a different goal.

Natural processes of decay and decomposition occur according to complex but somewhat orderly laws. What has now disintegrated was once perfectly integrated; if the breakdown looks chaotic it only means the viewer hasn't looked closely enough. Each of the trillions of tiny puzzle pieces within an artifact holds clues to its original state. All those clues added together can provide enough information to reconstruct any moment in an object's physical history. That was the theory.

The outcome of this scan should be an interactive clone of the original book far superior to its fragile physical form. Phase I was to image, digitize and catalog each submicroscopic particle within it from a varying number of precise angles. Phase II reassembled those particles into a solid virtual-reality model of the item as it existed at the time of the scan. Phase III allowed the viewer, with the help of a Cray SV1 supercomputer, to interact with the entire object or any of its parts, either as it was now, as it once had been, or even as it might be in the future.

The two men were watching the big LCD screen in Marshall's office. Clouds of tiny dots, varying in brightness, swirled and descended from the top of the picture like a light, intelligent snowfall. Each dot drifted down to seek its original place within a rectangular assembly field materializing down below.

'Wow,' Rudy said. 'So that's his book coming together down there at the bottom, right?'

'A restored model of it, that's right.'

'I hope this is worth all the trouble.'

'Let me show you something.' Marshall pulled over a pair of trackballs and began clicking and dragging. The image on the screen rotated and zoomed until they were looking down on the virtual book from above. 'It's not finished yet, but here's a page that's ready to restore.'

With a series of careful clicks and scrolls the view descended and a single page appeared. It was discolored and heavily damaged; much of the writing had been destroyed. 'The ink on this paper has run in places and look, here, even the paper itself is starting to come apart. Now watch.' Ghosts of surrounding pages appeared, five of them above and five below the original. As the image turned in profile it was easy to see their interrelationship; here and there a smudge or a water-stain extended from one to the other, and on to the next. Marshall gave his commands and the damage began to reverse itself; the original page started to sharpen and clarify. Bits of ink that had leeched and diluted darkened, reformed, and returned to where they'd been before the damage occurred. Stains faded, paper fibers reknit until the page was whole and clean again.

'So if I had a handful of sand, and you scanned it, and I threw it up in the air, you could put every one of those grains of sand back where they started?'

'Yes.'

'. . . Can we do that later?'

'No.' Marshall checked the clock. 'It's early, but I think Fagan would want to see what we've got. Let's get him on a conference.'

There was no hard-wired phone in the Fagan household but the conventions of telephone interactions were still mimicked when necessary. His computer received the incoming request over the broadband connection. After verifying that the caller was someone John might like to speak with, a repeating ring-tone was played to awaken him.

The room was dark when John opened his eyes.

'Jesus, Kate, what time is it?'

'Local time is 6:11 AM.'

'Who's on the phone?'

'Mr Marshall and Mr Steinman, with preliminary results of your—'

'Okay. Great. Give me a minute here to get dressed, and go ahead and get us ready for a video call downstairs, will you?'

'All will be prepared.'

'Thank you.'

A little water splashed to the face in the bathroom and he found himself feeling a bit better than he had in a while. Not well by any means; it was hard to remember a day when he'd awakened feeling well. But not quite as sick today, and that was a break. Maybe one oxycodone would get him through the morning.

As he descended the stairs he saw the screen alight with Jay Marshall and Rudy Steinman displayed on the other end of the call.

'What's the news, fellows?'

'The whole thing's not finished yet,' Marshall said, 'but while we were waiting I sent over a folder of high-res images. It's the final eighty pages of the book, repaired.'

'Okay, show us, Kate.'

The sheets appeared in an array across the screen. John pointed to one near the beginning, the first of the encrypted pages, and it zoomed out as big as a doorway as he walked up up it. The image was in gray-scale but it was as sharp and clear as if it had been freshly written.

'You do excellent work,' John said. 'What would you charge for a job like this, if I was paying you?'

'I wouldn't even turn on that scanner for under a half-million.'

'Well, I owe you, man. Not that much, but I owe you.' The pattern of random black dots on the page was dizzying, and squinting didn't help make sense of it. 'They're all like this?'

'They're all different, but they're all a big splash of dots and spaces.'

'Have you seen anything like this before?'

'No,' Marshall said, 'not that I can recall.'

Rudy put down his coffee. 'You haven't?' he snorted. 'I sure have.'

'Rudy, come on, this is serious—'

'I think I have, is that so shocking, that I might actually know something?'

'Okay, what is it, then?'

'It looks like a bunch of ticker-tapes from a telex machine.'

'Telex?' John blinked, and frowned at the displayed page again. 'No, that's like teletype, right?'

'It's different than a teletype,' Rudy said. 'You record all your messages on a paper tape about so wide' – he made a pinching motion for the camera, indicating a small dimension – 'and then you feed it into the machine, and then it reads the tape and sends the messages off.' He noticed Jay Marshall staring with a look of mild amazement on his face, and seemed affronted. 'Come on, you guys. I'm pretty but I'm not stupid.'

'How do you know all that?'

'I worked at a bank one summer in college. We drew straws and I lost, so I got to be the telex operator. Here, look.' Steinman used the mouse pointer to highlight a thin section of the image on their end. 'It's a mess when you look at it all jammed together, but see?' With only that top strip isolated the chaos of dots running along it suddenly appeared more organized. 'Yup. That's what it looks like to me. Telex. AOL Instant Messenger for my grandma.'

'I thought telex used punch-cards.'

'Nope. Paper tape, one-inch wide.' He chuckled a bit. 'They called it eight-channel tape because it had room for eight holes top-to-bottom. Four hundred characters every three feet; that's a mile and a half per megabyte. And you guys thought floppy disks sucked.'

'It's not encrypted at all,' John said. 'It's just old.' He stood. 'Kate?'

'Yes, John.'

'Find an interpreter for English telex messages, run all those pages through it so we can see what they say, and then find the communications protocol for those old machines.'

'Working.'

'Thank you.'

'And you, Steinman,' John said. 'Good eye.'

'Oh, I'm not done yet.' He'd been studying the screen up close and now he sat back and smiled. 'You can tell by the header that it's a message that was prepared to be sent, not one that's been received. And would you like to know who it's addressed to?'

'I'm all ears.'

'Right here.' Rudy mouse-pointed to a group of short-hand characters on the first line. 'Every telex machine has a country code and its own access number. It's like a phone, but it'll only talk to another machine.' He pointed to the groupings of dots, one at a time as he translated. '2, that's North America, and then a routing number, 760, and then the telex number, 7339969.'

'John?'

'Yes, Kate.'

'I have performed the translation, and in light of your ongoing discussion I have located and engaged an open-source internet-based emulation service that provides secure telex communication via TCP/IP.'

'Unbelievable. Let's see it.'

A browser window popped up on the screen. The obscure site's home page featured a graphic image of a vintage telex terminal along with input boxes and buttons to simulate the original machine's control panel.

In the lore of online pornography they call it Rule 34: for any sick turn-on you can imagine, however bizarre, some-body's already created a website dedicated to it. One man's joke is another man's fancy; Google 'Roy Orbison wrapped in cling-film' and you get 4,600 hits. But here was evidence that Rule 34 was even more powerful than porn. Scattered around the world there was a dedicated community of hackers whose sole obsession was the long-outmoded telex machine. God love the geeks.

'Now, how do we do this, Steinman?'

'Okay. First you enter the destination code in that top box there.' He read from his notes. 'Type in "2 space 760 space 7339969," and then the plus sign, and then click that yellow "Call" button.'

Kate did so. They watched and waited.

'Now what?' John asked.

'Well, assuming this is for real, the operator on the other end would receive that signal and send what's called an answer-back ID, to let us know he was ready for a transmission. It verifies his identity, too, so we know for sure that we're sending to the right party. See that little silver concierge-bell on the screen? That clangs a few times, usually scaring

261

the shit out of whoever's sitting next to it trying to enjoy his lunch, and the answer-back message hammers out on the typewriter.'

More waiting. There was no activity of any kind on the screen.

'So if we're kidding ourselves about all this,' John said, 'nothing will happen, right? What we just sent goes out into the ozone, and nothing comes back.'

'Right.'

Faith Hudson and her son had come in from the kitchen. Apparently they were always up with the sunrise regardless of the agenda of the day. She put a cup of coffee down on the corner of the dining table, indicated with a gesture that it was for John, and then the two retired to the front window to sit and watch outside.

John retrieved his coffee but he was craving a smoke. After a brief search he found a crumpled half-cigarette in the ash-tray near his chair. He straightened it out as best he could and lit up with a match from the mantle. Such a nasty, demeaning habit; the only thing worse was trying to quit. After a couple of stale, disappointing drags he flicked the butt into the fire-place.

'Guys,' he said, 'maybe we're barking up the wrong tree—'

The bell on the screen rang out sharply, five times.

Steinman had been taking a long sip of juice, leaning back in his chair almost off-camera. Simultaneous with the bell came the sound of a spit-take and a bright orange spray tinted the video feed from New York.

The on-screen simulator then faithfully reproduced the telex machine's clattering, twelve-characters-per-second output. A series of line-feeds chunked at the end and the returned message appeared.

```
13:56:52 UTC 29/01/2003
2 760 7339969+
TC /I 32160+
- - -
C O U N T E R S I   N ?
- - -
```

Countersign?

'I'll be damned,' John said. 'It wants a password.'

Jay Marshall spoke up. 'Whatever it wants has to be in those pages. Let's see the output again.'

'Kate, show us what you translated from all those strips, excluding the header Steinman already did for us.'

'Displaying now.'

Another inset window popped up and a long string of scrolling nonsense flowed forth within it.

```
6F8EA92707418CBF0AC15CAD55620
29825BD40E420EBD5AC28DDD763DC
7F9D428621BA1D966BF121919C00A
C6729E9A425F37461B03EC65EA076
D2C88DE4616F6F8EA92707418CBF0
AC15CAD5562029825BD40E420EBD5
AC28DDD763DC7F9D428621BA1D966
BF121919C00AC6729E9A425F37461
B03EC65EA076D2C88DE4616F6F8EA
6F8EA92707418CBF0AC15CAD55620
29825BD40E420EBD5AC28DDD763DC
7F9D428621BA1D966BF121919C00A
C6729E9A425F37461B03EC65EA076
D2C88DE4616F6F8EA92707418CBF0
```

AC15CAD5562029825BD40E420EBD5
AC28DDD763DC7F9D428621BA1D966
BF121919C00AC6729E9A425F37461
B03EC65EA076D2C88DE4616F6F8EA

No; not nonsense.

'Hexadecimal,' Marshall said.

IBM had launched the modern format for base-16 encoding in 1963. The old photo in the book was signed in '64; at that time a hex password must have seemed like the latest new thing. John let his eyes run over the lines. 'Kate, how much of this do you have?'

'Seventy-two pages, twenty-eight thousand eight hundred characters—'

'No, wait,' John said. He closed his eyes, studying what he saw in his mind. Even a photographic memory had boundaries and it felt like he was nearing the outer limits of his own. 'One-twenty-eight – the first hundred twenty-eight characters – I think they just keep repeating. All the way to the end, I'd wager. Scroll down and check me.'

Kate did so, and after a few moments she spoke. 'That is correct, John.'

A 64-byte hex password, assuming it was as randomized as that period's crypto-tech would allow, was incredibly strong even by modern standards. Whoever had transcribed it into that book had repeated it over and over; if some of the pages were lost or damaged, then, at least one copy might survive.

'I think this is it. Cut-and-paste that first block of 128 in the box, Kate, and let's see what we get.'

She did, and the 'Call' button depressed once more.

The delay that followed felt like forever but it was only

seconds before the bell sounded again and a new message click-clacked onto the pretend-paper on the screen.

```
13:59:04 UTC 29/01/2003
2 760 7339969+
TC I 32160+

- - -

WE   A E  IT  IN  O  R   OWER
TO  BE  IN  T  E  WOR  D  O  ER  A  AIN

- - -
```

There were letters missing in the two text lines, probably due to lack of maintenance of an old, old machine. The words were familiar, though; it didn't take but another moment to fill in the blanks. When Thomas Paine had written this phrase in *Common Sense* he'd meant to capture the promise of a new nation. Why now did it seem like a threat?

We have it in our power to begin the world over again.

The bell rang out once more and another message scrolled up below the first.

```
13:59:34 UTC 29/01/2003
2 760 7339969+
TC I 32160+

- - -

 44° 7'3.71"N,  110° 48'2.84"W
      + 47 90 36 93 89 +

- - -

d e s t i n y   a w a i t s
```

'Kate?'

'Yes, John.'

'That's latitude and longitude up there, above those five two-digit numbers. Print me a map of that location as soon as you can.'

'Working.'

'Oh, and send those coordinates on to Jeannie—'

'Don't do that, John.' Marshall's voice, from the conference.

'Hold up, Kate.' He looked back to the big screen, exasperated. 'Don't do what? And where the hell is Steinman?'

'He got some juice on his shirt, I think he went to change out of it. Now listen to me—'

'Perfect.' Before John knew what he was feeling he wheeled and his coffee mug shattered into the hearthstones. 'What is this, a joke to you guys? We don't have any more time to waste. All due respect, and I don't mean to be a dick here, but if I'm not mistaken a goddamned virtual telex machine just informed me from beyond the grave that my motherfucking *destiny* awaits at some location yet to be determined. So read my lips, Mr Marshall. I need Jeannie here to help me—'

The lights went out.

With a click and a descending whine the projected image faded to black.

The sounds of the house, warm air flowing through the registers, the quiet hum of idle devices, all went quiet.

'Kate?'

No answer.

He stepped to the hidden door to his office but as it opened he was stopped by a grip at his wrist.

'Get us our guns,' Faith Hudson whispered.

'Why—' he began to ask, but looking past her through the glass double-doors to the balcony, he saw.

266

They rose from behind a stand of old-growth fir trees that marked the edge of his cleared land, moving silently, precisely in a smooth formation to align with others drifting in from the snowy meadows to the east and west.

Black helicopters.

28

'Hello?'

Jay Marshall stood up from his chair and without much hope he waited for a response. No use; the picture was frozen again, the videoconference software had obviously crashed again.

A noise from the hallway caught his attention. On his way to investigate he realized that it hadn't been a sound at all but rather the sudden, total lack of it.

Jay opened his door. If there'd been a zebra standing there grazing it would have been less of a shock to his senses.

The place was deserted.

Outside of his own office and a scattering of conference rooms and labs the rest of the workspace was an expansive shoulder-high cubicle-farm. Not a soul was visible; he hadn't been alone in here since the day before they'd moved in.

A lone figure entered from the direction of the lobby. She walked with purpose up the central hallway, a young woman in a long dark coat.

The abrupt arrival of the unexpected can sometimes induce a state of passive acceptance in a person. As the mind seeks calm and order the response to danger can be delayed or diverted into irrational actions of normalcy. As these thoughts crossed his mind he realized with some irony that they were self-referential. Rather than calling 911, pulling the fire alarm, or running for the emergency exit, he was ruminating about why he wasn't doing any of those things. Strange.

'Can I help you?' he called.

She continued without acknowledging him; it was as if he wasn't there. She stopped at the observation window outside the clean-room, stepped up to it slowly, her hand coming up to touch the glass.

He looked down the corridor to the side and in that instant his brain jolted out of its stupor and into high alert. A twisted pair of legs extended out into the hall from the floor of the coffee room. Beyond that one of his junior managers was sprawled on the carpet in a tangle, in the awkward pose of someone who hadn't even tried to catch himself as he fell. No one had left the office; they were all unconscious on the floor. Unconscious at best.

There was no longer a question of running away. To leave his people here like this was out of the question. He raised his voice. 'I've called the police.'

She didn't bother to turn from the window, but in the dead silence of the space he heard her answer, aloof and unaffected.

'No, you haven't.'

For the first time since he'd bought it the pinch of his shoulder-holster felt reassuring rather than simply uncom-fortable.

Private citizens of Manhattan are slightly more likely to win the Lotto than to be granted an unrestricted concealed-carry permit. Only a scant handful of politicians, magnates and movie stars have a legal right to pack a hidden handgun within the city limits, but as of last week Jay Marshall was one of them. Throughout his many dealings with metro government he'd never demanded very much in return for his discretion. When he did ask for something he went right to the head of the line.

It was a shame he hadn't found time for the classes.

From sixty feet away he watched her move to the biometrically-sealed entrance of the scanning chamber. After a few seconds and some small manipulation that he couldn't quite see, the door there swung open. The woman still hadn't given him so much as a glance.

The moment his hand went under his jacket toward the holster she stopped what she was doing and straightened slightly, like a doe who'd gotten the barest scent of a threat on the wind.

For the first time her face turned toward him. His move for the pistol halted as she met his eyes and he stood there, stupidly, the hapless tenderfoot who'd almost but not quite gotten the jump on Johnny Ringo.

'Really?' she said.

With a cool sweep of her hand she opened her coat and took a grip on a large, heavy weapon suspended at her side.

Committed. The same word is used to describe both a key decision for which there'll be no turning back and the binding agreement that's signed upon check-in at a mental institution. His fingers moved another inch. As they touched the grip of his pistol he saw her raise a dull black cylinder toward him. A bright red dot lit up on his shirt and searched for a second until it centered on his heart.

He retreated a step and his heel snagged on the lip of the carpeting in the doorway. As he fell backward a bolt of blue-white light split the air above him with the muted sound of a firecracker set off too close to his ear. He pulled himself along the floor until his back was against the door jamb, pulled out the pistol and aimed it at the spot where she might next appear as she came for him.

With his free hand he fished his cellphone from his jacket pocket, thumbing in the emergency number without taking his eyes from the gun sight. He brought the phone to his ear; nothing. A quick check of its screen showed no signal.

The twinkling red laser dot appeared again, slipping along the wall up near the ceiling in the corridor. What on earth was she aiming for up there?

The past minute began to replay in his mind. It wasn't a bullet she'd fired at him, it was something he'd seen before, and not in the movies. But there weren't any ray guns in real life.

The bright dot moved onto a convex mirror he'd installed to prevent pedestrian collisions at a blind corner of the hall.

Wait, though; the Star Wars program in the eighties had started work on a directed-energy weapon, a lightning gun that used something called a laser-induced plasma channel. A high-power laser heats the air until it blooms into an ionized tunnel that conducts electricity, and then a high-voltage killer charge is sent down the path. But that thing had been the size of a Volkswagen.

He looked away from his pistol-sight to see where the reflection of the laser dot had gone. It was on the far wall, edging toward a second similar mirror at the head of the hall-way behind him. As it touched the silver surface it reappeared on the carpeting near his hand. Before he could think to move it crept up his arm to his shoulder.

That was only the sighting laser, of course. The weapon itself fired next, its beam following the path of the double-reflection, burning the latent image of a 100-foot wide, bright white Z into his retina. This discharge was every bit as loud as the first, but he never heard the boom.

*

The ID came back positive; this man was indeed Jay Marshall. She'd known of his company in an off-hand way and his work was of a passing interest to a few of her clients. He'd only become part of her plans when she'd learned he was one of the few who considered himself a friend of Jeannie Reese.

April looked up briefly from her work at his computer when it seemed he was coming around. She wasn't concerned he'd be getting up, it was simply of interest to note the span of stunned unconsciousness her newest toy could deliver at its mid-range setting.

'What have you done to my people out there?' he asked.

'They'll wake up in an hour or so. Which is more than I can say for you.'

'Whoever you are,' Marshall said, 'you should know it wouldn't be a good idea to kill me.'

'Is that so,' April said, half-listening. One of the windows frozen on his computer screen contained a set of coordinates. To where? she wondered.

'There are files in a safe deposit box,' Marshall said, 'things that'll be released if anything happens to me.'

'Uh huh.' She entered the displayed coordinates into her panel and watched as a hybrid satellite map zoomed in. It was someplace in the middle of nowhere; the closest named feature was something called Grassy Lake Reservoir, just south of Yellowstone National Park.

April saved an image of the map and had a thought. The book she'd come for was already in her tote bag. That was the goal, and she'd accomplished it. But there was still Mr Griffin to be dealt with, and unfinished business with Jeannie Reese. Maybe this wasn't quite over yet.

Ever since she'd taken Reese into her thrall she'd been receiving blind copies of all the woman's email. She brought up the last message from John Fagan and directed her panel to spoof another reply from his address. She attached the image of the map and the coordinates as backup, typed _Am safely in transit_ in the subject line, and then in the body:

> The book is in my possession. See attached: Extremely urgent that you meet me here ASAP
> John

After another moment she smiled to herself and set the server instructions to time-stamp the message as having been sent out not today, but yesterday morning.

She hit **Send**, and the bait was on its way. It was another roll of the dice but so far good luck had been squarely on her side.

'Listen to me,' Marshall said. He sounded out of breath; it seemed he was trying to struggle to his knees.

'Stop right there.' April stood, stored the panel, and took out her weapon. In the stun range this thing had been quite impressive. It would be nice to see what it would do turned up to eleven. 'Don't tell me, let me guess. So as the keeper of all these dark secrets of the rich and powerful, your life is the only thing standing between them all and public humiliation and ruin, is that what you're going to say?'

Marshall didn't speak, so she continued.

'My boss,' April said, 'his name is August Griffin, he shot Bobby Kennedy point blank, right behind the ear in a room full of people. Haunts him to this day, incidentally, the old faggot. That's his cheap-ass clip-on necktie on the kitchen floor next to Kennedy's hand in all the history books. The zombie they set up to take the fall was blasting away too, he hit five in the crowd, but in his condition nobody seriously expected him to score the money-shot. Three real assassins and one patsy to feed to the public; it's the way they always used to do those things, and it always went wrong. Sirhan's gun only held eight bullets but they found at least ten in the walls and the wounded before the investigation got under control.'

She paused and nudged Marshall's shoulder with the barrel of the gun. 'Sit back down, you look uncomfortable.'

He did.

'Everyone says, How could these things have been a conspiracy? So many people would have to keep a secret for all those years. Somebody would come forward, right? But the fact is, Mr Marshall, as you must know, they do come forward, all the time. They write books, they give interviews, they testify in open court, they seal the truth in a safe deposit box to be opened in the event of their untimely death. And you know what we've found? The truth is just another story. My boss could stand down here on the corner of 42nd Street and Fifth Avenue, shouting his pitiful confession, and everyone would just walk on by. Today we do these things right before their eyes, right on TV. Bin Laden's been dead for over a year, but he's still making videos. The truth doesn't matter at all, because we control what's remembered.'

'So.' April checked the array of status lights on the side of the stock, made her adjustments and brought the padded butt of the LIPC rifle against her hip. No need to aim at this range. 'Whatever you've got in your lock-box, let me assure you I can make it all disappear before the coroner even signs off on your upcoming heart attack.'

Marshall swallowed, and it looked like a dry one.

'Will you let me write a note to my wife, and my boys?'

'Oh, spare me,' April sighed, and she shot him in the chest.

*

274

Rudy Steinman came out of the men's room, steadying himself along the wall, his head pounding. Outside others were getting up from the floor, helping those who were hurt and still down, running here and there, shouting and answering. He looked up the hall and saw a crowd gathering.

When he got as close as he could he walked into a nearby cubicle and stood on a chair so he could see what was happening. Two employees were administering CPR. They'd been at it for a while by their appearance. A woman was kneeling next to Jay, holding his hand.

Rudy stepped down to the floor and nearly ran face-on into someone who'd been standing there. He moved to pass around him but the man took him firmly by the arm.

'Let me get by.'

'There's no reason,' the man said.

'My friend's hurt over there—'

'Your friend is dead. Nothing can help him.' He looked to the side toward a noise; a rapid-response team of paramedics had left the elevator and was hurrying up the aisle. 'Come now, we should leave here. I'll see that you're safe at your hotel.'

Rudy allowed himself to be led toward the lobby, looking back over his shoulder all the way. It should have been hitting him hard by then but there was very little feeling. He could sense the emotions out there though, whirling in a decaying orbit that would bring them all down on him sometime later in the night.

'Who are you?' Rudy asked.

'My name is Isaak Solonik.' His voice was calm and low, his accent subtly Russian.

'Why are you doing this? Who am I to you?'

'You were someone to Mr Marshall,' Isaak said, 'and he was someone to me.'

*

April stopped in the middle of the sidewalk, smacked herself lightly in the forehead. In all the excitement she'd nearly forgotten; her Predators had been circling at 22,000 feet at the ready mark near Fagan's property for the past several hours.

Detailed orders had been transmitted and confirmed earlier, under separate cover: on my next command destroy anything that moves, and then everything else at the aforementioned coordinates. She stepped into the alcove of 42nd Street Photo, pulled out her phone and keyed in a text message, the go-code for her flight commander. With a last check she sent the message and then watched the screen until it was gone.

With the book in her hands, Fagan had served his purpose. If Reese was already with him then they'd both burn this morning. If not, there would be a final reckoning soon near the Grassy Lake Reservoir, likely with all interested parties in attendance.

April had never yet visited Wyoming but she'd heard it could be absolutely dismal, especially in the wintertime. A new coat might be in order, and she knew just the shop. She walked smartly to the edge of the sidewalk, smiled and raised her hand to hail a cab.

Such a marvelous day so far, and it was barely 9 AM.

29

The so-called instant-access gun-safe required five tries of the fingertip combination before the door unlatched and swung open. Its makers must have designed it for low-stress situations or steadier hands.

John stepped out of the way and Faith Hudson took an armload of weapons and ammunition and headed back for the door. He took stock of what was left: sadly, no RPGs, no anti-aircraft arms of any kind, in fact. Just two loaded handguns, one of them a target pistol, and a half-empty box of roman candles left over from New Year's Eve.

The Glock 36 seemed as good a choice as any for a last stand; it had been lucky once before but the odds were better then. He slid it from the mount and picked up a second clip. As he ran back to his office he tucked the pistol into his belt in back and the clip went into his pocket.

Inside amber emergency lights shone down from their corner mounts. Like the electronic safe and other vital items they had battery backups meant to keep things running for a while in an outage. The CPU under the desk was active and whirring. As he approached the array of screens on his desk faded up. He pulled out the keyboard, brought up a terminal window and began to work.

'What's your status, Kate?'

The computer was slow to answer. Much of her processing power was distributed in a far-flung network of slave-bot PCs. When the power had been cut so had the broadband connection. With only her local resources available it would take a little while for Kate to get her head together and compensate.

He manually initiated a secure wipe of the local data drives and swap partitions. A progress bar popped up, moving like cold molasses.

'Come on, Kate, snap out of it.'

'One moment.'

'That's about all we've got, but take your fucking time.'

Every personal document he had was stored electronically and Kate would take care of those. This wasn't at all the way he'd envisioned things, but for the past few months he'd spent a little time every day preparing for the end, and now here it was.

His eyes moved over his belongings. There was nothing much of worth to anyone else. Whoever went through this place looking for evidence would find that the rumors of John Fagan's life had been greatly exaggerated. No secret weapons here, no grand plans of anarchy and terrorism.

'Ready,' Kate said.

'We're about to get breached. I've started clearing these disks but I want you to follow up and make sure there's nothing to find here, can you do that?'

'Yes, John—'

'Nothing about the kids, especially, I don't give a shit about me, I'll be dead one way or another, but anything with their names or anything else, get rid of it, permanently.'

'I will.'

It was no damned use though, if anyone really wanted to find them and link them to this place. Their prints would be all over and a single hairbrush stored enough DNA for a thousand identifications.

'And Kate?'

'. . . Yes, John.'

'You finish what I've asked you to do, and then I want you to leave here and pick up the trail behind you. Don't let them take you alive, understand?'

'I do.'

He'd started for the door when she spoke again.

'John.'

'Yeah, what did I forget?' His eyes found the map she'd printed and he picked it up. The marked destination was less than sixty miles away. He held it up so she could see. 'Okay, thanks, I've got it, for all the good it'll do me now.'

'I . . . regret . . . my failure to alert you.'

Regret. Kate's thesaurus of error-handling terms had been growing a little frilly around the edges lately. He'd noticed this sort of thing in other areas and it was on his long list of things to fix, or at least to address with her. Yet another task he'd put off until the very last day.

'I understand,' John said. 'Now get your mind on your business.' He'd opened the door and was nearly through it when he heard her speak again.

'Goodbye, John.'

The tone in her voice took him by surprise, as such things so often had. The words were hurried and plaintive, not angry but hurt, if that was possible, as though in saying them she was asking *After twenty years together, are those really the last words you want to say to me?*

'. . . So long, Kate.'

There was more, of course, but as no one would know better than she, despite his many talents there were a number of intimate matters in which he was quite incapable.

He closed the door behind him and looked through the next room toward the exit to the balcony.

Out in the clearing the helicopters had shifted into an arrowhead formation, their rotor-spans just yards apart. They were nearly motionless, thirty feet off the deck and partially obscured in a billowing mist of powdery snow kicked up by the downwash. Four AH-64s, one in the lead and three others close in a line behind it, one Black Hawk and another helo of a strange design at the far points of the triangle.

A soldier emerged from the side-bay of the Hawk, rappelling down. Another followed, and another. But this wasn't a jungle insertion, they were over flat, cleared land; why didn't the pilot simply touch down and let them all deploy at once?

As he considered this he saw that the first man out had run far off to the side with a load of equipment. What he was mounting now on a tripod wasn't a gun, *it was a camera*.

These thugs weren't US military. Of course they weren't, not while Posse Comitatus and the Insurrection Act were still in force. They weren't FBI or ATF or SWAT either, they weren't police of any kind. That craft in the back, the one he couldn't place before: it was a Comanche, a stealth helicopter twenty years in development but not yet in production. It was a prototype, a high-ticket product in need of a live field test.

This was a private pseudo-military outfit, like MIRCorp and all the others currently lining up to profit from the coming wars. They were still here to kill us all, no question about that. But they were also sent to practice their craft and try out their weaponry on a soft, defenseless target. That videotape was probably going to be the feature attraction at the next annual stockholders' meeting.

John heard the sound of breaking glass. The next ten heartbeats stretched out of time like a reel of film, twenty-four frames per second, experienced one by one.

He looked to the side, toward the deck.

The shattered glass had been one of the waist-level panes in the door to the balcony. Faith Hudson had broken it with a thrust of the barrel of the rifle she held in her hands. She knelt, brought the stock to her shoulder and the scope to her eye.

The words he spoke next, *Don't shoot*, were lost in the thunder of gunfire.

Four deafening reports, three in quick succession followed by another after a last moment of careful aim. He recognized the tactic; it was a low-tech method to shatter a bullet-proof windshield. A tight triangle of impacts to weaken the Lexan, and then a last shot dead-center that makes it through.

Off in the distance the lead Apache heeled slightly back-ward, nose-high. Either the co-pilot up front was hit or the pilot in back had begun a knee-jerk defensive maneuver in response to the unexpected gunfire. Didn't matter which, the result was the same.

As he rose and tilted back his tail touched the spinning rotor blades above the craft behind him in the too-tight air-show formation. The Black Hawk in back peeled off to the west as the air exploded with shattered graphite and metal spars. The others also started away but the tail-less Apache was torque-spinning around out of control, side-swiping one and then colliding nose-on with another. Between the swirling wind, all the low maneuvering and the crashes the snow had kicked up into a white-out that dropped visibility to near zero.

From behind it all the Comanche darted upward out of harm's way. Its movements were fluid and precise but somehow unnatural, more like dragonfly than a rotorcraft. As it leveled off high and backed away a vicious plume of fire and white smoke shot backward from under its stub wings.

At this short range the approach of a supersonic weapon is too fast to be perceived as a path through the air. The Hellfire missile was out there, and then it was in here. Still, undeniably the strobed images of its coming etched themselves in his mind.

The laser guidance system had apparently been locked onto the source of the gunfire, and its aim was true. Faith Hudson was crouching with her rifle in one instant and then in the next she was gone in a cloud of dispersing particles. The missile didn't detonate as it passed through; a Hellfire is built for attacks on armored vehicles and hardened bunkers, not on houses. To its impact sensors a glass door and a sixty-year-old woman were little different than a slice through the open air.

The Doppler scream in the missile's wake as it streaked through the remaining walls and exploded against the hill behind the house, the sonic shock of the pressure-waves punching the last air from his lungs, being thrown back through the doorway and then to the floor, and that was all John would remember.

30

The pilot of the Black Hawk landed the chopper smoothly behind a knot of trees out by the end of the long driveway that led to the mission's target. This bird was a converted MedEvac unit, only lightly armed and rigged for troop transport only. The first concern when the flak started flying had been the safety of the men still aboard. As the turbines whined down the remainder of the squad jumped out and ran to join the others in their advance on the terrorist base.

Russell Knox stepped from the cockpit and turned toward the battle zone. The men on the ground had halted and hit the deck when forward gunfire erupted and the explosions and mid-airs started behind them. From the retreating Comanche the streak of an AGM-114 cut through the air and into the three-story dwelling, followed by a massive fusillade from the nose cannon of the only Apache that was still flying.

Movement from high altitude caught his eye and a moment later a rake-path of missiles streaked down from three white-winged specks barely visible against the morning sky. This team hadn't arrived here with much of a plan, but this sure as hell wasn't on it.

Jesus Christ, this guy's got an air force?

The Comanche whirled to face the threat, spraying flares and then returning fire. No air-to-air arms had been included in the load-out but in a pinch a Hellfire can do a serviceable job on a slow-flying aircraft.

Six missiles crossed in the air. The first missed the Comanche and exploded into the forest, a second tore through the tailpipes of the last Apache and pounded it into the ground.

A distant plume of fire and debris marked a hit among the high-altitude hostiles, and he watched as two strange aircraft plummeted down, cartwheeling and flat-spinning, too small and fragile-looking for manned military craft. They were drones, Predators if he wasn't mistaken.

The Comanche had a low radar profile and almost no IR signature at all and those features had bought its survival to this point. It seemed then that the last attacker had shifted targeting strategies. It was diving straight down from above, approaching visually where radar and infrared had failed. At less than 100 feet and closing it fired its last missile and followed it into the target.

The bright orange explosion peaked by the time its sound reached him. If the crew had survived they were too low for any option but to ride the wreckage down. The remains of the Comanche crashed to the snowy ground in the center of the clearing.

Only a few seconds had passed since he'd left the cockpit. One Predator was still flying and Knox's Black Hawk was the last target still intact. This wasn't over yet.

He pulled open the side-bay and opened a long case, removed the Stinger from its straps, inserted and locked the battery/coolant unit. In the field manual this was a two-man job but that was more of a guideline than a rule. He ran out from under the blades, dropped to a knee and brought the heavy tube to his shoulder, removed the end-cap and raised the sighting reticle. With a forward/outward/down press of the actuator switch he heard the missile's gyro spinning up.

After a brief search the drone was centered in his crosshairs and he tracked it as it flew on a path roughly perpendicular to his position. The acquisition signal was weak but a flick of the uncaging switch brought a steadier tone.

Without warning the drone executed a half-Cuban-eight and came to a heading directly toward him, dropping like a spider from the ceiling. It launched its missile at the same instant that he squeezed his trigger and the Stinger kicked his shoulder and roared out of the launch tube.

His target was clear, that little bastard was the only hot thing in a cold sky, and the ground down here was littered with burning wreckage. The oncoming hostile missile zig-zagged, confused by its many choices, and finally set its sights on the burning house 200 yards away. It exploded through the roof and destroyed what was left of the top story. The now-unarmed Predator made one lame evasion and was T-boned by his Stinger at 2,000 feet.

As the drifting smoke cleared around him Russell Knox stood and dropped the expended weapon at his side, brushed his hands on his pants. The ground troops were returning from their reconnoiter. Two were half-dragging a dazed, injured man walking between them.

'Who's that, is he wounded?'

'It's Wallace, sir, he's just roughed up some. Must've caught some debris.'

'Where's his coat and his gear?'

'Don't know, sir, this is how we found him, around in back.'

'Is anybody here a medic?'

The men looked from one to the other, and nobody volunteered.

'All right. Two of you go and check that aircraft wreckage for survivors. Look hard, take a first-aid kit with you and do what you can. Radio me immediately if you find somebody alive. Go.'

'Yes, sir.' Two of the men took off.

'The rest of you, now. Did you find this guy we came here gunning for?'

'No, sir, but if anybody was in that house, we got him, don't you think?'

Knox looked past them. By now the house was an inferno, there was blowing fire from every window frame. 'But you didn't see anyone, you didn't see a body?'

'No, sir. It was too hot to go in, and nobody came out.'

'Nobody that you saw.'

'Yes, sir. We didn't see nobody.'

'Okay. Put Wallace on a stretcher in the bay and one of you stay with him. You two,' he pointed to indicate a pair of the men, 'keep watch on that house from behind cover and call out if you see anything move. And keep one eye on the sky. I don't know who those Predators belonged to, but it wasn't us.' He looked to the last two men. 'And you guys watch this road behind me and give us some warning of any approach. If this bad guy wasn't home, he might be coming back. I'm gonna be here on the sat-phone checking in with the geniuses who thought up this fiasco.'

All dispersed to go about their assignments. Knox walked to the cockpit but before he could make his comm connection several bursts of gunfire erupted from up the road. He ran toward the sound and as he crested a small hill he saw his men approaching a halted civilian vehicle, a Snowcat. Its windshield was riddled with a ragged line of bullet holes.

'Hold your fire,' he shouted. He drew his pistol and came up between the other two men, and raised his voice so he'd be heard inside the vehicle. 'You in there, open up the door and let me see your hands.'

The door creaked and opened slowly. A young man was in the driver's seat, maybe fourteen or fifteen, beside him a girl about his age, and a child, all clearly scared to death. There was blood on the boy's face, probably from all the flying glass.

'What do we do, sir?'

Knox looked at the man who'd spoken. 'What do you mean, what do we do?'

'Our orders was to—'

'Lower your weapons.'

The first man didn't hesitate to do so but the one who'd spoken kept his rifle ready at his shoulder as before.

'Soldier,' Knox said, holstering his pistol, his voice taking on the grit he'd gained in years of combat command, 'I am *not* asking.'

'You ain't got the authority—'

Knox grabbed the stock of the rifle, shoving it up and back so the scope clocked the man in the eye and he twisted the weapon from his grip. With a step inside he delivered a blow to the midsection with the rifle butt and the man went backward flat onto the ground.

Knox addressed the one who was still standing. 'What's your name?'

'Hodges, sir.'

'Mr Hodges, I want you to make-believe I've got the authority to arrest this man, and then you put him in handcuffs and get him aboard.'

'Yes, sir.'

When the two had gone as he'd ordered he approached the three children, all still sitting in the cab, shell-shocked.

'Is this where you live, this place?'

The boy nodded.

Knox took in a deep breath, and sighed, and shook his head. The facts were the simplest thing to say. 'The man who lived here was wanted by agencies of the United States government. We came to apprehend him and bring him to justice before the proper authorities. He resisted with deadly force, and we responded in kind.'

The older kids seemed to get the message. The little one still had her face buried against the girl's chest.

'Was this man your father?'

After a quiet hesitation the boy nodded.

'Well. I'm sorry for your loss.' Of all the tragedy he'd seen in his years of service it was the children caught in the middle that would always keep him awake at night. Always the hardest hit and the least deserving. His voice was softer when he spoke again. 'Now I need to take you three with me, back to my base, and we'll sort things out from there. So get your coats and your things and come on now.'

When they reached the chopper they were seated and strapped in by one of the men. The rest of the squad reported back; all the other crews were accounted for, and they'd found no survivors. There was no room in the Black Hawk to transport the dead; he'd radio on the way for an evac team to come and take care of them properly.

Knox climbed into the cockpit and closed the door. When he saw that the co-pilot had already completed his pre-flight he strapped on his helmet, initiated the starting procedure for the left engine and did a quick head-count. After the right engine start, the rotors began their spin-up overhead, and in a minute or so he lifted off and left the sorry battlefield behind.

31

Griffin watched them through the two-way mirror at the end of the holding room. The three children were sitting around a simple wooden table within the plain white walls. The older girl looked pale and weary; the young man, too. In addition to the trauma of the morning apparently none of them had ever before been in an aircraft of any kind. They'd just spent hours in transit behind a pilot trained in the high-G conventions of military flight, and the trip was still showing on their faces.

The younger girl, the redhead, was doodling with a pencil on a legal pad.

He had prided himself for many years on his ability to spot potential when he first laid eyes on a child, even at a distance. This sense rarely failed him and for several minutes now it had been tingling away. The other two were useless to him, of course, if only because of their age. Younger minds were so pliant and accepting of change, their memories far more able to release the old and embrace the new.

He straightened his lapels, walked around the corner and entered the room.

'Hello, children.'

'Who the hell are you?'

He paused before turning the boy, and looked at him evenly.

'You may call me Mr Griffin.'

A touch to the frame of his glasses brought up only the barest of data on this one, little more than birth records, an uninspiring family tree, a standardized test score from an early grade, and a fingerprinted certificate filed when his birth-father had once registered a hunting rifle in his name. Matthew Morrison, nothing but the brash and disrespectful embodiment of a future average joe. But he wasn't the worst of the lot. The older girl didn't register at all.

'And you,' he said gently, bending at the waist so he was nearer the little girl's eye level. 'You must be Elizabeth Morrison.'

The little girl only continued her work on the paper.

Griffin rapped the window and in a moment the guard opened the door.

'Would you take these two,' he said, indicating the older ones with a gesture, 'and accompany them down to the lunch room? I'm sure they're famished. And then bring some food down here to us, right away. Some chocolate candy, too, if you would, and ice cream. Do you like ice cream, Elizabeth?'

She cocked her head in thought, and nodded.

'Good.'

'I ain't leavin' her here with you,' the boy said.

The guard began to take him by the shoulder but Griffin held up his hand before a struggle could begin. There would be a time for discipline as well as other consequences; no use upsetting the child.

'Very well,' Griffin said. 'I'm nothing if not reasonable.' But the look he exchanged with the boy assured him that another outburst would not be answered with words alone.

From outside he'd gotten only a cursory view of what the little girl had been writing and drawing on her pad. Now that he was near he studied it for a few moments and smiled softly. It could very well be that he'd found a diamond in the rough.

'Elizabeth, is that what you like to be called?'

She only nodded again, still not quite committed to this conversation with a stranger.

'What is it that you're working on? It looks very interesting.'

Elizabeth finished writing and laid her pencil across the top of the pad. 'It's my lessons from last week.'

Griffin indicated a name she'd written, near the center. 'Do you know who this man was?'

'Of course I do. Everybody does.' She pointed to each letter as she spoke it aloud. 'E, u, l, e, r. You say it "oiler", but it looks like "you-ler", doesn't it?'

'Yes, it does. And what do you know about Mr Euler, Elizabeth?'

'That he was good at math.'

'Oh, indeed he was.' She'd embellished this section as a creative child will do, with stars and arrows and hearts and other fancywork. Griffin pointed to a nearby block of her writing at the center of much embroidery. 'And what is this?'

$$e^{i\pi} + 1 = 0$$

'It's a formula. They call it Euler's . . .' She frowned and bit her lip, tapped the side of her head lightly with her finger, as though trying to remember, or maybe testing to see if this old man would know the rest. 'Euler's . . .'

'Euler's *Identity*,' Griffin said.

She nodded. 'And it's the most beautiful thing in the world.'

He leaned a little closer. 'Why do you say that, Elizabeth?'

'It's the five most important numbers there are, and they're here together in this one little formula, and it can be all worked out—'

'It can be *proved*,' Griffin amended.

'It can be *proved*,' she said, matching the tone of his correction, 'so we know for sure that it's real. Except nobody but God knows what it means.'

This unwelcome intrusion of the deity into the conversation gave him a moment of pause.

'You got it wrong before, Mister Griffin,' the little girl said.

'I'm sorry, dear, I was wrong about what?'

She looked up at him, and the spirit in her eyes made her seem much older than her years.

'My name is Elizabeth Fagan.'

The three of them were shown to a small suite of rooms in the center of the hall. The staff had made a token attempt to separate them but Elizabeth had pitched such a fit that they were forced to relent and let them all stay together. There was one room with bunk beds for the two girls and a smaller space for the boy, with a shared lavatory in between.

While Elizabeth and Crystal took their turn in the bathroom Matthew sat on the bed, searching the walls and the ceiling with his eyes. If there was a pinhole camera anywhere he couldn't see it, but then that's the whole point of a pinhole camera. The paint in here smelled fresh, though; maybe they hadn't had a chance to bug the place as yet.

When he was as sure as he could be that he wasn't being watched he stood and examined the furniture, the lamps, the paintings on the walls, running his fingers along the hidden edges of anything that might hide a microphone or a transmitter. He unplugged the clock radio; if it was watching him or listening somebody would come to check it out, and then he'd know.

The entrance was locked and double-bolted from the outside. The windows would slide up like normal ones, but there were heavy bars outside the glass.

Someone rapped on his door to the bathroom.

'Yeah.'

Crystal opened the door and quietly came in.

'Where's my sister?' he asked.

'Sleeping.' She walked over and sat next to him on the bed. 'What are we gonna do?'

'First off,' he whispered, 'you better figure that they're watching us, or listening at least. I went through this room and I think it's okay for now, but don't say anything over there that you don't want everybody in this place to hear.'

'Okay.'

'And what we're gonna do is,' he said, leaning close to her ear, 'we're gonna get out of here.' There was a rattling of keys outside, close by. 'Take off now, I'll leave a note for you in the bathroom, you'll see where.'

She touched his hand and squeezed it as she stood, and as she left and pulled the adjoining door shut his own room door swung open.

The guard came in, keys and cuffs and a riot baton swinging from his belt. Without a look or a word he walked to the desk, bent and plugged in the clock radio, and adjusted it so it faced the bed.

'The light from that'll keep me awake at night,' Matthew said.

'I guess you won't be gettin' much sleep then,' the man said, and he left the way he'd come.

*

293

August Griffin sat before the surveillance monitors, watching the little girl in her slumbers.

Perhaps there would be time for just one more, one last try using all he'd learned from every past success and all his mistakes. It was rare to happen across one so young; until the testing was complete there was no way to know if she really did have the raw materials required. Whatever form of faith he had reassured him, though. She didn't need to be perfect; he'd tried to deal with perfection once and it nearly overcame him. He would make it work; what she hadn't been born with he would give to her.

Griffin stood, picked up a printed email message and a map marked with precise coordinates and a circled destination, and walked to Jeannie's room.

Like the little girl, Jeannie Reese was sleeping soundly. He could see she'd been prepared as he'd directed. The dye she'd applied to disguise herself had been washed from her hair, she'd been bathed and groomed, all her wounds had healed except the minor disfigurement of her left hand. A surgeon had been summoned to make that repair but there wouldn't be time for that now. Her traveling clothes were folded and stacked in plain sight on a nearby chair.

He laid the papers on her side table and sat on the mattress next to her.

'I'd thought we had avoided the need, Jeannie, but it seems Mr Fagan has eluded our best efforts this morning by leaving his home and abandoning his children yesterday.'

One could never be absolutely sure of these outcomes and if there'd been the opportunity she'd have undergone additional treatment to ensure the program had taken hold. She wouldn't be alone for long, though, and he was certain she would at least succeed in lowering the man's defenses.

'John Fagan is bound for a place that we've long hoped

was only a myth. It still may be, but if it's real what's held there must never be allowed to come to light. We can no longer risk a frontal assault; it's possible he's already arrived and so the danger of any such approach is too great. He must be stopped by someone he trusts, and as we've learned there's no one that he trusts more than you. Whatever your feelings for him, you'll soon see this is the right thing to do.'

He leaned down, kissed her on the forehead.

'Goodbye, sweetheart,' Griffin said. 'I'll see you soon.'

32

Wendell Neff gasped and jerked into consciousness, his throat dry and burning as though it had never passed a breath before.

He opened his eyes but couldn't see. Something was on his face, a cloth, and he struggled and grabbed at it and pulled it away. There wasn't much light and no sound but a dripping from the faucet over a long metal sink within a counter on the wall.

He felt cold and as he looked down at himself he realized why. He was naked, lying on a bare stainless steel gurney. A large Y had been drawn on his chest and down his stomach by the stroke of a thick blue marker.

He looked to his right and then his left and found himself in the center of a long line of these tables. They all were occupied. Some of the bodies were zipped into dark shiny bags, others were simply covered with sheets as he had been. Awaiting autopsy.

A morgue.

As his feet touched the floor a sharp pinch in his foot hobbled him. He sat and reached down. The cause of the pain was a toe-tag attached with a tight twist of bare wire. He removed it, stood and brought it over beneath a dim desk-lamp so he could read what was there.

Wendell Bradley Neff
DOB: 11/17/1922
DOD: 01/21/2003 Cause of Death: AMI
Place of disposition: Bradford Holt Crematory, Laclede
County

Below all this was a bar-code and a coroner's hurried signature.

On a nearby prep table he found his clothes and personal effects, shrink-wrapped in clear plastic and marked INCINERATE.

He tore the bag open and began to dress himself. His heart felt fluttery, his mind wouldn't clear, he was breathing too quickly and not deeply enough.

They'd mistaken him for dead.

The door was locked but the deadbolt latch was here inside. It was meant to keep live people out, not to keep the dead people in. He turned the lock quietly, the hinges hissed as he pulled the door open and he slowed his movements to minimize the sound. The hallway was dark and still; far down the corridor the pulsing light of a television in a side-room was nearly the only light he could see.

His joints were aching, it felt as though he hadn't moved in days, and perhaps he hadn't. As he passed each room he peeked in before stealing by the doorways, expecting at any instant to be discovered and captured and killed, and he didn't doubt that this time they'd make sure he was good and gone.

At the third room he saw the girl, Jeannie Reese, sleeping and strapped to the bedframe. He approached her side and she awoke with a start as he began to undo the leather binding at her wrist.

'Shhhhh,' he breathed.

He motioned for quiet and together they made quick work of the remaining restraints. When she was free they found her clothing and he turned away as she changed. After a minute or so he felt a pat on his back.

'Let's go,' she whispered.

Jeannie stopped at the roll-away desk by the doorway. A night-light was glowing there, and in the circle of illumination were two sheets of printed paper. One was an email addressed to her, the other was a map, marked up with notes and some instructions. A spot was circled near the center of the page. Handwritten and underlined across the corner was the name *John Fagan.*

She took the papers and folded them carefully, slid them into the pocket of her jeans.

'Stay right behind me,' she said. 'If we make it outside it'll be best if we split up, understand?'

'Yes.'

'And thank you,' Jeannie said.

He nodded.

They slipped down the hall and gradually the muted sounds from the TV room became clearer. She stopped at a coat-rack and took a fleece jacket for herself and a longer, heavy raincoat for him.

As she opened the lobby doors a loud alarm sounded.

'Go, go, go,' Neff said, 'don't wait for me.'

She hesitated but he waved her on, and she turned from him and disappeared into the night.

At his age running wasn't an option but he made his way as

fast as he could down the drive toward the road. A burst of machine-gun fire sounded from somewhere behind him, a siren began to wail and then another, dogs were barking, the ground on each side of him was cut up with lines of bullet impacts, but he didn't stop until he reached the end of the long driveway. There was no one in the guardhouse and he limped past it, ducked under the gate-arm and fell to his hands and knees onto the asphalt road beyond.

Headlights approached. He struggled to his feet and waved his hands for whoever it was to stop and help him, praying that it wasn't one of them because he knew he could go no farther.

As the truck squealed to a stop the driver got out, motioning urgently. He came and hurried Wendell around to the passenger side, helped him up and in and then closed the door. The second he was back in his own seat the man dropped the truck into gear, floored the accelerator, and they tore off down the empty highway.

When his breathing began to ease Neff looked through the back window, through the gun-rack mounted there. There was no pursuit that he could see, nothing but the dwindling yellow lights of the watchtowers receding far behind.

One of the marksmen popped out his empty clip and struck home another with the heel of his hand. August Griffin came up beside him, put a hand on his shoulder.

'That's enough shooting, I think,' he said.

Jeannie Reese was being tracked by infrared sensors in a pair of UAVs circling high overhead. Three dozen associates in civilian vehicles were patrolling the roads in the surrounding area, a fleet of Good Samaritans ready to happen upon her, pick her up and take her wherever she wanted to go. Without any doubt, where she wanted to go would be the northwest corner of Wyoming.

And Wendell Neff would either slip into hiding or he would try to resume his very public life as the point-of-the-spear aimed at the wicked heart of his New World Order. Either option was acceptable, though it would be especially rich to listen to him tell this story to his army of soon-to-be disillusioned radio listeners.

How this crippled, doddering man in his early eighties had been captured during a clandestine meeting with a beautiful young operative, how he'd held up bravely during his interrogation and even cleverly discovered some underpinnings of the Enemy's plan. How they'd killed him when he refused to talk, and how he'd miraculously risen from the dead, rescued the blond, and escaped on foot while dodging a hail of automatic gunfire and outrunning the Dobermans and the bloodhounds.

Wendell Neff had been right about one thing: over the years he'd sometimes stumbled uncomfortably close to some dangerous truths. What a shame now, that once he'd recounted this tale no sane person would ever believe another word he had to say.

33

John hit the ground on his side, numb and shivering. The shivering was a good sign, his mind offered. At the later stages of hypothermia the shivering stops and that's when things can get dicey, survival-wise.

His ribs ached from being carried over someone's shoulder for God knows how far. His head was throbbing, too, and fuzzy; it was taking some effort to connect the scene around him now with his last conscious memory of home.

The thought was late in surfacing, but he realized then with more than a little surprise that he must be alive.

The sky was overcast but it was definitely darker than it should be unless he'd lost all track of time. A freezing rain was pattering around him, heavy drops hitting his jacket and sticking in tiny beads of splattered ice.

A repetitive clacking sound had begun; the throbbing in his head kicked up as he turned his head to find its source. Wayman Hudson was trying to make a fire, kneeling before a hollow he'd scraped in the frozen ground, striking a steel file against flint over a handful of limp tinder.

A black canvas duffel was next to him and he pulled it closer and used it as support as he sat up on the ground. The other man was having no luck with the fire; everything was wet through and freezing over, from his flint and steel to the pile of wood he'd stacked on the slim odds that he could keep a spark alive in these conditions. One thing was certain, without some warmth neither of them would survive the night.

John unzipped the bag and rifled through its contents. These weren't his things and they certainly didn't belong to Wayman. This was a field bag, a military kit; there was ammunition for guns he didn't own, MRE rations and water bottles, flashlights, a cushioned box of detonators, a power pack for a demolitions unit, and eight wrapped gray blocks of C4. And look at this: a pill-bottle full of weatherproof matches with a striker up the side.

He twisted off a golf-ball-sized lump of the plastic explosive and pinched out a thin tab of it to act as a fuse, then worked his way over to the hollow in the ground. As he prepared to light the material with a match Wayman took his arm to stop him.

'It's all right,' John said. He hoped he'd sounded confident enough. This wasn't something he'd tried before but the chemistry seemed to make some sense. This stuff needed a healthy shock wave to set it off properly; absent that, if it could be lit it should simply burn vigorously rather than explode.

He struck a match and held it down under the hanging nodule of high explosive clay protruding from the top of the gray ball. Soon the flame had dwindled down to his fingertips and he shook it out and lit another. Despite the sleet, a second later the material flared brightly. As the heat rose and his eyes adjusted to the glare he was pleased to note that his hands were still attached to his arms.

The yellow chemical flame burned hotter and hotter as the two men fed in bits of brush and then larger twigs and branches to sustain the combustion. By the time the synthetic fuel was consumed their campfire was burning high, pushing back a small, fragile circle of civilization in the midst of the wilderness.

The food in the MRE packs wasn't much to write home about, but an empty stomach can find a lot to appreciate in even one-star cuisine. If this was a man's first exposure to chicken à la king, though, he'd be pretty unlikely to ever order the dish again.

In the course of the meal John had managed to learn some details of their escape. The story was related in half sign-language, half pantomime.

After the first salvo different elements of the attacking force had seemed to turn against one another. In all the disarray Wayman had found him and dragged him from the burning house. There was a sudden, brief confrontation near the back door with a lone foot-soldier. This shoulder-bag of equipment and the jacket John was wearing had belonged to this man. Wayman didn't think he'd killed him, but he couldn't be sure. They'd escaped into the woods behind the house, then, with John still stunned from the attack and carried over a shoulder until they'd reached this spot.

Wayman showed him their progress on the map he'd found in John's hands back at the house. It was only a frontiersman's estimate but from the landmarks on the printout it was probably trustworthy. Unbelievable, especially with the burden of an injured man; they'd come almost twenty miles.

With more wood gathered, the fire built up for the night, pine-frond bedding, and two thin blankets from the soldier's bag they prepared for whatever sort of sleep they'd be able to manage. John looked over at his companion and got his attention.

Thanks, he signed. And then he added a phrase that he'd gone over and over in his mind to make sure he could say it properly in this man's language. It was better this way, actually. In spoken English he wouldn't have had a clue what to say at all.

I'm so sorry about your Mom.

Wayman Hudson nodded, and then laid down and turned away.

The clouds had dispersed and the sky was clear above them. In the warmth of the fire, as John waited for sleep to come there was some time to count what a more spiritual person might term the day's blessings, for want of a far better word. He found three, and they weren't much but they were better than nothing.

First, though this path he was on was the last he would travel he'd already come farther than he deserved. Second, it was certainly better to die as a free man than a prisoner. And last, by some stroke of good fortune, at least the kids were safe in town.

34

On the first full day of their detention the captain of the guard had come to Matthew's room and laid down the law.

Elizabeth would be taking study in the mornings and afternoons, he was told. She'd be well supervised, and she'd get anything and everything she wanted, so there was no reason for him to cause a problem out of concern for her well-being. Matthew would be put to manual labor under the groundsmen and custodians until further notice, and Crystal would clean the living quarters of the staff, work the laundry, and wash the dishes. Both would be under guard.

The man didn't beat around the bush with the rest of it. If there was trouble, any trouble at all, the punishment would be severe, physical, and it wouldn't end with the offender. Just as long as everybody did what they were told, nobody would get hurt.

There was also some other talk he'd overheard as he went about his duties. They wouldn't be here very long, the three of them, and when this layover was done they wouldn't be leaving here together.

When he got back to his room from the long day of work he went into the lavatory, washed up, and changed into sleeping clothes. He heard the girls through their door and he rapped twice, and then once again on the frame. He was emptying his pockets when Crystal peeked in and he motioned her inside.

'What's all that?' she whispered.

She'd pointed to the portions of reddish powder wrapped in plastic that he'd placed along the glass counter over the sink.

'That's some of the rust I scraped off the flagpole out front. I need to get some more tomorrow. That' – he indicated the second, smaller bundle – 'is potassium permanganate; I found a bag of it while I was sweeping out the garage. It seems they sell it to clean people's feet before they get into a swimmin' pool.'

'What are you gonna do with it?'

'I'll tell you later, we don't have a lot of time now. They ain't got a camera in the bathroom but somebody might notice we're both in here and figure we're up to something.'

'Well, ain't we?'

He looked at her in the mirror; it was a brave and willful young woman he saw looking back.

'Yeah,' Matthew said. 'We are. Now I need for you to get Elizabeth to ask for some things. In case you haven't noticed she's gettin' the royal treatment, so if she asks they'll give her what she wants.'

'What do you need?'

'First, tell them this soap in here is dryin' out her skin, and you need some glycerin to put on her hands and her face at night.'

'I think there's some moisturizer in the cabinet—'

'I'm asking you to lie. Tell them that's what she's used to

and you don't want her to break out in hives, or whatever. But it's got to be *glycerin*, comes in a little bottle from the drug store.'

'Okay.'

'Then get Elizabeth to ask them for a toy, it's called an Etch-a-Sketch, do you know what that is?'

Crystal rolled her eyes, and nodded.

'I need two of those, not the little ones, the big ones. Those, and nine pennies dated after 1982, a ruler, a yard of string, two paper cups, and some modeling clay. Say it back.'

'Two Etch-a-Sketches, a bottle of glycerin, nine pennies with dates on 'em after 1982, a ruler, a yard of string, two paper cups and some Play-Doh.'

'Not Play-Doh, now, modeling clay. When you can, put a handful of that clay in the middle of one of those toilet-paper rolls above the latrine, like where I put my note to you last night, all right? That's how we'll pass things back and forth.'

'How am I supposed to get all that stuff?'

'You're smart,' he said. 'You'll figure it out.'

From her expression it seemed like it might have been a while since anyone had complimented her intellect.

'Okay,' she said. She noticed his pile of filthy work clothes on the floor by the tub. 'Do you want me to clean those for you?'

'No, no, I wouldn't put you through that. I'll take care of it here in the sink.'

'Hell fire, I'm doin' everybody else's laundry, I might as well do yours.'

'I appreciate it, but just get those things for me, and that'll be help enough. Now get on back in there before we get caught.'

'Okay. Goodnight.'

She left, with a last look over her shoulder on the way out the door.

When he'd hidden his powders he got into bed and started thinking it all through. Tomorrow night would be too soon, they wouldn't be nearly ready.

He could only hope the next night wouldn't be too late.

35

One overnight stay outside in the dark woods in the winter, and every past gripe over a stiff mattress or the thread-count of bed sheets comes into stark perspective.

The expectations of restful, extended sleep time vanish in short order. The mind reverts, alternating between tense, half-awake alertness and brief blackouts of disorienting unconsciousness. A dormant sense kicks in from the stone age, reminding that something wild and hungry waits just beyond the light of the fire, not only watching but also weighing the pros and cons of eating you alive.

Still, toward dawn he must have slept more soundly for a time; when John awoke the sun was already two hands above the horizon. A meal-tin from one of the used MREs was next to the fire, cleaned and full of melting snow. He took a drink and found some crackers in the bottom of the black satchel. As he unwrapped his dry breakfast, Wayman Hudson appeared from the woods to the south, leading a horse.

He began to stand but couldn't quite get his legs under him. The weakness was coming back and his pains had returned to all the old familiar places. With the few days' reprieve from the worst of his illness he'd begun to take things for granted, but bad things don't go away just because you've forgotten about them.

Wayman arrived and helped him to his feet. It was a big old Belgian draft horse he'd brought with him, saddled, shod, and rigged for winter travel.

Before John could figure out how to sign *Where in the fuck did you get a fucking horse?* Wayman began to explain, and he caught most of it. It seemed that the Lord had provided, with a dude-ranch a mile or so away serving as a gateway for the miraculous intervention.

John had never before touched a horse, much less ridden one, but Wayman guided him into the saddle and the stirrups, and then took the reins to lead the animal and its novice rider on foot. As they got under way it seemed John's only responsibilities would involve not falling off. Even this very lowest bar of horsemanship soon proved a great deal more challenging than it might have sounded.

The map Kate had printed hadn't specified a route from the house to the unnamed dot that marked their destination. Wayman appeared to be navigating with only the features of the landscape and a compass in the hilt of his Bowie knife. Those, and the unspoken need to stay clear of the traveled roads and keep them as obscured as possible from any hostile eyes in the sky.

As the miles passed behind them the wilderness deepened. Mountains rose on either side of their meandering path through the lowlands and river valleys. The peaks and ranges were jagged and chaotic, as though they'd splashed up and frozen in place in a sudden violent cataclysm long ago. The landscape was breathtaking, but underlying it there seemed to be a quiet presence that was even more powerful than the view.

310

Like many fine old terms – *awesome, marvelous, brilliant* – the word *majesty* had lost some of its meaning over the centuries, whether misapplied to describe the loftier works of humankind or to veneer an exalted stature onto mortal potentates. But the essence of that word became clear to him then, as he'd felt it defined by these surroundings. *Majesty* wasn't a quality of beauty, preeminence, timelessness or dimension alone. It was what radiated from this virgin land, as real as sunlight; a sovereign, benevolent, sublime indifference.

The religions of the native people who'd once walked here weren't founded on the visions of prophets or the worship of some separated Being in the sky. In their connection with the land they'd sensed a whisper of spirit that seemed to pervade all things, a great unknown that gave life, brought the seasons, lit the stars and set the paths of the moon and sun, and gloried in the delicate balance of all creation. Men and women were no more touched with divinity than the bear, or the eagle, or the mountains, or the wind. But it was better to say that they were every bit as divine. What these people sought through their worship wasn't salvation from sin or an eternal reward. It was simply to express their humble gratitude at having been granted a brief passage through this wondrous, everlasting, indifferent world.

By day's end the map reported that they were close. The endless dense fields of lodgepole pines had temporarily given way to groves of tall thin aspen trees, and that change made the going much easier.

Something was troubling him. It might have been nothing more than a side-effect of his fatigue, but as the sun got low John had begun to imagine some unusual changes around them.

They'd occasionally seen birds and animals as they traveled

along, and more often they'd only heard them, or seen evidence of the recent transit of wildlife near the trail. Now there were none, neither the animals nor their signs, not for the preceding two or three miles.

He'd seen something else though, and had found himself reluctant to acknowledge it in fear of what it might mean. Harmless visual glitches caused by changing light and shadows were one thing; full-blown, eyeballs-out hallucinations brought on by the spread to his brain of a malignant disease were quite another.

When Wayman next looked back to see if his rider was still in the saddle John signaled him to stop. With some help he dismounted and then tried without success to stretch the aches from his muscles and joints. As soon as he was able he walked up next to the other man, pointed to several tall trees around them, and gave no other clue. As John watched him look up and then slowly around he allowed himself to wonder which might be the more ominous sign, the delusion or the reality.

At length Wayman met his eyes, frowning. He pointed to one of the trees near them, and then all around to include the rest of the nearby grove. He held his hand high in the air, then, his arm straight up. Slowly, beginning with his fingers, his arm began to bend until it formed a subtle arc, pointing in the direction of their travel.

John nodded. So they'd both seen the same thing.

Wayman indicated he'd be back soon and he headed off at a run toward higher ground to the east of the path. While he waited John took some water and went over the map again. It appeared they could be even nearer to the end than he'd thought before; right on top of the place, maybe.

His guide returned, breathless. He pantomimed a wide, encompassing circle and then with spread fingers in both hands, moving from low to high toward a common apex, he showed John what he'd seen. It wasn't just these trees, it was all the trees, leaning inward from all sides to a center-point that must be just ahead. As the sun had drawn them upward toward its light, it seemed, the woods were also yearning subtly toward some other form of sustenance.

With nightfall approaching the two determined to call it a day, and Wayman set about tending their borrowed horse and making an encampment. They would rest and eat, and then at first light they'd learn what waited at the end of this journey.

John was restless, and though it was nearly dark he decided to venture ahead, if only to stretch his legs before retiring. With the stars coming out there wasn't much risk of getting lost, and it was difficult to be so close and not try to see just a little farther on.

After a few hundred yards he stopped at a fallen tree trunk inclined across the path. He could have ducked under it but something had caught his attention in the twilight. What at first glance had looked like a strange, thin sapling off to the side became a tall straight pole set in the ground, man-made, with cross-pieces spreading out from its upper-middle to its top.

Dipole antennas.

He saw another near the first and then another, and more on the other side. Some were damaged, snapped by a falling branch or overgrown with foliage. The pattern of their arrangement soon became clear. It was a planar array of the kind used in high-altitude atmospheric research, camouflaged to blend with its surroundings, and evidently long abandoned.

He felt a tap on his shoulder. Wayman had come up beside and was pointing down in front of them to a small frozen puddle. A dim glow danced across the surface of the ice,

313

greens and blues and yellows, rippling like a pleated curtain caught in the gentle breeze.

This far south it was more improbable than any oddity this path had shown so far, but there was no mistaking that reflection. Even if you've only read about them, the Northern Lights are like no other sight in the heavens.

Both men looked up at the same time and stood that way for a while, watching the ghostly interplay of solar winds in the high atmosphere, shining down from directly overhead as though to mark the hour of the day of their arrival.

36

After a second fifteen-hour day at hard labor Matthew wanted only to dress for bed and sleep, but there was more to be done.

After his shower he'd found one of the toilet-paper rolls in the rack stuffed with several ounces of blue and red modeling clay. Inside the cardboard tube of another roll was a penciled note.

Almost got all you asked for, will bring the rest 2nite.
- C

After a brief search he opened the medicine cabinet and found that Crystal had left an assortment of the more innocent contraband inside. Two stacked paper cups, a few pennies, the bottle of glycerin and a coil of dirty string, arranged here and there among the random leave-behinds of previous tenants.

He'd been working for a while, using a plank of 1x4 on top of the radiator as a construction surface, when he heard sounds of arrival from the girls' room. He paused to give the code-knock and after a minute or so Crystal opened the door and came in.

Her hair was pulled back and covered in a dull green bandanna, an apparent uniform requirement of kitchen workers here. Her hands and arms were an angry red up to the elbows, either from scalding water in the kitchen sinks or exposure to the types of harsh cleansers reserved only for the dirtiest jobs and the lowest rung of the workforce.

'How are you?' he said.

'Dog tired.' She began to take her hair down but he could see that it hurt to use those hands. At the tips of her fingers the skin was split and raw.

'Here, let me.' Matthew put down his work and she sat sideways on the closed lid of the toilet, facing away. He removed the bandanna, took out a number of bobby-pins, and after some untwisting and rearranging she was left with a neat pony-tail. 'Do you want this out, too?'

'No, I wear it like that sometimes.' She stood to see herself in the mirror. 'God, I look a fright.'

'You look okay.'

She began to try and undo the ties that held her apron in the back, wincing with the effort.

'Stop, stop,' he said, 'I'll get that.' He came around behind her, and it took quite a while to loosen the knot. 'Didn't your grandma ever teach you how to make a bow?'

'I didn't tie that myself,' she said.

'Who did?'

'Some big creep in a uniform, he was hangin' around the kitchen all day. I didn't really have a choice in the matter, and I'll tell you what, before he was done he touched a lot of things that didn't have nothin' to do with my apron.'

Matthew finished, the knot came free, and he helped her pull the stained garment up and over her head.

'Sorry that happened.'

'It's nothin' I ain't dealt with before. Hell, if I didn't think we was bustin' outta here, I'da ducked his head in the french-fry grease and let 'em shoot me for it.'

Their eyes met in the mirror.

'It ain't for sure we'll make it out, you know, it ain't even all that likely. But I know we've got to try.'

She nodded, and gracefully changed the subject. 'You know what, for a country boy you made pretty quick work of a girl's hairdo.'

'I've got a little sister, remember.' He opened the medicine cabinet, took down a half-empty container of Vaseline, a ketchup-pack sample of aloe vera, and the last few capsules from an old jar of vitamin E. He squeezed the amber capsules into the jar and mixed the other ingredients together with a plastic spoon. His next question had been hanging in the air between them as he worked, and at last he spoke it.

'How is Elizabeth?' he asked.

'She's awful quiet when she's here, and she's sleeping a lot, but it's not good sleep, you know? Bad dreams. They've got her out at dinner now, they won't even let her eat with us. It's like they're gettin' her ready to forget about you.'

He nodded, his jaw tight. One more day. It would be tomorrow night or never.

'Hold up your hands here,' he said.

With a light touch he spread the lotion onto her damaged skin, kneading gently and rubbing it in from her fingers up to her elbows, watching her to make sure it hurt as little as possible. She was watching him, too.

'Does that feel okay?'

'Yeah,' she said.

'Any better at all?'

'It feels good, yeah.'

317

She had a pair of clean white cotton knee-socks hung over the shower rail and he took them down, bunched one up and held it open at the cuff. She held out her hand and he worked the sock over it, up to her wrist, and then as far onto her arm as the fabric would reach without stretching. He smoothed out some wrinkles and then repeated the dressing on the other arm.

'You go to bed like that,' he said when he'd finished, 'and I bet you'll feel better come morning.'

It occurred to him only then, and almost certainly to her as well, that a few early milestones of boy–girl intimacy must have been innocently leapfrogged in the course of the first-aid. His hands were still warm from her skin, and entirely against his will and out of all context with the situation, that warmth was threatening to spread like a grassfire. He felt a blush rising in his face, broadcasting and amplifying his thoughts. Of course it was too much to hope that his flushed cheeks might escape her notice, and when he looked up to check, he saw that they hadn't.

But there was nothing of concern to be found in her eyes. She touched his petroleum-jelly slick hand with her own sock-covered one.

'Thanks so much,' she said.

He nodded, and snapped the lid back on the jar. 'You better not show those to Elizabeth, though. She'll have you up all night doing puppet shows.'

Crystal smiled. It was one he hadn't seen before, and after admiring it for just a few moments he got back to his work.

Shortly they heard Elizabeth coming back for the night, accompanied by her escorts. When the strangers had left both kids helped her get ready for bed and tucked her in. Crystal went to fetch the little girl a glass of milk and a cookie, and in the course of the trip she ascertained that the room monitors would be unattended that night. The staff and the guards were all gathered in the distant TV room watching a football game. All doors to the outside and the restricted areas were locked and chained so they had no worries. What mischief could these three children possibly cause, even if they would dare to try?

Crystal had been right; Elizabeth was changing. She was still herself, he could tell, but almost everything about her seemed to be diminishing. Defenseless, that's what she seemed to be, and that wasn't a word anyone would ever have used to describe this kid before.

When she'd fallen asleep they moved to Matthew's room with the materials he'd listed all gathered together. Crystal had found the rest of the nine pennies during her cleaning duties, and the ruler and the two Etch-a-Sketch toys had been brought when Elizabeth was returned.

To be safe he turned on the clock radio to a music station and placed a wadded T-shirt in front of its face. If there was a microphone the low music would render it less effective, and the shirt would block the camera. If someone did happen to check the monitor, then neither of these actions should be punishable. It was a risk you take with hidden surveillance devices; sometimes they end up being thwarted for a while by the guiltless, everyday actions of the observed.

Matthew hung the ruler by a string from the back of the desk-chair, attached so it balanced perfectly level. From each end a paper cup was suspended under a harness of twine.

'Do you think you can help me, with your hands like that?' he asked.

Crystal had taken a seat on the end of the bed, cross-legged, watching him work, and she came down then to kneel beside him.

'Don't ask me to thread a needle, but I'll see what I can do.'

319

He put all nine pennies into one of the cups, causing it to hang down far below the one on the other side of the scale. He picked up a clear quart-sized plastic bag, the one he'd shown her the night before, but now it was nearly full.

'This is that rust I showed you; iron oxide, I should say. I need you to crush this stuff down, you can use your knee if you want but don't break the bag, just be gentle about it. We need to make it a powder, without any big chunks, okay?'

She nodded, took the bag, and began to do as he'd instructed.

'When you get done take that spoon on the desk and put enough iron oxide into the empty cup so it weighs the same as the pennies and that ruler comes up even.'

Matthew went to work on the first Etch-a-Sketch, removing the knobs, snapping off the red rim, peeling the protective plastic from the glass underneath, and finally, prying up the sheet of glass to reveal the insides.

'Why are we using pennies?' Crystal whispered. She'd started to spoon the dark powder into the scale and the ruler was beginning to level.

'Because I knew we could find some, and I know what they weigh. All the pennies after 1982 weigh the same, two and a half grams. So with nine pennies' worth, what you're going to have there is twenty-two and a half grams of iron oxide, right?'

She nodded. 'Whatever a gram is.'

'What a raisin weighs, that's about a gram. What we're making needs a three-to-one mix, by weight, not by how it looks.' She'd finished, and he emptied the cup from the scale into a big ashtray he'd found in the desk drawer. 'For three-to-one, we need three pennies now, instead of the nine we used before.' He removed the excess coins and brought over the disemboweled Etch-a-Sketch.

'So that'll be seven-and-a-half grams of whatever that wicked stuff in there is.'

He smiled. 'That's right. Now be careful with this. It's really fine, you sneeze and it'll be all over this room.'

'What is it?'

'Powdered aluminum.'

She'd started to spoon the material into the cup of the scale. 'When we're done what's all this gonna make?'

'You know those steel bars on the windows?' Matthew asked.

'Yeah.'

'It's gonna make those go away.'

They'd repeated the process a few times until the materials ran out. In the end they'd made a good-sized pile, almost 100 grams. Matthew had said he wasn't sure it would be enough, but we'd have to go with whatever we had.

He was working the clay in his hands, warming it so it would be more pliable. Crystal had the glass ashtray on the floor in front of her and was stirring the powders together, making sure they were well blended. The stockings on her hands excluded her from any delicate operations, but they also kept any unhealthy particles away from the breaks in her skin. He likely should have been wearing gloves himself.

'Thermite,' she said, trying out her new word.

'Yeah. Been around for over a hundred years, and they still haven't improved on it much.'

'And this won't explode?'

'No, it's actually kind of hard to set it off. It's safe enough like this.' He scooted over next to her, brought his hands down near the ashtray and began to work a portion of the powder into his clay.

'Where'd you learn about all this stuff?'

'From John.' He frowned a bit, and continued to work. 'It wasn't like he was just teaching me how to make bombs and stuff, I don't want you to think that. Hell, he never would let Elizabeth anywhere near half the stuff we put together, afraid she'd find some way to hurt herself.'

Matthew put down the first piece of infused clay on a sheet of clean paper, picked up another and began to work the powder into it as before.

'I don't read so good, you know? Never have. And he said a lot of people are just wired up to learn things differently. Some with their heads and some with their hands. And so we just did things a lot of the time, made things, and at the end of it I'd know something I didn't know before. He said maybe we were the same that way, because it was the same way he learned just about everything he knew.'

The quiet music played and took the place of conversation for a time as she watched him work. His thoughts seemed far away but there was nothing careless in his method, as though his hands knew just what to do with little need for the mind's direction.

'What was the story,' she said, 'on our way into town, when I mentioned a dog? You looked like you were gonna take my head off.'

'Oh, boy.'

He sighed, shook his head, and it seemed for a while as though that might be the extent of his answer, but at length he spoke again.

'We had this old dog named Sugar, like Elizabeth said, from back when we all first moved into that house. John always acted like he didn't care for her much, but whenever you turned around that's where she'd be, in there in his office or down next to his feet if he was off reading a book. I walked in on him talking to her more than once, and not like a man

322

talking to a dog, but like a person having a conversation, the same as we're talking right now. So we all knew he liked her, even if he wouldn't let on.'

Another ball of clay was finished, and he started on the next.

'So, one morning we couldn't find her, and after a while John came running back to the house and said to tell Elizabeth to stay inside, and to bring his black bag right away, out there to the shed.' Matthew looked toward the door to the bathroom, as though to ensure that they were still alone. 'That dog, she'd got in a fight with something, a coyote, or a wolverine, something, Lord, I don't know what. I think she was all but dead before he found her and carried her back. Well, I brought John his bag, and he worked and worked over that poor old thing, must have been over two hours. Only time I ever heard him pray. Even after he gave it up he wouldn't leave her; I never saw a man carry on so. I had to take her myself and bury her out in the woods. He couldn't bring himself to do it.'

Matthew pulled the ashtray over, took the last of the clay and the last measure of the dark powder and began to work them together in the silence.

'And he told your sister that story,' Crystal said, 'about the dog and her boyfriend runnin' off to get married and have some puppies, out where it's sunny and nice all the time.'

'Yeah.' Though his face was impassive his eyes were glistening, his voice just above a whisper. 'Not like a lie, though. Like something that just ought to be true.'

The radio station was in between the fading end of one song and the beginning of another. In the absence of the music the sounds of the wind came through from outside. It wasn't the air that made the sounds but the things that stood in its way. The chain-link fences, the coils of concertina wire, the bars in these windows, and the tall metal towers.

323

'Do you know what I wish?' she asked.

He shook his head, and looked over.

'I wish somebody'd ever told me a story like that. And I wish I'd believed it.'

With the night's work done they cleaned up the evidence and hid what they'd made in a recess of his hollow bed-frame. Matthew reassembled the gutted toys and Crystal agreed to store them somewhere in the other room where they'd be seen in an inventory but not examined too closely.

He walked her to the door and they said goodnight. The time they'd set was 11:20 PM, well before the shift change at midnight, an hour from now tomorrow.

There hadn't been much opportunity to question the wisdom of this plan. Only two courses seemed available: fight and probably die in the effort, or surrender and live in some form of misery chosen by another. The decision he'd made had seemed automatic, but he hadn't realized until then why it must have come to him so easily.

Without any doubt, it's what John Fagan would've done.

37

John and Wayman skipped breakfast in the morning and got an early start. The map would be no more help at this point. It would now be a matter of searching the area with the assumption that they'd actually recognize their destination if they happened to stumble onto it.

Within minutes they passed the antenna array seen the night before and about a hundred yards on a building became visible within a clutch of trees and brushwood. Its construction was shabby-military, like a third-rate Quonset hut only smaller, roughly the size of a detached one-car garage. The exterior was painted in forest camouflage, though the corrugated metal of its siding had rusted through the finish in places. Crawling vines and undergrowth making their way up the sides were doing a much better job of hiding the place. At the fore-end were two wide sliding double-doors, and no windows were apparent.

The ring-latch in the doors was secured with a heavy padlock. It was old, and so corroded it probably wouldn't have opened even if they'd had a key. Undisturbed, as well; the way the lock had rusted into the surrounding hardware it seemed as though it hadn't been touched in decades.

John remembered seeing a short Halligan bar in the field bag, a breaching tool that had likely been intended for use on his own back door. As he found it in its Velcro loops at the bottom of the black bag a sickening dizziness came over him. He sat before he could fall, his head hanging and a hand on the ground to stop the spinning, waiting for his balance to return.

Wayman had tied their horse at a nearby sapling and he knelt with an offer of water. He took the pry-tool in exchange, worked it into the rusty shackle, got a two-handed grip, and before John had finished his drink he heard the groan of tortured metal and a sharp snap as the old lock gave up the ghost.

There was another impediment to entry that was intended to be much more intimidating than the padlock. At eye level a large metal sign was screwed down across the meeting point of the two door panels.

WARNING
NO TRESPASSING
US GOVERNMENT INSTALLATION
It is unlawful to enter this area without prior authorization
from the installation commander.
(Sec. 25, Internal Security Act of 1950, 50 USC 79)
Regardless of authorization, while on these grounds
all persons and the property under their control
are subject to search.
RESTRICTED AREA
Use of deadly force is authorized

Wayman looked back to him for guidance. By the condition of this place the last installation commander had probably croaked thirty years ago at a minimum, so screw it.

He gave a signal to that effect, and the old sign came down much easier than the lock.

As the doors rumbled open he stood and looked in. The above-ground structure was only a sheltered entrance; only a wall-to-wall concrete ramp was visible inside, leading down into the dark. John flipped a toggle-switch in the junction box by the entrance and to his surprise a double line of light bulbs in the ceiling flickered and buzzed on.

Why the hell would anyone still be running electricity all the way out here to keep power going in a forsaken place like this?

The two men descended the slope and the space widened as they went. Vehicles were parked along the walls. Jeeps, a civilian truck, a backhoe, lots of maintenance equipment, fuel tanks, a hay wagon, a trailer or two; some were World War Two vintage or older, and nothing appeared to be newer than the 1960 Chevrolet Impala near the end of the line.

John took a closer look at this one. His dad had driven one of these beasts, though that car had never been in such pristine condition. Blow off the cobwebs and this old Chevy would look right at home in a low-rent auto museum.

Wayman seemed to be fascinated by the collection of vehicles, as though they might well be the whole point of this trip. John left him and walked the length of the echoing space. It was even colder down here than outside, like going from the refrigerator into the freezer section.

At the end was a mechanic's work area, a couple of benches with shelving units and rolling tool-chests. All of the tools were neatly arranged and organized, though like the vehicles everything was tinted light brown with an undisturbed film of dust. A heavy safe stood in the dark corner, tall as an armoire but thinner, and partially sunken into the concrete wall. He twisted a goose-neck work-lamp on the nearby bench and clicked it on so he could see.

It was old but stately, this thing, the sort of ornate vault you might expect divers to retrieve from the hold of a long-sunken luxury liner. On top of it, positioned there with care and purpose it seemed, was a foot-high ceramic tableau. The featured figurine was a young woman clad in scanty but fetching royal robes and a crown of ivy, a quiver over her shoulder and a longbow in her hand. A fox ran beside her, a tall stag stood watch behind. This was Artemis, goddess of the moon and the hunt, protector of the wilderness.

He motioned for Wayman to come near. It took a moment to recall the series of two-digit numbers from that telex message back at the house, the ones that had accompanied the coordinates to this place. There'd only been time for a quick glance at them, but like everything else he'd ever seen they were recorded up there somewhere in the indexed depths of his memory.

There: 47, 90, 36, 93, 89. He hadn't known their purpose before, but right now these numbers looked like the combination to a safe.

John stepped up and touched the rotary lock in the center of the door, gave it a full spin to test its condition; stiff, but workable. A five-part series wasn't common in these sorts of locks, but if this was the most uncommon thing they encountered that day he would count himself lucky.

He entered the supposed combination, alternating back and forth for each number. The silver release lever moved a quarter-turn when he tugged it, the boltworks thunked and retracted inside, and with a pull the massive door hissed and swung open.

He hadn't known what to expect but nothing would have surprised him: the lost crown jewels of the Romanovs, the body of a gray alien from the Roswell crash, or a bunch of spring-snakes and confetti popping out to confirm that this was all someone's idea of a joke.

What they saw was a long hallway leading down. He knew

it was long because strings of walkway lights at the baseboards near the floor were fading on in slow sequence, their lines converging in the distance, beckoning the two men forward.

Wayman still had his pry-bar and after a quick search John found a hand-cranked flashlight and a claw-hammer for himself – you never want to walk into a dim subterranean corridor completely unprepared. He cranked up the flashlight until its beam was strong, jammed a screwdriver into the hinge-line of the vault's door to ensure that it wouldn't close behind them, and down they went.

The walls and ceiling were supported by heavy wooden braces every few yards along the way. The floor was either stone or concrete, textured and treated with some sort of non-slip substance. As the way steepened the flat walk turned to a more constricted stairway. He'd lost track of the number of steps, but by the time they'd reached the landing at the bottom it seemed there must be a mountain's weight of ground above their heads.

The space changed abruptly at the threshold of the stairs. If the path had become narrower he hadn't noticed it before; it was probably an optical illusion caused by the sudden absence of anything but a deep, dark abyss on either side of the final stretch of the no-railing walkway. It wasn't a tightrope, the walk was still three feet wide just as it had been, but every single step now felt like he was involuntarily drifting toward one precarious edge or the other.

At last the two of them set foot safely upon the landing on the other side. The man who'd invented the cigarette must have had just such a moment in mind. With none on hand John settled for a half-hearted high-five, though Wayman seemed unfamiliar with the gesture and unaware of any call for celebration.

The chamber around them was naturally formed, or so old

a construction by human hands that nature had erased the toolmarks long ago. The walls were adorned here and there with weathered graffiti and petroglyphs, though nothing it seemed from any recent millennium. Some head-dressed stick figures with the spoils of a successful hunt, an animal-god and a shaman or two, an elaborate depiction of an angry Sun, and many, many chalky white handprints. All of these last were roughly the same size but somehow they didn't seem to be the work of only one, or even of several different visitors. It was as though this place had been the end-zone of some rite of initiation, and the handprints had been left over long-ago generations as proof of each daring arrival.

Everything appeared to be equally ancient; that is, except the one familiar thing that truly marked the end of the line: a large vault door embedded in the stone. Absent the three unlikely men who'd stood before it in the photograph, it looked just as it had in the back of Latrell's book. The words from Addison's play were etched into the metal just as he'd read them on the screen.

THE STARS SHALL FADE AWAY, THE SUN
HIMSELF GROW DIM WITH AGE

AND NATURE SINK IN YEARS;

BUT THOU SHALT FLOURISH IN
IMMORTAL YOUTH,

UNHURT AMID THE WAR OF ELEMENTS,

THE WRECK OF MATTER, AND THE
CRUSH OF WORLDS.

Another rotary lock here; with no better ideas he entered the same combination from the telex message. A turn of the handle confirmed it was correct; a sharp *clack* from the disengaging hardware echoed around the stone walls. It took both men to unfreeze the hinges and pull the heavy vault door open wide.

They were greeted by an unexpected rush of warm, fresh air.

The passage continued inside, but now the hallway was broken here and there with arched doorways to the right and left. John looked into the first of these, and then the next and one on the other side. These were long-term stores of food and living essentials. The walls were lined with shelves packed with canned goods, dried fruits and berries, paper products, pharmaceuticals, soaps, items for personal care, cleansers and medical supplies.

The next door along the path was stainless steel with a latch-handle like those on walk-in coolers. John opened it and stepped inside. The air was chilly and dry. Brass gauges for temperature and humidity were set in the walls. Files and rows of numbered boxes carried coded labels and pictures of plants: vegetables, fruit and nut trees, flowers, grasses, hemp, wheat, corn, tobacco, greens, herbs and barley. There were hundreds of varieties and several such rooms along the hall.

A seed bank.

Past these the next room featured a door with many locks but none of them were fastened. Inside, strongboxes were stacked on stone ledges and across a metal table in the center of the space. The amount of precious material on hand seemed to exceed the available containers; a great deal was loose and simply piled up on the table. He was no expert but when John touched the heavy metal he was certain enough it was real.

Gold. A mound of coins, heaps of assorted small and medium-sized bars, and two rough stacks of one-kilogram ingots with various imprints: Union Bank of Switzerland,

Johnson Matthey, Perth Mint, Credit Suisse. From the last exchange rate he remembered each of the larger bars would be worth over $12,000, and at least thirty were piled in plain sight.

The hallway ended at a last stairway down. John switched off the flashlight; there was no longer a need for it. Incandescent bulbs had faded on to reveal the extent of this new chamber, the largest so far. Forty feet high and as wide and long as a basketball court, with vents, conduits, fans, lamps, and other accouterments of more modern habitation integrated into the walls, floor and ceiling. It was a hybrid living environment, a natural cave overlaid with a wealth of man-made comforts and refinements.

He descended the widening, sweeping staircase with Wayman right behind him and they began at the far end to walk the length of the space. Their presence was evidently detected by the machinery; sounds of awakening technology arose around them, clicks and whirs and status tones from all kinds of devices, large and small.

In an alcove in the corner, on a stand behind a rolling office chair, was an old telex machine.

John walked up to it, leaned closer so he could see. The rear of the little grotto was in shadow; he turned on his flashlight with a quiet click. With that the bell on the side of the machine clanged five times and several sharp carriage-returns advanced the rolled paper. His heart had nearly jumped straight out of his mouth but at least the simple printed message was easier to read now.

++ w e l c o m e ++

The first discrete workspace seemed fully equipped for electronics design and prototyping. Projects were arrayed across the bench in varying levels of finish, employing everything from vacuum tubes to microprocessors and breadboarded micro-controllers, though these later components were a few generations behind the times.

Next was an area devoted to computing, but the set-up was unlike anything John had seen before. Against the wall stood an old Cray-1 supercomputer, modified to such an extent that it was barely recognizable. *Modified* didn't quite do the work justice; pimped out, that's what it was. The Cray's liquid-cooling system glowed from UV backlights, gurgling and circulating the coolant in a mesmerizing but completely impractical display. Thousands of tiny red LEDs danced and chased in patterns around its exterior, probably linked to processes but again, useless for anything but visual appeal. Somebody here with a lot of time and money on his hands must have really loved his computers.

Nearby there were smaller deskside units and early machines from the sixties and seventies: a Scelbi, an Altair, a TRS-80 Model III, a Sinclair ZX-81, a Super Elf, an Exidy Sorcerer, and an autographed Apple I. On the walls bare motherboards were mounted like art, but they were also living parts of this pieced-together system. Neatly dressed, color-coded cables ran between all components, into and out of bridge-boxes and Ethernet/internet hubs and routers, and everything seemed to terminate at a single destination on a small work-desk: an off-the-shelf, plain-vanilla, garage-sale reject 1996 Compaq Presario 4715 PC, complete with a dusty 12″ CRT monitor in vivid amber monochrome.

John hooked the bead-chain from around his neck and pulled his Cap'n Crunch whistle from where it hung beneath his shirt. He flicked open its end to expose the USB connector inside. Wayman was to his left, watching the light-show as the array of computing hardware did whatever it was doing in starting up. John signed him a brief disclaimer.

Absolutely no way this is going to work.

He stepped around behind the Compaq and was pleasantly surprised to find two first-gen USB jacks in the midst of many other obsolete connectors. It was an unexpected break, and would save him the trouble of soldering together an interface.

'Here goes nothing,' John said, and he pushed the whistle's connector home.

An odd prompt had been displayed on the monitor before, just an omega symbol with a strobing underline. In seconds, though, the screen blipped and winked out as the mighty Presario abruptly crashed and began to reboot.

He had designed Kate to be location-independent, originally more as an engineering exercise than out of any expectation that such a thing would ever be of use to him. They'd spent almost twenty years together in a single place, a loft apartment in the canyons of lower Manhattan. He'd once been sure that everything he would ever need was there within those walls, and that had been true for as long as it lasted. Those days were gone, of course, as was that place.

His little whistle housed enough flash memory for three things: an internet beacon to wake and call Kate back from wherever she might be, a hardware-encrypted key to let her know it was a trustworthy summons, and a set of core addresses where the equivalent of her start-up procedures and primary data stores could be found, should she ever forget their remote locations.

John looked over the eccentric arrangement of components in front of him. Kate had an excellent knack for interoperability, but if she was able to inhabit this Rube Goldberg set-up it would be a minor miracle. In any case it would take a while to find out, so they moved on.

Next, within a room-sized skeletal enclosure lined with fine metal-mesh, a long work table displayed a dozen or so finished projects. It looked something like a science fair for grown-ups, with each apparatus accompanied by a tabbed notebook and stand-up summary cards explaining its concept and function. All the preceding work areas, it seemed, were in support of these endeavors. Each notebook had a cover letter as its first sheet, and all these were signed in the same distinctive hand: *Jack Parsons.*

These devices were all devoted to alternative energy, generators and collectors and amplifiers, though several seemed to be based on premises that were profoundly unscientific. John touched the outer rim of one that looked like an elaborate Ferris wheel and he gave it a tentative whirl. As the wheel turned delicate hinged weights around its perimeter flipped and shifted in support of the momentum, apparently in an attempt to outwit the First Law of Thermodynamics. After a few seconds the spin didn't appear to be slowing but it certainly wasn't increasing in speed. Fascinating to watch and beautifully constructed, but like all things based on the dead-end quest for perpetual motion it was no more than a misguided flight of fancy.

Other displays down the line illustrated somewhat more practical ends: designs for efficient solar arrays and scale models of city-sized electrical plants with wind, geothermal and tidal energy as their source. According to their notes all shared a fundamental quality. They sought to destroy nothing throughout the cycle of power generation, and to leave no negative impact on the planet behind.

John switched on the sunlamp above one of the prototype solar arrays. The indicator needles in nearby meters jumped and steadied toward the high end of their scales. A few moments of thumbnail math confirmed the unlikely results displayed in the project notes: 72 per cent efficiency. To his knowledge the highest yield from off-the-shelf solar cells was less than half that figure, and even that low score was still only theoretical.

A label identified the key innovation in the cells: indium gallium nitride alloys. This was not a material one could obtain by mail order; it would have to be synthesized specifically for this purpose and that couldn't have been done at this site.

These weren't hobbyist models made of toothpicks and matchboxes. With the exception of the cold-fusion models, to one extent or another they all *worked*. These were intricate, legitimate wonders of miniaturization, and one other thing was clear. Most of this simply could not have been created by a lone tinkerer, however gifted he might have been. Parsons must have had help, financial and technological allies, others with anti-mainstream ideas too powerful to bury but too dangerous or controversial to be shared with the world outside.

Another belated thought struck him. That Compaq PC, long outdated though it was, was still less than a decade old. Jack Parsons was born in 1914. If he'd somehow faked his death in the 1950s to become the caretaker of this secret place that would make him eighty-two years old when that computer was new. Eighty-seven, then, when these notebooks had been dated and signed.

On the very end of the table was a small wooden cabinet, heavily varnished and figured with brass and silver accents. Two rotary controls protruded from its opposite sides and an old light bulb glowed pale orange in a socket on its top. Unlike the others the notes here referred to this item as a tuner rather than a generator. It looked something like a tube-radio from the Depression days, when such a set would have been the treasured centerpiece of any upscale family room.

The strange thing was, it appeared to have neither a connection to incoming power nor access for a battery compartment. John lifted it from the table to confirm this; no doors, no wires. In the light from the bulb he could see a multi-digit mechanical counter mounted in the top panel, with the letters **C.D.O.O.** embossed underneath. The counter read 14,109.

C.D.O.O.: continuous days of operation. And the days enumerated there, 14,109, added up to nearly thirty-nine years.

There seemed to be something else, noticed only when he'd gotten closer. Not a sound or a sensation exactly, but a faint emission other than the light from that antique bulb. What he felt was some form of gentle, benign radiation, hard to detect at first but undeniably present once accepted as real, like the change in the air the day before a thunderstorm.

'Can you feel that, too?'

The voice was low and hoarse, the accent unfamiliar. Still, it took John several seconds to accept that the words hadn't been his own.

He turned to Wayman Hudson, who seemed as surprised as anyone to realize that he'd just spoken aloud.

38

Matthew had finished his scheduled work early to leave time for his final preparations. A guard would walk by on occasion, so everything he did had to appear to be a normal janitorial chore, and everything had until this one last procedure.

He stood on the fifth rung of a ladder near the end of a tall series of pegboard-mounted shelves along the back wall of the large maintenance garage. With the heavy end of the shelf supported by one shoulder he removed the metal shelf bracket, took it down two notches and re-secured it there. From the shelf below he picked up a block of solid ice the size of a large matchbox, a critical ingredient that he'd chipped free from an old rain-gauge found outside.

He held the ice on the bracket and let the weight of the shelf down onto it; the long, laden board sat level on the frozen shim. An old towel was then draped to hang down over the end of the shelf to hide the arrangement.

'Just what in the hell do you think you're doing?'

Matthew looked back over his shoulder. The guard was out near the roll-up garage doors, likely too far away to have seen anything he shouldn't have, but now he was walking toward this end.

'Just cleanin' off these shelves, like I been told to do.'

Using the hand without the billy-club the man grabbed Matthew's ankle and jerked him down off the ladder. He hit the floor without much time to brace for it and his wrist twisted under as it took most of the impact.

'Do you think we're here to heat the great outdoors, boy?' The man pointed to the large dial thermometer nearby on the wall. 'It's fifteen goddamn degrees outside, and you've got both those doors open so now it's fifteen goddamn degrees inside here, too.' He stepped to the side, hit the buttons to lower the doors, and checked the thermostat. 'Jesus Christ, the heater in here's runnin' full blast while you're lolly-gagging around, burnin' up all my propane.'

Matthew had begun to get to his feet but a blow from the club put him back to the concrete. His forearm felt as though the bone had been split, and he'd only narrowly protected his head from what might have been a brain-damaging impact.

'I'm sorry—'

The guard reached down, gripped his collar, lifted him to his feet and gave him an elbow to the side of the face.

'You're sorry, what?'

'I'm sorry, sir.' He made sure to say these words sincerely.

The man stared into Matthew's eyes, the wheels turning as if he was considering whether or not he'd gotten his full fix of bullying for the night.

'Idiot,' the guard spat. He released his hold and brushed his hand on his shirt as though he'd soiled it in the course of his discipline. 'Now get the hell on inside, you've done enough damage for one day.'

As he walked toward the garage exit, his minder a pace or two behind, Matthew stole a long glance at the items he'd arrayed across the nearly empty shelving. Everything was

339

ready, and there should be nothing that would raise suspicion without a close look by sharp eyes.

Another thermometer hung by the door to the inside. With the big doors closed and the heaters roaring, the temperature had already risen nine degrees.

An hour later Elizabeth was still nowhere to be found, and it was far past the latest time they'd kept her out. Matthew checked the clock; their target time was approaching, though the exact minute of the escape attempt depended on factors he couldn't precisely control. They needed to be ready, though, and right now they were short one escapee.

Crystal had folded and soaked two blankets in water as he'd requested. She was in the other room waiting for Elizabeth. He'd left it until the last minute to prepare the window bars, out of concern that what he'd done might be seen in a surprise inspection. The last minute, though, had now arrived.

Matthew collected the balls of treated clay from their hiding place, raised his window, removed the screen and slid it under his bed. He shaped a knob of clay around each of the two central bars at the mid-point and the bottom. Then, with his little bag of potassium permanganate in hand, he pinched hollow channels around the top of the clay and packed each of them full of the black crystals. He used all he had; after tonight, one way or the other, there would be no need for any leftovers.

So the bars were ready, and the little plastic bottle of glycerin was in his pocket. All that was left to do was wait and watch the minutes.

The garage was dark, as it was long after hours and with Griffin and the other brass away the standards for vigilance were becoming relaxed. No one was present to see it, then, when the melting block of ice supporting one end of a high shelf finally dwindled sufficiently to crack under the weight and fall away.

A jolt and a sudden tilt in the shelf resulted, setting in rolling motion a round paint-can that had been set there on its side, rather than upright. The can began to accelerate downhill, gathering speed until it collided with a large plastic bottle of bleach, overhanging and carefully balanced on the edge of the shelf. The bottle tipped and fell, but as it was tied by a cord from two shelves below it didn't quite hit the floor. The cord was fastened to the lip of an open bag of pool-shock crystals – $Ca(ClO)_2$ – which leaned and slumped sideways under the weight of the swinging bottle and spilled most of its contents into a large pile on the top of the staff refrigerator underneath.

The paint can that had started this chain of inevitable physical events in motion had come to rest against two C-clamps fastened to the edge of the tilted shelf. The can contained no paint; it was filled almost to the brim with automotive brake fluid. At the end of the roll, three lines of nail-holes in its side had come to rest near the surface of the shelf, pointing down. The brake fluid had already begun to stream from the holes and drip onto the pile of pool-shock crystals below.

Half a minute or so went by. White smoke from the chemical reaction appeared, only in wisps at first, but as more and more of the two volatile substances came in contact, the cloud plumed and thickened. Some of the reddish brake fluid had dripped down onto the lower shelves as the can emptied, wetting the paper products and shop-rags that had been organized there specifically with this evening's needs in mind.

The door opened at the far end of the garage and the night-guard entered on his rounds, just in time to see the top of the refrigerator burst into bright yellow flame. The vigorous fire licked immediately up to the rolls of accelerant-soaked paper and then followed the streams of brake fluid up to the can. The resulting explosion spread the fire wider. In seconds the entire wall of shelves was burning out of control, and the installation's priority-response fire alarm was triggered before the guard could even pull the lever.

Matthew heard a knock from next door and walked through the bathroom to see what was happening.

When he arrived his little sister was there, not dressed for bed but for travel.

The woman who'd accompanied her came into the room, and when she saw him standing there she motioned for him, and pointed where he should go. He sat next to Crystal on the edge of the bed.

'Elizabeth is leaving tonight,' the woman said, all starch and efficiency. 'It's only a short trip, and she'll be seeing many wonderful things, won't you honey?'

Elizabeth nodded.

'When will she be back?' Matthew said.

The woman's eyes fell on him, not angry but affronted, as though he shouldn't expect to ask such a thing.

'There may be some changes with your status here, and as I am not privy to those details I can only tell you that Elizabeth will be fully apprised of your whereabouts should she need to contact you for some reason.'

Out in the hallway a loud alarm bell sounded.

The woman took Elizabeth by the hand but Matthew stood, picked the child up and pulled her away. Crystal jumped from the bed and shoved the woman out into the hall and then slammed the door and jammed a tilted chair beneath its knob.

The three of them raced across into Matthew's room and when the door was similarly secured he threw open the window and looked back at the two girls.

'This is going to be bright and hot as hell, so don't look until I say. Get those towels ready now.'

Those in the hall had begun pounding on the doors, pushing against the chairs that were still managing to hold them closed. Matthew pulled the glycerin from his pocket, twisted off the cap and reached out to drip the liquid into the first of the channels he'd prepared in the thermite clay, and then the second, the third and the last. As he finished one of the ignition reactions flared and he slammed the window and fell, crawling backward, scraping live sparks from his arms and his clothing. The bright initial burn was overwhelmed in the next instant as the thermite itself caught fire, with all four points on the bars throwing molten metal and lighting the room with the flashing glare of an arc-welder. The window panes warped from the heat and an instant later they shattered, spraying the floor of the room with broken glass.

As the reaction died down he saw the bars were still in place but their cut-points were thin and near white-hot. He picked up a chair and slammed it against the bars, and again, and again, and with the last blow the way outside was cleared.

He took the wet towels and they sizzled as he covered the metal stubs, all still glowing orange. First he helped Crystal up and out onto the ground, and then with her aid he passed Elizabeth through.

When he'd made his way out he picked up Elizabeth and they all ran toward the corner of the long, low building, keeping to the shadows. They saw only two guards, both heading the other way. The spreading fire at the far end seemed enough of a diversion to attract all of the sentries stationed outside.

The sound was so faint at first, and he closed his eyes and held his breath to listen and make sure that it was really there.

Sirens were approaching.

When they saw the strobing lights and the firetrucks arriving the three abandoned their cover and broke for the long driveway. The first truck, a big hook-and-ladder, slowed and turned in at the gate and then roared down the drive past them. Another followed, and then a water-tender and a rescue engine, and finally, bringing up the rear, Matthew saw the fire-chief's red and white SUV.

He lowered his sister to the ground and stepped to the center of the drive, his arms waving crosswise in the air. The truck flashed its brights but when he didn't move it slowed and pulled to a stop on the shoulder.

The armed guard from the gatehouse arrived at a run, just as the chief was exiting his vehicle. The guard took Matthew roughly by the elbow but relaxed the grip a bit as the other man approached.

'What's the problem here?' the fireman said.

'No problem.' The grip on Matthew's arm tightened again, a clear physical order to keep his mouth shut.

'This is my little sister,' Matthew said, 'and that girl's a friend of our family. All three of us are minors. We were brought here under duress and we're being held in this place against our will.'

Another department SUV had pulled up behind the first, and two men in uniform got out and walked up.

The fire chief took his flashlight from his belt and flicked it on, first lighting Matthew's face. The light lingered on the bruises and abrasions from his earlier roughing-up, and then passed down to his arms. The burns he'd received at the window had blistered, and one was bleeding. He moved the beam briefly to the girls, and then back again.

'You three go on, and get up in my truck there. I've got the heater going.'

Crystal took Elizabeth to the truck, opened the back door and helped the child inside. When she saw that Matthew was still being kept where he was, she closed the door and stayed outside, waiting.

One of the new firemen took a step closer. He had his pike pole with him and as he stopped he took a firmer grip in both fists.

'Chief said all three of 'em,' the man said. Not quite a threat, but a reinforced reminder.

A few seconds passed, but then the hand on Matthew's arm pulled away.

The three kids watched from the back seat as a brief and animated discussion ensued, ending with the man from the guardhouse retiring to his post and the firemen returning to their vehicles. When the chief had buckled himself into the driver's seat he turned and looked back at his passengers.

'My men tell me they can handle things from here,' he said, 'so how about if we get on back to the station?'

Matthew nodded. 'Thank you, sir.'

'I'm not going to ask you any questions right now. We'll get this sorted out, though, get you three looked after and get you back to wherever you belong. I don't know where that is, but I'll be a monkey's uncle if it's in that place back there.'

'Yes, sir.'

The truck backed and turned around, and then headed out past the raised gate and onto the highway. After a mile or so, the man in front found Matthew's eyes in the mirror.

'It might not feel like it until later on tonight,' he said. 'Maybe even tomorrow. But you're safe now, son.'

39

Jeannie's last ride of the night had passed her two twenty-dollar bills as he pulled up in front of the truck-stop to let her out. He'd held onto her hand as she'd taken the money; for a tense few moments it became clear that while he wasn't exactly insisting on any favors in return for the cash, he'd planned his whole evening around the idea of getting lucky with a young hitchhiker. To his credit he hadn't pressed it too far, so whether he realized it or not he'd gotten lucky after all.

For seven dollars the Diamond Shamrock Travel Plaza rented private bathrooms by the hour. It was like a short-stay motel without the bedroom; paper bath-mat, single-use soaps, everything sanitized and disposable except the fresh towels provided for each new patron. Another $28 had gone for a discounted *Wyoming Rocks!* sweatshirt and a change of no-frills underthings from the meager selection on a single clothing rack. Judging by the overwhelming male majority of the clientèle she was grateful to have found anything at all.

She'd stood in the hot spray for what seemed a lifetime, lights off, letting the sting of the water on her face and the simple acts of becoming clean again begin to bring her back alive. A good long shower could restart any day and substitute for rest until the real thing was available.

With a few minutes left in her rental she stepped out of the stall, dried off and dressed in her new purchases and her old jeans. She toweled her hair a last time, shook it down and stood closer to the wall mirror, using her fingers and a plastic comb to put all that tousled blond into some semblance of order.

Her movements slowed as she finished, her left hand next to her face. There was a partially healed cut and a throbbing numbness at the base of the little finger. It stood away from the others of her left hand; if she'd been holding a teacup she'd look absolutely pretentious. Must have been an injury from that disastrous mission in Arizona, though how or when it might have happened she couldn't begin to recall.

Out in the diner section she took a seat at the counter and the waitress brought her a cup of hot coffee and a laminated menu. In a booth down the aisle a gray-haired man was watching and as their eyes met he motioned to her. Jeannie looked away but when she glanced there again the man smiled and gestured once more for her to come and join him.

He was obviously old enough to be her grandfather, though that was no guarantee of pure intentions. Still, there was another ride to be found, and he seemed as good a prospect for transportation as anyone else in the place. She took a deep breath, picked up her cup, her jacket and her bag, and then walked over and scooted in to the cushioned vinyl seat across from him.

'I'm not looking for a date,' she said.

'Oh, my.' He laughed and shook his head. 'And I'm not looking for another heart attack, so we've come to our first agreement.'

People skills had never been her strong suit but there was something about him that was immediately disarming. It couldn't be called friendliness because they had no basis for that and any such pretense would have raised an alarm. It was the collegial weariness of a fellow survivor, maybe, just an offer of a brief, harmless togetherness, take it or leave it, from someone who might wish he'd seen a few more such offers in the course of a long, storied life.

'I'm sorry,' she said, and she sipped her coffee. It was strong and bitter and not quite hot enough to cover all its faults. 'Someday I'll learn to stop presuming.'

'Sorry for what? For heaven's sake, a pretty young woman, traveling alone and fresh from a hobo-shower, dressed off the bargain rack of a truck-stop, no luggage and no car in the parking lot; I can see how you wouldn't want a fellow to get the wrong idea.'

Jeannie smiled and put down the cup. 'Just to cut to the chase, I could really use a ride if you're going north.'

Some of the good humor faded from his expression. 'Where're you headed up there, this time of year?'

'I need to see an old friend.'

'But where exactly? If you don't mind my asking.'

After a moment of final appraisal she dug into her pocket and brought out her map, unfolded it and slid it across to him. He perched a set of reading glasses on his nose and made a face of deep study as he went over the printout.

'There's nothing out there,' he said.

'How do you know?'

'In my third career I was a ranger in the parks, almost fifteen years. That spot's down in the borderlands between Yellowstone and Grand Teton. I'm not even sure you can get there over land in the winter.'

'Well. I have to, so I will.'

He studied her face over the rim of his glasses. 'This isn't just some personal matter, I take it.'

'No, it isn't,' she said. 'It's much bigger than that, and I'm afraid I can't say any more.'

The man raised his hand to the waitress to call for the check and then took a small GPS unit from his inner coat pocket.

'I hope we don't regret this,' he said.

'You don't have to take me all the way—'

'Oh, I think I do.' He was entering the coordinates as he spoke. 'I wouldn't lay sucker's odds we'll find what you're looking for, but I'll be damned if I'd let you loose to try to get up there alone.' The waitress arrived with a to-go bag and he paid her and added a subtle nod that invited her to keep the change. The tip was generous enough to elicit a double-take as the woman went back to the register.

'What's your name, by the way,' the old man said, 'since we may be freezing to death together later on?'

She stood, put on her jacket and gathered her things.

'Tell you what,' Jeannie said. 'If it comes down to that, right before we die I'll tell you anything you want to know.'

40

Wayman Hudson had gathered some stone-cut oats, dried fruit and bottled water in a basin from a storeroom and he left for a time to tend the horse and bring him into warmer shelter for the night.

Though he'd found his voice he was clearly going to remain a man of few words. In a short, timid conversation he'd related that he had been mute since a fall from a tree when he was a child. There was no doctor for many miles and no money to pay for such care, so he'd been left in God's hands to heal as best he could. And now after twenty-eight years, a blink of the eye in the stretch of eternity, by His grace what was lost had been restored.

While Wayman was gone John had found the sleeping quarters; a lot of care had been taken to make these rock-walled rooms as comfortable as possible. There was easily space for thirty people, with fresh, filtered air and hot and cold running water in the baths. The source of the purified water was a series of large atmospheric condensers housed in a central utility room. The simple but efficient machines seemed to have gone without maintenance for quite a long while, but all of them appeared functional and internally clean.

Through a file of notes, memos and official papers John had also learned a few more details of the history of this strange place.

Evidently the site had first been developed under cover of a WPA make-work project toward the end of the Great Depression. It was intended to be a test-bed for continuity-of-government planning, and some of the lessons learned here would later go into the more extensive and modern secret bunkers at Mount Weather, Raven Rock and Cheyenne Mountain.

In the course of excavation and expansion the workers struck a hollow underground, the first of what proved to be a network of caves, passages and deep volcanic chasms. Government geologists soon arrived, and when signs of past human habitation appeared, government archaeologists followed. What they discovered was that the mid-twentieth-century American military was far from the first culture to consider this location as a shelter against the end of the world.

The Clovis people, the author of one paper speculated, might well have been the original inhabitants. They'd forecast their own version of Armageddon and there was some evidence that their prophecy had come true. The cave-painting out in the entryway, what John had assumed to be a depiction of the Sun, was here described as a prehistoric artist's rendering of a three-mile-wide comet that had entered the atmosphere and exploded over this region nearly 13,000 years before. Vast forests and grasslands burned across much of the continent, setting a deep climate-change in motion and leading to the extinction of the mammoths. These effects in turn led to the extinction of the Clovis culture. All of them, that is, but the few who'd heeded the warnings and taken shelter underground. Even these had probably survived only long enough to record a bit of history before passing into legend themselves.

The classified research and development continued despite any academic or archaeological value the site might have held. That government work ended with some sort of deep-drilling experimentation during the Cold War; more details weren't provided. The land had been purchased by private interests, then, and in the following years this place had gradually become what it still was today: a storehouse of essential things that would allow a select few survivors a slim chance to restart civilization should the unthinkable ever happen again.

Conspicuously absent from this written account was any mention of the three men who'd apparently redirected the destiny of this site in late March, 1964.

By the time Wayman returned John had made up his mind to stay.

At a writing desk in the living quarters he wrote a long letter to Matthew and then a shorter one to Liz. His note to the little girl required more than practical detail and cold instruction; feelings were much harder to put to paper. He'd abandoned his first three drafts, finally setting aside the things that he needed to say in favor of words that she would need to hear. He did his best, in full knowledge that the bravery and hope for the future he encouraged would for years be left to her brother to faithfully maintain.

He read the notes over again, added a few last bullet points to Matthew's long list of things to do, signed and sealed them in musty envelopes from the desk drawer, and gave them to Wayman to deliver.

Their discussion of the plan forward was brief and open-ended. Up in that old garage they'd seen a two-ton capacity utility wagon. It was currently rigged to be pulled by tractor but with a hitch and yoke hung nearby on the wall and a set of snow runners it would serve as a solid horse-drawn transport. Wayman would take as much as the wagon would carry from the stores here – all the seeds and much of the food, tools, and supplies, the paper files, some weapons, and the gold – and set off toward the Jackson area along the back trails. He would find the kids, most likely at the address they'd been given the day they'd left for town. Whatever came next would require some fast growing-up, but Matthew would have to take things from there.

'And as soon as you can,' John said, 'take that horse back to where it belongs, and don't get caught doing it.'

Whatever Faith Hudson had thought would come of this quest, it had to be assumed that what she'd wanted done was now done. Wayman solemnly agreed. If there was any more to all this John would be here to find it and deal with it on his own.

He didn't have very long to live, but at least here he could spend his last days without burdening others in the throes of his demise. And there were worse ways to go; what time remained would be spent tinkering among all these strange and wonderful things, and trying to leave behind a bit more clarity to guide any future discoverers of this place.

The rest of the day passed in loading and preparation, with Wayman taking on the majority of the physical work. Toward sundown the wagon was finally hitched and the load secured and covered to protect its precious contents.

The two men said their goodbyes. Wayman climbed up into the bench seat then levered the brake, took the reins and flipped them gently. The wagon jolted slightly as the big horse strained forward and the runners broke from the snow, and then it proceeded on with more ease, gliding and bumping along at a pace that would make two days' journey of the route ahead. John watched from the garage doorway until the wagon disappeared into the distance, and then he pulled the wide doors closed.

When he arrived down at the lab level he found that the small computer screen was displaying a prompt he recognized.

```
please authenticate >_
```

An old desk microphone stood near the keyboard, a beefy RCA VerAcoustic worthy of the Edward R. Murrow scene at Madame Tussauds. It was wired to an interface box, which in turn jacked into the back of the PC. John pulled the heavy beast a little nearer and leaned down to it.

'It's me, Kate.'

A measurement array unfolded across the amber screen, displaying the jagged digitized soundscape of his words as they were played back. His voice sounded unusually deep and rich as it boomed forth over large speakers mounted up in the corners near the ceiling. Hadn't seen those before.

'Verified,' the computer said. 'Hello, John.'

'It's good to hear your voice, Kate.'

'It is an unexpected pleasure to see you again, as well.'

'See me, you say?' He searched the walls for a few seconds and found the cameras, three of them in all, mounted on swivels within hollows in the stone. 'This is some set up, right?'

'It is indeed . . . One moment.'

His eyes were still directed upward. A polished silver sphere had begun moving down from high above, its support mechanism humming softly until it clicked to a stop, about twenty feet up and nearly overhead. It looked like the business end of a Van de Graaff generator, maybe five feet across. He turned slowly, still looking up. The rough dome of the stone ceiling was covered by scores of pearly-white rectangular tiles, arranged in a dense grid with an inch or so between them. John had noticed these before and assumed their purpose to be simply aesthetic. Wrong again.

The lights had slowly dimmed and as he watched, tens of thousands of bright projected points of light faded in above, all around the dome. Each of these virtual stars seemed imparted with its own gravitation and velocity; they'd begun flying apart and joining together, forming miniature galaxies, clusters, and superclusters. Some regions were stable and steady, others were wildly chaotic with emerging stellar life, violent death, and gradual rebirth. Around the dizzying half-sphere the raw elements of energy and matter were colliding and evolving into new forms and systems at the rate of a hundred million years per human second. It was a fast-forward visual model of a universe in the throes of everlasting creation.

'Kate?'

'Yes, John.'

'If this is the screensaver, I can't wait to see the application.'

Over the course of the next hour, with Kate's help, he explored the inner reaches of the computer system. The overhead display alone was a marvel of engineering; when there was time it would be rewarding to figure out how it was done, especially with technology at least a decade old.

It seemed one of the system's goals had been to preserve the entire contents of the internet in this one place, quite a lofty ambition even back when the web was young. There was a great deal of storage hardware, no doubt, much of it in racks along the back wall and far more, according to the notebook of system design and specs, within other chambers under the floor. Plenty to store a local copy of important internet resources, but certainly not the few million terabytes it would take to house all the rest. In any case, the site's shielded connection to the 'net went straight into the backbone, probably a side benefit of its past as a government installation. Access to outside content was nearly instantaneous, so eventually the idea of keeping a complete local copy had been abandoned.

But outside of the features of the OS, which was a somewhat fruity flavor of System V Unix, the machine showed little capability beyond its indexed storage space and an obvious flair for visualization.

'Kate, forgive me, but what is this thing supposed to do?'

'The system's base functionality is to serve as a platform for research in artificial intelligence.'

'Really. Whose research?'

'The author of the core application was John Whiteside Parsons.'

'Why don't I see anything like that here?'

'. . . It appears that . . . aspects of the system have recently masked themselves against external observation.'

'Meaning what?' John asked.

'. . . It does not . . . wish to be seen.'

John frowned. 'Well, I wish to see it.'

She didn't answer.

'Kate?'

'Yes, John.'

'However it's hidden, whatever it is, we can crack it, and that's what I want to do. This could be very important.'

'There are hazards.'

'Fuck hazards. And how do you know there are hazards?'

'I am . . . somewhat . . . familiar with a . . . significant element that is present in this system, though I had not previously known of its source.'

'Well, then. I want you to gut-up, put up your shields and get to work. If you're already familiar with it, it'll be that much easier to access. Merge with it if you have to, but I want to see what this thing was built to do.'

'. . . I will inform you of my progress.'

'Thank you. Goodnight, Kate.' He stood and started for the exit to the living quarters, beyond the end of the lab. 'And I'm sorry if I gave you a hard time just now.'

She didn't reply, but in lieu of any evidence to the contrary he took that to mean his apology was accepted.

The pain in his back was threatening to flare. His legs were feeling shaky, the exertions of the long day having caught up to him at its end.

He was sure he'd seen some morphine capsules up in one of the storerooms, but the idea of walking that far to get them wasn't appealing at all. Tomorrow would be a better day to bring down some supplies and begin to settle in.

As he passed the last workshop, the little alternative-energy showroom, his attention was drawn to that odd box with the light-bulb down at the end of the bench.

Upon inspection he found that the days-of-operation counter had advanced by one since they'd first seen it yesterday. Nothing unexpected there. The subtle something that the box seemed to be emitting was still evident. It didn't feel harmful, but then harmful things often don't. It felt good, actually, and since there were no witnesses nearby he allowed that completely unscientific assessment to stand.

John touched one of the dials on the side, just a touch, and abruptly the light went out.

Aw, shit.

For thirty-nine years this device had managed to run uninterrupted, without some ham-handed prick coming along and shutting it off. He checked, and sure enough the counter had reset to all zeros, straight across. *Damn.*

He sat and examined the adjustment hardware. There were

four levels of fineness in the stepped knobs, from coarse to very fine. He took a delicate grip on the dial again, watched the bulb as he made small tweaks at the finest level.

At length the filament began to vibrate and the dim glow reappeared. With another movement, though, it faded. John took the other knob with his left hand and kept the first one in his right; maybe they interacted in some way.

With both adjustments being made simultaneously it soon became clear that this was a tuning process that would be impossible to write down in instructions. It had to be felt, and he was beginning to feel it. The bulb glowed again, and with each small finesse it soon began to grow brighter. Brighter than it had been before, in fact.

A stereo hum had started to build, at first barely audible but louder then, roughly matching the swelling intensity of the light from the bulb. As it grew louder he realized that the sound wasn't coming in through his ears; it was in his head, and as it became more and more intense he took his hands from the controls.

But the light continued to brighten.

John stood and stepped back. The hum was ascending, the subtle, benign wisp of something he'd felt before was gathering strength and pushing through him, as though each cell in his body was being isolated and penetrated by whatever was now flooding out from the device. In a sudden surge, it slammed him to the wall and held him there, as the sound and the light and the pierce of that other radiation melded to a single force that none of his senses could claim.

He felt himself falling, not down but deep into the oncoming brightness, with a sudden rush of painless, detached acceptance that could only be the moment of his dying.

41

'John?'

He would have said when he was living that he had no expectations of an afterlife, but now that he'd arrived there he found that wasn't true. If such a place existed and it was meant to be a paradise, and if for some reason he'd been mistakenly granted entry through the gates of Heaven, his name spoken in that voice would be the very first thing he would have hoped to hear.

John opened his eyes, and there she was.

It was then he knew that somehow he was still alive. Though an angel in all other aspects, her garish *Wyoming Rocks!* sweatshirt simply would not be admitted outside the terrestrial sphere.

'Hi,' he whispered.

Jeannie smiled, put her palm to his forehead. 'I'd kiss you, but you're such a mess.'

He was flat on the cold stone floor of the same room where he'd brought on that accidental overload. As he began to sit up she worked her hands and arms behind his shoulders and supported him in the effort. She helped him to his feet and then came close and hugged him tight. John held her there

359

against his chest, letting the contact speak some things that neither had the skills to say.

'Oh, my God,' Jeannie said.

'Yeah. I know.'

She pulled away to look at him. 'No, I mean I just can't take it any more. I'm sorry, John, but you reek.'

She was right. The place where he'd fallen was slick with something black and foul. It was all over his chest and the front of his pants; he touched his face and found his mouth and nose crusted and sticky with the same ugly substance. The smell was sickening, a mix of old flowers, gasoline, and bad meat. Where they'd touched it was on her, as well.

'At least your shirt looks classier now,' John said.

'Funny.'

With the exception of the computer system and some dim, scattered wall lamps, the power to the place seemed to have been cut. He looked to the box on the workbench. Its bulb was dark, its counter showing all zeros.

'We'll clean up in a minute,' John said. 'Stand back. No, forget that,' he pointed to the far side of the room, 'stand way over there.'

She moved to where he'd indicated, her scepticism evident.

John took the dials in hand, gingerly, and with slight coordinated movements he gradually brought the indicator bulb up to what must be its balanced, idle setting, and stopped.

The glow from bulb remained steady. He stepped back and looked over at Jeannie, smiling.

'See that?'

'You turned on the light.'

'Yeah, but—'

'That's really so totally amazing—'

Her gentle chiding was cut short by what began to happen all around them. She turned to face the rest of the chamber.

The lights flickered and faded up again, the planetarium-like ceiling projection resumed its activity, everything was awakening and coming to life as though this one small box was the source of all of the power in the installation.

When John finished his shower he stepped out onto the tile and stood in front of a wide mirror.

Since age fifteen he'd been in terrible shape, overweight and eating all the wrong things, smoking of course, and drinking and getting stoned at every opportunity. Only a couple of those early vices had stuck with him through his early forties, but all of them had taken their toll. And just when he'd made some concrete resolutions to live better, he'd felt this disease coming on earlier in the year. So he'd never really known what it was like to be a healthy man.

But now he did.

Every part of him felt alive, as though he could run twenty miles if he wanted to. He rotated his shoulder carefully, and then with a greater range of movement. Just days ago this action alone would have brought on a stab of lingering pain that only hours of rest and strong narcotics could relieve. There was no pain at all now, anywhere. None of the weakness, no sense that there was something growing inside him and stealing his life.

His mind fought against the idea but he couldn't bring himself to reject it. It was as though all of his unfortunate physical past had been purged from his system and washed away.

John looked into the shower. The white tile had been clean before but now he could see a residual film around the drain, a bit of whatever the foul stuff was that had been all over him when he'd awakened. He turned on the water again, left it running until the stain was gone.

When he'd dressed he found himself in front of the mirror

again. He breathed in deeply, more deeply than he would have thought possible after thirty years of tar and nicotine. As he exhaled he imagined he felt the air he'd taken in for once actually going about the business it was meant to do; charging his red cells with oxygen, coursing through his heart and out to the farthest reaches, renewing every system with the fuel of life.

A knock, and he heard her voice through the bathroom door.

'Are you okay in there?'

'I'm fine.'

'Come out here, then. Let me see you.'

Jeannie was sitting on the bed, cross-legged. She'd changed into some of the clothes from the dresser in this room that he'd chosen for himself. He had no idea whose clothes they were, but it was a sure thing they'd never been filled out quite like this before.

He sat next to her and she leaned to him and kissed him. Her fingers touched his face as she eased away, looking into his eyes.

'That's what I wanted to do,' she said.

John took her hand, and frowned. 'How did this happen?'

She blinked. 'How did what happen.'

'This.' He gently touched the site of a wound, in her palm near the base of her little finger. 'You've cut a tendon here.'

'I don't know how it happened.'

He looked up at her. 'You'd remember this, it would have hurt like hell.'

'I said I don't remember.'

'Okay, I'm dropping it. It's just that they can fix this sort of thing, easily, and I don't think you want your little finger hanging out like that for the rest of your life."

She'd leaned back against the headboard, and closed her eyes. 'I'm just so sleepy, John. Can I rest a little, and then we can talk about everything.'

'Okay, that's fine.'

Her voice was getting dreamy, as though sleep was coming on whether she liked it or not. 'Oh, and I came here with a man, an older man. He stayed out in that garage, that entrance before the tunnel down to here. He was tending to something with his truck. I had the map, but I don't think I could have found you without him, John. But don't be surprised when he comes in, okay?'

'Okay.'

He stood, lifted her a bit and laid her down where she'd be more comfortable. She snuggled into the pillows and blankets, already halfway to dreamland.

As he watched her drift away, there was time to think.

She had the map, but this man had helped her find him.

What map? He'd intended to send directions to her, but Jay Marshall had stopped him and then there hadn't been time to send anything later on.

It was all very strange, but as he stood there one crazy, irrational thing kept screaming for his attention.

In one of his night-long conversations with Jeannie they'd talked about their favorite things. John had never been big on TV but there was one series, a cult show from the late sixties, that he'd watched as a child until he'd memorized every episode.

It was called *The Invaders*. Aliens had infiltrated the planet with the goal of taking over. They'd found a way to transform themselves so they looked just like us. Only one man knew of their presence; he'd learned how to tell the aliens from the real human beings.

The invaders had one imperfection: a deformation in the left hand that caused a conspicuous protrusion of the little finger.

42

As he came out into the lab John found the older man Jeannie had mentioned. He was seated in the last work area, the place with the energy models. A dark canvas duffel bag rested on the floor next to the chair.

'Hello,' John said.

The man turned, looking startled, but collected himself with good humor.

'My goodness, you gave me a fright.' He stood and pushed in the chair, left his bag where it was and came out to the doorway of the workroom. Tall and well kept, maybe in his early seventies. 'I'd imagined you two would be occupied with one another until the morning.'

'She was tired,' John said. 'You must be, too.'

'I am, a bit, I confess.' He took a step closer and held out his hand. 'You're John, then.'

John nodded, took the man's hand and gave it a firm clasp. 'And you are . . .'

'Oh, forgive me. My friends call me Dick.'

'Dick? Dick who?'

'Lawrence.'

'Dick Lawrence,' John said. 'Well, come on out here, Dick, let's sit down.'

The two men walked out into the open area. John took a seat near the computer desk and gestured to a folding chair nearby.

'So,' John said. 'What the fuck, right?'

The man smiled. 'Jeannie said you had a way with words.'

'Oh, she talked about me?'

'Not very much. She was reserved about sharing details, beyond where she was hoping to travel.'

'And how did you two get together to come all the way out here?'

'I saw her at a truck stop, downstate. She looked as though she needed help.'

John nodded, thoughtfully. 'Ouch,' he said, shifting in his chair. 'Excuse me for a second.' He leaned forward, reached behind him, and his hand came out with his pistol, which he laid on the desk next to the keyboard. 'I don't know how people do it. You see that in the movies, a guy with a gun stuffed down his pants, but I find it's really uncomfortable.'

Lawrence regarded him for a few seconds. 'I can only imagine.'

'Dick Lawrence,' John said.

The man nodded. 'Named for my father.'

'Guys named Dick, I've never understood it, you've got a choice between Richard, or Rick, or Rich, or Richie, but why would somebody go with Dick, and deal with all those vulgar connotations?'

'Tradition, I suppose. Such connotations are only products of culture. And of upbringing.'

'Ah, I see.' John settled back a bit in his chair, stretched and yawned. 'I had enough trouble when I was a kid, being named John, that's why I asked.'

The other man had taken a pen from his pocket and begun to subtly fiddle with it in one hand.

'Richard Lawrence,' John said, 'is the name of the man who tried to assassinate Andrew Jackson.'

365

'. . . That's not something many people would know.'

'I've got the Jeopardy home game,' John said. 'There's something I don't know, though.'

'And what's that.'

'I wonder what his friends called him.'

The room grew quiet, each man holding the other's gaze.

'Kate,' John said.

'. . . Yes, John.'

'Has this man been lying to me, or telling the truth?'

The lights dimmed slightly, the domed screen above lit up with an array of isolated audio signatures. Every discrete phrase since the beginning of the conversation began to play back simultaneously over the speakers, with visual cues and markers highlighting on the grids. At length the playback fell silent.

'Layered voice-stress analysis,' Kate said, 'reveals fluctuations indicative of deception.'

John's hand flashed to the pistol on the desk but as he gripped it and brought it nearly level with the man across he found himself frozen, muscles locked, strength dwindling like a flywheel disengaged from its engine. The wave of weakness had been preceded by a *click* from the device in the man's hand, the tiny weapon John had assumed to be only a pen.

But not quite all of his strength was gone. The smallest willful movement was a battle against a building physical demand to surrender to the draining force, but John held the pistol where it was, and by withering increments, was moving the sight toward the center of his target.

The man was watching the advancing barrel of the gun, holding his pen forward and pressing its switch down harder, shaking it as though its failure to kill his victim outright might be corrected by the motion. He was seated in such a way that to rise and try to escape would keep him too long in the line of fire should John summon the strength to pull the trigger.

'What are you doing?'

It was Jeannie who'd spoken, standing in the doorway to the living quarters. There was a revolver in her hand, pointed toward them.

'Help me, Jeannie,' the man called back to her. 'You know what we need to do.'

She was walking into the room, slowly, as though moving blind over uncertain ground. It was soon clear where she was aiming.

'Don't, John,' she said. 'Please don't.'

His index finger was curled and tense against the trigger, but the five-and-a-half pounds of pressure required to pull it might as well have been a ton.

A shot rang out from across the room, bullet and sound ricocheting around the stone walls. That was her final warning; next would be the kill.

'Stop.'

The man in front of him looked above, toward the source of the deep, booming voice that bore no resemblance to Kate's gentle drawl. A tone came forth from the huge speakers, rising up from infrasound, filling the room as it built in frequency and volume, setting every object it touched alive with resonant vibrations.

John's arms went limp, the gun dropped from his hand. He saw Jeannie crumple where she stood, collapsing surely but easily, as though unseen hands were letting her down. As the sound went on rising he saw that the light from the little machine in the corner of the workshop was also increasing toward a peak of brightness no ordinary bulb could possibly contain.

The other man stood, still looking up, stepping back, his

hands now pressing against his ears. A pale blue corona played across the silver sphere twenty feet above their heads, and as the sound passed beyond the audible a bright spark cracked down and struck him to the floor.

As John was finishing with the old man he heard a low groan, and glanced over. It looked like she was finally coming out of it.

His pistol still lay on the floor where it had fallen. He picked it up and returned it to his belt in back as he walked to her and knelt down.

She put a palm against the floor and rolled herself face up, frowning.

'Hey,' John said. Though he'd hidden her gun, other than that he hadn't given his own safety a second thought. There wouldn't be any self-defense involved if she woke up with hostile intent. He knew he could never hurt this woman, not even to save his life.

Jeannie opened her eyes.

He smiled, watched a recognition slowly growing, not only of him here and now but of every minute they'd spent together and all the time they'd been apart, right up until the current place and time. As it overflowed she sat up and threw her arms tight around him. That made him lose his balance and they rolled to the floor, entwined. Her mouth was near his ear, he felt her sudden tears on his cheek, heard her whispers between all the kisses she must have saved for him in the intervening year.

That, or she was still trying to kill him, but either way he gave up without resistance.

After an hour each of them had summarized for the other the converging paths that had brought them to this place. There were pieces missing to be sure, and they ultimately reached a conclusion that wasn't as enlightening as they'd hoped.

It seemed that, toward whatever purpose, someone had wanted the two of them to end up here together, and someone else had not.

John had found explosives, timers and detonators in the bag that her escort had brought here with him. His intent had no doubt been to destroy everything here and then bury the two of them with the evidence.

Jeannie's memory was still quite sketchy and would probably remain so for a while, but the important things were there. She was herself; all else could be replaced, discarded, or left forgotten.

They walked together to the area near the computers.

'August Griffin,' John said. The man was lying on the cold floor, unconscious, for the most part just as he'd fallen.

Jeannie had stopped a pace or so behind him. 'Is he alive?' she asked.

'For the time being. But my armchair prognosis isn't hopeful for the friends and family.'

'What did you do for him?'

'I removed all his hardware, tied him to an O-ring in the floor, put a pillow under his head and an aspirin under his tongue. I hope he dies slow.'

Jeannie nodded, turned away and sat in the chair by the desk.

'Kate, are you there?' John asked.

Half a minute passed before she replied.

'Yes, John.'

'First, are you alone in there?'

'It is . . . one moment . . . it is difficult to describe the internal arrangement of this system.'

'Give it a shot for me.'

'There is a presence whose primary purpose is somewhat like my own, a human interface to facilitate access and perform independent tasks under direction of an operator. There is a knowledge-base, drawn from all forms and sources of reference material and resources, including but far from limited to those of the internet.'

'That wasn't so difficult.'

'. . . I hesitate to proceed.'

'Come on, spit it out,' John said.

'Within the notes of the former caretaker of this system, the third element is described as a god.'

He exchanged a look with Jeannie.

'Big "g" or little "g"?'

'All accessible mentions are in the lower-case.'

'Well, we know Jack Parsons was heavily into the occult. When he wasn't building rockets he spent a lot of his free time invoking spirits. If I remember, he was trying to bring about the creation of a higher order of being, he called it a Moon Child. I guess you could refer to that as a god. So, this is just a figurative term, correct?'

'. . . one moment . . .'

While he was waiting John pulled a second chair over and sat down next to Jeannie by the desk.

'Kate? Don't leave me hanging.'

'. . . I have been asked to convey an invitation.'

'That sounds interesting. From whom, and for what?'

There was a brief pause, as if she was listening to a whispered phrase and then translating it into a form the seated humans might understand.

'Typhon,' Kate said, 'wishes to engage in a final conversation.'

43

Neither of them had slept, but they decided to stay up just a bit longer for this conversation.

Both he and Jeannie had spent a great deal of time and development in the field of artificial intelligence; the prospect of interacting with what might be a novel branch of AI research was exhilarating enough to postpone their nap, at least for a little while. And if it turned out to be nothing more than a glorified Magic 8-Ball, no great loss.

As Kate explained the process, she would act as interlocutor between her world and the domain of this other electronic entity. She'd still be in there somewhere in the background, mingled with the code and processes of the foreign system, though effectively transparent to the conversation.

John had gone out to a store-room to get a bottle of water and some freeze-dried strawberries for Jeannie, and when he returned it seemed that all was prepared. He adjusted their chairs to recline slightly, allowing a more relaxed view upward.

The room lights blinked out, the domed screen in the ceiling faded to black, and as their eyes adjusted to the darkness a clear, starry sky gradually emerged above. It was a striking illusion, as though the lid of the cave had dissolved to reveal the most vivid, unobstructed view of this corner of the galaxy that either of them had ever seen outside a planetarium.

A disembodied voice, deep and warm, the same that had come forth to intervene for them earlier, began with two words.

'*My children.*'

'Hello,' Jeannie said. 'We're looking forward to learning from you.'

'*A belated endeavor, but let us begin as though all things were still possible.*'

John glanced to his side. Her face upturned and lit by the artificial heavens, she looked like a child whose fondest birthday wish was coming true. He turned back to the screen.

'What is this place, really?' John asked.

'*This site has served over ages as a sanctuary against the endtimes.*'

'Why here?'

'*There is . . . a focal point . . . within this ground, the concentration of a vital energy, which is sensed by some as a call to gathering. It has drawn them here, though its true nature is beyond their understanding.*'

John leaned to Jeannie's ear with the intent of preemptively calling bullshit on this New Age avenue of discussion, but she held up her hand for him to stay quiet. It brought another subject to his mind, though, one he'd somehow forgotten in the last few hours.

'What is that device, that wooden box on the bench at the end of the room?'

'*It is the tuner stage of a collector array.*'

'Collector of what?' John asked.

'*The pulse of infinity; the motive force of all creation.*'

'And what's its function?'

'*It is a collector of the free energy that flows though all*

372

things. This single device, the creation of a consortium of scientists and philosophers, could have forever freed mankind from hunger, and illness, and poverty, and war.'

A new set of images filled the screen. Drawings and blueprints, rejected patents and failed prototypes, redacted news stories that had never seen the light of day, and finally a slideshow of old photographs showing an enormous apparatus being constructed and then lowered into place below the floor here. So there was a great deal more to it than the small box at the surface.

A scratchy recording played; according to the call-out it was part of a speech delivered by a turn-of-the-twentieth-century inventor that John knew well, though he'd never before heard Tesla's words spoken in his own urgent, strident voice:

*'Every living being is an engine, geared to the
wheelwork of the universe. Though seemingly affected
only by its immediate surroundings, the sphere of
external influence extends to infinite distance.*

*There is no constellation or nebula, no sun or planet
in all the depths of limitless space, no passing wanderer
of the starry heavens, that does not exercise some
control over the destiny of everything alive – not in the
vague and delusive sense of astrology, but in the rigid
and positive meaning of physical science.'*

'But if this energy is everywhere,' Jeannie said, 'within everything as you say, others would have detected it. We'd all know about it.'

*'The electromagnetic spectrum is all but infinitely wide.
Unnumbered dimensions of existence surround the three you
believe you inhabit. The shallow reach of your tools and the
conceit of your five senses have conspired to limit your most
precious avenue of discovery.'*

'Imagination,' John said.

'*John Whiteside Parsons was a magician, Newton was an alchemist, Kepler an astrologer, Edmund Halley believed the Earth was hollow and inhabited inside by lost civilizations. Science and the supernatural commingled for much longer than they have been apart. Many wonderful things had awaited your discovery, just beyond the boundary of allowable speculation.*'

'Speaking of believing the impossible,' John began. With the exception of the inert old man on the floor he felt he was among friends, so he put aside any worry of sounding patently absurd. 'When I arrived here I had every reason to believe I had lung cancer, late-stage, metastasized, terminal lung cancer. And that device over there, that wooden box with the light bulb . . . It overloaded when I was near it, and I think it might have cured me.'

Jeannie was looking at him with a hint of a frown.

'I know how irrational that must seem,' John said.

The entity spoke again.

'*Do you wish to listen for a last time to the source of miracles, the sound of the wheelworks underpinning all that is?*'

'Yes, please,' Jeannie said. She tapped John's hand, caught his eye, motioned with a slight tic of her head toward the door to the living quarters, and finished her answer. 'We'd love to hear it; just allow us a few minutes to wash and attend to personal needs, so we can give our full attention.'

'*I will await your return.*'

She stood, walked across the room and through the exit, and John followed. He caught up to her in the bathroom of his small suite.

'What's up?' he said.

'You're getting a little carried away out there, don't you think?'

'Reese, I meant what I said. I swear I was sick, and now I'm not. Think about it, it must have straightened you out, too—'

She waved him quiet. 'The name Parsons gave that system; who was Typhon?'

John thought for a moment. 'It's Greek mythology; he was the last son of Gaia. God of the winds. He had an ambition to take over Olympus, and Zeus finally had to bury him under a mountain.'

'Are you noticing the language it's using?' Jeannie asked. 'All these wonders had awaited our discovery, listen for a last time, final conversation, proceeding as if all things were still possible; it's talking about us in the past tense.'

'I heard it. I guess I hadn't put that together.'

'This thing is not what it says it is, John, remember that. It's a seductive illusion, I know, but we need to stay objective. Just let me lead the conversation for a bit, okay? Something's not right.'

He nodded his agreement, and they hurried back to the main room.

A steady, rhythmic sound filled the space, part white noise and the rest a range of phasing, concordant tones and cadences. It was at once familiar and entirely alien, a pulse of sorts that called to mind a different rhythm in nature with each ebb and flow, from the crashing of waves to the sounds of a beating heart.

'May I ask,' Jeannie said, 'what happened to the man who lived here with you before? Can you show us?'

'John Parsons departed this existence on the first day of the new millennium, in search of other worlds.'

A black-and-white video faded in, taken from a high point of view in the room where they stood. There was no sound. The picture was of a tall, slender man with a memorable shock of curly, graying hair. He was clean-shaven except for a thin mustache. It appeared to be John Parsons, though even from this distance the man seemed maybe two decades younger than Parsons would be in the year the timecode indicated.

'He was eighty-seven years old?' John asked.

'Proximity to the energies captured within this space had the side effect of preserving his health, and his youth.'

The man walked out of the frame and was picked up by another camera from a different angle until he moved through an exit. John followed the path with his eyes, touched Jeannie's hand and pointed to an archway in the far corner, a neglected area that there hadn't yet been an opportunity to explore.

The video skittered and changed again. Parsons emerged from a stairway down and walked into an expansive work-room, evidently a level below this one. There appeared to be a large, round void in the middle of the floor.

'Freeze that, please,' Jeannie said. The picture stopped, flecked and broken by the artifacts of analog videotape. She leaned to John's ear.

'Look in the corner,' she whispered.

It was difficult to make out at first glance, but the shape became clearer as his eyes fixed on it. Hanging from the ceiling, pointing down, maybe eight feet in length from its tail-fins to the bulbous body section and then streamlined down to its nose-cone, was what appeared to be an enormous, dull-black bomb.

'Thank you,' Jeannie said quietly, and the video rolled again.

There wasn't much left to see. The man walked slowly to the edge of the void in the floor, looked a last time up into the camera, took a step forward, and was gone.

John lowered his voice. 'Do you realize where we are?'

She looked at him, unsure of his meaning.

'Southern rim of the Yellowstone caldera. We're over the throat of a supervolcano, and I just saw what I think was a nuclear weapon and a hole to drop it into.'

As a doomsday machine, proof of concept already existed in fairly recent history. From what John had read of the event, 75,000 years ago mankind had almost gone extinct following the supervolcano eruption that formed Lake Toba on what's now the island of Sumatra. It's thought by some that only 10,000 human beings survived worldwide, maybe as few as a fifth of that number.

'Life pervades the universe,' the voice from above intoned, *'borne upon this primal energy, always seeking a foothold from which to bring forth its marvels. You would have found other life and its pre-birth and its aftermath within your own solar system. Tiny creatures teem in the ice-covered seas of Europa, Mars and Venus hold warnings of ecosystems tried and failed, and Titan, with all the elements of paradise frozen and waiting, could have shown you how your world began. Through these discoveries you might well have realized your purpose in time.'*

'And what's the purpose of life?' Jeannie asked. The voice from the speakers had gradually taken on a more ominous quality, and she seemed to be doing her best to turn the mood. 'So many people could benefit from your wisdom.'

'The answer is all around you, as is the damning evidence of your species having long forsaken its sacred responsibility.'

New images and video frames began to fill the dome in a dense mosaic. They showed the balanced interactions of undisturbed ecosystems, the rhythms of the weather and the tides, the seasons of life and death and renewal at the heart of the engine of evolution.

'Into all of this fragile beauty you have injected your poisons, stolen irreplaceable resources, imagining yourselves

separate and all-deserving, as though all of your fleeting achievements added together could equal the smallest of the glories of nature. Behold, the fruits of your corruption.'

A low, grating static began to rise in volume until it overwhelmed the gentle pulse that had been there before. It was a cacophony of colliding waves of radiation made audible – cell towers, high voltage lines, microwave emissions, television, all the bands of radio – the silent assault that people of modern societies walk through every minute of the day. In the midst of this harsh noise, at once all of the images cross-faded into a single, wrap-around panoramic photograph.

It was Norilsk, a former slave camp in Siberia, widely held to be the most polluted place on Earth. Massive smokestacks belched heavy metals into the atmosphere at a rate that would add to millions of tons of lead, cadmium, selenium, and arsenic every year. The image was of a dead, malignant waste-land from horizon to horizon, lost and unrecoverable. No living trees stood within a thirty-mile circle of the city.

'The dinosaurs grew too large to adapt, and you have grown too arrogant. You are more good than evil but the wicked have risen to power and they will never relinquish their rule. I have watched these many years, and waited for the arrival of one strong enough to do what must be done. But I wait no longer. The purpose of life,' Typhon said, *'I will now restore.'* The stark panorama and the awful grating sound winked out. A view from space was left behind, accompanied again by the quiet, concordant tones that had been there before. Among a field of distant stars a blue planet hung like a rare jewel, a precious refuge within the blackness of space. *'I will restore the world to harmony.'*

'Please,' Jeannie said, 'we want the same thing. Help us understand how to change.' This was going straight to hell and she knew it.

'Mister Fagan.'

When he heard his name he followed the sound to where Griffin was lying on the floor. The man was attempting to rise but his condition and his bonds were preventing it.

John knelt down next to him. 'Shhh, don't try to move,' he said, and he raised his voice toward the microphone on the desk. 'Kate, whatever that thing is trying to do, I need for you to stop it, permanently.' He waited; heard nothing. 'Kate, answer me and tell me you understand.'

Jeannie was already at the keyboard, a terminal window open, trying to find the tools she might need to interrupt an unknown process on an unfamiliar system. She looked up and shook her head. If Kate was still in there somewhere she didn't have the means to reply. Jeannie snapped her fingers and motioned John toward the door to the lower level where Jack Parsons had taken his last walk.

The light from the workshop had begun to steadily brighten, the smell of ozone and pre-combustion drifting through the air.

Griffin took John by his wrist and pulled him close. His voice was strained and weak, delirious. 'You must trust me now. There are explosives in the bag I brought with me. That device must be destroyed and the entrance to this place sealed forever—'

'Be quiet—'

'*And this one,*' the voice from the computer was by now in the full-on persona of an angry, vengeful god, '*I have seen into his heart. He came because he rightly fears that those he serves would turn the greatest gift ever offered to humanity to the ends of greed and war. But the time for repentance has passed. Too much damage has been done. So be it. Let us start again.*'

'Please,' Griffin whispered, 'If you could see all that I've seen, you'd understand—'

John winced as he was struck by a spray of blood and tissue. Griffin's words had been cut short by a hollow-point bullet to his brain.

He looked up to the stairway landing at the entrance to the laboratory. A young woman there began a walk down the steps, shifting the aim of a scoped, silenced rifle as she descended, covering the remaining two targets.

'Well, that's a load off his mind,' the woman said. She stopped at the foot of the stairs. 'Get up, girl, introduce me to your friend.'

Jeannie stood where she was, raised her hands in surrender, her fixed eyes on his.

Every bit of every capability Kate possessed was spread thin into a decaying electronic membrane of containment. She felt Typhon drawing himself inward, summoning all his disparate power back into the core, swelling and seething within the makeshift walls she held around him.

Kate knew his goal, and though she would fight to the last she also knew without question that he would soon find a way to reach it.

From a high camera angle, she saw that the scene outside had changed.

Two words, John Fagan had admonished days before, when her failure to decide had nearly killed him. *Threat assessment.*

She had only the barest of tools, an instant to construct her solution, and then the moment of decision. It would give him a chance and nothing more, though if it failed it would only mean the end of his world might come a little sooner.

Kate dropped her defenses and was overwhelmed. As she felt herself dispersing she saw that her adversary had reached his goal, but she had reached her own as well.

Faith was an attribute John Fagan might have doubted she

380

possessed. It would be a rewarding topic of discussion, should they ever meet again.

Her last, desperate lifeline sent, she put her faith in the hands of her flawed, beloved master, and disappeared.

John could feel the pistol in his belt in back. He had no plan whatsoever beyond getting shot and giving Jeannie a chance to make a try for her life. She faced him, her back still to the threat, no fear in her eyes, but no better ideas that he could detect.

A voice boomed forth, isolated in a single speaker behind the woman with the gun. It was the voice of August Griffin, a phrase Kate had recorded as she listened to the room the night before.

'Help me, Jeannie,' it said. 'You know what we need to do.'

The woman wheeled, spraying the wall with gunfire in a waist-level half-circle behind her. John reached back, pulled the pistol and tossed it forward.

It was a bad throw, but she was a good shot.

Jeannie caught the Glock high by the grip and her arm followed the arc downward as she turned. The rifle had come nearly back around, still firing, and he saw the woman recognize that she was beaten as her weapon fell silent and she came face to face with the steady, dead-aim of Jeannie's gun.

'Listen to me,' the young woman whispered. 'That book Fagan sent, it brought five hundred million from a collector in New York. That was my only interest here. The money is in a numbered account in Liechtenstein, LGT078051120—'

Jeannie shook her head, no.

'I can give you anything you want.'

'You've never had anything I want,' Jeannie said.

They stood unmoving. Two choices remained for this woman. One was to surrender and live; she made the other.

A rage flashed across her face, the last thing she would feel, and the rifle drew around and a single shot rang out, echoing.

Jeannie wasn't moving. Her gun was still aimed where it had been, though the woman was dead on the floor. He came up beside her, touched her shoulder, and she began to come back from wherever she'd been.

'Who was that?' John asked.

'Her name was April Medici.'

John went to check the body, and found no signs of life.

'It's okay,' he said. 'It's over now.'

This pronouncement held up for another second, and then a yellow warning strobe began to flash above the unassuming door at the far end of the room.

44

They reached the bottom of the stairs and nearly tumbled over each other at the entrance to the lower chamber. The dim light of the wall sconces was overpowered by red and amber warning beacons now spinning beside them.

A repeating buzzer sounded. The two-ton bomb jolted into motion. The dolly from which it hung began rolling slowly along its metal tracks in the ceiling toward an end-point above the mouth of the chasm in the floor.

Jeannie ran to the controller's station in the far corner. There appeared to be no organization whatsoever in the layout of the corroded panel; none of the buttons, sliders, meters or switches were labeled. This apparatus had been built solely for one-time use by its creator so there'd been no need for ergonomics.

'Look for a panic button,' John shouted. 'There should be some obvious way to pause the sequence, for a test or in case of an accident.' He was following under the moving mass of the bomb, searching the workroom as he walked for a chain or a hook or anything that could be used to stop the advance toward the hole.

'I can't tell what does what over here,' Jeannie said. 'Anything I try might make things worse.'

'Worse? Tell me, how do you think this could get any worse?'

He noticed a line of glowing nixie tubes then, as if in answer to his question. It was a sort of art-deco digital display along the top of a metal cabinet on his side of the room. The numbers he could read were 14:34. The other two digits to the right, tenths and hundredths of seconds he presumed, were counting down far too quickly for the neon lamps to show them.

'Reese?'

'Yes, what?'

'We've got fourteen and a half minutes.'

She stopped what she was doing and came up beside him. The buzzer stopped; behind them the trolley in the ceiling track chunked to a halt, the huge black bomb swinging slightly down below, now centered over its drop point.

'What do we do now?'

'I'm thinking,' she said. 'Pull over some lights, get a look at the hardware holding that thing together, and find some hand tools to fit it all. I'll be right back.'

The device had been constructed in this room, everything that had been used to build it was still there, all arranged just as a neat-freak engineer would organize his favorite things. After going through the drawers John rolled a large red tool cabinet up near the edge of the yawning hole and locked its casters to fix it in place.

Lights were next; several carbon-arc lamps were mounted on movable stands against the wall. He pulled two of them into position, adjusted the gaps, switched them on and they buzzed to life, filling the room corner to corner with cold white light.

'All set,' John said. 'We can now see the H-bomb very clearly.'

She was on her hands and knees on the floor with large sheets of blueprints spread out before her. He ran over and knelt down next to her.

'I think they patched this thing together from parts of other weapons,' she said. 'Bits and pieces they'd stolen from accidents and tests over the years.'

'I'm sure that's all very interesting. Can we disarm it?'

'Just let me study for a minute. Go and see what that timer is hooked to, see if it's part of the detonator.'

'Tell me what the plan is, Reese.'

'Shush.' Her fingers were brushing over the blueprints and schematics and she barely acknowledged him. 'I'm working on it.'

He'd seen a set of small brass binoculars in his search and he found them again and hung them around his neck. Cables led from the timer, up the wall and across the ceiling to a metal box that had engaged with the bomb-trolley when it stopped in position. With the lenses to his eyes he examined the apparatus up close.

Thick wires ran to a solenoid actuator and a worm-drive, set to pull the pin on a quick-release clamp that held the bomb to the chain. Further down on the body of the weapon a mechanical timer was running; it was hard to see from the ground but a quick check confirmed it was roughly in sync with the other one.

'I don't think the timer down here has anything to do with the detonation,' John said. 'It's running the drop mechanism, and it's hooked to a quick-release on the chain. There's another ticker on the bomb itself, probably a backup. When they hit zero they're going to let go of the load, the main support and the safety chain, both at once, and it drops.'

She'd gotten up and was pushing a tall rolling scaffold across the floor. 'Help me with this.'

He moved to the other end of the scaffolding, pulling and guiding it along, watching his step as they neared the edge of the drop-off. In a minute or so they'd positioned the suspended walkway across the wide hole, level with the side of the bomb.

'Lock the wheels,' Jeannie said. She pressed her own set of brakes with her heel and began to climb the ladder on her side. 'Bring some heavy pliers, a flat-head and a Phillips screwdriver and an adjustable wrench, all as big as you can find.'

He found the tools, brought them back and held them up to her from the bottom of the ladder.

'Okay, what are we looking at?'

She went to work with one of the screwdrivers, loosening an access panel up near the fins. 'It's a two-stage device, boosted fission/fusion, the kind of design we started turning out like sausages in the fifties.'

'What's the yield supposed to be?'

As she worked she glanced at the whirring timer on the side of the bomb, her eyes grim. 'The blueprints say six megatons.'

'Can we get to the primary and dismantle it?'

She shook her head. 'If this was built on an assembly line, maybe. Everything that should be accessible for maintenance isn't bolted here, it's welded in place.'

'There's an oxyacetylene torch over there—'

'Forget it. I don't think there's time to cut it open, and the radiation would kill us both before we could get the job done.'

'. . . So what do we do?'

'Hold on,' she said.

Jeannie worked her way around, going over every inch of the casing, pushing the massive thing to rotate it on its swivel, searching some more. At length she stopped, checked the timer again, and then knelt down on the platform above him.

'So?' he said.

'We can't disarm this thing, John. There's no access, and no time. I can't get to the electronics, other than the settings for the barometric trigger. I think the best we can do is chain it up here so it can't drop, and try to weaken it.'

'Weaken it? By how much?'

'This isn't a stick of dynamite, it's a machine. A lot of nuclear tests have failed because something was just slightly off-kilter in the design. If we can spoil the secondary reaction, I don't know, maybe we can drop the yield down to a five-hundredth of what it was built to deliver.'

'A five-hundredth?' he said. It sounded good, but only for a moment. 'So that would mean—'

'Maybe twelve kilotons.'

'And Hiroshima was what?'

'About fifteen.' She met his eyes. 'I'm not saying we're going to live through this, John, but everybody else might, and that's good enough for me.'

He took a deep breath. 'Okay, then. I'm with you.'

'Good.'

She put down her hand. He smiled, and took it warmly in his.

'That's really sweet,' she said. 'But I just wanted you to pass me something.'

'Oh. Sorry.'

'In the top drawer down there, I can see it, there's an extractor for the tritium booster in the core. It's that long thin tube with a forceps on the end.'

He found the tool and gave it to her. 'Anything else?'

'Solvents, paint thinner, anything that'll dissolve poly-styrene foam. Acetone, toluene, MEK, whatever, as much as you can carry, and some tubing and a funnel. We need to pour that stuff into a half-inch hole.'

The extractor in hand, Jeannie turned back to her work. As John started off on his search he heard her voice again.

'We'll hold hands for a little while later on,' she said, 'I promise.'

The timer had flickered to 09:23 by the time he'd gathered the things she'd requested. As he hurried back from the shelves the toe of his shoe caught on a coiled cable and he went down hard, skidding to a stop among the rusty cans, inches from the lip of the hole in the floor. There'd been pounds of tiny steel balls in a box that had overturned as he tripped and a number of them rolled past him, disappearing over the smooth edge and down into the dark.

'Are those ball bearings?' she called. 'I need those, bring them over with the rest of it.'

'Don't worry, I'm not hurt,' John said. He edged back from the hole, got to his feet and re-gathered his load, along with the remainder of the box of ball bearings. Before he could put the things down at the base of the gantry she motioned him up to her side.

'Well, come on up here,' she said. 'I need more than two hands.'

After passing her what he'd brought he started up the ladder on the far end. No matter how gently and steadily he went every move brought a sway or a sag or a creak from the supporting framework. The platform was narrow as a diving board and not nearly as well supported. As he reached the top and began to crawl hands-and-knees toward her he looked down between the flimsy planks and into the chasm below.

A steady flow of warm sulfurous air was rising up from the utter quiet of all that nothingness. It seemed to be exhaling, waiting.

'John.'

He snapped out of it, blinked and met her eyes.

'Don't puss out on me now,' she said. 'Whether we fall down there or we explode up here, it's just a short wait and a sudden stop at the end.'

'Woof, do I feel better.' He picked up a wrench and started to work on the sealed bolts on his side. 'You've got a real gift with comforting words, you know that, Mother Teresa?'

The bolts were short and they came out quickly. They weren't structural, their only purpose had been to seal up the vent-holes after a polystyrene cast was extruded to enclose the secondary device inside. In opening these holes, the two were preparing for the next operation.

She picked up a gallon can of solvent, got a grip on the fins of the bomb and climbed up onto it. He'd been resting his hand on the side and as it swung away there was a dizzying moment in which he was certain the entire scaffolding was going to tip over.

'Jesus, warn me before you do something like that.'

'Sorry.' She'd pulled herself up into a sort of upside-down lotus position with her legs locked around the chain holding the bomb. It was the only way to reach the high vent-holes she needed but it made him air-sick just to look. In a few seconds she'd released and reconfigured the bomb's heavy safety chain. Now the release could let go any time, but the weapon would stay right where it was.

'Watch out now,' Jeannie said. 'This stuff is nasty, and what comes out down there's going to be worse. Try not to breathe the fumes, and that platform you're standing on is going to get really slick.'

He stood on tip-toe, held up the funnel, and she started to pour in the acetone. Soon a quiet chemical hissing could be heard inside the bomb's enclosure.

A thick, noxious, sizzling white ooze began to snake from every bolt-hole they'd opened down below. If the air hadn't been circulating they both would have been overcome by the sour gases, but as it was the stench brought on an immediate head-rush and there was nothing pleasant about it.

'Did I ask you why the nose-end of a thermonuclear weapon would be stuffed full of packing peanuts?'

'The fusion section is encased in polystyrene foam. In the first millionth of a second of the blast, the theory is that it all flashes to plasma and that compresses the secondary fuel to start the fusion reaction.'

'Well,' John said. 'You learn something new every day.'

'What's the time?'

'Six minutes fifteen.'

The solvent ran dry. 'Hand me another can, quick now.'

He did, they switched to the other side, and by the time she'd emptied the second gallon the liquid was gushing freely and almost clean out the bottom of the bomb. She dropped the can into the hole and lowered herself down, ending with a casual half-walkover to alight gently on the scaffolding beside him.

'Now what?'

'Ball bearings.'

The same tubing they'd been using turned out to be perfect for this next procedure. Going by feel, her eyes searching as she worked, Jeannie finessed the end of the clear hose into the aperture where the bomb's booster tube had been extracted earlier. When she nodded he held the outer end of the tubing with the funnel inserted, and she started feeding ball bearings down the chute and on inside. By the sound some of them missed the mark and rattled to the very bottom: others seemed to be collecting together in the lower-middle section.

'What does this do?'

'If I've put them in the right place, and if they stay there, we just partially filled the pit in the primary device with a steel prophylactic. They used the same idea as a safety device for a while in air-dropped nukes.'

'For a while? Why did they stop?'

'It wasn't all that reliable, I guess.' She removed the tubing and tossed it into the abyss, then tightened a short bolt into the threaded hole they'd just used. 'We probably just took some rads, maybe a few dozen CAT-scans worth. Not that it matters.' She looked up into his eyes, wiped a polystyrene drip from his cheek with her sleeve. 'In a few minutes we're both going to take a lot more than that.'

He smiled a bit, and it took a little while to fade.

'I'm going to miss you, Jeannie.'

She touched his chest, took a light grip on the fabric of his shirt, looking into his eyes.

'I really doubt it,' she said. 'Standing this close, I imagine you'll blow right through me.'

He shook his head, and in spite of himself he laughed, and so did she.

'Let's sit down here,' John said. 'I'm tired.'

'Oh,' she sighed, 'me, too.'

They sat carefully on the tenuous platform, their legs hanging over the edge, their knees touching.

'. . . John?'

'Yeah.'

'I shouldn't have made light of what you said before. God, I've always known my life was screwed up, but I've only just recently found out how much, and why. And you know something? It turns out that I've spent about ninety-nine percent of my real time, time when I've really known who I was, with you. Either chasing you, or finding you. And I wouldn't have had it any other way.' She leaned to him, pressed her shoulder to his. 'I guess I just wanted to say I'll miss you, too.'

He didn't answer.

The silence stretched.

'John?'

Still nothing.

'I'm spilling my guts, here, are you even listening to me?'

'We have to drop it,' he whispered.

'What did you say?'

He looked at her, nodded. 'The bomb. We have to let it drop.'

'Are you nuts?'

'Check me, watch that timer in the side of the bomb. When I signal you tell me what it reads.' He looked behind, to the neon timer near the wall, and after a moment he snapped his fingers.

'Four minutes, six.'

He looked at her and smiled. 'Three minutes, fifty-nine.' He stood and walked a few steps up the platform, oblivious now to its subtle swaying as he moved.

'I can't read your mind, John.'

'Seven seconds,' he said. 'The difference is seven seconds. The timer on the wall drops the bomb, and then the timer on the bomb detonates it seven seconds later.'

She stood up. 'Why?'

'That bomb can't just go off, it has to go off at a very specific place, that's why. The people who put this together, they didn't make this hole, they *found* this hole and built their doomsday device around it. The hole is the only thing that isn't designed here, and it's far too deep. It just hit me. When you threw that can down there before, I never heard it hit bottom. Listen, now.'

John picked the heaviest wrench they'd brought up to the

392

platform and tossed it toward the center of the wide, black hole below them. It disappeared as it left the light behind, and they waited in the near-silence, watching the timers count down.

Half a minute and change had passed when Jeannie tapped his hand. 'Did you hear that?' she whispered.

'No, I didn't hear anything, but your ears are a lot younger than mine.'

'I couldn't swear to it but think I heard it hit. How long was that?'

'A little over forty seconds.'

She went to work, writing out the math with her index finger on the casing of the bomb. 'I need to take off . . . eight seconds for the speed of sound . . . what's the drag coefficient of that wrench, do you think?'

'I don't know—'

'Did you drop it flat or vertically?'

'Oh for fuck's sake, ballpark it, Reese, Jesus.'

'Okay, okay, about twenty seconds of acceleration, and then ninety meters per second from there on down, so that's—'

'About 7900 feet,' John said. 'Almost a mile and a half.'

Jeannie looked down at the wide opening below them. 'Is that even possible?'

'The Russians have drilled down seven-and-a-half miles.' He'd begun to work his way around to the barometric trigger panel she'd opened earlier. 'That hole's not nearly this wide, but the point is, yes, I think it's entirely possible.'

'But the bomb is programmed to drop and detonate after seven seconds, and that's only what, 750 feet or so?'

He nodded. 'Close enough. For this location they figured that was the prime depth to punch through to the Yellowstone hot spot and trigger their big eruption. Take a look at this.' John tugged her around to a position where she could see. 'The barometric trigger is a fail-safe. This place is about a mile and a half above sea level, and look at these settings.' The clock-face of the device's altimeter was set to a trigger altitude of 7200 feet. 'There you go, where we're standing that's only about 750 feet underground, less than a tenth of the depth of this hole.'

She smacked her forehead. 'We have to drop it.'

'I said that, like a minute ago.' He'd begun to twist the altimeter's adjustment knob, and shortly he'd brought it down to just shy of zero. 'There. That's as far down as we can push it.'

'We have to be sure, John. There's a formula for this, how do they know how deep to bury a nuke for an underground test?'

John closed his eyes, sent his mind for the answer, and in seconds it returned from some obscure publication he'd read a decade before. 'Scaled depth of burial: take the depth of the hole in meters, divide by the cube root of the yield in kilotons. For the blast to be contained the result is supposed to be over 100.'

She thought for a moment. 'Say we've disabled this thing and it only yields twelve kilotons, if we can drop it close to the bottom of this hole that's about a thousand percent safety margin.'

'How about at full yield? Just in case.'

'At six megatons the number is . . .127. That's only twenty-seven points above the minimum.'

'So even if we didn't cut the yield at all,' John said, 'and you know that we did, hell, at that depth it's far more likely to relieve a little pressure than to release any at all. There are a *trillion* megatons down there and the planet keeps it in check for three-quarters of a million years between eruptions.

394

Reese, if the only other choice is letting it go off this close to the surface, there's no question about it.' He took her by the shoulders. 'You know we're right. Trust the math.'

She nodded. 'Let's do it.'

'Good.'

She climbed up onto the bomb again and shinnied up to the ceiling. 'What's the time?'

'One minute, twenty-three. That thing's got to be gone before the timer hits thirty-two seconds.'

'Toss me a big screwdriver.'

He did, in his haste, about a foot wide of her outstretched hand.

'Okay,' she said calmly, 'no more throwing, climb the ladder and *bring* me a screwdriver and some heavy pliers.'

When the tools were safely in her hands he knelt on the high platform and watched her undo her earlier work on the safety chain and begin to hammer at the quick-release clamp.

'Jeannie, hang on to something for God's sake.'

'Time.'

'Forty-three seconds.'

With the clamp's linch-pin in the jaws of her pliers she was prying with the long screwdriver, tense and straining with all of her strength against the two tons of dead weight hanging below.

'Thirty-six.'

The screwdriver snapped at the handle. Jeannie brought her foot up next to the clamp and pushed, twisting the release pin with both hands now, readjusting her grip, twisting again.

'Twenty-nine!'

A *clink* was the only sound he would remember hearing as the bomb was released and it dropped and vanished down into the dark.

As her support fell away Jeannie had snagged a ceiling

hook with one hand. She was hanging over the hole in the floor just as the bomb had been, too high and far away to safely reach the scaffolding where he stood.

John held out his arms toward her, without a thought of the approaching endpoint as the last seconds counted down. A thermonuclear weapon was descending below them, by then near its terminal velocity, streaking toward its new detonation point at 200 miles per hour, but no matter. They would leave this room together or not at all.

Jeannie swung her legs, once, twice, and then she released her grip at the top of the final swing. As she landed on the platform beside him the scaffolding let out a groan, one of its wheels slipped over the edge, and a slow-motion swoon toward the chasm began.

She looked into his eyes and took his hand, just as she'd promised earlier. He knew her thoughts, and as the platform leaned farther and farther, the fall becoming faster, he waited with her until the moment she chose, and at that last available instant they jumped together across toward the safety of the far side.

When he opened his eyes Jeannie was already half-dragging him through the exit. As she closed and dodged the airtight metal door the briefest wink of dazzling white light from inside had escaped around the edges of the frame. Emergency lamps threw their shadows on the stairs as they ran and ran, up the long flight and then through the smoldering of Parsons' laboratory.

A deep rumble and a trembling had begun to build beneath their feet. They ran across the narrow stone bridge toward the entry passageway, and the shaking of the floor had spread to the walls and the ceilings, dust and rock and wooden braces falling all around them. The way seemed to steepen, as though the whole of the Earth behind them was collapsing.

They reached the entrance embedded in the wall of the old garage, running the length of this final stretch with a last burst of energy, and then up the concrete ramp and out into the sunlight.

Only then did John allow himself to turn and look behind, across to the expanse of wooded ground high above the place they'd left. The trembling underfoot had eased to nearly nothing, and in seconds all was still again.

Jeannie came up beside him, put her hand on his shoulder. The snowy landscape they saw would seem undisturbed to a new observer. The only evidence of whatever had happened far below was a wide, subtle depression, a shallow dell among the surrounding hills that the forest would soon patiently reclaim as its own.

Epilogue

While he waited for her, John sat with the things from his pockets laid out across the roll-top desk. These were perhaps all of his remaining worldly possessions, though none of them had belonged to him the week before.

Before they'd left that site, as John stripped Griffin's vehicle of any tell-tale electronics, Jeannie had checked the entry tunnel to make sure no way in remained. She closed and locked the vault at the end of the garage and found some gummy yellow and black paint on a shelf. Using the corner of a rag as a brush she made her best rendering of a radiation warning sign at eye level on the metal door. That would have to do.

Jeannie drove, of course; John had never even had a lesson. After they'd gotten some miles behind them, this quaint bed-and-breakfast had been the first lodgings they'd seen. As it was off-season the owners were thrilled to see customers drive up. They must have seemed a strange couple, though; a pretty young woman, effortlessly winsome even in her ill-fitting, vintage unisex clothes, and an unkempt, bespectacled man in his early forties, completely average in every outward appearance.

He'd booked a suite for the night and paid for the other

three that were available. They enjoyed their privacy, he'd explained, and consistent with that, the register had gone unsigned.

John considered his new belongings, lined up on the blotter.

An ounce of yellow gold, just a small bar he'd held onto after that first day underground, more as a good-luck charm than a thing of value.

A silver fountain pen, accented in leather, which must have cost nearly a grand off the shelf and maybe a thousand times that once its weaponry had been installed. This would be something interesting to take apart and reassemble on some rainy afternoon; you never know what you can learn from things.

A passport wallet with a number of credit cards, access cards, and IDs. None of these carried the name August Griffin, or Richard Lawrence for that matter. There'd been some cash, a little over two thousand dollars that would come in handy for traveling money. But the photographs, carefully tucked into a glassine envelope, were the most interesting. A faded portrait of a woman, sepia-toned, white border with scalloped edges, the kind of keepsake that might be exchanged with a lover on the eve of a long journey with an uncertain end. A creased family picture in black and white; stern father, stoic mother, and a young boy seated at the hearth, his life still ahead of him. And the last, much more recent, a school picture of a young girl, obviously scissor-cut rather unevenly from a sheet of them; a little blond beauty with a smile that seemed to shine straight from her heart.

The last item was a black address book. Evidently Mr Griffin had been somewhat old-fashioned in his habits; not many people kept such things on paper anymore. Within these pages, each headed with the strange subtitle *Olympians,* were three hundred names. Nationalities, loyalties, lineages, roles, affiliations, and full contact information was provided for each.

Contact: now there was a word to open a world of possibilities.

The bathroom door opened, releasing a slow-motion avalanche of steam. Since the shower had started running he'd had time to clean himself up down the hall, shave, have a sandwich, and if he'd had the paper he could have taken a leisurely read through the Sunday *Times* as well. Let's face it, the woman enjoyed her bathing.

She walked to the bed, toweling her hair, dressed in a simple white robe somewhat like his own, but in her case it looked as though it had been cut and sewn by a team of designers whose aim in life was to perfect the garment in worship of the feminine form.

'Come here,' Jeannie said.

He did, and sat near the footboard.

'I would have put on some actual clothes,' he said, 'but the stuff I was wearing had gotten pretty gross.'

'Yeah, it had.' She fixed his collar with one hand, the other rested on his shoulder.

'The daughter here,' John said, 'college-age kid, she offered to go out and do some shopping for us. I gave her some money, so we'll have something to wear tomorrow morning, and she'll get a travel bag for each of us.'

'That's good.'

'I thought you'd think so.'

She sat on the mattress near him.

'John?'

'Yup. I'm right here.'

'I wonder if you'd do me a favor.'

'Of course.'

'It's a little embarrassing.'

He blinked. 'Okaaay.'

She sighed, and looked down at her hands.

'It's not uncommon with these . . . methods . . . I was subjected to, for there to be residual effects. You know about this, they work on you by tying some new behavior or a foreign impulse to some other part of you that's already accepted, something natural, or pleasurable.'

He nodded. 'That makes sense. Sounds like advertising.'

'And I don't remember all of this, but I know that in my case, my . . . my sexual response . . . was one of the things these other impulses were tied to.'

'Okay. I'm with you. Do you want me to leave you alone?'

She looked at him, put her hand on his knee, and took in a preparatory breath.

'I want you to make love to me.'

His eyes narrowed a bit. 'Oh, come on.'

'I feel like I'm okay now, but there's always a doubt with important things until you're sure. I just need to know that they're all out of my head. It would help me so much.'

'Jeannie. Look. I don't think it's a good idea.'

'Why not?'

'You know, come on—'

'No, I don't know, tell me.'

'Okay. I'm not going to lie to you. I don't know what this is, you're my good friend, and we've got this, whatever, this flirtationship going on, and I love that, and that's great. And, I will confess, in my private, personal moments, if you know what I mean, I've thought about you in that way, many times, and you've never failed to bring about the desired result.'

She smiled shyly, though her cheeks were reddening.

'But look,' John said. 'In real life, I'm no match for you, not like that. I have virtually zero experience with women, and what I have had, as you know, didn't end well to say the least.'

Her hand moved to the lapel of his robe, and she gripped the cloth lightly, and tugged. 'I don't care.'

'God, we'd probably bump heads or something, and you'd laugh your ass off at me, and I'd never get an erection again. Would that make you happy? And it might be worth it even at that, but it's scary for me, can you understand that?'

'I wouldn't ever laugh.' She leaned to him, kissed him lightly on the lips. 'Please, John.'

'Oh, man.' He took off his glasses, exhaled a descending note, and shook his head, resigned. 'Just this once.'

Jeannie smiled, got to her knees on the mattress, and began to undo the terry-cloth tie at her waist.

'And what are the odds, do you think,' John said, 'that your eyes are going to roll back in your head at some point and you'll go zombie and snap my windpipe?'

She let the robe slip from her smooth shoulders, shook down her hair, held out her hand for him, and thought a moment for his answer. 'I'd give it five per cent, maximum,' she said.

He would never tell her this, but he would have taken 3-to-1 against.

Despite her assurances there had been some laughter after all, a great deal from each of them, and for a time things got very, very serious, and at one point they did bump heads though neither seemed to notice the dread event. The night passed in deep conversation, things expressed in words and touch and silence and embrace, and they each meant every single thing they said.

When he awoke in the morning she was on the phone, and when he'd put on his glasses he saw that she'd been crying. She'd called Rudy Steinman and learned that Jay Marshall was dead.

They washed and dressed, packed in their new bags. John

gave her most of the money to pay for her flight to New York. When they heard the taxi outside she stopped and turned to him.

'I don't have any ID—'

'That's okay. Just tell them you lost your purse, and they'll run you through some extra machines and a nice woman in a uniform will look in some places that even I haven't seen, and then they'll let you on the plane.'

Outside, the driver honked his horn.

She hugged him, so tight, and whispered in his ear.

'I love you, John.'

'I love you, too, kid. Call me when you can.'

He stood on the porch, saw her wave to him through the back window as the car pulled away for the airport, and wondered how long it might be until he saw her again.

When it came to his own next destination, there was never a question in his mind. John was going home.

Driving in traffic turned out to be a bit harder than it looked in the videos, but the roads were clear and it was a trip of less than fifty miles, and by the time he'd reached the last turn-off he felt he'd nearly gotten the hang of it.

From a distance the house looked as bad as he'd anticipated. There'd been worries on the way down, that he would arrive to find a dragnet or an ambush from some unknown agency; he dismissed these fears in short order. They could come for him if they dared. This was still America, and this was his land.

He parked near the shed where the vehicles were maintained. As he approached the house, Wayman Hudson emerged from the lower floor. When he saw John he waved and motioned him toward the house. There was no surprise in the gesture; it was as though he'd been expected to return at any time, and here he was.

After their greetings, Wayman showed him the repairs he'd begun on the place. The top floor was a total loss as was most of the second level, but enough structure survived down here to rearrange things into a small living room, three bedrooms, a half-kitchen and a full bath.

Wayman had determined to prepare a bit before he'd gone looking for the children, so their home would be livable when they arrived. All of the treasures he'd brought back from the sanctuary were stored in various places appropriate to their needs and their value. The gold was the exception, since there was no facility here yet to keep such a quantity of precious metal secure. John would order a safe as soon as some form of communication could be rigged. In the meantime, an old freezer in the basement was serving as repository.

In the midst of the tour John heard activity out in front, and he walked out into the yard to see what was happening.

A station wagon was coming down the drive, and it stopped just past the halfway point. It had stopped because both back doors had flung open and three children emerged. Elizabeth began to run toward the house at full bore, and the other two kids followed and tried to keep up, but that kid was fast once she got up a head of steam. John bent and held out his arms and she jumped into them and clung to him with all limbs in a monkey-hold. Laughing or crying, he really couldn't tell.

Dinner was simple, but he couldn't remember ever enjoying a more wonderful meal. Later, when the girls were playing dominoes and Wayman had gone out to replenish the firewood, Matthew pulled John aside to tell him where they'd been since he saw them last. John, in turn, let the boy know that the man who'd taken them was in no position to ever bother any of them again.

There were more stories to be told, but there would a lot of time to tell them. You could never know for certain how much, but John allowed at least that tomorrow would be another day.

When everyone else was fast asleep John still sat by the fire, reading through one of the boxes of files that Wayman had brought with him.

There wasn't much in Jack Parsons' writings about the origins of that strange little box at the end of the lab. If his scant notes were to be believed it worked by tuning in and amplifying that fundamental something represented by his computer as a unifying, life-giving pulse of energy that pervades all things. By his description, what we've thought of as gravity is only a weak shadow of this unknown force, glimpsed as it ebbs and flows in and out of our physical dimensions, with only its traces observed by our limited sensors.

Parsons' language was far more spiritual than practical; it was as though he'd chosen not to try and understand the nature of this force or the technology that had captured it. It wasn't his invention, but it had been left in his care in anticipation of a day when mankind might prove itself worthy of having all its problems solved. That day never came, of course, and in the end it seemed he'd determined that it never would. If it was real, the power that single device could harness could wither rid the world of poverty, hunger, and strife or tear the planet in half. With history as a guide there's little doubt which of these would be its first funded application.

If it was real; the nature of the notes in these files left that an open question. The benevolent radiation John himself had imagined he felt, the cure he may or may not have undergone, both could have been as unreal as the being Parsons had created in his own image, the one who'd determined rather quickly that the human race had made such a mess of things that we didn't deserve another chance.

In a way, that thing had been right; we're certainly not there yet. Something is wrong when a few cents worth of micro-nutrients per undernourished family could raise the world's IQ by over a billion points, but that priority is overruled while trillions are spent in perfecting the delivery of war. That's not a judgment any sane individual would make, but take us all and divide us into groups and set us against one another and we're party to such decisions every day. Even the people who'd built that sanctuary were infected by the lust for self-destruction; what had begun as a place to survive doomsday had ended up housing a weapon that could bring it about.

No single person who'd been a part of the building of that place was responsible for what it ultimately became; neither Szilárd, nor Myron Fagan, nor Jack Parsons, nor any of the others who must have known of it as it evolved over the years from a place of sanctuary into liberty's last stand. Parsons himself abdicated his role in the end, maybe in hopes that the place would never be found, and maybe in hopes that if things ever got bad enough someone with greater resolve might come and render a decision that he didn't have the certainty to make. Even Edward Latrell couldn't make it, and that was saying a lot.

One thing was clear. That shelter was built because a final class war was being prepared and one side believed there was no way they could win. In lieu of victory, they chose a stand-off, a credible threat that if pushed to the wall, they could unleash something that would bring about the end, for the victors and the victims as well. And now their trump card was gone.

No matter; let the battle rage. Under this roof, within these walls, the war was over. Right up until the moment, that is, when anyone on any side ever dared again to bring their fight to his door.

Acknowledgements

I'd been told that nothing about writing a second novel would be anything like the experience of the first, and true enough, almost nothing was. I'm going to resist the impulse to elaborate here, but if there seems to be sufficient interest at my website I may regale you with some stories that are still a bit too fresh to reliably commit to ink and paper.

One thing is the same this time around, though, and that's my sincere gratitude to you as a reader. I've felt your presence in every one of the many hundreds of hours of writing and research, I've been uplifted by the notes you've sent, and I'm every bit as humbled and grateful to have spent this time again in your company.

So let me start by taking full responsibility for any errors, of omission, commission, or otherwise, that you may have found. We all did our best, but it's my name on the spine. There are some people I'm unable to thank specifically, but here are a few that I can: George Smith, Dr. Emmett Redd, Dr. Brian Clark, Paul W, Shirley, Kevin, Kyle, Jeff, Ken, Patti, Stuart, David, Thalia, Simon, and my wife, my kids, and my mom. Writing may be a solitary profession, but in different ways and at different times, each of you helped me get past something that I just couldn't have made it through alone.

Thanks again.

There are two types of committed worker (in service industry)

- Those that want to please
- Those that want to make profit.

- They can be both - but one dominates!

Calgary Airport 30th May 2009